BOOKS BY SUZA KATES

The Savannah Coven Series
Whisper of a Witch
Conviction of a Witch
Binding of a Witch
Haunting of a Witch
Possession of a Witch
Deception of a Witch

The She Series
She Who is Hidden

Single Titles
Hallowed Eve
The Penance Stone

DECEPTION OF A WITCH

THE SAVANNAH COVEN SERIES

SUZA KATES

ICASM PRESS
SAVANNAH

Published by Icasm Publishing LLC
5710 Ogechee Rd. Suite 200 #278, Savannah, GA 31405
www.icasmpress.com

Library of Congress Cataloging-in-Publication Data

Kates, Suza
Deception of a Witch / Suza Kates
    p. cm.

ISBN-13:978-0-9889809-2-1
ISBN-13:978-0-9889809-3-8 (ebook)
I. Title

Printed and bound in the United States of America

10 9 8 7 6 5 4 3 2 1

THE COVEN

Anna St. Germaine
Hair: Long, straight, sable brown
Eyes: Sapphire blue
Color: Sapphire blue
Cat: "Ivy" gray female with lime green eyes

Anna sees visions of past, present, and future. She is the coven's head witch and is a descendant of the three women who originally banished the demon Bastraal three centuries ago. Her ancestral home is on an island off the coast of Savannah, Georgia and now serves as coven central.

Claudia Grant
Hair: Straight, long, flaming red
Eyes: River green
Color: Coral
Cat: "Rowan Von Ashbi" coloring of an American Wirehair with yellow eyes

Claudia is a history professor who only needs to touch an object to sense its past and previous surroundings.

Hayden Wells
Hair: Brownish red "caramel"
Eyes: Golden brown
Color: Pale pink
Cat: "Daisy" black tortoiseshell with yellow eyes

Hayden is a medium from San Francisco who sees and talks to spirits/ghosts.

Kylie Worthington
Hair: Long, wavy golden-blonde

Eyes: Hazel
Color: Yellow
Cat: Sassafras "Sassy" also a long-haired blonde but with bright yellow eyes

Kylie is a college student who's "on a break" to do her part for the coven and is able to control electricity in any form.

Lucia Ruiz
Hair: Long, wavy deep brown
Eyes: Brown
Color: Red
Cat: "Iris" black Persian with blue eyes

Lucia was born to privileged wealth in Spain and has the ability to find anything that is lost. She is an adventurer, world-traveler, and renowned relic-hunter.

Paige Reilley
Hair: Shoulder-length, white-blonde with ragged bangs
Eyes: Turquoise blue
Color: Turquoise
Cat: Tiger Lily "Tiger" brown and gray with white chest and belly, bright green eyes

Recently discharged from the military, Paige is a soldier in every way with the added abilities of super-strength and speed.

Shauni Miller
Hair: Long, straight, black
Eyes: Emerald green
Color: Green
Cat: "Cuileann" black short-hair with green eyes

Shauni is a nature-loving biologist from Colorado and communicates with animals telepathically.

Viv Sakurai
Hair: Shoulder-length, black, angled bangs
Eyes: Gray
Color: Purple
Cat: Kikoku "Kiko" orange tabby with yellow-green eyes and a grumpy disposition.

Relocated from Chicago, Viv is a physicist searching for an explanation for her own special power of telekinesis.

Willyn Brousseau
Hair: Wavy, shoulder-length, light blonde
Eyes: Pale blue
Color: White/cream
Cat: "Snowball" pure white with golden eyes

Willyn is a nurse, a mother, and a Christian. Raised in Alabama, she uses her healing powers to help those in need. She came to Savannah with an additional package, her young son, Tadd.

THE GUYS

Dr. Michael Black   *Whisper of a Witch*

This tall handsome veterinarian fell in love with Shauni in the first book of the series. He has dark blonde hair and gray eyes and is able to read a person's aura. He's a pretty calm guy until someone messes with his witch.

Dare Forster   *Conviction of a Witch*

Dark and handsome with deep blue eyes, this male witch came to the coven's island with his own plan. He wanted to partner with one of the women, but he never expected to fall in love. Especially with a gentle, Christian soul like Willyn. Now married, the two have made a family with Willyn's small son, Tadd.

Nick Reagan   *Binding of a Witch*

The coven likes to hang out in their favorite pub, and the owner of the bar always liked looking at Viv. His eyes are the color of the whiskey he sells, and his past is one of struggle. One night Nick finally got the nerve to approach the Asian beauty, but he got a lot more than he bargained for. The demon Bastraal had been destroyed once before, and his remains had been buried. Beneath Nick's very own pub.

Trevor Roch   *Haunting of a Witch*

One of Savannah's finest, this homicide detective clashes

hard with the coven's ghost whisperer, convinced she's a con artist. Hayden has no choice but to work with the annoying man and find a serial killer who's working with the Amara. Staying true to form and following the coven's pattern, the two fall in love. Against their better judgment.

Quinn St. Germaine

Quinn is the younger brother of the coven's head witch, Anna. With sable hair and cobalt eyes, he is the masculine and handsome version of the siblings. His knowledge runs to occult history and magical languages. He assists the coven in all things, and though he has his eye on a particular witch, he does his best to deny it.

Ethan Drake *Possession of a Witch*

This demon hunter is well-acquainted with evil and has been chasing his own monster since childhood. When he offers to help the coven with their demon infestation, he has no idea he's about to be taken on the adventure of a lifetime. Lucia Ruiz is hard to resist, and is the one woman who might be able to save him.

1

Cole glanced at his watch and noted the time, jerking one side of his mouth up in irritation. He only had half an hour before he was scheduled to meet his partner for a witness interview across town, and his spur-of-the-moment lunch date had yet to show.

She's only ten minutes late, and traffic is pretty bad this time of day. The half-hearted excuse he made on her behalf didn't alleviate his annoyance, so he glanced again at the 1960's-styled watch on his wrist, dragging a fingertip across the plain black band and unadorned face.

Sure, he could use his phone to track time, as so many did today, but the watch had been his Scottish grandfather's and was symbolic on multiple levels. So he wore it proudly, as a reminder of both tradition and family.

"More coffee?" the young waitress asked as she passed his table on her way back to the serving bar. Cole lifted a hand and shook his head to refuse, but then he graced her with a smile in an attempt to hide his foul temper.

After all, it wasn't her fault he was stuck waiting, and the staff here was exceptionally friendly. When he'd first entered the café, he'd cast a rueful eye at the bright green walls and muttered, "Interesting color." The girl had cheerfully explained the shade was called *Anjou* before seating him at a re-purposed metal table of bubble-gum pink.

Swearing to himself he'd never again agree to meet anyone in an unfamiliar place, Cole studied the vibrant walls and wondered if he'd ever actually seen a pear that color. He didn't think so.

The coffee-slash-smoothie bar was vintage-inspired but with the palette of an Easter-egg basket. Aromas flowed from fruity to coffee-laced depending on whichever beverage was being prepared behind the counter. At the moment, the air was heavily scented with strawberry.

He squirmed in the dainty chair that his body was much too big for. The place was definitely a female haunt, and the surrounding high-pitched chatter made him run a finger inside his shirt collar. He was beginning to feel claustrophobic.

Good thing his partner Trevor wasn't here to witness his discomfort. Big, tough homicide cop getting edgy because he was flanked on all sides by women.

Normally the attractive company would be his proverbial day at the beach, but something about the pastel atmosphere here was just...wrong. He felt an overwhelming need to fix a pipe or adjust his jock.

Suddenly, the idea of being stood up held a certain appeal. He'd give Rachel five more minutes. Then he was *out*.

A tinny little jingle rang out as the café door swung open, and Cole looked up to see if she'd finally arrived. When he saw the familiar face in the doorway, his chest lightened along with his mood.

He smiled and waved to get Kylie's attention, then nodded as Lucia strolled in behind her. *Witches on a smoothie run.*

Would he ever get used to that reality? Not only was there a coven of witches living in Savannah, but they'd been tasked with saving the city from demonic destruction.

And Cole was honored to be one of their inner circle. To be

considered a friend.

Before Trevor had fallen for one of the witches, both he and Cole had been dragged into the middle of a supernatural war. One neither of them had ever suspected was going on in the city they were both sworn to protect.

Knowing what they did now, the two of them accepted the existence of demons and magic as easily as they did beer and Monday Night Football. Well, almost as easily. It would help if they could actually *see* the monsters like the witches did, but he and Trevor were only human.

Cole stood when Kylie bounced over to greet him, her face lit up with a bright grin. The energetic blonde was the youngest of the coven, and her unabashed vitality was always uplifting. "Hey, handsome." She gave him a one-armed hug as Lucia sidled up behind her.

The tall Spanish woman was mildly subdued, and Cole had a feeling he knew why. Two weeks had passed since Lucia had returned from South America in search of an ancient, prophecy-fulfilling dagger. Like the witches before her who'd been called to face an individual challenge, Lucia had found a man and fallen headlong into love.

But unlike the others, she had yet to complete her trial. Time was ticking by, and with every day that passed the coven grew more anxious. Trevor had been giving Cole status updates as he received them from his girlfriend, Hayden. She was the coven's medium and was as concerned as everyone else.

Lucia had no idea what was left for her to do or how she could win another victory for their side. Neither did any of her friends. All they could do was wait, and brainstorm, and research, hoping for a flash of insight or the discovery of a new clue.

For that reason, Cole was surprised to see them in town and was about to broach the topic when the door jingled again. He glanced to check for his late date, but the woman he expected to see didn't walk in.

Instead, a third member of the Savannah coven breezed into the café, and a hell of a lot more than Cole's collar tightened up. He should have been able to control this response by now. He was a cop, trained to disguise initial reactions and strong emotions when they arose.

But as Claudia Grant's long—*long*—legs carried her to his table, the only logical thing he could think to do was raise his coffee cup to keep his jaw from hitting the cotton-candy-hued table top.

Her hair was red as a desert sunset and complimented her ivory skin. She always reminded him of peaches over ice cream, but considering Cole's two weaknesses were women and sugar, the analogy was fitting.

She was dressed up, as usual, and wearing some sort of light-colored dress with pale green stripes down the side. A flower design was barely visible on the fabric, but the detail was lost on Cole anyway. All he noticed was the length of the dress, fascinated by the way the hemline stretched across the front of her thighs as she took a step forward.

Cole set his mug down and forced his eyes away from Claudia and back to Kylie. Safer territory. "What brings the three of you out today? Taking a break from…" He thought better of the careless question and glanced at Lucia.

The brunette witch only shrugged. "They're trying to make me feel better." Her light brown skin still managed to appear wan, and her lips were absent their signature bright red paint. Cole could see why her friends were trying to cheer her up.

She rolled her dark brown eyes toward Kylie. "As if the answer to my trial will be found beneath a new pair of high heels."

Kylie made a face and waved away Lucia's cynicism. "We aren't trying to solve your problem by shopping. The point is to *forget* about your challenge for a day." The younger witch huffed. "Or at least for a few hours."

Ignoring her friends as they glared at each other, Claudia let her gaze travel around the candy-colored room. Then she smirked at Cole. "I didn't realize cops hung out here. I had you pegged for a smoky tavern and a super-sized *Arran* ale."

Cole grinned, more delighted than he had any right to be that she'd referenced a Scottish beer. The red-haired witch was always quick on her feet, and her wit could either be charming or sharp as a blade. He figured he'd just gotten a taste of both.

"I'm meeting someone," he said, but as soon as the words were out he wanted to knock them out of the air where they hovered, begging for a follow-up response. He didn't want to tell her he was on a lunch date, but he refused to acknowledge the reason why.

Thankfully, Claudia didn't ask anything else but bobbed her head as if he'd provided a full explanation. Kylie, however, was not as tactful. "Got a hot date, Cole?" She winked and bumped his shoulder with her fist. "A little afternoon—"

"Kylie," Claudia cut in, smooth as butter but with a meaningful tilt of her head.

Though Cole's throat felt clogged, and he was wearing what now felt like a choke collar, the exchange had at least one desirable effect. Lucia tossed him a sly smile as her cheeks pinkened.

And he knew he'd willingly be the butt of every single joke if it helped lighten her load even a little.

He could laugh at raunchy, locker-room stories as loudly as the next guy, and without a hint of embarrassment. So he knew his current discomfort wasn't due to the fact he was meeting a woman, or even that the date was going down in this ridiculous Candy Land-themed café.

No, he wasn't bothered by who he was having lunch with.

But who he *wasn't.*

The first time he'd met all the witches, he thought he'd

died and gone to a Miss America pageant. Then over time, the
women had become his friends, and in some rare and dangerous
instances, his battle-buddies. Demons kept cropping up in the
area, and he and Trevor were always ready to lend a hand.

Cole had established a deep respect for each and every one
of them, from Willyn's sweet, motherly ways to Anna's cool
elegance. He felt fraternal affection for the coven and could
place them safely in the friend category without a second
thought.

All of them, that is, except for Claudia. The intelligent
history professor with an eye for fashion, whose hair was as
hot as the fireballs she blasted from her perfectly-manicured
hands.

He had no business looking in her direction, not with
everything she was dealing with. The prophecy, her friend's
incomplete trial, and not knowing when she would be called to
stand on her own against the waking demon.

Not to mention the Amara, a.k.a. the bad guys. They were
a sordid collection of black witches, a shifter, and some freaky
tattoo woman Cole still didn't understand, mixed in with a
few other mutants. Their plan was to help the demon Bastraal
enter this world and wreak pain and suffering on mankind.

And Cole had thought *he* had a tough job cleaning up the
streets of Savannah.

Claudia eased away from his table after declaring she
wanted a lime-mango-banana smoothie, making Cole glad for
his simple black coffee with sugar. He lowered his eyes but
stole a surreptitious glance at the hem of her dress as she
approached the bar, just to see how it looked from behind.

Too good was the answer, each step revealing her toned
thighs and slim calves. Between that and her straight-as-rain
hair in a sleek, fiery ponytail, the backside visual almost did
him in.

Keeping his stare down, he studied the dark brew in his mug

and reminded himself that Claudia was somewhat spoken for. Her life was already mapped out, and fate had laid the plans.

When her challenge arrived, she'd inexorably meet a man and fall in love. Providence had decreed this pattern for the witches. For the women of the coven. For the nine.

And despite the sexual attraction that gripped him by the ba—*ahem*, by the *throat*—whenever Claudia was around, Cole just wasn't a one-woman man and had no plans to become one anytime soon. All things considered, he'd be wise to steer clear of the sexy witch.

Her *and* her romantic destiny.

He enjoyed his bachelor lifestyle. He enjoyed the company of women. It was that simple.

As if on cue, the door jangled again, and this time it was the fresh-faced pharmaceutical rep who'd requested Cole meet her at the café. Her blue business jacket was appropriate, but tight enough to flatter her figure while the matching skirt did the same for her legs.

Rarely did Cole wish for an emergency summons, but he could really use one right about now. He didn't know why the air crackled with tension as Kylie and Lucia eyed the approaching woman, or why he wanted the sassy blonde to be anywhere but here.

"Hey," she said, slinging her bag into a nearby chair and leaning forward to give him a peck on the cheek. She didn't sit down but stood and looked expectantly between Kylie and Lucia. Cole coughed and made brief introductions.

The pause he took before saying Rachel's name earned him a look of disapproval from the efficient yet perky sales rep, and he suspected he'd hear about it later. They'd only gone out a couple of times, but waves of territoriality were rolling off of her as she openly scoped out the other two women.

Lucia smiled before turning to Cole. "Well, we're heading out." She jerked a thumb toward the bar where Claudia was paying for her smoothie. "She was just in the mood for something fruity."

The awkwardness was apparent, and he couldn't blame the witches for bolting. Kylie patted his cheek before she walked away. "Buh-bye, handsome," she cooed, and he wondered how much of that had been for Rachel's benefit.

With a relieved breath pushed out her nose—because her lips were pressed shut—Rachel took the seat across from him and lifted one brow. "Friends of yours?" Her tone carried a heavy dose of insinuation.

"Yes," he told her matter-of-factly as he sat again. "Good friends." Hoping to steer the conversation away from the departing women, he offered Rachel a laminated pink menu. "I only have time for coffee."

When she made a sound of disappointment, he worked up a smile. "Sorry."

She still wasn't appeased, blowing air through her nose again in a habit he'd never noticed before. "I guess I'll have a salad, then." She dropped the menu and tossed her hair over one shoulder.

Cole might have reminded her that she was the one who'd arrived late, but there was no call for rudeness, and he'd had manners drilled into him from an early age. Both his mother and his father had rigid opinions on chivalry.

He could hear his father even now. *If in doubt, treat every lass as you would your màthair.*

As Kylie, Lucia, and Claudia made their way to the front door, Cole scanned the redhead's mile-long legs again and absolutely refused to think of his mother. Re. Fused.

Fingers snapped in his face, so he swung his eyes quickly back to Rachel. "Want me to call the waitress?" he asked, all charm and innocence but suffused with guilt inside. He'd been looking. And he'd been busted.

"Sure." She narrowed her eyes at him. And blew air out of

her nose.

Catching the attention of the friendly young server, he channeled every ounce of patience he possessed. Rachel was revealing a new side of herself, and if there was one thing he couldn't abide in a woman, it was jealousy.

As she pointed to the menu and gave the young girl her order, Cole wondered how this lunch date would end. A glance at his watch and he immediately had his answer. The proof was in the chagrined inner voice that consoled him with a countdown. *Only fifteen more minutes.*

The change in Cole's attitude wasn't entirely Rachel's fault. He hadn't expected to run into any of the witches today, and seeing Claudia had rattled him. She'd come out of nowhere with that siren's face and bright, silky hair. Like a sucker punch thrown from his blind side.

Then her leg-baring dress had been the kick while he was down.

Cole sipped his coffee and searched his mind for small talk, hoping he could salvage Rachel's feelings if not her meal. He'd agreed to this date and would see it through, though he predicted this would be his last with the pert woman.

No, it really wasn't her fault, but neither was it Cole's. He hadn't planned to see his friends, and he sure hadn't invited them there. So when Rachel fixed her gaze on him, he did his best to appear interested in what she had to say.

He did his damnedest to admire her blue eyes and petite frame. To recall the appeal of her shiny blonde hair.

And to tell himself he preferred it over red.

2

"I don't like her." Kylie had her hands cupped around her eyes as she tried valiantly to peer through the glare on a picture window. She'd spied a color-blocked dress inside the boutique but couldn't make out the price tag.

Claudia wasn't interested in clothes at the moment—an occurrence as uncommon as a swamp-ape sighting—but the younger woman's statement caught her attention. "Who are you talking about?"

"The girl Cole's dating." Kylie scrunched her nose. "She's not his type. She's too...I don't know. Something."

Claudia sighed. "I didn't really notice. Besides," she said, pulling Kylie along to keep up with Lucia once that one started moving along the sidewalk, "I'm not sure Cole has just one type."

As they caught Lucia at the crosswalk, Claudia envisioned the brisk blonde she'd seen at Cole's table on the way out of the café. Because she *had* noticed.

She'd known Cole for a couple of months now and had always found him attractive in a bad-boy-turned-hero kind of way, but the hollow feeling in her belly was brand-stinking new.

And she didn't much care for it. Not at all.

Her worry over Lucia had been an ever-present knot in her

gut, as it had been for all of her coven sisters, but the sensation she was experiencing now wasn't the same. The emptiness had come over her in an instant, with one quick glimpse at Cole.

She'd meant to wave good-bye but hadn't been able to catch his eye. He'd been too engrossed in conversation with the woman who'd joined him. Talking to his *date*.

Which had been absolutely fine until he'd given the blonde a taste of that heart-wrenching smile of his. And Claudia had felt a quick pinch of longing in her chest that had nothing to do with drinking her cold smoothie too fast.

She couldn't attribute the feeling entirely to Cole either. At least, not directly. She'd known him for a while now and, as far as she could tell, he'd never lacked for female companionship. So she didn't feel the pang of loss from jealousy...but envy.

For the flash of possibility she'd seen in Cole's smile. Detective Lonergan was a good man, a rare breed, and one day he would smile at a woman and mean it for a lifetime.

Claudia just wouldn't be that lucky girl, for him or any other man. And occasionally, on days like today, she let herself acknowledge the vacancy that would always be inside her. The yearning for what she would never have.

Even if the absence was a result of her own choices. Her own reasons.

Shaking off the thoughts of gloom and doom, she focused on the warm sun falling on her bare arms and the steady stream of tourists on Broughton Street. The air was sweetened by parks filled with fragrant magnolias and candy stores offering up freshly-baked pralines.

Spring was her favorite time of the year, and in the South the sun came early, bringing azaleas to life with white, pink, and lavender blooms. Claudia preferred the coral variety, though; petals of softened orange so like her own signature color.

The same peachy shade as the center stone in the necklace she wore. Her amulet had been created centuries before, an intricate silver piece crafted to hold nine gemstones. Nine different hues signifying nine different witches.

Eight smaller stones ringed the light orange stone in the middle, connected by silver swirls just as she was connected to her coven. One day her stone would sing out a one-time song of victory, assuming Claudia got her chance to stand at trial. And, of course, assuming she passed.

Claudia tracked Lucia's steps as they quickened, and her gut constricted with concern. She'd never seen the Spanish woman so confused. So anguished. Or so lost.

The last part was the worst, because Lucia was never, *ever* lost.

"What's up with her?" Kylie voiced Claudia's exact thoughts before calling out to their friend. "Lucia, where are you going?" Her young face was marred by furrowed brows. "Lucia's tight black pants are on fire over something. Let's go."

Claudia didn't have to be told twice. She crossed the street, despite the flashing yellow hand, and defied any cars to run her down. While Kylie's phrasing differed from her own, the blonde witch had been right about one thing. Lucia was definitely moving with purpose. As if her pants were indeed on fire.

Excitement stirred inside Claudia. This was the most motivated she'd seen Lucia in over a week, so she jogged until she was close enough to touch her friend's long brown curls. "Do you feel something? An object?"

Lucia's gift granted her the ability to locate any lost item, living or inanimate, and she'd done plenty of that in the course of her challenge. Another reason the women were so bewildered that she had yet to complete her trial.

"I can't explain it." Lucia stopped and swiveled her head, looking first down Broughton then across to a street that led toward the river. "You know this isn't how it usually works. I have to be familiar with whatever I'm looking for." She shook her hand and clamped a fist to her stomach. "But I've got a burning sensation right here. It's like it's...pulling me."

Her eyes locked with Claudia's. "I have to follow."

"Yes. Yes. We're right behind you." When the light turned, Claudia hurried across Broughton with Lucia and Kylie, speed-walking in high heels as easily as she would in tennis shoes. A talent that required practice.

The three of them reached the next corner, and Lucia skidded to a halt. She turned toward a set of double doors as if led by a magic string. Pulling one glass door open, she stepped inside, but now her steps were hesitant. Cautious. Like moving too fast might break the connection.

Claudia and Kylie shared a glance before charging in after her. As soon as they crossed the threshold, Claudia's gift kicked into high gear as well.

They were standing inside an antique store.

The floors were a simple beige tile, but the rest of the rooms were the color of milk. From the walls and their wainscoting to the painted doors and ceiling. The design was genius, really, since the clean backdrop accentuated and showcased the gleaming antiques.

The store was a true find, full of authentic period pieces and rare treasures, but Claudia didn't have to study the collectibles to know their value. She didn't need to scrutinize the furniture for tongue and groove workmanship or the glassware for specific patterns.

All she'd done was step inside the store, and she could *feel* it.

Stories and vibes from past occurrences tickled at the edges of her mind. The sensation wasn't unpleasant, but to read an object's history, she actually had to touch it.

The presence of the antiques wasn't what bothered her, but in addition to Lucia's agitated state, a feeling of unease was crowding in the back of Claudia's mind. Like her friend, she was picking up a strange, pulsing energy.

The kind each of the women in her coven had learned to

identify. And to never ignore.

Magic was hiding among these fine collectibles, inside the enchanted item that was calling out to Lucia. And crawling like infection into Claudia's brain.

In need of a balm for her discomfort and hoping for a pleasing vision, Claudia spied a wash basin and pitcher set. She stepped closer. Cobalt-blue flowers rimmed the edge of the white porcelain, giving it a dainty, feminine flair.

She stroked the curving handle and opened her inner senses, letting the history of the antique wash her tainted mind, just as the set had once helped another cleanse their hands and body. The scent of roses flooded her, along with the image of a young blonde woman.

The genteel lady was washing her arms and shoulders with rose-water, an expensive and cherished gift from her husband. The very same soldier who'd just returned from war, taking a furlough from the nation's bloody battle of brother-against-brother. North against South.

While the backstory was bitter, the moment in time Claudia was witnessing held no hate or anger. Only love. She could almost feel the woman's nervous smile. See how full her heart was as she readied herself to be cherished by her one special man.

Claudia broke the connection then, having learned from experience when to extract herself. The lovely picture had done its job, and she'd been given a brief reprieve from the strange power she'd felt before.

But where was Lucia? For that matter, where had Kylie gone?

Claudia edged around a large armoire and caught a glimpse of Kylie's flowing golden hair. She could only make out her shoulder, but the bounce of the younger woman's curls as she nodded vigorously gave away her identity.

Claudia eased up beside her to see what Lucia had found.

The Spanish beauty was shaking as she held her palms out like radars. She swept her hands back and forth over a long glass counter where a variety of jewelry and other small treasures were on display.

"It's in here," Lucia said hoarsely. "Whatever it is, it wants to be found." She slowed her frantic waving and began using only her right hand. She expelled a full breath and set her palm atop the glass just as an older woman arrived on the other side of the protective case.

"Can I take something out for you?" The woman smiled, offering assistance without presumption. Claudia could see this was a lady who knew both her trade and her clientele. No pushy sales tactics would ever flow from those perfectly lined lips.

Claudia felt her heart kick when Lucia tapped the glass with one fingernail. "The pocket watch, please." A sudden sense of calm seemed to have conquered the Spanish woman's anxiety.

But as Claudia let her gaze fall to the intricate watch, a trembling sense of awe blossomed deep inside. Here was the force that had beckoned to Lucia. And here was the magic that filled Claudia with dread.

The saleswoman retrieved the watch and held it out to Lucia, the burnished gold still nestled in a purple velvet bag. Lucia worried her bottom lip as she held the antique with reverence, but then she cast apprehensive eyes to her friends. "I don't feel anything."

The lady behind the counter wrinkled her forehead briefly before stepping aside to give Lucia some time with her potential purchase. Claudia knew some collectors could be odd ducks, and the woman was likely used to strange behavior.

Kylie nodded to the watch in Lucia's hands. "Take it off the bag and touch it directly."

"Yeah." Lucia licked her lips. "Good idea." Her nervousness had made a reappearance and was evident in her quivering fingers.

Claudia was worried as well. What if Lucia was wrong and they ended up leaving the store without an answer? She'd performed more tasks than any of the other witches before her. Yet her amulet remained stubbornly silent.

Claudia would bleed for Lucia if she thought it would help her—her friend, her sister in magic—but there was nothing she could do to assist in her challenge. Nothing anyone in the coven could do.

It felt as if they'd abandoned a fallen comrade on the field to fend for herself, and the hole in Claudia's chest grew bigger every day. Every week, as Lucia's trial extended.

Would they know if she'd already failed? Would they be struck down by blue lightning or eradicated from existence? The waiting and the not knowing were worse than any demon's wrath or black witch's spell.

Suddenly the ticking watch seemed to be counting down to their doom. Was that why the ancient piece had struck Claudia so strangely? What would happen when Lucia touched it?

Tick...Tick...Tick...

She almost reached out to stop her friend. They really didn't know anything about the ancient timepiece. "Lucia—"

But Claudia was too late. In one rapid move, Lucia plucked the watch from the velvet, holding it tightly in her bare hand. Instead of closing her eyes, the Spanish woman stared at the watch as if daring it to respond.

After a few seconds, she shook her hand. "Come on. Do something." Her nerves were frayed to the breaking point, and the saleswoman looked as if she might comment on the rough-handling of the expensive and delicate piece.

"It's okay, Lucia." Claudia touched her friend's shoulder and smiled at the clerk in assurance. She spoke softly so only the two witches would hear. "Are you sure this is what drew you here? Maybe you should check again."

Lucia ground her teeth. "I'm sure."

In an attempt to distract her friend, Claudia looked more closely at the watch. "I don't know much about the mechanics, but this looks pretty old. Open it, so we can see inside."

"How do I open the thing?" Lucia's voice was brittle with frustration. "Here." She offered the piece to Claudia. "You know antiques, and I'm not feeling very careful right now. You take it."

Claudia paused, her bottom lip falling open slightly. She didn't know why she hesitated, but her need to soothe Lucia quickly overrode any misplaced fear. What was wrong with her? She loved antiques.

And she loved her friend.

"All right." She turned up a palm to receive the gleaming watch, and as soon as she captured it between her fingers, a vision overwhelmed her. The watch's history crashed through her, and she was helpless to control it. All she could do was hold onto the golden timepiece and grit her teeth.

Because the pain was excruciating.

Someone moaned as Claudia was consumed by her magical gift, and she had the impression the sound came from her own mouth. That her lips were releasing the agonized groan.

Before she could think any further on the noise, she pushed herself through some type of mental barrier and exploded out the other side.

She was instantly free of the burning pain. But she was no longer standing in the antique store.

Her head swiveled as she took in her surroundings, noticing now that the edges of her vision were blurred and sparkling. As if she were standing inside a prism looking out.

"Where am I?" Her words floated through the air, thick and unclear. Echoing. Then she took a more scrutinizing look at the room and stumbled backward as she understood. The question wasn't *where* she was.

But *when*.

Visions had always come to her in various forms. Sometimes she saw a clear picture, a brief glimpse of history as she had with the water pitcher and bowl. Other times she only caught a scent or a sound, depending on the strength of emotion still attached to the item she touched.

Often, though, she was simply filled with that emotion. A child's barrette could make her laugh, while a widower's belt buckle could drown her in grief.

But she'd never experienced this before. A complete and overpowering consumption by the past. She didn't know where her body was, but her mind was far, far back in time.

If she had to guess based on the bedroom's décor, she was standing in a seventeenth or eighteenth century home. A noise behind her startled her, and her head—such as it was—swung around to witness a maid enter through the doorway.

Claudia froze, hoping her lack of corporeal form would also mean she was invisible.

The woman in a black dress and white apron walked close enough to pass through Claudia's shoulder, but when she did so without pause, relief returned full force. The maid couldn't see her.

Claudia kept her gaze clapped to the woman as she took quick steps to a handsome dresser on the far side of the room. The wood was dark and finished with a burl ash veneer, and Claudia admired the craftsmanship as the maid slid open one of the top drawers.

She lifted a bag from inside, and Claudia would have gasped if she could. The bag was small and made of purple velvet. Now she understood her presence here. The antique watch from the store had brought her to this specific place in time. But how? Why?

Just as the questions whirled in her head, an undulating amber glow caught her eye. Above the dresser, something was shining like sunrise over a lake. Shimmering in waves of orange and green.

She zeroed in on the radiant space, and as she did, the colors lightened, leaving only a glistening outline. The strange colors encircled a painting on the wall, and an inner voice prompted Claudia to pay attention.

To remember.

A man's bellow carried from the other side of the door, from the hallway, and the abrupt shout caused the maid to jump. She cried out before cutting the sound in half by clamping her lips. Quickly she placed the watch on top of the dresser and rushed to stand beside the door.

Bowing her head, she waited, presumably for her employer. The man coming down the corridor.

The small woman was clearly afraid, and Claudia wondered what type of brute would instill such terror in the people who served his household. And why she'd been summoned—against her will—to watch whatever was about to unfold.

This time when the door swung open, she was calm and prepared, certain she wouldn't be discovered. Sure she was safe.

A tall man with raven-black hair filled the doorframe, and just as the heavy door slammed against the silk-papered wall, his eyes looked straight ahead. And focused on Claudia.

Trapped inside this foreign place, her mind scrambled for a way to escape. But she couldn't move. She had no control and could only stare back in horror. *His eyes. What color are they?*

In the depths of the stranger's glare, all she saw was fire.

Then his mouth opened, and pure black power permeated the room. Small stinging particles swarmed like a million sins.

The rush of malevolent energy catapulted her backward, and her untethered essence rolled and twisted through the air, into a void where she could no longer see the horrifying man. Or hear his poisonous rage.

Again she was wrapped in the scalding pain, but only briefly before the sensation vanished and she became aware of the ground beneath her back.

When Claudia opened her eyes, she found two worried faces hovering above her own. Lucia and Kylie. She was back.

Her breaths came rapidly now, in and out with urgency, but Claudia was just thankful she could feel her lungs working again. That she could sense her body.

Behind her friends, the antique store came into focus, and she realized she was lying on the floor.

Then, through the burning in her head and the roar in her ears, she heard an unmistakable sound. The precious song of a mystical jewel. A trial reaching completion.

Lucia gasped and looked down at her necklace. The crystalline sound seemed especially loud as the crimson stone rang out, and over Kylie's laugh and Lucia's triumphant, "Yes!" Claudia could still hear the clear note of victory.

Even the amulet seemed to be yelling *Finally!*

"I can't believe it!" Lucia's eyes filled with tears before her gaze returned to Claudia. "Oh. But are you okay?" Still, she couldn't stop the laugh from rolling again. "But I can't believe it!"

"I'm okay. I'm pretty sure." Claudia patted her friend's arm, giving her permission to enjoy the long-awaited moment. "I'm just going to take a minute. My head's still spinning."

"You passed out." Lucia's eyes had gone from exhilarated to troubled in a heartbeat. "As soon as you took the watch."

"Hmm...About that." Claudia had plenty to share with them both, but she was in no rush to relive the experience she'd just had. And she wanted to make sure she wouldn't fall again. "How long was I gone?"

"Um." Lucia shook her head. "About three seconds. We caught you and lowered you to the floor. Then your eyes popped open."

Claudia squinted into the bright light spilling in through the windows. "That can't be right. I was there for a few minutes, at least."

"We can figure this out when we get home, but right now, you should get up." Kylie's mouth had formed an anxious moue.

Claudia's head still felt like a water balloon, so she held up a hand to her friend. "I think I'll lie here for a minute."

"You should get up," Kylie repeated more fervently.

Lucia frowned at the blonde witch. "She doesn't feel well, Kylie. Give her a minute."

"Fine." Kylie's tone carried a warning of dire consequence when she spoke to Claudia. "But you're lying on a dirty, public floor. In your brand new *Elie Tahari*."

And with the grace borne of a ballet-filled childhood, Claudia gained her feet in one smooth motion. She pivoted so Kylie could check the back of her dress. "How is it?"

"Looks good." Kylie lightly dusted her fingers over Claudia's derriere. "I keep your priorities in check, even when you can't."

The two fashionistas shared a smile while Lucia rolled her eyes.

Still, the Spanish witch was worried as she put her arm around Claudia's back. "You think you can walk? What happened?"

The saleswoman spoke from behind Lucia, and the three of them turned to find her standing nearby. Claudia couldn't tell if she was more concerned about the fainting customer or the costly watch still clasped in her hand.

"We'll take the pocket watch," Claudia said, carefully handing the antique back to the store clerk. She didn't look at Kylie or Lucia, but she could sense her friends' surprise.

"I'll package this and ring it up." The clerk accepted the watch and bustled away, but her wide smile told Claudia that she just might faint again after all. Once she saw the bill.

"You're buying it?" Lucia asked, her arm still firmly

supporting Claudia.

"Yes. We need it." With a pounding headache growing stronger by the second, Claudia put one hand on Lucia's arm and used her other to reach for Kylie. "I just had a run-in with a demon."

While her sisters stared with shocked expressions, Claudia took a deep breath. "I think I just met Bastraal."

3

While Kylie went straight upstairs to deposit her shopping bags in her bedroom, Claudia and Lucia detoured to the kitchen. They found Paige and Mrs. Attinger preparing a veggie tray.

Only the maternal housekeeper could get away with batting Paige's hand away as it reached for the freshly-sliced carrots. "If you eat it all before we get it to the others, we'll just be back in here filling up again."

"You forget." Paige grinned. "I can whip this up in a flash." The ex-soldier stood at least six inches over Mrs. Attinger, but the wink she gave the silver-haired lady was equal parts mischief and affection.

The housekeeper considered all of the witches her honorary children, and there was no one who could keep a coven in line like Mrs. Attinger. She pointed a cautionary finger at Paige. "You'll keep that super-speed out of my kitchen. I like the walls where they are."

A grin tugged at Claudia's lips when Paige only grunted in response. The female banter and cozy kitchen environment were helping to improve her mood. Masonry of beige and gray rocks arched across the ceiling, ending in a wall of the same workmanship.

The kitchen was one of the coven's favorite hangouts. The

space was warm and inviting, with Anna's familial home punched up and brought into the twenty-first century by a few stylish additions.

The kitchen island was the same gray found in the stonework, but the oversized granite piece curved in the shape of a crescent moon. Plenty of seating for nine women. And their cats.

Anna had added her own touch of style with spots of color throughout the space. There was a gleaming farm sink of cobalt and three hanging lights with glass pyramids. Each shone its own bright hue of red, blue, or yellow.

Lucia cleared her throat to draw the two women's attention and snapped Claudia out of her drifting thoughts as well. "Is there a party somewhere?" The Spanish witch gestured to the food when two sets of eyes swung her way in surprise.

"There you are!" Mrs. Attinger tossed them a sunny grin.

But it was Paige who answered the question in a brisk tone. "Not a party. Exactly." She eyed the broadly smiling Lucia with suspicion. None of them had seen her so relaxed and happy in weeks.

"I just came for wine," Claudia said quickly, stepping to the cabinet that housed the glasses and trying to head off Paige's interrogation. She knew Lucia wanted to share her good news with everyone at once, and Paige was studying her shrewdly.

The others would all be ecstatic to learn that Lucia's trial was actually, thoroughly, completely *over*. And verified by a gemstone solo that had truly been music to the ears.

Claudia really did want that wine, though. She had a terrible headache, and while a little juice of the grape wouldn't cure the pain, it would certainly numb its sharp edges. And she would need the liquid analgesic soon, because after Lucia shared her joyous news, Claudia had an announcement of her own.

She was thrilled for Lucia, and relieved her friend's trial was over after all she'd battled through. A trip to Peru that had begun with a plane crash. A run-in with the Amara in the depths of the Amazonian jungle. A harem of flesh-eating half-demons—who could also turn into spiders—that guarded the ancient dagger Lucia had been sent to find.

And last of all, a soul mate who'd been saddled with a demon of his own. If any of them deserved a respite from this prophecy, it was Lucia. So there were no misgivings on that front.

Claudia just wished her call to trial had been a little less… torturous. Her summoning hadn't been the sweet and fuzzy kind that some of the others had experienced.

No magical hummingbird, prophetic vision, or messages from an ancient book. Even nightmares and ghosts seemed preferable to the agony she'd gone through, only to end up face to face with the creature they all feared most.

Bastraal. Demon from the underworld currently scheming to enter the human realm. Just as he had three centuries before, only to be defeated and banished by the original Savannah coven. Three witches, three sisters, who'd left a prophecy behind to be fulfilled.

Now, as Claudia poured herself some shimmering Chardonnay, she wondered what the St. Germaine sisters from so long ago would think of their modern-day counterparts.

"So where is this not-exactly-party?" Lucia asked as Paige hefted the veggie tray.

"In the library." Paige gave them a lop-sided grin when she made her way around the center island and out the door. Then she called back to them, "With a candlestick."

Lucia put her hands on her shapely hips. "What does that mean? I don't get it." American expressions and pop-culture sometimes eluded the Spanish beauty.

Claudia sighed, letting the chilled wine bathe her strained throat. "I'll explain on the way."

Most of the mansion's residents were piled into the library, the perfect place for such a crowd considering the vast space and variety of seating areas. But the reason for their gathering in the bibliophile's haven wasn't for books. At least, not today.

Two massive desks had been cleared of the usual clutter to make room for a board-game tournament. One held the typical cardboard square, and Paige's earlier comment made sense when Anna declared, "Mrs. Peacock, in the conservatory, with the wrench."

Willyn's husband, Dare, tossed down three cards and frowned at his childhood friend. His eyes of deep-sea blue accused, while Anna stared back innocently. Albeit a bit smugly. "Tell me again that you're not using your psychic powers." His mouth flattened with chagrin as he gathered the cards to shuffle.

Anna laughed and cocked her head. "You always were a sore loser."

Paige took the empty seat between the two of them, returning the number of players to four. Lucia's boyfriend, Ethan, sat at the table with his back to the doorway where Claudia and Lucia stood, still unnoticed.

Kylie slid up behind them quietly, waiting for Lucia to take the lead. This was her show after all.

Claudia looked to the other game area where colored dominoes formed long lines or "trains," each player doing their best to be the first to lay down all their tiles. It was then that she realized how the coven was separated. The pattern was surely unintentional, yet her skin chilled and ran with goose bumps.

All of the women at the domino table had completed their trials. Shauni, Willyn, Viv, and Hayden were engrossed in the competition, but it was their number that gave her pause. Four of them, now five with Lucia's success, had gone up against evil, and had won.

They were over halfway through the tests the coven had to face. One step closer to defeating the Amara. The group was led by Ronja, an ancient witch who'd only grown more ruthless over the passing years, and the very immortal who planned to raise a demon from the underworld.

Bastraal.

Somehow the name held more menace for Claudia now. Meeting his handsome human form hadn't made him less terrifying, but more so. His black hair, chiseled face, and lean physique were attractive by human standards.

But the demon fire in his eyes had scorched Claudia to her marrow. To the deepest, darkest place inside her soul. One that should have been protected, but against his strength, was as vulnerable as newborn flesh.

Quinn was the first to spy Claudia, Kylie, and Lucia loitering on the edge of the crowd. He sat in a chair near the windows on the far side of the library holding Willyn's son in his lap. Six-year-old Tadd supported a book half his size, and given the aged cover's cryptic writing, he was getting a lesson on magical writing from the coven's resident expert.

Quinn notched his chin up in greeting. "Hey. Did you guys bring any real food back from the mainland? Mrs. Attinger is treating us like a bunch of rabbits."

His remark drew everyone's attention to the three women standing in the doorway, but Ethan was the first to leap from his chair. He'd turned slowly in his seat, searching for Lucia, but with one glance at her face, he knew.

His wide smile matched hers, the Spanish witch who'd fought so hard for his love. "You've done it." The surety in his voice and gleam in his eye spoke of how well he could read Lucia's expression.

When she nodded in response and her eyes glistened with happy tears, Ethan gave a great whoop and rushed to lift her in his arms. He spun her full-circle before setting her back on her feet.

The room erupted with questions, and Claudia found herself getting caught up in the heightened emotion. After all, they'd left the island for a little retail therapy, and had returned with another victory for the coven.

Kylie chose that moment to send a satisfied grin to Claudia as the others clamored to offer their congratulations. Pride was written all over her face. "Never doubt the power of shopping," she murmured, holding out her palm for a high-five.

Shaking her head and chuckling low, Claudia allowed herself a moment of job-well-done and slapped her hand to Kylie's. Who would have guessed dragging Lucia out of the island home for a day would yield such excellent results?

She let the joy wash through her as Ethan and Lucia embraced again. The relief in his expression as he held on tight made Claudia's heart release with a bittersweet sigh. Lucia was a lucky woman, and now, at long last, she could relax and enjoy her newfound love.

Hugs and laughter continued for a moment, when amid the raucous excitement, Lucia gently extracted herself from the center of it all. Her smile dimmed as she gazed expectantly at Claudia.

"What? My turn already?" Claudia's forced laugh felt anti-climactic, but the details of how Lucia had completed her trial had to be shared with the rest of the coven. And that included Claudia's vision.

"Why do I get the feeling there's more to tell?" Paige asked, always the one to cut to the heart of a situation, even if the slice was painful.

Lucia moved to stand elbow to elbow with Claudia before addressing the curious group. The air of happiness in the room had veered swiftly to concern. "I didn't know how to end my challenge, but I was supposed to find a particular object. One I didn't even know I was looking for."

Her eyes were empathetic when they fell on Claudia. Each trial proved more difficult than the one before, and Claudia's had begun with an even greater level of distress. "This has never happened before," Lucia said. "My trial ended," she turned back to the coven, "when Claudia's began."

Her words were met by stunned silence and a few gasps. Hayden shook her head, caramel-hued hair falling around her shoulders. "But that's so fast. No time at all in between."

The accelerated pace was a worry to them all. Yes, the women had learned a lot about their powers in the last year, discovering new strengths and hidden magic, but the ever-changing pattern kept taking them by surprise.

Kylie squeezed Claudia's arm encouragingly and went to sit in a chair. Her action served to calm the rest of them, and they resumed casual positions.

Willyn and Dare leaned against a desk together, while Quinn left Tadd to flip through the huge book by himself. Lucia went back to Ethan, and the other women all settled into seats.

Removing the black glasses perched on her nose, Viv put on her scientist face and leveled Claudia with a stare. "I take it the object Lucia was talking about is in that bag?"

For a moment, Claudia felt as if she were facing her first full lecture hall of students. Her knees quivered and her chest constricted. She wasn't nervous about speaking to a crowd, but she was about to share one hell of a history lesson

"Yes. It's a pocket watch." She let the breath roll out of her as she launched into a recap of the day's events. She reached into the bag for the watch, now safely ensconced inside the purple velvet wrapping as well as a jewelry box.

She was actually afraid to touch it again, and the fear left her unsettled. The talent she'd always appreciated had suddenly become a source of anxiety. Her gift now seemed like a curse, lying in wait to drag her back down. Through the overwhelming agony.

And back to the monster.

She cleared her throat forcefully. "When I took the watch from Lucia, I traveled through some sort of portal, but only my mind went back in time. Not my body."

She spoke rapidly, pouring out the awful memory before anyone could interrupt with a question. "I could see and hear everything that was happening, but the people there couldn't see me." *Not the real people, anyway.*

"Where were you?" Shauni asked, petting her cat as the feline twined around her ankles. Cuileann's black hair and emerald eyes were a reflection of her human's and, as if summoned by the important meeting underway, the rest of the cats began filtering into the library.

"Um," Claudia lost track of her thoughts as she searched for her own Rowan Von Ashbi. Funny how she was surrounded by friends—essentially family—yet she still sought the comfort of her cat. Her loyal confidante and all-around best guy.

"I was still in Savannah." She saw Kylie's golden girl, Sassy, leap into the blonde witch's lap as Lucia's black Persian perched gracefully on Ethan's booted foot.

Just as irrational panic was clawing its way through her abdomen, Claudia felt a silken caress against the back of her legs. Then the low rumble from Ashbi's chest as the stately tomcat took a dignified seat next to her and gazed upward. She would swear he was offering his support.

She almost asked Shauni to tell her what the cat was thinking, but remembered she had more critical information to share. "The vision." She looked to Anna, their leader and owner of the ancestral mansion they all called home. "I was still in Savannah, but not the present. I went back to the seventeen-hundreds."

"How could you tell?" Paige leaned forward, propping her elbows on her knees as she listened intently.

Here came the hard part, Claudia thought. Her news would be a shock to the coven, just as it had been to her. "The furniture and dress of the maid I saw there gave me clues, but the owner of the house was someone..." She stalled, hoping to ease them into acceptance. "Someone who was alive at the same time as the original Savannah witches."

Anna's shoulders went rigid, and Claudia knew she understood. "I was in Bastraal's home," she confirmed. "I saw his human form. Rather, I saw his victim's stolen body."

Paige's face turned to stone. "Oh, shit."

Kylie nodded. "Oh, yeah."

Bastraal's ultimate goal was to return to this world in corporeal form, in a human body. Just as he had three centuries ago, when he'd performed unspeakable atrocities during his short visit.

The original three St. Germaine witches had put him down then, but had left a prophecy behind. They had known the demon would try to return one day, with more power, a better plan, and his own hellish army to back him up.

The fiend had been preparing for three centuries.

The coven had been together for one year.

"Touching the watch took you to him," Anna said on a breath. She rolled her shoulders in an attempt to release tension. "Well. I guess we were bound to have direct contact with him at some point."

Grateful for the slow, trickling effect of the wine she was drinking, Claudia took a deep breath and readied herself to tell them everything. Bastraal's reaction when he saw her, the painting and its apparent significance, and of course, the difference in her gift. The vortex that had thrown her back into history, and straight into the demon's path.

Then there was the discomfort she'd felt. Oh, who was she kidding? Not discomfort, but a blood-searing burn that made her quiver at the mere memory.

"I'm ready for my challenge." Claudia meant the words, though she took a quick sip of Chardonnay to back them up. "But I am worried about one thing."

"You?" Kylie hiked a blonde brow. "You're not the worrying kind."

"Well, I am now. I'll probably have to find that painting, and I think my test will involve locating certain items Bastraal owned when he was in this world as a human. I don't know all the answers yet, but I'm going to figure it out. The watch is the first step, but definitely not the last. I'm sure I'll have to handle antiques, gaining what knowledge I can from each one."

Clenching her jaw, Claudia voiced her greatest concern. "I'll use my gift. It's what I'm meant to do."

Anna sat with her back straight, like the true lady of the manor. "What is it that frightens you, Claudia?"

"When I held the pocket watch, I didn't have control of the vision. Not like I normally do." No amount of wine could lessen the impact of the truth. "The vision had control of me."

4

The sun was strong and climbing up one side of the sky when Cole stepped off the white boat and onto the dock. Trevor had called him earlier to invite him to the island house for lunch, assuring him the request was from the coven.

The two detectives had worked late into the night after their witness interview had led to an arrest, a brief interrogation, and a babbling confession from the suspect. Cole smirked as he followed the trail through the forest. Most criminals weren't nearly as clever as the ones on television.

As a result, he and Trevor had this Sunday off, free and clear. So he had no reason to turn down the offer of a meal with the coven.

He was well-rested, as there had been no late-night activities beyond the paperwork he'd had to write up. No time spent at his favorite bar. And no date with Rachel the Perky.

That had been his decision, though, since her nose-breathing had really started to get to him. At least that's what he told himself. The same way he argued with his inner voice that he was always glad to hang out with the witches and their men. That he wasn't any more eager to visit the island than any other time.

Even if the weather was warming up. And the short skirts

were coming out.

Unsure if he was attending a special occasion of some kind, Cole had opted for a plain white shirt and dark gray pants. He'd even taken the time to shave his I'm-too-busy-solving-murders stubble he'd ignored for the past few days.

Despite Anna's previous insistence that he make himself at home at the mansion, Cole rang the doorbell next to the wide double doors and waited for someone to answer. He admired the mix of stone and dark wood that made up the exterior, marveling at the elegance and architecture.

A few of the women called the place the St. Germaine "castle." He could certainly see why.

As he waited, he grinned to himself, comparing the massive entryway to an advent calendar. With all the people residing here now, he never knew what he'd find when the door opened.

When Trevor swung one of the massive oak panels wide, Cole grunted and frowned. "Aw, hell, that's no fun. I see you all the time."

"Good to see you too, partner." The blonde giant who'd been tamed by a ghost-whispering witch crossed thick arms over an even thicker chest. "Or were you just hoping to be greeted by someone prettier?"

Because the wisecrack was too close to the truth for his comfort, Cole lifted a careless shoulder. "Never hurts to hope."

As they moved inside and crossed through the foyer, Trevor tossed a glance his way. His tone was half warning, half jest when he said, "I don't want any of the girls ending up in that digital black book of yours."

Cole ignored his partner and waved aside the comment as they strode through the great room. He knew his way around the lower floor, and would rather find one of the women to banter with than his over-protective partner.

Trevor's distrust of him was ironic, since Cole had been the one to welcome Hayden when she'd first come to offer information on a case they were working. When his doubtful colleague had shunned her, Cole had been the open-minded one.

Even though her information had been supplied by a ghost.

Eventually, though, his partner had come around. He'd learned to believe in Hayden, and in the end, had taken a rocky tumble into love with the pretty medium.

Now he viewed all of the witches as sisters, of a sort, and felt the need to repeatedly remind Cole that they were off limits.

Despite the fact they needed no protection and could all throw fire and freaky blue light from their palms faster than Cole could unholster his Sig.

Cole decided he had a response after all. "You wound me, man. You really do. I'm not good enough for one of the witches, but you are?" His tone was light, but inside he was growing increasingly defensive about Trevor's jokes.

"Not what I'm saying. I know you're solid. Any woman would be lucky to have you." His partner led him down a wide hallway and toward the back of the home. When Trevor stopped just inside a set of French-paned doors leading to the gardens, he gave Cole a meaningful look. "That is, once you decide to settle on a woman. And *only one*."

Now Cole bristled. He pushed out the door and into the light, but not before flinging back at his friend, "I don't mistreat women, and I don't lie or cheat."

Wanting to put the discussion behind him, Cole veered straight to the woman he'd just mentioned. Hayden was beaming at him and holding out some kind of champagne flute. "Mimosa?"

With a lift of brows as answer, he took the drink and downed it in two long sips.

As soon as Trevor showed up with a glower on his face, Hayden looked up at her boyfriend and pursed her lips. "What did you say to Cole?"

When the big guy threw up his hands, Cole couldn't stop the laugh that rumbled from his chest. Then he leaned over and gave Hayden a smacking kiss on the cheek. "You really shouldn't let Trevor answer the door, you know." He jerked his head toward his partner. "Good thing I'm used to him."

Trevor only grunted before wrapping his arm around Hayden's waist and responding to his friend. "Does that mean I'll eventually get used to you?" He lifted one side of his mouth, and Cole knew there were no hard feelings.

It took a lot more than a few words to come between the two men. The two partners, who'd seen more corruption of the human race than anyone should ever have to, and who were always ready to take a bullet for each other.

The courtyard where they stood was paved with flagstones that were much older than any of the people currently living in the mansion. A long table had been set up, and Mrs. Attinger was bringing out covered silver platters.

Though not one for fancy trappings, Cole took a moment to study the white tablecloth and colorful setting. He noticed straight away that the long runner down the middle of the table was deep red. Lucia's color. As were the ornate goblets sitting in the two o'clock position in relation to the white porcelain settings.

Three crystals bowls had been placed on the runner, one in the center with the other two near the ends. The flowers they held were in the shape of stars—he didn't know their name—but the petals were a different color. Not red, but a pale orange.

And that was Claudia's color.

"Why didn't you tell me?" he asked Trevor, feeling the grind in his jaw as he spoke. When his partner only furrowed his brow in confusion, Cole clarified, "That Claudia's trial has begun."

Trevor shrugged. "To be honest, I don't know. I didn't even think about it, and we needed you here today anyway."

Now Cole's back muscles bunched. Claudia. Her trial. Now

he was needed for something? This didn't bode well.

He was attracted to the redheaded history professor, but considering the coven's pattern—every witch called to her challenge was ultimately paired with a mate—he wasn't comfortable being summoned to help. Or put into the line of fire.

He wouldn't deny the women anything they needed to defeat the Amara, but if he were smart, he'd keep some distance between himself and the witch whose time had finally arrived.

The witch who made his body tighten in response whenever she was near.

And speaking of the devilishly gorgeous, Claudia Grant chose that moment to stroll from the house carrying a small platter of sliced meats. She was wearing another short dress— the sadist—of a purple so dark it was almost black.

Her straight hair flamed brighter against the color, and as her heels clacked across the stones, Cole spoke aside to Trevor and Hayden. "What exactly am I needed for?"

"Your expertise." Trevor slapped him on the back as Anna waved them to come over and take a seat at the table. "What? Did you think the ladies just longed for your company?"

Without explaining further, Trevor walked away, but Hayden looped her arm through Cole's and gave him her sweet, patient smile. "Friendship is one of life's precious jewels, isn't it?" Her eyes sparkled in the sun.

Cole shook his head and laughed. "With Trevor, sometimes it's more of a dirty rock."

Drawing closer as the others started taking places at the long table, Cole and Hayden automatically deviated toward Trevor, who stood at the opposite end from Claudia.

However, his course was interrupted by Anna's serene voice. "Cole, take the chair by Claudia, if you don't mind."

At the mention of his name, Claudia's head snapped up. Her eyes widened almost imperceptibly, but Cole registered her surprise.

"Cole." Claudia's voice was smooth and luxurious, like velvet sliding over his already-heightened senses. "I didn't realize you were coming."

Yeah. He'd guessed as much.

Choosing to confront the mystery head-on, he moved her way. "I think you and I are both being kept in the dark." He gestured to the peach-hued napkins and floral centerpieces. "I see it's your turn."

A shadow passed behind her eyes, but she recovered quickly. "Lucky number six, I guess."

Cole nodded as Trevor jumped in to clarify. "I forgot to mention to Cole that your trial had started, but after Hayden told me about the antique watch you found and how everything went down..."

"Watch?" Now something other than Cole's apprehension was stirring. He was immediately intrigued, and slightly relieved. "Now this is all starting to make sense."

Claudia was already seated, so he took the chair next to her and explained himself. "I know about clocks and watches. My grandfather taught me his craft, and restoring old clocks is a hobby of mine."

If she'd been surprised before, now she looked stunned. "You're a...*clockmaker*?"

Her glossy lips smiled as she said the last, making Cole feel like a doddering old man who had a handlebar mustache and wore lederhosen. He cleared his throat. "It can be a welcome distraction. The work gets my mind off of other things and helps clear my head." *And tonight I'll be nose-deep in minute wheels and hairsprings, trying to forget about your legs.*

Deciding to divert his attention from said appendages, he reached for the napkin tented on his plate, but froze when he caught a whiff of her perfume. Either he'd leaned too close or the breeze had shifted, but a gentle cloud of fragrance passed over him.

Cole reached deep for control, hardening his face into a mask that showed no reaction. First Claudia's color was everywhere. Then she just had to be wearing a thigh-high dress. Now he was to be tempted by her sweet scent.

He shot a dark look to Trevor. His partner was a dead man.

Cole didn't know much about perfume, but she smelled of barely-there flowers mixed with something citrusy. Whatever it was, she smelled too good. And this luncheon was turning out to be a special kind of torture.

He'd been accused of having a silver tongue, but the lump in his mouth felt tarnished at the moment. Claudia Grant and her sky-high IQ always had that effect on him. She made him jumpy. But as always, he did his best to hide it.

The meal was getting under way, and Mrs. Attinger waved Shauni and her boyfriend to take a seat. The two animal-lovers were the last standing, so the tall blonde vet helped Shauni into a chair before leaning down to kiss her cheek.

Thankfully, Mrs. Attinger instructed everyone to dig in, saving Cole from any further conversation. He focused on the meal before him instead of the woman next to him, and let one primal need take the place of the other.

He needed to get himself together, take a look at this watch they'd mentioned, then make a hasty exit out of there. The vibe he normally felt around the coven had changed, its intensity increasing to an uncomfortable level.

Like a cable stretched too tightly, Cole felt like something inside him was ready to snap. And proximity to Claudia was directly correlated to the tension.

Despite her nearness, he made it through the salad, entrée, and dessert, while small talk with the other men passed the time. Quinn was next to Trevor, and Nick and Ethan had also joined the day's impromptu celebration. Dare was at the far end of the table, never one to wander too far from his wife,

Willyn.

It was a packed house today, and the lively group helped Cole loosen up. As did the amazing gardens, bright and cheery with an assortment of blooms. The wind was light, the sun was warm, and everything else was picture perfect.

Until coffee arrived and Claudia touched her hand to his arm. Every ounce of repressed desire rushed back when her long, delicate fingers brushed the underside of his forearm.

"Ready to see the watch?" She started to rise when Quinn spoke up. "Anna asked me to get it when I went inside." He reached over a basket of rolls to set a purple bag on the table. "Hope that's okay."

"Of course. It belongs to the coven, even if it is part of my challenge. Just like the book and dagger." The smile Claudia gave Quinn made Cole's heart kick hard. She'd smiled at him just like that. In the beginning. But the last few times he'd seen her, something had been different. More strained and awkward.

She indicated the bag, presumably with the watch inside. "Go ahead."

Cole wondered why she didn't reach for it, opting instead to keep her hands tucked carefully in her lap.

As requested, Cole set aside his dessert plate and eased the bag open. A box slid into his hand, so he lifted the lid to find a gold watch in excellent condition. "What period did you guess this was from?" he asked Claudia.

She leaned closer to study the face with him. "I thought early eighteenth century. Possibly even older."

The plain gold casing and black filigree hands didn't give a fair representation of the complexity that Cole knew lay inside. "You were close. I believe this is a fusee with a mock pendulum, sixteen ninety to sixteen ninety-five." He flipped the watch over to study the back. "Odd. I don't see a maker's mark, so I can't tell you who made it."

When he started to open the watch to inspect the inner workings, Claudia sucked in a sharp breath. "Careful," she whispered, but again, Cole noticed she kept her hands a safe distance from the piece. The pocket watch was important to her, but she didn't want to touch it.

His eyes clashed with hers then. In question. And in challenge. "You could tell me just as much about this watch as I can tell you."

Claudia simply gazed back at him, her river-green eyes giving him no clue to what she was thinking.

"Oh, there's more to tell, all right." Kylie lifted her coffee cup to punctuate her declaration.

Cole kept his stare glued to Claudia, his previous urge to leave now crushed beneath the weight of curiosity. And for reasons he couldn't identify, he was troubled.

Closing the black box with a muted *click*, Cole reached for the coffee pot to refill his own cup. "It's Sunday, and Trevor and I just closed a case." He winked at Kylie then turned to Claudia. "So I've got plenty of time to discuss the watch. And you can tell me everything."

5

"Why are you afraid to touch the watch?" Cole was right behind Claudia as they walked down the hall toward the great room. She didn't feel like answering his question, and besides, today was supposed to be about Lucia. The luncheon was to have been a celebration.

Claudia didn't feel festive anymore. Then again, she hadn't felt lightness in her heart since she'd been blasted back through time to face Bastraal. But she'd hoped to forge her way through her trial in her own time, her own way.

Now here Cole was, pushing himself into her business. And without any tact whatsoever.

"That doesn't matter." She whirled to face him as she came to a stop in front of the majestic fireplace. The hearth was empty, since the southern heat of spring had arrived, aside from a multitude of flaming candles sitting in place of burning timber.

The absence of sound was disconcerting. No snap and crackle, no shifting logs. No warmth.

And Claudia was so cold inside, even with the bright, sunny weather. "Can you tell me about the watch or not?" she asked him, dodging his query with one of her own.

His eyes narrowed momentarily, then he relented with a

sigh. "Fine." He wasn't happy about giving in first, and Claudia suspected he wasn't finished with his interrogation.

Cole was her friend and a man she trusted implicitly, so why was she suddenly so standoffish with him? He had knowledge to share about the antique watch. Knowledge she needed. But her gut was screaming at her to stand back.

Actually, it was shouting for her to run.

Cole was a good-looking guy, hardened by the misery he'd seen in his line of work, yet he managed to maintain an almost irrational optimism. And empathy in those gray-green eyes of his. Unique in color, and unsettling in their intensity.

"Let's sit down. I don't want to risk dropping the watch on this slate floor." He held out a hand in a ladies-first gesture, so she had no choice but to sit on the green velvet couch.

When they were seated—entirely too close for her comfort—Cole resumed his lecture on the pocket watch. "There's not much I can tell you other than the time period it appears to have been made, that the creator left no stamp or trademark to stake his claim, and that it is a verge fusee. Verge refers to the mechanism that controls the advancement of gears inside. To keep it simple, it helps control the ticks."

"I'm familiar with the fusee part. Not sure where I heard it, though." Claudia hazarded another glance at his face. He was absorbed in the timepiece he was telling her about, while his strong, rugged hands inspected the watch with delicacy.

She wondered if he'd be the same way with a woman. Rubbing her forehead to cast out the lurid images dancing in her mind, she continued. "Fusee has something to do with the pulley inside." She exhaled. "And that's the extent of my education on watch innards."

"Good thing you have me around, then." Cole offered her a friendly smile, but she could only focus on what he'd said. No, it was *not* a good thing to have him around. Not when he was so charming, and helpful, and so, so...overpoweringly *male*.

He lifted the front of the watch and pointed out a few of the parts, explaining how they worked. She caught the terms *escapement* and *mainspring*, but his voice was mostly just a buzz in her ears. A deep and sexy buzz.

And backed with all that knowledge she never even knew he possessed. A completely unique aspect of him that had nothing to do with collaring perps, or whatever real-life homicide detectives called the apprehension of murderers.

Cole was supposed to be the ladies' man hot cop, not an intriguing person with complexities she might find fascinating, and multiple facets that deepened his character. Imagining him as simply "Trevor's partner" had been her ward against his physical appeal.

Maybe she should perform a real spell. One that would make him repellent instead of captivating.

Claudia huffed softly. Cole Lonergan needed to get himself far from her presence and stay that way henceforth. At least until her trial was over and she was safe again. Safe from the vagaries of that force called fate, which so enjoyed playing matchmaker with the witches in her coven.

She waited for Cole to finish his spiel and, once he had, he fell silent and looked at her expectantly.

"Well." Claudia lightly slapped her thighs, then stood. "I appreciate your help, Cole. If I have any questions, I'll let you know." He only sat there staring, so she tried another tack. "How about some more coffee?"

"How about you tell me why you won't touch this watch?" Now his smiling eyes were resolute, and she could see he was going to be stubborn.

What did it hurt to tell him? He knew everything else anyway. Then he'd be satisfied. Then he'd be *gone*.

"You know about my talent for seeing the history of any item I touch. How I get glimpses of the past." She started to cross her arms over her chest but felt the move was indicative of vulnerability. And she didn't want to appear weak. "I had a very strong vision when I touched this watch, because it once belonged to Bastraal."

"The demon?" Cole leaped up and came face to face with Claudia. "What did you see?"

She wanted to retreat a step, but forced her feet to stay glued to the floor. "I saw him, his bedroom, and his maid." As she revisited the experience, the words burned her throat. "The visit to his time period was unpleasant, to say the least. So I don't touch the watch, because I don't want to go through that again until absolutely necessary."

"What do you mean, his time period? I thought you only saw things, like flashes from the past."

Now she did cross her arms, but casually. "That's how it normally works, yes."

Cole studied her face and seemed to be searching for what to say or ask. Instead, he closed the jewelry box soundly and placed it back inside the purple bag he still held. Finally, he set the bag and its contents on an end table.

Voices suddenly floated from the back corridor as the others filed in from the gardens. Cole nodded to Trevor as he and Hayden entered, with Kylie and Anna close behind. Shauni and Viv followed Mrs. Attinger to the kitchen with dirty dishes.

"Claudia was just telling me about her vision," Cole said, looking briefly to Trevor, then back to Claudia. "And about Bastraal."

Hayden's grin faltered. "Oh. It was awful from how she described it. The pain and passing out the way she did."

Cole stiffened. "She failed to mention that part."

Claudia waved her hand as if to dismiss the severity of what she'd gone through. She worked up a rueful laugh. "Details, and not important ones. We all go through something during our trials. I just wasn't prepared." She smoothed one hand down her dress, as if securing an invisible shield. "Now I am."

"Right," Hayden agreed. "And when you find the painting, we'll all be here to help you."

"Painting?" Cole perked up.

Claudia grimaced. "Hayden. As much as I adore you...you're going to *have* to stop talking now."

Sporting an apologetic smile, Hayden sidestepped and made a sharp right turn. "Um...I'll just go see what I can do in the kitchen." She latched onto Trevor and tugged. "You should come with me. We've both interfered enough for one day."

Cole opened his mouth, but before he could speak again, the rest of the party trooped inside, giving Claudia an extended reprieve. That is, until Kylie and Anna descended on her. "We want to help you look for the painting you saw in the vision," Anna said.

Anna was an artist herself, so she and Claudia had already decided to peruse some of her art books to see if any of the works looked similar to the one in Bastraal's bedroom. The one that had shimmered mystically, declaring itself the prominent part of the scene.

"We can wait until after the celebration." Claudia sent a steely gaze toward Anna. Her sister of the heart and very dear friend. Who was mucking things up just as badly as Hayden had been. "After the *guests* have all gone."

"Maybe I can help," Cole offered, the mocking half-smile on his face telling Claudia he knew she was hoping to get rid of him. "I've been all over Savannah searching for rare clocks and working with other collectors. If your painting is in this city, I might be able to point you in the right direction."

"You don't have to do that," Claudia said. "You've already been a big help, and I can take it from here." Her clipped tone and the set of her jaw relayed what she wasn't saying. That she could handle her responsibilities. That she preferred to do so. *Alone.*

"I think the more heads working together, the better." Anna

lifted one brow in question.

Gritting her teeth, Claudia slowly inclined her head. "Okay, then. Let's go."

Determined not to waste any more time, she made a beeline for the library but slowed her pace when the *click-clack* of her heels resonated throughout the long hallway like stiletto firecrackers. She might be agitated, but she didn't have to show it.

The heavy double doors were open, and she entered the room to find Quinn, Dare, and Willyn already gathered around one of the desks. Apparently, she was going to have *lots* of heads working on this.

But at least she and Cole wouldn't be in here alone. The physical tension between them had included too many accidental touches and stolen glances.

Cole had never been shy about sharing his love for the female sex, in all its forms and flavors, but his eyes on her had felt different today. And her duplicitous body had responded. Everywhere he'd looked, her skin had grown hot, as if being stroked by his hands instead of his gaze.

Well, she decided, there would be no more of that.

Conjuring a cheerful expression for the others, Claudia asked, "Are those all of the books?"

Willyn cast eyes as blue as the summer sky over to her friend. "Just the ones Anna recommended we start with." The blonde woman was a healer and instinctively compassionate. Of all the women, she understood the predicament of using her magical ability only to be met with agony.

But the pain Willyn used to feel after healing people had lessened over time. As the witches had grown into their magic, becoming more in touch with their true power, her discomfort had disappeared altogether.

Claudia told herself that she only had to make it through her challenge. Then she would return to normal, as would her gift. She had to believe that, because she was bereft without it.

"Here," Willyn said, hefting a large book and carrying it to another desk. "This one focuses on an individual artist in each chapter, so you can see their paintings all at once. Maybe you'll notice a particular style."

"Perfect." Taking a seat at the wide wooden table, Claudia flipped the heavy cover open and turned to the first chapter. When a chair scraped up next to hers, she cast a warning look to her left. But it was only Kylie.

"Hey, Teach. Can you describe that picture to me again?" The younger woman had her hair in a blonde braid and a notebook in her hand.

"What are you doing with that?"

Kylie tapped her pen to the paper. "Taking notes for an Internet search."

"Oh. Right." Claudia bobbed her head like a doll's on a spring. Why hadn't she thought of that?

Most likely because she was completely out of sorts, and unable to think straight. *I've been muddled before. I just have to remember how I made it through grad school. Formulate an outline, and take things one piece at a time.*

Only difference was that if she'd gotten a less than perfect grade on a history paper, she wouldn't be sentencing the city of Savannah—not to mention all of her friends—to a horrific and bloody death at the hands of the Amara and their pet demons.

And then there was Bastraal. The master of them all.

Focusing on the task at hand, she described the portrait to Kylie. "The scene was fairly simple with an olive green background. A single woman was sitting in a chair. Her dress was royal blue, her eyes and hair both brown."

She took one long nail, painted plum to match her dress, and pointed to the next empty line of the notebook. "Put an asterisk by this. A golden owl was perched on one of the woman's fingers. Despite her expensive clothes and haughty expression, that owl was the main character. The wise one."

"Got it." Kylie hopped up and headed toward one of the computer stations, leaving Claudia to continue studying the book at her own pace.

The group worked quietly for a while, and she was relieved to see Cole and Quinn scanning another art book at a distant table. She liked Cole; he was a good, reliable friend. But she'd be more at ease when the danger of her trial was over.

And she wasn't referring to Ronja the evil witch or the Amara. Or even Bastraal.

Scrutinizing the colonial portraits, Claudia tried not to think of how her friends would react to her secret fear. The topic of romance was bound to come up, and she was afraid they'd think her silly. Irrational.

She could count on Paige to be on her side, though. The woman who took feminine independence to an entirely new level. But even the coven's anti-love crusader might scoff at her reason.

It was nothing world-shattering or unheard of. In fact, the problem was quite common. Claudia had been cheated on in her younger years, and while many women had felt that particular sting to their heart and pride, she didn't know anyone who'd experienced the betrayal quite like she had.

Nothing drove the anguish of infidelity home like picking your high school boyfriend's letterman jacket up off the floor and getting a visual play-by-play of his weekend in the arms of Cindy Barker, homecoming queen and—even Claudia had to admit—an extremely talented contortionist.

Putting her cool fingers to her temples, she blocked the memory and told herself she'd moved past that time. She'd been young. He'd been young. And everyone involved had moved on. Claudia had even allowed herself to fall in love again.

In college. With a frat boy. So she shouldered half the blame for that one.

Yes, she had her reasons, but her fellow witches still might not understand. Particularly those who were practically glowing with love themselves.

No matter how happy the others were, Claudia was determined to keep her heart intact, and that meant staying away from any man who might prove tempting. Especially a man like Cole.

She peeked at him from beneath lowered lashes. He was arresting, with his dark good looks and drop-dead grin. His light-colored eyes that promised any woman a night she'd never forget.

And therein lay the problem. Cole couldn't help it if he was female catnip, but Claudia could certainly limit her participation. She couldn't let herself be attracted to him.

And that woman at the café. Rachel. *Hmph*. She'd only reinforced Claudia's assessment of Cole. A very good man, who wasn't nearly ready to settle down.

Footsteps caught her ear, and Claudia snapped out of her mental haze to find Cole approaching. He held one of the books, fingers of one hand marking his place between the pages.

When he drew near, he set the book beside hers and showed her what he'd found. "These are by Willem van Haecht. They had some of the qualities you said to look for."

Swallowing the nerves that clamored when he got too close, she ran a palm over the page. "Close, but I don't think so."

"Bam!" Kylie cried abruptly, slapping her hands on the desktop. "Am I good or what?"

"*You* seem to think so," Quinn murmured with an irritated scowl. Claudia and Cole shared a smile. Kylie and Quinn were always at each other.

And the rest of the innocent bystanders couldn't wait for the two of them to finally get *at* each other. There was one match of soul mates that everyone had figured out. Everyone, that is, except Quinn.

Or maybe that's why he gave the younger woman such a hard time?

"Never mind that. I've got my own problems," Claudia muttered under her breath, pressing her lips together as she stood and ignored the quizzical expression Cole sent her way.

She crossed the library to where Kylie sat, looking over her friend's shoulder to see what she'd found. "That's the one!" She was incredulous. "When we beat the Amara and their big, bad demon, I want you to transfer universities, Kylie. I need a research assistant like you."

"It'll cost you, Teach." Gleeful from her success, Kylie stood to let Claudia sit in her chair.

Once she had a chance to read the website Kylie had found, Claudia realized her good fortune. "I won't say I'm surprised by the timing, considering we're all just pawns on prophecy's chess board, but this is definitely the painting I saw in Bastraal's bedroom."

She swiveled in the chair to face Anna, who'd come over with all the others. "And it's being auctioned off next weekend."

"Next weekend?" Anna leaned in to get a better look at the web page, much like Claudia had before. Her lips moved as she read silently to herself. She pointed to a line at the bottom. The words were in bold red letters. "But it says tickets are sold out."

"What?" Claudia looked back in panic. "Well...we're the Savannah coven. I mean, surely we—and by we, I mean you, Anna—have some strings we can pull."

"I'm sure we can figure something out." Anna's mouth was twisted as she bit her bottom lip. Then she read aloud from the page. "A silent auction...as part of the fundraising gala to benefit Big Brothers Big Sisters of Savannah."

Behind Claudia, Cole made a strangled noise before coughing. When she and Anna faced him, he stuck his hands in his pockets and rolled back on his heels. "Ahh...I have tickets."

Claudia's face felt like acid was rushing through her veins, and her vocal cords couldn't be convinced to work.

Luckily, Anna spoke for her. "Then you and Claudia can go together." The head witch turned to where Claudia still sat, flummoxed by the turn of events. "And I want to contribute money to help buy the painting. In fact, I want to help with the watch too."

"No. I made the decision to buy the watch, so I'll cover it." Claudia's voice was weak. "We can discuss the rest. I hate to admit it, but if this keeps up, I'll have cleaned out my savings in no time."

"I have some money to give," Kylie piped up, only to have Quinn mock her. "You mean your daddy's money."

Kylie glared at him and said silkily, "Oh, I'm sorry. I didn't realize you built this palatial home with your own two hands."

"Enough." Anna raised a hand. "We can talk about the financial needs later." Her eyes fell to Claudia. "At least we know what comes next."

"Yeah." Kylie rubbed her hands together. "And we know who you'll be spending more time with." She wiggled her brows at Claudia, then stared boldly at Cole. "Dummm-da-dum-dum."

"Stop trying to embarrass us, Kylie." Claudia's face was now corroding from the inside out. Sometimes having the typical redhead's skin type was like carrying around a flashing red warning light in her head. "It's not a date."

"Okaaay. You'll both be getting dressed up and going to a specific place at a pre-appointed time." Kylie gave them a doubtful look. "But it's not a date."

"Kylie…"

"Why don't we change the subject?" Dare seemed as uncomfortable as Cole and Claudia. He even went so far as to give Cole an I-feel-you-bro expression before looking back to his wife. Though for her, he winked.

"Right." Willyn was going to play savior too, it seemed. "Why don't we talk about a happier topic?" The gentle witch and loving mother turned to Anna's brother. "So, Quinn. Have we found any more demon portals?"

6

Kylie was in the small elevator that would take her from the foyer to the upper floors of the mansion when Quinn forced his hand inside the closing door. He stepped in beside her and hit the button for the top floor.

His face was grim, and he shot cobalt daggers with his glare. "Why did you say that about Cole and Claudia dating? Couldn't you see Claudia was uncomfortable?"

Of course his foul temper was directed at her, Kylie thought. Always, it seemed, at her. "I was trying to lighten the mood. *Because* I could see she was uneasy."

"Always the funny one. Never taking anything seriously." He stepped closer, crowding her in the small space.

She put a hand on his chest and shoved, but he didn't budge. "Get out of my face, or I will push you back. Even if I have to use magic."

"No, you won't."

He was right, and that he knew her well enough to call her bluff made Kylie seethe. Impossible man. "You're a lot more upset than Claudia was. Believe me, she has no problem speaking for herself and calling it like it is."

"Normally, maybe." Quinn shook his head and looked down on her as a parent would a rampant teenager they just couldn't understand. "She's not herself and, whether you want to see it or not, she's scared."

"I know that!"

"Then why don't you try acting like a friend instead of a spoiled little girl who only wants everyone's attention?" His words carved her up inside, and his obvious contempt made her slouch against the wall.

Still he moved closer, sparing her no consideration. "I know you're young, Kylie, but you need to get your priorities straight. And you have to accept reality."

Her voice shook when she asked, "What reality? I didn't do anything—"

Cutting her off with a slice of his hand through the air, Quinn finally eased back. But he wasn't done with his lecture. "Not every one of you is destined to fall in love. The pattern changes every time."

"But that doesn't change. Love is the only thing that's happened to every witch who's faced her trial." Her heart felt tenderized, bruised, like it had gone up against a meat mallet and lost.

She knew what he meant. And why he was telling her.

"I can promise you one thing, Quinn St. Germaine." She swallowed and forged ahead. "If love comes my way, I'll accept it and be grateful. I won't run or try to divert what's meant to be. No matter what you say." She narrowed her eyes, but he matched her heated glare with one of his own.

She felt a sob in her chest but hammered it back down. Was it always going to be this way between them? Was she wrong to care for him?

"That will be your choice," he finally said. "But this one is Claudia's, and she doesn't need any more pressure." The elevator door opened on the top floor, where Quinn's bedroom was located. And Kylie's.

He stepped out and waited for her to join him in the hallway.

Rich mahogany wainscoting ran the length of the corridor, and landscape paintings hung in heavy gold frames on blue silk-papered walls.

"I'm not adding any pressure." Kylie lifted her eyes to the man who could so easily trample her emotions. And without the slightest hint of concern. Anna's younger brother treated all of the other women with respect. Like sisters.

But he treated Kylie like an enemy. The bratty *little* sister that he couldn't stand to have around. And it sucked. Especially since she didn't view him in a brotherly way. Not in the least.

Quinn nodded his head one hard time. "See that you don't."

With that, he turned on his heel and stalked off, leaving Kylie standing alone. She stared at his retreating back for a moment, then turned and marched to her own room.

With anger and hurt feelings still choking the air, the two went their separate ways.

~~~

Ronja was certain she could still feel the scent of brimstone burning her nasal passages as she exited the pit beneath her refurbished plantation house. Communing with Bastraal was more intimidating than ever, because she and her followers had failed the demon a few times too often.

Though Bastraal hadn't dealt her any torment in the last several days, his moods had become unpredictable. To humans, the notion of a moody demon from the underworld might sound comical. To Ronja, however, the reality wasn't remotely funny.

Her meeting with him today had gone well, better than expected, and she'd come away with a stroke of brilliance. A new plan of attack to be carried out against her most hated enemies. That damned coven of witches led by Anna.

Ronja lifted her head as if actually looking down her nose at the good witch. The white mage who was far too arrogant for one so young. And still so *human*.

In contrast, Ronja had been paying her magical dues for a millennium, first suffering loss of family and flesh before being rescued by the very demon she still often feared. It was ludicrous to believe that a coven of women—each having lived fewer than thirty years!—could triumph over her dark power and wealth of experience.

No. She tapped a fist to her thigh as she walked from the dirt floor into the dungeon of stone. She had waited too long for Bastraal to rise again. The demon had promised her magic beyond measure, and she would perform the vilest deeds to ensure that power became hers.

Ronja entered the darkened room lit only by a few torches— she loved the old-world feel of flame light—and eased over to the captive standing against one wall. She was more than happy to adjust her previously laid plans. And eager to free the handsome man shackled in the corner.

"Tyr." She spoke softly. "I have good news." Moving toward his tall, muscled form, she dragged her gaze over his body appreciatively. Yes, even after all she'd done to him, her proud warrior still stood firmly on his own feet.

With his arms suspended, her lover could do nothing to stop her from creeping closer. But he had his eyes on her, watching like the hawk he was. He showed no fear, or anger, as she took full advantage of his helplessness.

Gradually, painstakingly, she moved in closer and closer, until her nipples were pressed against his blood-covered chest. Tyr looked down to where their bodies made contact. Then he groaned.

Ronja lowered her eyes as well to see the crimson liquid soaking into the pale blue silk she wore. The stain spread slowly, and as it did, a sweet copper scent filled her senses. She thrived on the aroma. The one that spelled pain. And death.

Thrilled by the degeneracy, Ronja leaned forward and ran

the tip of her tongue over her prisoner's firm lips. In return, Tyr kissed her savagely. She gladly reciprocated, growing more aroused with every rough swipe of tongue or lip.

Then she bit down on one side of his mouth until warm saltiness spurted inside her mouth. Tyr shook but didn't attempt to pull away.

When Ronja released him and kissed his torn flesh, he lowered his eyelids seductively. And smiled.

"You see, Tyr." She tossed her golden mane back with one hand. "That's why you're just no fun to torture."

His black, soulless eyes pierced her. "Why? Because you know you'll just heal me afterwards with a sip of your immortal blood?"

She patted his sharp, tanned cheek, proof of his Native American ancestry, as lust swirled its liquid heat between her thighs. "No." She pushed away from him and offered him a truly wicked grin. "Because you enjoy it too much."

As she removed one heavy metal cuff, Ronja did her best to form a pout, but any show of docility was unnatural to her. Her very marrow was made of sharp, piercing barbs. Or so she preferred to believe.

"You know I had to punish you for your most recent failure," she purred. "The Spanish witch should have died down there, in the bowels of the jungle. Yet somehow..." Ronja's voice became cool. Dangerous. "Somehow, she survived."

Tyr bowed his head. "I deserve your wrath." He offered no justifications or pleas for mercy, because he knew she would accept none. Even an attack by a harem of flesh-eating spirits was no excuse for his failure in Peru.

He let his free arm drop to his side, proof of his continued submission. Behind him, blood spatters painted the gray stones from his days of torment, but Ronja knew there were no tears staining the wall. Not a single one.

"Yes, darling," she whispered. "You did. And as the saying

goes, bodily fluids trickle downhill." She crushed her eyes closed, recalling yet another lesson received by her master. "Bastraal demonstrated his disappointment in me."

She uncuffed Tyr's other arm. "So I showed you my dissatisfaction, and for the very same reasons. We must maintain unity in our quest. We all strive for the same reward."

Taking his fingers as lightly as a mother would her newborn child's, Ronja guided Tyr through the dungeon, around the assorted "play" areas, and to the bottom of the staircase. "We'll get you a drink, so you can heal before your shower. Water on those open wounds will sting, and I don't want you to suffer."

With a meaningful look she added, "Needlessly, that is."

"Of course not." He took the steps as if unaffected. As if the soles of his feet weren't torn open and raw. His calf muscles not stretched to the point of rupture.

But that was one of the traits Ronja cherished in her bronze-skinned companion. Tyr thrived on pain, even his own.

"I thought I would have to heal on my own this time," he said. "After my failure."

"You would have." Ronja was glib as she pushed open the door on the main level and glided into the hallway. "But plans have changed, and I need you back to your full power sooner than anticipated. We have a new strategy, and you'll play an integral role."

She quirked a suggestive brow. "Not that I won't enjoy your renewed...stamina...for more personal reasons."

They passed Ross in the foyer, and the shifter dared to sneer at the disheveled Tyr. Ronja stilled, unappreciative of the blonde man's judgment. He should learn to control his animal instincts.

Grabbing him by the throat, she lifted Ross off his feet and held him aloft easily with one arm. "I find myself without a warm body in my dungeon. Would you care to take Tyr's place?"

The man's pool-blue eyes bulged and his face ballooned, full and pink. He tried to shake his head in the negative.

Ronja dropped him to the floor, but he landed on his feet and doubled over at the waist, sucking in some much-needed air.

"Then mind your arrogance, shifter, or I'll chain you up like the mutt you are." She whirled, the bottom of her blue dress billowing around her ankles as she headed for the winding stairs.

Tyr didn't spare Ross a glance, as well he shouldn't, considering the crazed man wasn't half as powerful as the ancient warrior. No animal form of Ross's could compare to the deep wells of might that lay in wait within her dark lover. Strength just waiting to be released.

But only when absolutely necessary, because after that, there would be no going back.

Ross lowered his head and wisely remained silent as Ronja and Tyr climbed the gleaming wood of the steps.

At the landing, she turned down one corridor toward Tyr's room, which was on the same side of the house as her own chambers. She entered his bedroom and went to the en suite bath.

Once inside, she made preparations at the counter. She would feed Tyr, allowing her demon-enchanted blood to heal his cuts and gashes.

The essence flowing inside her would close his wounds, return his strength, and, as it had for centuries, prolong his life.

When she raised the blade to her brachial artery—a convenient vessel and expedient point of delivery—Tyr grasped her wrist. "Will you tell me of this new plan? Tonight?" He lowered his voice, the deep timbre rumbling through her body. "In bed?"

He brushed the fingers of his other hand over her blood-soaked gown, teasing her sensitive breasts. "I want to prove that my full strength has returned."

"Oh, yes," she whispered, her breath tingling inside her chest at the idea. Nothing turned her on more than curing the pain she herself had inflicted, then riding out her fury on her renewed and vigorous mate.

"In fact, I'll explain everything while you bathe." She walked around the half-wall of beige and brown tiles, then turned on the shower. Several jets erupted at once. Because Tyr deserved the very best.

She dropped her gown and retrieved her knife once again, readying herself to deliver as promised. "The idea is simple, really. I'm surprised I haven't thought of it before." She beckoned him with one finger.

Watching with pleasure as Tyr stripped off his destroyed and stained garments, she said, "The coven grows stronger with every challenge."

Tyr stared greedily at her naked body. Her bare arm and pulsing artery. "Yes. They have learned much, but the prophecy has yet to be fulfilled."

"Their strength," Ronja said, "their intelligence, and their," her lip curled, "*powers*, will be the very things that serve us now."

Her resilient lover frowned and met her gaze. "I don't understand."

"Along with their successes, they've discovered something else." Ronja smiled. "Hubris."

Stepping backward into the steaming sprays of water, she scraped the side of the knife up and down her inner arm, teasing him as the shower wet her long flaxen hair. "This time will be different," she said, slicing her arm and offering it to Tyr.

"This time," she gasped when his mouth latched on, "we will use their strengths against them."

7

Cole's formal black shoes clip-clopped against the brick sidewalk as he walked through the neighborhood in the historic district of downtown Savannah. While many of the houses he passed were Victorian style with ornate wooden porches and multiple pointed rooftops, the place he was destined for this evening had been modeled after an entirely different era.

He came to a stop in front of the looming stone structure, its clean lines and English Regency architecture making it stand out like a fierce soldier at a ladies luncheon. Two curving staircases with green iron railings curved up to meet beneath a grand portico with stone columns in the same mustard-beige as the rest of the building.

Once again, he told himself the sensation in his stomach had nothing to do with the woman he was meeting here tonight. That the yearly gala held to benefit Big Brothers Big Sisters always made his gut feel like an overfilled helium balloon.

But that was a lie, and just one more in a long line of untruths that he'd been feeding himself since the previous weekend. Ever since he'd watched Claudia's face blush like wildfire and her utter loss for words when Kylie mentioned the word "date."

Not that he was any more interested in a romantic fling than she was, but he wasn't thrilled by her obvious repugnance either. He'd gotten the impression she'd rather meet up with one of the city's invading demons than spend an evening in his company. And that stroked his ego like a hand wrapped in barbed-wire.

Straightening his black tie, he chose a towering oak to stand under while he waited. Spotlights were aimed from the front gardens up to the house, highlighting the entrance and the elegantly dressed visitors who'd come to mingle and make donations.

He couldn't care less if they were only here for a good time, as long as their checks were big enough to get the charity through another year. He'd first become a Big Brother while still living in California, after his days as a beat cop showed him just how many young people were in need of role models.

Or at the very least, someone who just gave a damn.

Savannah, unfortunately, had its share of misguided youths as well. So he would continue to do his part. Children, he believed, were everyone's responsibility.

Moving from his tie to his cufflinks, he twisted and turned them until they were perfect. When he realized what he was doing, he promptly dropped his hands with a scowl for the empty street. *It's only Claudia. A woman I've known for too long to be nervous about seeing.*

He rolled his shoulders in an attempt to look relaxed, but the sound of a single set of female footsteps approaching made him freeze and glance to the shadowy street corner. She emerged from the dimly lit sidewalk, and the sight of her bright hair pinned up to reveal graceful white shoulders made his chest start to burn.

No more telling himself that it was only Claudia, and he shouldn't be worried. As he took in her tall, slim figure and the beautiful face he knew so well, the truth popped that helium balloon so it landed back in his gut like a pile of rocks.

Look at her. How have I been able to keep myself from her

for as long as I have? This wasn't the pre-planned encounter of two casual acquaintances. Not for him. And it wasn't a simple date either.

The truth couldn't be denied. Tonight, he was here with the most amazing woman he'd ever met. *Claudia.*

And suddenly Kylie's ridiculous tune popped into his head, but this time the song played out in heavy, reverberating notes. *Dummm-da-dum-dum.*

Man. He was so screwed.

"Don't you look nice," she said in that husky voice of hers as she came to a standstill beside him.

"Thank you." Cole found a smile for her, hoping to hide his shameless thoughts. Like slipping his hand into that coil of flaming red hair she had done up so stylishly as they took advantage of the bench he'd spied on the side of the house.

"You look *brèagha,*" he said, but when she furrowed her brow, he explained, "It means splendid." He sure wasn't going to tell her he'd meant the other meaning of the word. That she was beautiful.

Her laugh was rich and infectious. "If you speak Gaelic, I'm going to feel like I'm out with James Bond's Scottish younger brother." She indicated his sleek tuxedo. "Not that I'm complaining."

When she turned to admire the house in all its glory, Cole took a moment to appreciate just how *brèagha* she really was. In addition to her shoulders, her arms were bare, except for a bracelet on her left wrist that glistened with diamonds.

The only other jewelry she wore was her silver amulet, the peach-hued stone at its center glistening proudly.

Her floor-length black dress was made of a shiny material like silk or satin, and the strapless bodice cut straight across her chest. The material fell in straight lines below her waist, where something sparkled at the area cinching just above her hips.

The same stones glittered across the top as well, as if the designer had meant to draw the eye to the most alluring areas. Well, Cole admitted, it was certainly working on him.

Offering her his arm to escort her along the path and up the stairs, he struggled to keep his gaze on more appropriate places. The manicured hedges, looming trees, or the colossal estate in front of them.

They sailed through the open doors and into a foyer like none he'd ever seen before. The walls were a forest green and set off by two white columns that supported another set of dual staircases. Dark wood paneling lined the bottom half of the walls, and the floor was an intricate parquet with a tile mosaic in the center.

Tracking directly upward from the elaborate design, Cole spied a massive crystal chandelier. All he could think was that he'd hate to be underneath the monstrosity if it ever fell.

Glancing aside to Claudia, he saw she was taking in the lavish surroundings with rapt attention to every detail. "Are you getting a vibe from this house?"

"No." She shook her head. "I can control what gets in. Well, I usually can."

Cole remembered what she'd told him about the vision and getting sucked into a room with the demon. He decided to distract her. "How about a tour?"

"Yes, let's." Her lady-like response brought a gleam of humor to her eyes, and Cole found himself amused as well. He enjoyed playing dress up, but one night a year was about all he could take.

They turned left and found themselves in a sitting room with pink walls. Cole immediately wished for the green from before.

Pastel petits fours were arranged on silver stands, along with other desserts situated on a main table. Interspersed were various vegetables along with their appropriate dipping sauces, and small finger sandwiches fit for a queen. Or at the very least, a dowager duchess.

"Beverages must be in another room." He indicated the sweets. "You hungry?"

"Not really." Her hand settled on her midsection. "I'm actually a little light in the stomach. I think it's nerves."

Cole was never one to turn down dessert, but he could tell Claudia was on edge. "Let's put ourselves out of our misery and find what we came for."

The breath she exhaled and her quick nod told him she was in full agreement. The painting was their primary objective, and she would probably feel more at ease once they confirmed its presence.

In a back room on the same side of the mansion, they found the punch bowl along with an open bar. They both looked at the shining bottles of liquor, shook their heads at the same time, then laughed. "Probably not a good idea," she said.

"Probably not." Putting his hand on the small of her back, Cole pretended not to feel her flinch at the contact. Then after they eased into the next room, he removed it just as casually.

The gardens in back were a maze of stone walkways and neatly trimmed shrubbery. Flowers burst with color near the center where a fountain arced high into the crisp night air. Claudia paused to admire the view. "Ooh, it's gorgeous."

Cole remained silent and waited for her to lead the way. When her steps resumed, they found themselves on the opposite side of the house and in another spacious room. Here the furniture had been cleared out or moved to line the walls.

Long tables had been set up in the center and were covered with white linen. The items on display were for the silent auction. Almost immediately, Claudia spotted the painting. She perked up and moved to get a closer look.

The woman with the brown hair and an owl on her finger was encased in a gilded frame and propped upright. In front of the antique portrait sat a white sheet of lined paper for interested bidders to write their names and corresponding offers.

Only two people had bid so far, but the price had already risen to over a thousand dollars. Claudia was unfazed, however, and withdrew a pen from her small black purse. She scribbled her name and a higher bid.

She sighed. "And so it begins." Meeting his eyes, she visibly relaxed. At last. "Now let's eat."

Cole swept his hand out in a debonair fashion. "A woman after my own heart." And again he caught her anxious reaction. "It's just an expression."

"I know. It's just…" She looked around to all the nearby people and fell silent.

Without another word, Cole guided her to the beverage room, stopping only for two glasses of punch before moving on to food. After they'd had their fill—though she barely touched her cucumber sandwich—they wandered back to the bidding room to check the status of the painting.

The first bidder had returned with a higher price. Claudia swiftly countered.

"What now?" she asked. "A walk in the gardens? The bidding has another forty-five minutes until closing." She shook out her arms. "I wish I could get rid of this nervous energy."

And that was all the opening Cole needed. She'd studiously avoided the front room where several couples were dancing, but now he took her hand and propelled her in that direction.

"Oh, but…"

"Too late," he said, when they'd crossed the threshold to hear a waltz flowing from the musicians seated in a corner. "This will expend all that energy and still keep you close enough to watch the painting. As soon as anyone bids, you'll be ready to one-up them."

Her eyes lifted to the ceiling before finally admitting defeat. "I can't argue with that logic." Holding her purse in one hand, she laid her arm over his shoulder and moved in.

Cole softly enveloped her, as if holding a fragile figurine, but the intense heat of her skin beneath the black silk shocked him into stillness.

"Are you all right?" She eased her other arm around him as if to offer support, but the increased contact only jolted him further.

"I'm fine." His voice sounded husky even to his own ears. "I wasn't sure I was holding you the right way. I mean, for this dance."

"You're good." She started moving lithely across the floor, and Cole felt like an uncoordinated ox in comparison to her gracefulness. He focused on moving in time with her, and slowly the classic dance eased him into a calmer state.

Then Claudia spoke, and the tension ransacked him again.

"I've done a lot of thinking since we last saw each other, and I've decided we should confront this issue head-on." Her features were cool and serene, but distress swam behind her eyes.

"What issue would that be?" Cole played dumb. But considering how they'd been reacting to each other all night, he was pretty sure he knew what she meant.

She cleared her throat and met his gaze. "You know what I'm talking about. You've been around for two trials now, and you're well aware what...*happens* to each of us when we face our individual challenges."

Cole chuckled, but the act felt forced. "You make it sound like a traumatic event."

"For some of us it might be." Her delicate features grew solemn. "For me, love is like a train wreck, and if you've ever seen a derailed locomotive and the cars that followed helplessly, you would have to admit it's pretty traumatic."

"Sounds like," he agreed, though inside he wondered just what kind of collision she'd suffered in the past. He felt sure it hadn't been the automotive variety.

"Besides," she continued, "we both know what's important. Finding Bastraal's lost belongings is all that matters. Helping the coven and saving the lives of innocents. We both care about doing the right thing and, if this is the last time we're brought together by my trial, then I'll gladly thank you for your help."

"And if this isn't the last time?" he asked, because she was right. He did know the coven's pattern. Trial, danger, love. But not always in that order.

Her green eyes—the color of the Savannah River in full sun—softened with apology. "I'm afraid the answer is the same. I'll gladly thank you for your help."

"But you're not interested in the fringe benefits of completing your challenge."

She tilted her head slightly to the side. "No. I'm not."

"Whatever you say," he replied, but his spine still bristled. "You seem to forget that I didn't ask for this either. Yes, I want to help the coven, and I'm happy I could be of assistance by bringing you here tonight. But that doesn't mean I'll be buying red roses in the morning."

She smiled gently. "Now I've offended you. I'm sorry. The threat of a love that can't be denied tends to shake a person up." She repositioned her hand on his shoulder. "And I get grouchy when I'm worried."

Willing to let her previous comment pass for the time being, Cole returned her humor. "I get grouchy when I'm hungry, but a candy bar usually makes me right again."

She lifted her arm and wiggled her wrist with the glistening bracelet. "For me it's shopping."

Feigning an alarmed expression, Cole said, "You're one of those? Good thing we're not going to fall madly in love, then. I'm not sure I could afford you."

With the tone between them affable again, they danced until the song ended, then clapped politely. When the next started up, Claudia shrugged her lovely shoulders and held out her arms. "What else have we got to do?"

Cole slid his arm around her tiny waist again, and thought, sure, he could take the torture for another three to five minutes. Then he inhaled the sweetness of flowers and citrus. *Or maybe not.*

"I'm glad we're of the same mind," Claudia told him as they whirled closer to the long gold curtains hanging from an embellished rod. "I feel better about working with you. Now that you understand where I'm coming from."

She nodded as if affirming her own opinion. "I like you. We get along well, but neither of us wants a committed relationship."

Cole didn't remember saying anything about not wanting a relationship, casual or otherwise. Not exactly. He watched her closely, wondering why he was suddenly feeling possessive.

"We should be okay," she went on, oblivious to the determination that was burgeoning inside her dance partner. The more she disclaimed any possibility of their being together, the more it began to piss him off. "We're already good friends, and it's never been a problem."

Maybe not for you. Why did she have to look so damned relieved? Cole knew he was getting worked up when his inner voice started cursing.

He decided to take the lead, and he wasn't talking about the dance. "Is it just me, or do you plan to avoid forming an attachment to every man that crosses your path in the next few weeks?" Had that sounded sarcastic? Judging by her frown, he guessed it had.

"If that's what it takes."

"So, you plan to spend the rest of your life loveless and alone?" The more he thought about what she was really saying, the more irritated he became.

Claudia gave him an insulted *hmph* that would have done any Victorian matriarch proud. "Why shouldn't a woman be happy by herself? Where is it written that a man must be present for complete life fulfillment?"

Cole couldn't resist the challenge. "In about ten billion romance novels. Books, by the way, that your kind love to read." He let his hand fall to her waist. "That's where."

Her smile was at half-tilt, as if she enjoyed his response but didn't want to let him know it. "That, my dear Cole," she spun out in a tight circle, then back into his arms, proving she could free herself from his grasp, "is why I prefer text books."

Just as he was thinking up his own witty response, a woman in the front of the room screamed. She stood near the door to the foyer, pointing up to the ceiling. "What is that?!" Her voice was shrill with terror as the white-haired man beside her looked up at the coffered ceiling in confusion and then back to the woman, presumably his wife.

The man spoke to her, but Cole couldn't hear what he said. As one, he and Claudia edged closer. Both of them had well-honed intuition, one a cop's and the other a witch's.

And they both sensed evil at work.

"Can't you see it?" the woman cried, clapping her hands over her eyes against whatever horror she was witnessing.

"Looks like Mrs. Heller's had too much to drink," a man said within earshot. By this time, the older woman had fallen into her husband's arms, burying her face against his shoulder.

Finally she peeked up again with one eye, and her shoulders slumped. "It's gone. Praise the Lord. It's gone." The white-haired man bolstered the woman and led her through the room. As the couple passed, Cole heard him promising his wife that some fresh air would make her feel better.

"I don't think the air was the problem," Claudia said, and the rigidity of her shoulders told Cole that something else was wrong. Very wrong.

Her stare was glued to the doorway where the older couple had been standing. Two different people filled the space now, and Cole instinctively put his hand on Claudia's back. "How do you want to handle this?"

Claudia fumed beside him, her chest rising and falling with frustration. "In whatever way I have to, I guess. Because I'm not leaving empty-handed."

He glanced around. "We have to make sure no one gets hurt."

Claudia nodded and shifted closer to Cole, making them a unit. They stood together, ready to deal with whatever madness came their way.

He reached automatically for his Sig but found only his crisp cummerbund. Not that he would fire a gun in here anyway. And not that bullets would have any effect on his intended targets. Turning to Claudia, he said, "Now, I guess I'll follow *your* lead."

This was her battle, after all, and she was no longer the only witch in the room.

Standing in the doorway, and looking straight at them, was a strikingly handsome couple. That reeked of dark magic. Even Cole recognized the black-haired man and his beautiful companion.

Ronja and Tyr had arrived.

8

Claudia wouldn't have been surprised if Ronja had shown up wearing red. Blood red. However, she was decked out in royal blue, the color of sapphires, and seeing Anna's symbolic hue on their nemesis made Claudia's blood vessels feel like they were pumping fire.

With the poor Mrs. Heller removed from the room and free from whatever spell Ronja had cast, Claudia made short work of weaving through the crowd to confront the blonde woman with the black soul.

When she neared the queen of the Amara and her evil lover, Claudia would have taken one step closer, but Cole's arm hooked around her waist. She was close enough that their lowered voices wouldn't carry over the music to others, but still just outside of Tyr's reach.

Claudia didn't delude herself. If Ronja wanted to touch her, she would use her magic without a qualm. Just as she had done to the innocent woman only moments before.

Claudia drew herself up and was pleased that her height allowed her to literally look down on the corrupt witch. "Lowering yourself to attacking defenseless humans, Ronja?" She sniffed haughtily. "That seems beneath you."

Ronja's laughter was silky yet full of the desire to inflict damage. Most likely to Claudia, since she had dared insult the ancient *seiðr*. Ronja's blood thirst and desire for revenge on all mankind went back a thousand years.

Plenty of time to feed off her demon savior, Bastraal, and increase her lethal power.

Her eyes were the color of stone bathed by blue moonlight. Her hair a gold many women would envy. "All humans are beneath me, so why the surprise?" Her malicious gaze traveled around the room, devouring all the people mingling nearby. Those she so despised.

Then she settled on Claudia. "Would you like to pick the next one? I don't really care. One sow is as good as the next when it comes time for slaughter, wouldn't you say?"

Fury roared inside Claudia. "Why don't you and I take this outside?"

"Careful there." Ronja straightened the length of her silk gloves. "I have about nine hundred years on you. If Anna can't beat me, a youngling like you certainly can't."

"Why, with power that great, you should be able to wipe out our whole coven with a swipe of your hand." Claudia tapped a finger thoughtfully to the side of her cheek. "But you haven't done that, have you?"

Though her eyes glittered with hatred, Ronja didn't take Claudia's bait. She allowed a brittle smile to shape her pink lips and turned to study Cole instead. "Is this your boyfriend?" She laughed caustically. "Your fated love?"

Claudia ignored the instant fear that knotted in her chest. She didn't want Ronja's attention focused on Cole.

So she hid her anxiety and met the woman insult for insult. "Boyfriend? Probably not by your twisted standards." She smirked. "Since he doesn't bite me and suck my blood like a swamp leech."

Anger sparked and ignited behind the stony blue, but still Ronja kept her voice civil. "No one *bites* me."

"Well, why didn't you say so? That makes it all better, then." Claudia wanted to hurt Ronja, or at least let her know she wasn't intimidated, but she felt Cole's firm grip on her hip. A non-verbal warning to settle down.

And she would do well to be cautious. Prudent. No chess game was ever won with bravado, and she needed to take tonight's match. And the painting.

"I'm sure a woman with her power would rather face us fairly," Cole said, eyeing Ronja and Tyr. "You obviously know what we've come for."

He smiled, like a boxer did an opponent he knew had a shorter reach. "May the best checkbook win." With that, he nudged Claudia and maneuvered them around the pair and into the foyer toward the pink room.

"I don't need a snack." Claudia's dress suddenly felt too tight, as if she were having a panic attack. "I have to keep an eye on that portrait. You know she's going to bid on it."

"Exactly." Cole rubbed her lower back, a soothing gesture and not the least bit sexual. Claudia was grateful for his support. Thankful he was here with her.

And wasn't that a change in her untiring pessimism? At least where he was concerned.

"A leisurely stroll through the house and gardens," Cole explained, "will give you time to cool off, Ronja an opportunity to place a bid, and me time to figure out how much bankroll I can kick in."

A resistant smile spread over Claudia's lips. "Yes. If it's one thing Ronja has, it's money, but Anna and the others have also pooled some of their funds. We should be able to match her."

She swiped and gulped a punch as they breezed through the beverage room in the rear of the house. "I hope."

"Regardless, I'm here. Just in case." Cole winked, then stole a sip of her drink for himself.

As they walked down the stone steps into the gardens,

Claudia mused silently. Wasn't that always the way with Cole? Quietly standing by, making jokes as needed, but ready to throw himself into the action when his friends called?

She really didn't want to like him any more than she already did, but he just kept revealing those facets of himself. First she'd known him as an upstanding and trustworthy detective, as well as Trevor's partner and best friend.

Then she'd discovered his interest in antique clocks, his traditional side—which Claudia had also—and now it turned out he volunteered to help troubled youths. Frankly, she didn't think she could afford to like one more thing about Cole Lonergan.

She dipped her head at two women as they passed her and Cole in front of the fountain, noticing that both of their stares lingered on her handsome escort.

And therein lay the rub. He was a ladies' man with a healthy dating life. Love life. Sex life? She sighed and downed the rest of the punch, wishing she'd spiked it with a little vodka after all.

A slow turn around the fountain, with just enough nip in the air to calm her ire from the confrontation with Ronja, and she was ready to go back inside and check the bid sheet. Cole had stayed at her side as they perused the azaleas and gardenias.

He was silent and thoughtful, yet present. And that's what counted.

They returned to the room where the silent auction was still underway, and Claudia spotted Ronja and Tyr in the far corner. The witch lifted a mocking brow, as if encouraging them to check out her offer. To see what they were up against.

Claudia moved to the portrait and accompanying sheet to examine the dollar amount written there. She almost choked.

Maintaining her dignity, she removed her pen once again and retaliated. But not by more than a few hundred dollars. She didn't want to seem concerned, and why jump the bids to an overinflated price just yet?

They still had another fifteen minutes until the auction closed, and Ronja would definitely make another move. *Please let me win. I have to win.*

Doubt rang inside her head like a death toll. Her hands started to shake, so she turned to move in the other direction. To hide any sign that she was daunted by the evil woman's presence.

A strong, warm hand slid into hers, helping to steady the tremors racing up her arm and toward her shoulders. Cole's gentle touch grounded her, centered her. Without dispute, she let him lead her to their own corner.

Where they waited for their rival's next move.

This time Tyr made the trip to the table. In his usual stoic manner, he spared Claudia and Cole nothing, not a glance, or even a superior grin. No acknowledgement at all. The Native American man's cryptic ways were somehow more menacing than Ronja's outright threats.

"Don't make your move yet." Cole spoke calmly to Claudia.

She nodded acquiescence, fully in line with his plan. "I'll let the clock run down a little more." She was still holding his hand, so she slipped it away from him under the guise of patting her hair to make sure her coiffure was still in place.

"While we wait, tell me what time period you visited when you saw...you know who." Cole frowned, as if he didn't even want to think the demon's name, let alone speak it aloud.

Especially while Ronja was in the vicinity.

Taking a deep breath, Claudia told him the same thing she'd already revealed to her coven. "Unfortunately, somewhere in the mid to late seventeen hundreds."

Her tone of disappointment drew a lazy grin from Cole. "Why unfortunately?"

"As it turns out, the three original St. Germaine sisters *did* settle on the island off the coast around 1738, several years after Savannah was colonized, but they didn't battle Bastraal until they were much older." Her mouth tugged to the side. "The timeline wasn't quite what I expected. That's all."

"I see." Now his smile spread. "Your three-centuries-old prophecy is actually *almost* three centuries old."

"Hmm. I know. Just doesn't have the same ring, does it?" Claudia rolled her eyes when he burst out laughing, then she noticed the annoyed expression Ronja was throwing their way.

So she started laughing along with him, just to irritate the bitch.

Taking hold of his wrist where he wore his watch, Claudia rotated his arm and checked the time. She decided to wait a few more minutes, unsure what to expect as the clock ran out.

Paige really should have had this task. At least she could super-speed write and make sure she had the last bid.

When she let go of Cole's arm, she couldn't help rubbing the pads of her fingertips together, marveling over the heat his flesh had transferred to hers.

In a move that surprised them both, an unknown man stopped in front of the portrait. After only seconds of scrutiny, he too scribbled an offer on the paper.

"This could get interesting," Claudia said. Then she realized Cole was watching her instead of the new player who'd joined the game.

His eyes seemed darker than normal, as if he were as cognizant of the energy between them as she was. He leaned closer, clenching his jaw. She thought for a second he might say something, but then he shifted his attention back to the bidding table.

Finally she released the breath she'd been holding. Thank goodness she didn't see Cole dressed this way very often. Overlooking his desirability had become routine for her on the few occasions he'd visited the island with Trevor.

But ignoring him in a tuxedo was more than should be asked

of any warm-blooded female. She actually felt flustered. At least, she assumed that was the emotion making her cheeks burn and her pulse race.

If she was indeed flustered, well...there was a first time for everything.

She tried to focus on anything else in the room. Anything other than the portrait she so desperately needed, Ronja and Tyr in the opposite corner, and now Cole, stretching the black fabric over his shoulders and arms in a manner far too delicious for her comfort. Too provocative.

"There she goes."

Claudia flinched when his deep voice warned her that Ronja was on the move and going back to the bid sheet.

"Two minutes," he told her, giving her a countdown.

"I might as well see how she's going to play this," Claudia responded, easing toward the painting to see what the damage was. She clamped her teeth together and made sure her facial features were impassive, refusing to let her adversary see her reaction.

When she read the paper, she saw that Ronja had only outbid the previous man's offer by a hundred dollars. If she didn't intend to financially force Claudia and the other bidder out, then what was the wicked woman's game?

Would she use magic? Here, in a public place? Surely not, because drama at an event like this would make news and draw more publicity than even Ronja would be able to make disappear.

Unless she planned to leave no evidence she had been the culprit. Or no witnesses.

No, Claudia rationalized internally, that didn't make sense. So breathing deeply and channeling her Zen—as Hayden would say—she reached slowly into her purse for the pen. She wrote her bid nonchalantly. In no real hurry. She was trying to run out the clock.

Then she would see just what the Amara's nasty queen had in mind.

Movement in her peripheral vision alerted her that Ronja was moving in, with Tyr trailing a couple of feet behind her. And in the opposite direction, Cole was closing in as well. She eyed the blond woman gliding regally across the room, and waited until she was standing next to her at the table.

Ronja made a big show of pulling out a silver pen and waving it in a circle before she leaned down and put one long fingernail on the corner of the bid sheet. Then she pulled it toward her and wrote her name.

With an additional five-thousand dollars added to Claudia's last offer.

More resolute than ever, Claudia narrowed her eyes and smiled. She eased the sheet back in her direction, the paper sliding against the tablecloth with a slight *hiss*.

Again she breathed deeply, counting to three and fighting off the pounding of stress and fear in her head.

"You'd better be quick." Ronja's voice mocked her. "I see the young lady standing in the doorway, ready to call for the close of the auction."

Playing it cool, despite the fist of anxiety clenching in her gut, Claudia asked sweetly, "Oh? How long do I have?"

"Write your bid and find out." Her opponent didn't seem worried at all.

And that worried Claudia.

She tossed a glance to Cole, and at his quick nod, she put her pen back to paper. She met Ronja's expensive offer but only topped it by another hundred. Her pride would not write a check she couldn't cover. Though truth be told, she was still a far cry from her maximum number, thanks to the combined forces—and bank accounts—of her sisters.

"Lovely," Ronja said, waving her pen back and forth between them. "Do you have any idea what this painting is?" She cocked one perfectly curved brow. "You don't seem very nervous."

In a flash, Ronja snatched Claudia's hand and squeezed, crushing her fingers into the pen she still held. "You should be."

Shock cost her only a moment before Claudia sent her coven's blue magic down to her palm like a loaded cannon. She didn't want to draw anyone's attention, but neither would she let the murderous couple hurt her or anyone else.

She would die defending these people, though she knew none of them, other than Cole. That was the destiny she'd accepted last spring, when she and her friends had gathered in the great room for their first taste of pure magic.

They'd learned what they could accomplish. Together. And over time, came to understand everything they stood to lose.

"You think that little blue spark will scare me?" Ronja's pupils grew large, and tiny bolts of lightning seemed to flash in their depths.

"Ladies and gentlemen, the silent auction is now closed. Please allow the attendants to collect the bidding sheets." A middle-aged woman stood on one side of the room as other volunteers quickly went down each table to gather the papers. "We thank you all for participating. And for bidding generously."

Laughter tittered around the room, and Ronja lifted a shoulder in resignation. But loathing still raged from her eyes of stone. "Looks like you won this round. I should know better than to let my emotions get the best of me. Maybe next time." She snickered. "In fact, I'll make sure of it."

Whirling with a flourish, Ronja took Tyr's offered arm and exited by way of the dance area.

Claudia stood immobile, still unable to believe she'd won. A young man came for the portrait, and she had to stop herself from demanding to know where he was taking it.

"Good job," Cole said next to her ear, breaking her from her trance.

"I can't believe it." She clasped her hands together. "I got it. I really got it. And I don't mind telling you I was scared."

"I never saw it," he assured her, but his grin said he was a liar. "Let's go make the arrangements, so we can claim your prize and get out of here."

Relieved and ready to vacate the premises—and to get some real food—Claudia let out a breath. "Yes. Please." With an eye on the milling crowds, she followed Cole upstairs where a room had been cordoned off for auction winners to make their payments.

The stairs were the only open entry, and she'd be keeping an eye on them.

She couldn't let her guard down. Not yet. If one thing could be said about Ronja, the witch was tricky. Claudia expected her to come blasting up the wooden steps at any moment.

Finally the painting was ready and boxed safely in protective packaging. She wrote her check and thanked the young man as he started to hand the portrait over, but Cole swooped in and took the box. "Let me get that."

With their small audience, Claudia didn't want to argue, but as soon as they were downstairs and in a relatively isolated spot, she stopped and met him eye to eye. "Why did you do that?"

"I don't want to take any chances. You might get a read off of the portrait, even through the packing material." He glanced around at the still-thriving party. "This isn't the best place for you to pass out."

She had to give the man credit for thinking ahead. She had been more than ready to hold the box herself. "You're right," she admitted. "Especially if Ronja and Tyr are still lurking around."

He cleared his throat. "Exactly. Which is why we're going out the back."

When he advanced toward the doors that led into the

gardens, Claudia was right on his heels. "The back area is enclosed. We can't get out that way."

"Yes, we can." He was so sure of himself that she didn't bother to argue further. Better to get clear of the mansion, the horde of innocent bystanders, and the possibility of a surprise attack by the strongest of the Amara members.

She'd wondered if that shifter, Ross, was up in a tree somewhere, spying with a birdy pair of eyes. The Amara didn't often travel alone, and the painting Cole was carrying was far too valuable for them to lose.

"Maybe they don't know who I am," Cole said. "And if they don't, they won't know where I live. At least, not inside the next hour. We should be safe until Joseph can come to pick you up."

Her heels clipped across the stone walkway, though she tried to tread softly. "I drove myself."

Cole grunted. "Of course you did."

"Why wouldn't I? My car's been parked at the mainland house for a year. The garages are large enough to hold us all, but my baby needed a warm-up."

He stopped mid-stride and turned back to her. "I've absolutely got to know what kind of car you call 'baby.'" Casting a hesitant eye over her shoulder and back toward the mansion, he pressed his lips together. "But later. After we're secure."

Claudia wasn't fond of directives, and his controlling attitude was beginning to rankle. "I have faced the Amara before, you know. And back when I had a lot less power." She snapped her fingers and an orange flame leapt half a foot from her crimson fingernail.

She'd always had an affinity for fireballs.

"Put that out," Cole hissed. "Damn. Remind me never to take you on a stakeout. Besides, the painting is what's critical here. Not your pride."

She almost sniped at him but had to bite her tongue. Because he was right.

Cole wrapped his hand around her forearm, as if he didn't trust her not to run back and call Ronja out for a garden duel. But she wouldn't antagonize him. His last remark had gotten through.

She had to protect the painting above all else and get it back to the safe haven of the island.

But when she saw the shrubbery Cole expected her to squeeze through, she froze like a show dog on command. "That's holly. The leaves are sharp." She tried to jerk her arm away from his vise-like grip. "I'm not going through there in this dress."

When he only tugged with more insistence, she spoke in a hurried whisper, her words jabbing at him in the dark. "Do you have any idea how much this dress cost?"

Heaving the weary sigh of the put-upon, Cole took off his jacket and turned it inside out. Then he shielded himself and leaned heavily against the offending bush, creating a narrow opening. "Hurry up."

Because she didn't want to seem too much like a girl, she sucked in her stomach and lengthened her torso as much as possible, then slipped through.

Cole came out behind her and kept the jacket slung over his arm. Claudia couldn't help staring at the way his broad shoulders filled the starched white shirt. Moonlight shining on Cole was worth a moment's pause.

Even if the Amara were after them.

"My car should be right about," he did a slow pivot and pointed, "there."

The old but restored Range Rover was a surprise to Claudia, but then again, Cole was proving to be quite unpredictable. They hurried across the street, and he opened the back to ease the box with precious contents inside.

"Why don't you just take me to the yellow house?" She climbed into the passenger seat when he opened the door for her. "Joe and Claire are there, and it's only a boat ride to the island."

Cole shook his head. "No. The Amara would probably be expecting that." He shut the door on her protest and walked around the front to the driver's side. When he got in and started the car, his tone brooked no refusal. "My place will be the safest. For now."

She straightened her dress and got comfortable in the soft leather, but even the luxury automobile didn't soothe her. "How can you be so sure?"

Cole slid easily away from the curb. "Because I just bought it."

9

Claudia was practically on the edge of her seat when Cole pushed a button on the electronic controller to make an elaborate metal gate to slide to one side. "This is your house?" she asked, not even trying to hide her disbelief. "No offense, but on a detective's salary—"

"How can I afford it?" He grinned at her, not insulted by her blunt curiosity. "It's a bit of a fixer upper."

Claudia knew a little about Victorian homes, and the large house in front of her was of the "Romanesque" style, so titled because it resembled a small castle. And it was located on Forsythe Park, some of the most desirable real estate in the historic district.

When she scoffed and gave him a doubtful look, he laughed. "And my parents went in on it with me. As an investment."

"Now that makes more sense. I was going to give you a hard time for insisting we come to your place," she gasped as she took in the wide wrap-around porch and stone columns, "but you're officially forgiven."

Once he parked the car, Claudia hopped out without waiting for him to open the door for her again. No sense encouraging any more of his *date* etiquette.

The evening was almost over, she'd come away with her

prize, and this would be the last time she worked with Cole on anything having to do with her challenge. And not a moment too soon, because his rough-and-tumble good looks mixed with his dry humor and all the interesting tidbits she'd been discovering about him... Well, it was adding up to a dangerously potent mix.

"Wow," she murmured, forgetting about the threat of Cole's sex appeal when she got a good look at the gorgeous house basking in the moonlight. This style of architecture often used rough-faced, square stones for construction, but she'd never seen the deep reddish-brown color before.

"We can go in the back." Cole tossed a hand out to indicate the sidewalk, then strode that way, assuming she would follow.

She did, but at a more leisurely pace, craning her neck to study the round tower with its cone-shaped roof. Even the back entrance had been done up properly. A contrasting white pilaster around the door performed double-duty, providing support along with style.

Cole stepped inside and left the door open for her, his footsteps resounding across the hardwood floors. Echoing, she soon realized, because the house was completely empty.

"When you said you'd just bought it, I didn't take you quite so literally." She admired the classic details as she trailed behind him toward the middle of the house, down a hallway, and into the room where he'd obviously set himself up.

Given the built-in bookshelves, the space could be used as either a small library, or a very large study. Cole had a desk situated on one side, and on top was a clock that had seen better days. Its insides had been gutted and were spread out in front of the hollow shell.

On the opposite side of the room was a queen-sized bed, simple and without any type of frame. "This is your bedroom, I see." She gestured to the mattress and box springs.

"The bathrooms upstairs need a lot of work, so I didn't see

the point in cluttering the whole place up yet." He put his hands on his hips and surveyed the study. "This room was in the best condition, so I cleaned and painted to make it more livable. This, the guest bathroom, and the kitchen are where I've put all my energy so far. The basic comforts."

Claudia nodded, secretly approving of the khaki-colored walls. Against the darker toned wood shelves and mouldings, the soft brown created a sophisticated setting.

She could envision a massive desk against the windows, antique collectibles interspersed with leather-bound books, and of course, a couple of vintage wingback armchairs in the corners, where the lord of the manor might retire for his evening cigar.

Or where the lady of the house might sneak in an afternoon read while her husband was out.

She smiled as her own fantasy world filled in the blank spots, and found herself with an acute case of house envy. "I love it, Cole." She spoke with unabashed honesty. "I absolutely love it."

He shuffled on his feet and seemed to search for words. "Then you'll have to come back when it's finished. Though that might be a while."

Taking a few steps back toward the open door, Claudia glanced over her shoulder to him. "Do you mind if I get a better look at the house? You know, in my special way?" She considered it rude not to ask, even though he had just purchased the home and probably hadn't established any memories there yet.

"Go ahead. I'd be interested to know what you see." He stayed where he was, near the foot of his bed, but his light green gaze tracked her as she moved. "Maybe you can tell me if it's haunted or not."

"Sorry. That's Hayden's department." She swallowed against the tickle in her throat. Cole. Handsome in his tux. Standing in her version of a dream house. *Ahem.* Was the room suddenly getting stuffy?

She wandered into the hallway, mainly because the older wallpaper still remained and would give her a better read on the house, but also because she needed to get farther away from Cole.

His spicy cologne had captured her interest more than once as the night had worn on, but while he was so close to a bed and...well, all the other inviting things she'd listed in her mind, the need to breathe a different cloud of air was vital to her peace of mind.

When she lifted her hand to press it against the faded paper with blue flowers, she felt a hitch in her stomach. One that reminded her of how her last peek into the past had gone.

She dropped her hand and cursed Bastraal for making her fear her own talent. The gift she'd always been fascinated by, had always cherished, and been grateful for.

At least she was only going to *feel* a house. A fairly safe object to help her get back on the proverbial horse. Personal possessions tended to hold onto emotion more so than buildings, but for a trial run, the papered wall was as good a place to start as any.

Sucking in a quick breath, she channeled courage and placed her open palm against the wall. Almost instantly, the image of two teenage boys running down the hallway overwhelmed her. They were laughing and dressed in what she guessed were late nineteenth century school uniforms.

She felt sure she was getting a glimpse of the first family who'd resided here, as the Victorian home had likely been built in the 1870s. And while other people had lived in the house since, she was content with the sense of carefree abandonment she got from the two happy-go-lucky kids. Young and innocent, hopeful, and looking forward to summer break.

She withdrew her hand, having seen enough. She would take that joyful feeling and tuck it close to her heart. Her personal magic was still her own to control, and that made her feel as elated as the two boys she'd seen.

Turning to Cole, she formed a full smile, ready to burst with relief. "You've bought a healthy history with this house. Good times have been had here, and I hope you get a chance to do the same."

"I'll give it my best," he said, finally moving from the bedroom to join her in the hall. "We have some time to kill. You want some coffee or something?"

"Sure." She held out a hand to stop him. "You did say you have at least one working bathroom?"

"Yeah. A guest bath in the front corridor." His chuckle rumbled, low and sexy. *Damn him.*

"Okay. Just making sure. In that case, I'd love some coffee." She watched as he retreated to the kitchen near the back, appreciating the sinewy roll of muscles beneath the white shirt and the cut of his black pants. *Oh, dear.*

Waving her hands to fan her face, she returned to her scrutiny of his living space. She wished for a chair so she could slip off her heels and have a seat. To relieve the slight ache, she stood on one foot, and then the other. Even she preferred bare feet some of the time.

After blood was flowing into her toes again, she did a more thorough examination of the contents of his desk. But she didn't dare touch anything. The pieces and parts weren't organized as far as she could tell, but a few were cleaner and shinier than others.

As much as she loved antiques, she had no desire to learn the mechanics. If they required a specialist to ensure they worked, then that's who she'd gladly turn them over to.

She could see the beauty hidden in the old clock, though, and believed it was a lantern style, one of the oldest of the kind that were small enough to sit atop mantles or desks, but large enough to make a statement.

Her musings about antiques reminded her that the painting she'd been so frantic to acquire was sitting on the floor propped next to the bed. Cole had been right to keep the box from her while in public, but if she was to complete her trial, she had to inspect the portrait sooner or later.

Tapping her pointed shoe against the floor, she cocked an ear for sounds of Cole's return, debating the wisdom of taking a look inside. It wouldn't hurt to slide the top off and steal a small peek.

The more she considered it, the more she wanted to make sure they'd come away with the right item. What if Ronja had managed to pull a switch of some kind? She was a ridiculously powerful witch.

And she'd been far too cool and composed after losing the bidding war.

Certain now that she'd been duped, Claudia lifted the box and set it gingerly on the mattress. The coverlet on the bed didn't look terribly expensive, or even new for that matter, but she'd still be cautious not to snag the fabric.

Testing the corners, she figured out how to ease the lid of the container to one side, and was glad the arrows and markings told her which way was up. As soon as she cleared the packing material from the portrait, she blew out a breath and let her ebbing panic recede completely.

This was the right painting. The peevish woman with an owl on her finger stared back at her from inside the box.

Claudia eased onto the bed beside her purchase, leaning over to inspect the pattern of the brush strokes more closely. The artist had used oil-based paints, and the resulting effect was beautiful. Masterful. Mesmerizing.

Without thinking, she brushed a finger over the owl's golden wings.

And pain crashed all around her, into her, churning like a tidal wave of agony until she had no choice but to let herself fall into the waiting darkness. She couldn't fight her reaction to the portrait, and the only way out of this turbulence was to push herself straight through.

To the other side of time.

When she emerged, she found herself in a study not very unlike the one she'd just left. Only this room *did* smell of cigars and lemon oil. Just as she'd imagined Cole's might.

Again, she had no solid body to control, but she managed to move her—essence, she guessed was a good word for it—to a corner where she could hide behind an enormous potted palm. She never would've pegged Bastraal as a plant man, or plant demon, but there was no guarantee she'd even come to his home this time around.

Maybe she'd gotten lucky? Examining the carpet and architecture, she decided this building had been built before the Victorian era. But that was bad news. Bastraal had been in Savannah in the mid to late 1700s, so this could very well be another section of the home she'd already visited.

Okay, I need to focus on why I'm here. None of this is coincidental. With renewed determination, she took in every corner of the study, each table or piece of furniture, and every small item.

If she could find whatever she was meant to see—assuming this vision would work like the last—then maybe she could get back to the present before anyone even realized she was here.

Claudia hated the cowardice she sensed rearing up, but she simply didn't possess the bravery to face Bastraal again. Not when he had the upper hand. She'd never felt such an oily black malevolence like the filth the demon had spewed from his mouth during their last encounter.

And if she had her way, she never would again.

So she needed to crawl out of her hiding space and search the room. Nothing glimmered like the painting had, or at least, nothing she could see from this vantage point. So she maneuvered herself through the room and closer to the desk.

Blank parchment lay on top, along with a quill pen and capped bottle of ink. A ledger of some sort sat to the right, but there were no adornments of any kind. Straight and to the point. All business.

Now that was more like the Bastraal she'd pictured in her head.

Should she open the drawers, or would they be locked? Deciding to see for herself, she reached for the top left handle, and was shocked to see her hand materialize. She wiggled her fingers, and sure enough, they worked.

Perhaps this time-traveling trick of hers was a case of mind over matter? Regardless, she wanted to get out of this place as quickly as possible, so she put her wraith-like hand to the test. The drawer didn't open, but only because it was indeed locked.

She tested the one below it, and was rewarded when it slid free. Old-fashioned files were inside, but she didn't waste precious seconds perusing them. Nothing was glowing, and if it didn't shimmer, she wasn't interested.

The top left drawer wasn't locked either, and inside she found a peculiar looking box. Wooden, with a foreign and unintelligible script embossed on the top. The lid lifted easily on smooth, well-oiled hinges, indicating the item was well-cared for.

As soon as she saw what lay inside, she knew she'd found what she'd been brought here to discover. A dark red candle sat on one side. No. She peered into the small chest. Not a candle, but a wax stick with a wick, used for sealing letters.

Now Claudia understood the ring resting atop a folded cloth, the very object that shimmered in that familiar wavy aura she'd been searching for.

The silver-toned piece of jewelry was a signet ring, used to press into the wax after it had been dripped onto an envelope. The design on the ring would not only seal the correspondence, but would identify the sender as well.

She shivered as she reached for the heavy ring, an intimate and important item. One that belonged to the demon himself.

The seal signified his position in society. His power.

She picked up the ring, obliged to study the signet and commit its design to memory. The ring was thick and flat, and the metal appeared to be silver. A tree had been etched into the center, its leafless branches spreading in various directions. A sword had been driven into the thick trunk.

Claudia frowned. She'd expected something more gruesome, more ominous. But at least the picture was simple and easy to remember.

She set the ring carefully back inside the box and closed the lid, only to feel the distinct tendrils of time transportation as they reached for her. She was about to be sucked through the vortex once again.

Having learned to shut her eyes and mentally relax, she let herself go limp, so the process would be more bearable. Then she waited as the black tunnel began to consume her.

Out of nowhere, two heavy arms wrapped around her, capturing her in a vise-like grip. Trapping her. With shadows still clouding her eyes and terror racing through her, Claudia screamed.

10

Fearing the demon had somehow crept up to catch her before she could escape, Claudia arched her back and fought against the constricting embrace.

"No!" she cried, alarm skittering down her spine as her captor increased his hold.

"Claudia!"

She stopped struggling and opened her eyes, chest heaving from exertion. Instead of eyes full of flame and murder, she saw the loveliest shade of green, like peering through bottle glass into a stormy sky.

Cole was the one holding her, supporting her.

Fear-induced exhaustion overcame her, and she leaned into him, needing his strength and compassion as much as she did the air she was gasping into her lungs. "Cole. Oh." She buried her face into the crook of his neck. "I'm so glad it's you."

"It's me. I've got you." He let her hang on and gulp a few more ragged breaths. Though he rubbed his hand in slow circles over her back, he sat rigidly, his spine stiff.

Easing away and putting a few inches between them, Claudia put a hand to her chest. "You almost stopped my heart." She licked her lips and willed her body to stop quaking. "I thought you were Bastraal."

If she'd seen stormy skies before, now his expression thundered with fury. "What the hell is wrong with you?" The bass in his voice vibrated through her, causing her distress to spike again.

She knew exactly what he meant. "It was an accident. I didn't mean to do it."

"The packing box *accidentally* opened itself?"

"No, I just needed to make sure—"

"Claudia," he reached for her and grabbed her by the shoulders, "there's a fine line between daring and idiotic, and you just sailed right over it."

"I told you I didn't mean to touch it." She brushed one of his arms away. "And stop yelling at me. I'm already shaken up." The admission of insecurity flew out of her mouth before she could think better of it.

But if she'd expected guilt to replace his ire, Cole was proving her wrong again. The anger still simmered beneath his exterior, but alongside it was real concern. What must he have felt when he'd come back to his study to find her passed out on the bed, her hand still draped across the portrait?

She was the one overcome with guilt now, but as much as she felt the need to apologize, her stubborn tongue just wouldn't form the words.

"I don't know what's wrong with you," he said, repeating himself. Then his hand returned to her shoulder and slid up her bare neck, resting on her nape where his fingers splayed gently but firmly. "And I don't know what's wrong with me either."

Closing the distance between them, Cole pressed his lips to hers lightly, as if tasting the wares. Then before she could protest, he angled and pressed deeper inside. His taste was an explosion in her mouth that wound its way through her to settle somewhere south of her belly.

The intense pleasure coiled there and waited, urging her to

take more. Her hands dipped to his waist of their own accord to test the hard planes of his stomach before slipping gradually around to his back.

She delighted in each rise and fall of his well-honed physique, shivering over the complete absence of softness. Every inch of him was unyielding, a hidden toughness beneath the always-smiling charmer the coven had come to know.

A groan tore from Cole's mouth just before he ripped his mouth away. He released her as if her skin was scalding hot, shaking his head without speaking.

Embarrassed and frustrated at once, Claudia immediately went on the defensive. "I knew it. I knew it!" She scrambled to her feet and took three strides across the floor, putting a safe distance between them.

Her long black dress whirled around her ankles when she turned on him. "I could feel trouble brewing from the minute you stepped into the courtyard for Lucia's luncheon." She crossed her arms and accused him with her eyes. "I thought we understood each other. That we were on the same side."

"We are. We are." Still sitting on his bed, he reached for the lid of the box and made sure the painting was fully enclosed once again before standing and casting serious eyes her way.

But he still didn't look guilty. He raised a hand and dropped it carelessly. "I'm sorry. I couldn't help myself."

Claudia gaped at him, completely affronted by his dismissal of what had happened. He seemed to be shrugging off what could potentially be the first step down the road to her destruction.

"That's all you have to say? That you couldn't help yourself?" Fine. She'd show him the kiss hadn't meant anything to her either. "Come on, Cole. I'm sure a guy like you can come up with a better line than that."

Now his hand fisted against his thigh. "A guy like me? What is that supposed to mean?"

"You know exactly what it means. You were just with that

other woman at the café last week." She faltered as she gathered words, so upset by his nonchalance that she was unable to keep her injured pride from overruling logic. Or courtesy. "And probably a different one last night."

"Wait just one—"

She cut him off. "No. I don't care, because it doesn't matter. You and I feel a basic sexual attraction for one another, but since we both cringe at the thought of commitment or, heaven forbid, the development of real emotion, I think it's safe to say we just made one colossal mistake."

Cole's jaw tensed. "I agree."

She gave a sharp nod. "Which is reason number eighty-four why tonight is the last time you and I will see each other until my trial," she crossed her arms in an X, then slung them out to her sides, "is over."

Shoving his hands into the pockets of his black pants, Cole crooked his head to the side as if stretching out a kink, then let out a harsh breath. "You're right. About everything."

Without taking a single step in her direction, he crossed to the door and looked out into the hallway. "I still think you should avoid returning to your car tonight. I'll call Joseph to come pick you up."

"Good idea. And Cole," she said when he started to walk away, "I do appreciate your helping me tonight. But I can take it from here." She knew the words were cold and dismissive, but there could be no uncertainty left between them after what had just happened.

The cord between them had been sizzling hot, dragging them toward each other with a terrifying intensity. So it had to be severed. Quickly and cleanly.

When his retreating steps echoed with a harsh finality, she told herself it was for the best. That it would hurt a lot less now than it would later on.

But if she ever let him kiss her again, she would be doomed.

~~~

Cole waited until the gate closed behind Joseph's departing car. As the red glow from the taillights disappeared, he finally let down his guard.

And soundly cursed himself.

He couldn't blame Claudia for being so enraged, because he was just as disappointed and angry. Why had he kissed her?

During their honest discussion at the gala, she'd confirmed her reluctance to spend any time with him. Hell, she'd plainly stated that she wasn't interested in any kind of ill-fated love affair.

Particularly with him.

And while he didn't begrudge her the desire to remain unattached, the attack on his character had been completely uncalled for. First Trevor. Now Claudia. They both seemed to view him as a confirmed bachelor. A real lover boy.

After slamming the back door when he went inside, he instantly regretted the show of temper. He'd only just started rehabbing the place and didn't need to cause any damage that he'd have to turn around and repair.

Blowing out a defeated breath, he ambled into the kitchen. Why did their opinions irritate him so much? Before, when Trevor had teased him about women, Cole had always laughed it off and shot right back that his partner was just "jealous."

And the only reason he'd been able to take the disparaging comments so lightly, was because there was so little truth in them.

Did he date women? Sure. But taking a casual date or two to the physical level didn't happen nearly as often as Trevor evidently believed.

And now—Cole opened his fridge and pulled out a beer—Claudia believed it as well.

When she'd looked at him tonight, as if he'd put some sleazy playboy-style moves on her, Cole had felt a flash of mortification. Even though her assumption was entirely false.

He'd never intended to cross the boundary she'd so clearly laid out, or the one he'd set for himself since first being introduced to the coven. The red line he'd reinforced over and over again. Every time he'd seen Claudia.

He hadn't let desire confuse the issue, telling himself all of the witches were strictly off limits. He would support them all, as well as Trevor and the other men, until the Amara and their demon were put down for good.

He'd never taken issue with those restrictions. Until tonight, when Claudia had looked at him with those eyes of hers. She'd been so scared, distraught. Worry for her had overridden all his good sense, and everything inside him had damned his own advice, as well as her warnings.

He'd needed to know that she was all right. That her heart still beat with life, that her blood still ran warm. And boy, had it.

The stark truth was, he hadn't had a bite of anything other than candy for quite some time. Womanizer? He huffed over the rim of the green beer bottle. Yeah. That was a good one.

With the plan in his mind to have another beer, then sit down to do some work on the clock in his study-slash-bedroom, Cole loosened his collar and reached again for the handle of the refrigerator.

The chime of the doorbell stopped him midway.

In no real hurry, but wondering what Claudia could have forgotten, he made his way to the foyer. Swinging open the door, Cole was confused by the woman he saw standing there. With a wicked grin on her face.

Sweet perfume carried to him on a gust of wind, teasing with its sultry mix of musk and flowers. Against his will—and his better judgment—Cole's stare turned greedy, traveling the length of her body.

From her strappy high heels and all the way up, he took in her curves, then settled once again on her face. There his gaze fastened on seductive eyes of violet. They were feline in shape, with thick lashes accentuating the upturn at the ends.

She breezed past Cole, into his home, stroking her palm over his jaw and down to his shoulder as she went. "Hello, lover." Her voice was like a drug as it shot straight to the base of his brain and rushed to every nerve-ending in his body.

As she made herself at home on the staircase, crossing her legs and leaning back, Cole stared outside and into the night. Unsure what to do, he took his time closing the door, then hesitantly allowed acceptance to take hold.

He threw the dead bolt to lock the door. Against the stars, the moon…and a lingering sense of hope. Then he turned.

And went to her.

11

Two days after the gala, Claudia was scouring the island mansion for Anna. She finally found her in the greenhouse, along with Willyn and Paige. Anna was a devout botanist, and it was easy to picture motherly Willyn planting flowers around a sweet little cottage in the woods.

But Paige?

Claudia crossed her arms. Paige had surprised them all. The ex-soldier could punch through a brick wall unscathed, but those same hands of steel held seedlings with tender care. She had an affinity for growing things and, apparently, a naturally green thumb.

"Is it time for those to go outside?" Claudia asked, edging into the greenhouse carefully, making sure she didn't brush against any of the soil-laden tables. Anna was meticulously clean in most things, but when it came to gardening, she was a real free spirit.

"Yes, it is." Anna beamed as she held up a small pot. "We're just talking layout and design. You sure you don't want to join us? Nothing eases the soul like getting your hands in the dirt."

Claudia pinched her lips together. "I'm not dressed for it."

"Are you ever?" Paige asked, waving a filthy finger at Claudia's white capri pants and sea-green top. She paused in the act of cracking a grin and looked Claudia over more critically. "Are you going somewhere?"

"That's what I came to tell you." Addressing their leader, chosen by both providence and inheritance, Claudia continued. "Anna, we can't find anything about the signet ring in the library here. I'm going to the downtown library with Hayden and Viv. I just wanted to let you know we'll be out."

Anna rescued a small plant that had somehow fallen over and was dangerously close to being uprooted. "I hope you find something."

"Me too." Claudia took a few more steps into the room. She didn't mind working with plants; in fact, the practice seemed like second nature. The loamy smell of the greenhouse was always soothing, with the warm, moist air and fresh soil practically serenading her inner witch.

"I also had a theory I wanted to run by you before I go." Claudia nodded to Willyn and Paige. "You both can weigh in too." Trailing a French-manicured nail along a glossy green leaf, she said, "Something occurred to me when I first saw the ring in Bastraal's office. My immediate thought was that the signet was representative of his position. And in a way, his power."

Anna stopped pressing her fingers into the soil and looked up. "Go on."

"Well, what if each item is supposed to symbolize a different aspect of the demon? If the ring is power, the painting could be—and I hate to admit this—his human side that appreciates art and the beauty of this world."

Willyn furrowed her blonde brows. "Maybe the beauty is part of what he envies. One of the reasons he wants to be here."

"Or why he wants to destroy it," Paige countered.

Claudia was inclined to agree. "Yes, that's more likely. The pocket watch is the one I can't figure out, though. I would say that it represents time, obviously, but I can't find a way to connect that to Bastraal."

Anna shrugged. "His ability to defy the passing of time? I mean, he's been around, in some form, for longer than we can even fathom, yet he keeps returning. And at various points in time." She met Claudia's gaze with her calm stare. "But I think you're on to something."

"I had a feeling, but I wanted your opinion." Claudia stepped on something round and hard and moved her foot to find a piece of mulch. Oh, yes. Free-spirited Anna.

"At any rate," Claudia said, "they're important to Bastraal in some way. They may even be the key to his destruction." She played with the tip of her braid that lay down the front of her shoulder. "That would explain why Ronja wanted to get to the painting before I did."

Paige dusted off her hands, but she looked overjoyed to be getting so dirty. "So when Claudia gathers all the pieces, however many there are, maybe we can have a great big bonfire and cast Bastraal into the netherworld forever?"

Anna stared at Paige then Claudia. With her mouth in a flat line, she shook her head and resumed her work on the plant. This time she seemed to be laboring with repressed frustration. "I really have no idea."

Paige waved a hand. "Easy on that seedling."

Curling her fingers, Anna paused in her mission to tamp every bit of dirt to the bottom of the pot and looked at her friends. "I don't like having to say that I'm totally in the dark any more than you like hearing it, but it's the truth I've come to accept. When you all arrived last year, none of you even realizing you were witches, I thought I knew so much more than any of you." She shook her head. "But not anymore. Now I'm clueless half the time."

"But you're still the strongest of us." Paige's voice was firm. "You're the one who will have to face the toughest trial, and I think we can all admit that now." The warrior broke into a wide smile. "But I'm still faster, so don't let any of this go to your head."

"Oh, Paige." Willyn took off a glove and tossed it at her friend.

Claudia grinned. At least one of them had the good sense not to ruin her nails.

She started backing out of the room, careful not to trip over any stray pieces of bark. "I have time to figure out the rest. Hopefully I'll know what to do with the antiques by the time I find the final piece."

Anna waved goodbye with a confident smile in place. "You will. Like I have to keep reminding myself lately, everything will reveal itself in due time."

With a quirk of her lips, Claudia saluted with one finger and turned to go back inside the house. She hoped Anna was right.

~~~

"Now that's what I call a library." Viv shaded her eyes as she trailed her gaze up the white Georgia marble covering the stately edifice.

Claudia, always the history professor, shared a bit of the massive building's background with Viv and Hayden. "This library was originally built in 1916 and later expanded to bring the square footage to a whopping sixty-six thousand. The design is neoclassical and, as you can tell," she flicked a hand to encompass the sprawling lawns with fountains, seating areas, and moss-covered live oaks, "the people of Savannah put it to good use."

Visitors to the library stood chatting in small groups or ambling along the curved sidewalks. Sunshine cast the marble in a heavenly light, and the yards aptly reflected the structure's beauty and grace.

After a few moments of quiet admiration, they agreed to

return for a stroll through the park after they'd finished their research. If Claudia was going to locate the signet ring she'd seen in her last vision, she had to learn more about it.

Hayden and Viv had opted to help, and as they climbed the wide steps in front, Hayden broached the second-most disturbing topic on Claudia's mind. "Are we still banning any conversation about Cole?"

Claudia barely hid the grimace that wanted to clench her facial muscles. "Only if anyone links his name to destiny, love, or my ongoing trial. If you want to talk about a case that he and Trevor are working on, that's fine, but none of the other."

She pulled the glass door open and held it, glancing back and forth between her friends. "Any other questions?"

"No, Ma'am," Viv said. "I can remember how I felt when …" She trailed off. "Never mind. That draws a comparison between Nick and me and you and he-who-shall-remain-unmentioned. So I'll stop there."

"I appreciate it." Claudia stepped inside and was just starting to take in the stylishness of the huge building when Hayden gave an exasperated huff.

Claudia turned to the caramel-haired woman in time to see her frown pitifully. "But I like Cole. I really do. I don't understand why you're so against him."

Claudia sighed. "I like him too, and it has nothing to do with him personally. It's the whole destiny thing. A prophecy-enforced romance is simply not my cup of tea."

"But look how happy we are." Hayden wiggled her thumb between herself and Viv. "And neither of us went easily down that path. Especially Viv."

The Japanese physicist frowned at Hayden, then lifted one shoulder in acceptance. She faced Claudia. "I hate to admit it, but she's right. If anyone can identify with the abhorrence of having someone or something else make your life decisions for you, it would be me."

As her semi-good mood began to fray at the edges, Claudia drew on what was left of her patience and held up both hands. "It's not exactly the same for me, and I really, *really* don't want to talk about it. Okay?"

The two women nodded, though Hayden did so with reluctance.

Claudia gestured to the long corridor before them. "Now, I would love to get started on the research." She winked. "And get a look at the mural in the children's section."

Hayden bobbed her head back and forth as she studied the lofty ceilings and chandelier high overhead. "This place is amazing."

They followed the tiled hallway to the center area. An attendant sat behind a wooden desk on one side, while a staircase rose near the opposite. Warm honey-toned walls made the busy hub inviting, with doors that branched off to separate areas.

After confirming that every floor offered computerized card catalogues, they decided to find a spot on the second level. Claudia set her purse in a chair as the other two did the same, claiming the corner table for themselves.

This was a research project best kept private.

"Quinn suggested we start with local history books that focus on collectibles and museums, so I'll go see what I can find." After running a search on the in-house system, Claudia came back with a list of potential books.

The three of them spread out to collect texts from various locations, then regrouped to create two intimidating stacks. Hayden pulled her hair back in a tail. "I say we start with pictures."

"Let's hope it's that easy." Viv dove in and selected a small tome off the top of the nearest pile. "I still think we should try a search for tree, sword, ring, seal...or any combination of related words, even though we couldn't find anything on the

Net."

"That'll be the next step if we don't find anything in these books." Claudia watched as Viv donned her black glasses to get down to business. "But I think focusing on local history will get us there faster."

After a long period of mostly silence—except for the flipping of pages and occasional shifting of bodies in their seats—Hayden lifted her face from the book she was reading. "Claudia, are you in danger of losing your professorship since you've taken an extended leave?"

More than ready to take a break and rest her eyes, Claudia leaned back in her chair. "It's possible. My position was probationary anyway. I haven't gotten my doctorate yet, but the rarity of my area of concentration weighed in my favor. There aren't many historians who put emphasis on physical objects and their impact on past societies."

Viv chuckled. "You do have a certain advantage in that field of research."

Rolling the crick from her neck, Claudia let a small smile play on her lips. "Yep. And I don't feel a bit guilty about using my gift that way. How else are artifacts and antiques supposed to get their version of the story out there?"

"That's a unique perspective." Hayden eased closer to the table. "You know, between your visions and my ghost interviews, I bet the two of us could re-write large chunks of history."

"One corset at a time, my friend." Claudia laughed despite the fact they had yet to find anything related to the ring or its emblem.

Until Viv sat straight up and put her finger to a paragraph in the book laid out in front of her. "There's a description here that fits what you told us." She made a give-me-that motion with her hand. "Where's the sketch you made?"

Pulling a piece of paper from her purse, Claudia unfolded

it and gave it to her friend. She listened as Viv read from the text. "The presence of a sword in what was an apparent representation of the 'Tree of Life' led to a title. The insignia was thusly referred to as 'The Death of Life.'"

Viv's head popped up so quickly that her glasses slid to an angle on her nose. She nudged them back into place. "What do you think? It sounds exactly like what you saw."

"And the 'Tree of Life' reference," Hayden said excitedly. "That can't be a coincidence. The tapestry where we found the clues to the book, the blade, and the burial ground was a picture of the same thing."

Claudia felt a tingling sense of premonition in her gut. During Willyn's trial, the nine had joined hands and channeled their combined magic into a tapestry in Anna's home. A hidden message had lit up for all to see, and had ultimately led them to discover those specific items.

Three pieces that would be required to defeat Bastraal.

The St. Germaine sisters had left clues for the modern-day witches, pointing them in the right direction to help fulfill the prophecy. Hayden had made a crucial connection. The 'Tree of Life' reference was the key they'd been looking for.

"We need to narrow our search." Claudia stood but motioned to the stacks of books on their table. "Let's keep these for now, and I'll see if any others pop up with the new search parameters."

It only took a few minutes for her to find mention of the symbol in a newspaper article about an estate sale held in October, 1952. The words "Death of Life" had promptly returned a link to the publication.

An estate sale often meant family heirlooms and valuable antiques. "Hot damn," she said automatically, then she swiveled her head to see if anyone had heard her swear. No one was around.

Returning to the table, she grinned at Viv and Hayden,

slung her purse over her shoulder, and hefted one of the book piles. "Let's go."

"You got something?" Viv asked, mimicking Claudia's routine. Smile. Purse-sling. Book-heft.

Then Hayden did the same, helping to clear the table. Together they moved to the rolling cart that held books needing to be re-shelved, and as they loaded it up, Claudia filled them in on what she'd found. "We have to go to the microfiche storage room. Old newspapers are housed in that format."

"And once we have a copy of the article?" Hayden asked, trailing the other two back down the staircase.

Claudia shook her head. "I guess we'll find out."

Familiar with the machine and film that it used, Claudia made short work of inserting the appropriate microfiche and scrolling to the sought-after article. She scanned each paragraph, enthralled by the tale of the Havens family and the wife's revenge on her late husband.

She had inherited the family home, but he had brought money to the marriage, allowing them to keep the house in good repair. A marriage of convenience. One that had been a little *too* convenient, in the wife's opinion.

As revenge for her husband's multiple mistresses, the widow Havens had decided to sell off his collection of "obscure artifacts." Claudia lifted her brows. Well, at least the woman had left this one small clue behind for the witches to discover.

When she scanned the end of the article, she found a note of extreme interest.

> The following items will not be available due to previous purchase arrangements between Mrs. Lida Havens née Davidson and local collector William Clermont.

Within the list of items already sold to Mr. Clermont were the words that had identified the article during Claudia's search.

```
    …one silver "Death of Life" insignia
  ring…
```

She rolled her chair back and clapped her hands. "Now we're getting somewhere." When Viv and Hayden crowded around her to read over her shoulder, she pointed to the passage. "Now we just have to find out what happened to this Mr. Clermont."

"To him," Viv said in a deadpan voice, "and all of his belongings."

Hayden straightened and stretched her arms over her head. "Then I say we do a quick genealogy search and cross our fingers that the man's descendants are still around. And afterward, we relocate to a more beverage-friendly environment."

"I'm with you there," Viv said. "To the coffee shop."

~~~

Two hours later, after an exhaustive search for family records and contact information, the three women sat at a round high-top table with their drinks and sandwiches. Viv and Claudia had cappuccino and espresso respectively but, since the shop didn't serve canjee, Hayden settled for a chai tea latte.

They allowed themselves enough time to eat their food before Claudia retrieved the notes they'd taken of local names and phone numbers. If their luck held, one of these people would be able to tell her where the ring was today.

"It's got to be here," Hayden said, her voice full of encouragement. "The 'Death of Life' is a pretty obscure symbol, and the only reason we even found mention of it is because the signet originated from Savannah."

Viv swallowed the last bite of her tuna sub. "And because the ring belonged to Bastraal. Maybe all of his items that we need have been kept here by...other means."

"Like a mystical magnet?" Claudia liked the optimistic viewpoint. "Making sure everything we need to defeat the demon stayed close enough for us to find? Sure. I'll go with that theory. It's nice to think the metaphysical powers that be might lend us a hand occasionally."

Hayden snorted. "I know, right?"

Taking another sip of her espresso, Claudia picked up her phone and punched in the first number on the list. "Then here we go."

After three calls with no useful information, she finally reached an older woman who was more than happy to relate how the collection of her grandfather, the same William Clermont, had been passed down from first son to first son and was now the property of her second cousin. The "lunatic," as she put it.

Once she got the man's name, Claudia thanked the woman and checked her list. "Here he is. Nathaniel Clermont." She looked hopefully to Viv and Hayden. "Doesn't sound too bad."

"Yeah." Hayden nodded. "He's probably fine. The lady was just miffed she didn't get the inheritance."

"I'm sure that's it." After skipping down the list to locate the name and number, Claudia dialed and waited. When a man answered, she tried to infuse her voice with charisma. "Yes, am I speaking with Nathaniel Clermont?"

He answered in the affirmative.

"My name is Claudia Grant. I teach history at a university in Pennsylvania, and I'd be interested in speaking with you about an item you might have inherited from your grandfather, William Clermont."

She drew a breath to continue, but was brought up short when the man asked sharply, "Do I know you?"

"Um, we haven't met, but I'm—"

"Are you from Savannah?"

Claudia shifted her eyes to Viv then Hayden, but had no choice but to answer the brusque question. "No, but—"

"Fine." He cut her off again. "Then is your *family* from Savannah?"

"No." She was trying to keep a lid on her frustration, because she needed to get this rude man to talk to her. More than that, she needed to see the ring. And somehow convince him to sell it to her.

So far, she'd barely had a chance to tell him her name.

But Nathaniel Clermont, gentleman of the South, didn't give her another opening. "Then I don't know you. Good day." He hung up without another word of explanation or apology.

"Wha—" Claudia held out her phone and glared at it, affronted. "How rude!"

"What did he say?" Viv was scowling at the phone as well.

"Not much, but he made it clear that he wouldn't talk to me because I'm not from here." She added in a snooty tone, "Since my family isn't from Savannah either."

Hayden bested the both of them, pulling her own phone from her pocket and holding it up. "He wants an old Savannah pedigree, does he?"

She hit a button on the little pink smart phone. "I happen to know a good ol' Savannah boy, whose family probably put up one of the first tents next to the river."

Viv worked up a mischievous grin as her pewter-gray eyes slid over to Claudia. "Trevor."

Deflated by the man's horrible attitude, Claudia could only flicker a smile in return.

As Hayden waited for her boyfriend to pick up, Claudia envisioned the brawny blonde man and was glad they had him on their team.

Then she pictured his partner. Today was a workday, so

wherever Trevor was, it was likely that Cole was with him.

Pointing a finger at Hayden, she issued a caveat. "All right. You can bring Trevor in on this." She gulped the rest of her espresso and shivered at the overdose of such a strong brew. Then she pointed with more insistence. "But *only* Trevor."

12

The car door of Claudia's silver convertible closed with a solid *thunk,* like only a well-built car from the 1960s could. With her sunglasses on to combat the midday sun, she took in the country estate and the tall black iron gate barring her from entry.

Mr. Clermont, it seemed, was protective in more ways than one, and she was surprised he lived so far outside the city of Savannah. Considering his ingrained prejudice against...well, anywhere that *wasn't* Savannah.

Waving away a fly and considering waiting in her car with the air-conditioner on full blast, Claudia contemplated her foul mood. She couldn't blame the heat, the imposing gate that made her feel like a trespasser, or even, for that matter, Nathaniel Clermont himself.

The man had a right to his privacy, as everyone did, so his high-handedness didn't bother her enough to ruin her outlook on this lovely day. No, she'd blame that on someone else entirely.

The rumble of a car coming down the old paved road—so worn the gravel was poking through—alerted her that someone had arrived.

Trevor had known exactly how to get Claudia in to see

this Mr. Clermont, all right. And the backstage pass would be delivered via the one man she had no desire to see at the moment.

As it turned out, she required Cole's help one more time.

He pulled his Range Rover to the side of the road, parking beneath the tall breezy pines and on top of the untrimmed grass. Claudia leaned against her car, in a stance she felt was the perfect blend of casual and defensive.

When he exited his vehicle, irritation was etched into the handsome lines of his face. "Before you say anything, I just want to clarify that I already know what you're thinking." His eyes were slightly glazed.

"Are you sick?" Claudia asked. Brushing off the guilt that tweaked her conscience, she spoke in a forthright manner. "If you don't feel well, your...*friend* can get me inside, and you can go home."

Based on the rancor that rolled off of him, he hadn't forgotten their hostile parting after the benefit the other night. Claudia drew herself up. Well, neither had she.

He walked toward her, but angled closer to the gate, apparently trying to leave a wide berth between them. "I'm sure you'd prefer me to leave, but that wasn't the deal I made."

She sniffed and adjusted her sunglasses. "Fine. We'll get in and get out. I hate to keep repeating myself, but I don't need your help."

Cole's attention was on the woods across the street, but the scoffing sound he made was for her benefit. "Yeah. That's what you keep telling me." His laugh was short and sarcastic. "Then I get another phone call."

Standing up, because the metal of the car's hood was heating her behind, she strolled to the street and looked down the road. They were still expecting one more.

What was Cole's problem anyway? She chose to bite down the snarky response that flitted into her mind, instead turning back around to peer through the gates and down the winding drive. But behind her dark lenses, her gaze remained on Cole. He was a bit rough around the edges today, both in appearance and attitude.

Suddenly groaning, he bent his head and rubbed his forehead. "You're right. I'm not myself today. I must have picked up some sort of bug."

Her concern was real when she asked, "Will you be able to go home and get some rest after we meet with Mr. Clermont?"

Cole shook his head. "Nah. I'm not actually sick. Just a little more tired than normal. Nothing for you to worry about."

She did worry, though, and hated the thought of his having to be out here in the heat when he didn't feel well. She just didn't know how to show her concern without appearing too invested.

Cole wasn't her enemy. He was a friend, but after their impassioned kiss, their friendship was blazing like a hot meteor toward more. A hot lot of *more*.

Claudia's mouth twitched with the urge to frown but she stifled it. Having him thrust into the middle of her trial again had put her on guard. There was no question that fate was playing games with them both, so she needed to be extra-vigilant.

Cole had ended up here today in lieu of Trevor, because the woman who could get them past those tall gates owed Cole a favor. And coming face to face with one of his *female acquaintances* was compounding her rotten disposition.

A noise caught her attention as he reached into the pocket of his jeans. He withdrew a small bag of blue plastic that crackled when he stuck his hand inside. He offered her one of the round pieces of candy. "Here. This will cheer you up. They're sweet and tart."

Her annoyance was that obvious? Then she'd unleash it. Her tongue lashed at him before she could stop herself. "Hmm. *Tart* being the operative word of the day."

His pissed off look was back again, and he was leveling it straight at her. "What do you mean?"

She gave him a cold shoulder. He acted as if they weren't waiting on another woman, one who was probably one of his past conquests. "I know we're only getting in to see Clermont, because you called in a favor. From a female *acquaintance.*"

"You mean Jean Atmoor?" Cole's jaw dropped. "You know, Claudia, you've got a dirty mind. I never realized that before. Or what a snob you are."

"A snob?" Now she was insulted. "I'm no such thing."

"Really? Let me give you some examples. How could a lowly detective possibly afford the house I bought?"

She cocked a hip and put one hand there. "I never said lowly."

Cole ignored her rebuttal. "Not to mention how shocked you were that I have an interest in antiques and restoring timepieces. Or that I volunteer my time to help kids in need. Why, I'm surprised I can manage it, what with all the skirt-chasing I do every day."

"I never said—"

Now his genial mood vanished completely, leaving his face marred with a scowl. "You said something pretty close. If I remember correctly, the phrase you used was 'a guy like you.'" He popped another piece of candy in his mouth and chewed it up before adding, "And now you've called Mrs. Atmoor a tart."

Mrs.? The woman must have gotten married since her time with Cole. "Okay, maybe I shouldn't have said that. I apologize."

She abruptly reconsidered taking a piece of that candy, because the regret she was swallowing tasted bitter. She really had to stop letting her fear translate into anger and taking it out on other people. "I know I keep apologizing, and no excuse I make is—"

"Speaking of which." Cole wasn't listening to her anyway. He pointed down the drive. "Here comes the tart now."

A shining white car, long like a Cadillac, was coming down the country road at a leisurely pace. Claudia took off her glasses, curious to see what kind of woman drove a tank like that. The car was well-preserved, but obviously over twenty years old.

"You aren't the only one who drives a classic." Cole jerked his chin toward her convertible.

"It's a 1966 Alfa Romeo Spider, to be precise." Claudia was proud of her baby.

Standing tall with a cocksure flip of her hair, she reminded herself not to let anything the woman might say or do get under her skin. So what if Cole was throwing an old flame in her face? It's not like Claudia had any claim on him.

They were the furthest thing from it, in fact, and she intended to keep it that way.

The shiny Caddy eased to the side of the road, and Cole hustled to the driver's side to open the door.

Claudia *tsked* with her tongue. *Please. What a show he's putting on.*

But she felt the first stone drop in her belly when she saw white hair. The second, even larger chunk of granite, crashed to the bottom once she got a good look at the woman vying for Cole's attention.

His lady friend was obviously charmed by the attractive detective and offered him a sweet smile as he helped her walk to the call box on the gates. She relied on Cole's assistance instead of the cane hanging from her elbow.

Mrs. Jean Atmoor—the *tart*—was approximately eighty years old.

And there went the red alarm in Claudia's head, only this time it was one-hundred percent shame. When the older woman smiled and called, "Hello, dear," Claudia wanted to bang her head on the brick columns flanking the gate.

That would be far less painful than dealing with Cole's self-righteousness.

Until her face cooled down and the blush of humiliation receded from her cheeks, she would wait by her car. She would be unobtrusive. Chewing the inside of her cheek, she longed for a huge hole in the ground to hide in.

Mrs. Atmoor spoke into the intercom to announce them and a male voice responded. Soon after, the black metal gate swung open, but the genteel woman crossed her hands over her midriff and stood quietly, unmoving.

Claudia finally asked, "Should we drive up to the house?"

"No need." Mrs. Atmoor straightened the sweater of her yellow twinset. "They'll send a cart for us."

It was about that time that Claudia heard the familiar high-pitched whir, and a golf cart rounded the bend of the black asphalt drive. A man dressed like an old English butler was driving the cart, and the older woman greeted him, calling him Charles.

When the esteemed Mrs. Atmoor took the front seat, Claudia had no choice but to climb in back with Cole. The cart was clean—pristine, actually—so at least her dress wouldn't get dirty.

When the cart jolted over uneven ground and caused her naked thigh to bump firmly against his, she wished fervently for pants. His blue jeans didn't do much to keep his heat from penetrating through to her, but another layer of fabric would have helped. Cole's hands gripped his knees, and tension racked his shoulders. He seemed to be as uncomfortable as she was. *Only a few minutes more and we can resume a safe distance.*

They both heaved a sigh when the cart rolled up to a looming brick house and sweeping front steps. Verandas lined the upper floor with potted and hanging plants surrounding outdoor seating areas.

Claudia almost made a statement about Mr. Clermont inheriting a lot more than his grandfather's collectibles but realized that would be in poor taste. She shot a look to Cole as they climbed out of the cart. He only shrugged.

Once they were inside the house, they moved past myriad rooms and passageways. Claudia sent Cole a more direct and questioning glance. She wondered what kind of place they'd walked into, as the layout seemed to stretch on forever. Or had they simply taken multiple turns?

Finally they came to a massive metal door with bolts screwed in near the edges and a seam down the middle. A grinding noise began below their feet and climbed higher, until the opening split to reveal an industrial-sized elevator.

Claudia speculated about the safety of the contraption—or the wisdom of getting inside the peculiar Mr. Clermont's device—but Mrs. Atmoor was nonplussed and glided aboard in her lady-like way.

So Claudia gave in and joined her. When Cole came on last and the doors shut, Mrs. Atmoor patted Claudia's hand. "Don't worry. You're in for a treat." One of her white eyebrows winged up. "And you'll see why a trip to Mr. Clermont's is by invitation only."

When they touched down somewhere below ground, Claudia understood Mr. Clermont's reason for building a home outside of Savannah. He admittedly loved his hometown, but he couldn't have built this kind of underground hideaway so near the coastline.

They traveled west, farther inland, where the wealthy man had carved an entire level of rooms beneath the ground. And, judging by the length of the tunnel before them, the basement area was vast.

The channel was rounded at the top and clearly manmade, its cement having been stained brown and coated with a shiny sealant. Busts and statues lined both sides of the wide shaft, and still there was room enough for Claudia, Cole, and Mrs. Atmoor to walk alongside each other. Recessed lighting in the ceiling highlighted each work of art they passed, but the shadow effect on the walls was somewhat eerie.

At the end of the tunnel, they exited into a room with higher ceilings. Here again, the walls were reinforced by cement, with metal girders and wooden beams mixed throughout. To Claudia it looked like the man couldn't make up his mind on any particular design.

The underground refuge was a clash of old world and futuristic. She couldn't wait to finally meet the architect of this strange domain.

They passed through larger items first, including a few ancient barrels that had likely held whiskey. Farther down she spied a pile of cannon balls that she guessed were remnants from the Revolutionary War.

Square brick support columns had been painted the color of good claret, but in the gloomy chamber, the wine-colored posts reminded her of blood before it reached the heart. Lacking oxygen and life. Dark.

Cole edged closer to her as they walked, allowing Mrs. Atmoor to take the lead. "What do you think's back there?" His eyes traveled to indicate an opening with light glowing from within.

She shook her head as tingles of excitement and nervousness competed inside her tightening chest. "I don't know."

A wall had been erected outside the final set of pillars to cordon off another section. Still barging ahead like the queen of the palace, Mrs. Atmoor strode through the entryway with Claudia and Cole close behind.

When they crossed the threshold, the atmosphere changed. Here were the smaller items, the riches and treasures that deserved—and created—luxurious surroundings. Lush carpets covered the floor, and the fixtures on the walls cast a soft ambiance from elaborate golden lanterns.

A matching chandelier hung in the center of the room,

and glass-enclosed cases each held their own small bulbs to highlight the treasures within. Amazement paralyzed and muted Claudia instantly.

The place was a museum. No, forget that. There were museums that would envy the rare and special prizes this man had amassed. There was a lot more at work here than wealth and pomposity. The person, or people, who'd created this collection were certainly masters of their trade. And true historians.

A man reclined in a chair in the center of the space, where additional chairs circled a massive coffee table in the shape of a giant tortoise. While the creature might seem eccentric to some, Claudia could sense the piece's age and value.

A screen of carved sandalwood fit for a Chinese emperor stood in a corner. Weapons and full suits of armor were affixed to the cement walls, along with so many more items that Claudia's head literally began to spin.

"Mrs. Atmoor," the man boomed in a heavy accent, not the fake kind of Southern-speak that they always put in the movies, but a careless drawl that spoke of lazy days and lemonade. Debutantes and etiquette school. A sound that was rare today, even in the strongholds of Southern culture.

"Nathaniel," the older lady responded in a prim voice. "I understand you refused my dear friend, Ms…." Mrs. Attinger faltered, then looked to Claudia. "What was your name, dear?"

Claudia smiled at the brash woman. "Claudia Grant."

"Yes." Mrs. Atmoor tapped her cane one time on the carpet. "You refused Ms. Grant, and she being a professor of history." Her tone escalated at the end in righteous indignation.

"Now, Jean," he cajoled, swirling a tumbler of brown liquid in his hand, "you know I don't allow strangers in without a recommendation." He set the glass down and stood. "But now that you've vouched for her, Ms. Grant is welcome to take a gander."

He crossed his arms and thrust one shoulder forward, angling his body dramatically toward Claudia. "You do know that gander means *look*?" He licked his thin lips. "Not touch."

"I appreciate your letting me view your collection." How should she approach this unconventional man? He wore a starched white shirt with a dark brown vest, and his mustache was the quintessential handlebar.

She didn't want to make a wrong move and get herself booted from the property before she had a chance to locate Bastraal's ring. So keeping quiet—which was never her strong point—she deferred to Mrs. Atmoor and took behavioral cues from Mr. Clermont's trusted guest.

Around the large room they walked, she and Cole paired up behind the other two. Their host regaled the older woman with tales of his most recent acquisitions.

And Claudia kept her eye out for the signet ring.

Still, she listened politely as the man described everything from gemstones to furniture. When they came upon a small purple purse with brass trim, Mr. Clermont grew even more animated.

"This type of thing is all the rage these days." He opened the purse once, then again, revealing a hidden compartment with a small pistol, also trimmed with small decorative panels of brass.

"This is the real deal and, since the Steampunk lifestyle has taken off, I've gotten some outrageous offers." He wiggled his mustache. "But I won't sell." He shook his finger. "Not from my personal collection."

The distinctive wail of a bomb dropping echoed in the depths of Claudia's head. It was the sound of her own destruction. Her utter failure.

Because if she couldn't get Mr. Clermont to sell her the ring, she was finished. So was her trial, and the coven along with it.

She'd never fully comprehended the pressure each of her

sisters had faced during their challenges, but the enormity of her task weighed on her. The burden felt far too heavy to carry alone.

She touched the amulet hanging from her neck and pictured her friends. Her stone would sing, she silently cheered to herself. She wouldn't let her coven down.

She was about to address Mr. Clermont directly when Mrs. Atmoor patted the man's arm. "Yes, that is fascinating, but I'm afraid that's not what we came to see today."

She cast keen eyes toward Claudia, as if to say, *This is it, girl.*

Claudia stepped up. "I understand you have a signet ring, one that has been in Savannah for over two centuries and was passed down from your grandfather. The insignia stamped on the front has been referred to as the 'Death of Life.'"

She thought of showing him the copy of the newspaper article in her purse, but there was no need. He clapped his hands together and gestured. "Of course. Right over here."

A display case sat next to one of the claret-colored support pillars that were in this room as well. Mr. Clermont moved to the case and lifted the glass lid. Despite Claudia's eager smile and hopeful expression, he left the ring nestled around the velvet nub that held it in place.

Claudia bit the inside of her cheek. Should she risk touching the antique? What if she passed out and broke something in the fall? She'd lose the ring, not to mention any chance of purchase.

Whether she dared hold the piece was inconsequential, though. Mr. Clermont closed the case before she could form a strategy. "Remember. Touching is not allowed."

"I was actually hoping to—"

The man swept past her and re-engaged Mrs. Atmoor in conversation. As if Claudia hadn't even spoken, he led the older woman to a table with a golden box sitting on top. "So much for that," she muttered to herself.

Cole put his hand on her arm and propelled her forward. "We aren't out of here yet. Get back in there and do what you came to do."

Encouragement despite having insulted both Cole and the sweet elderly lady? Either he was trying to drive the guilt-stake clear through her heart, or he was back to his old self. Dependable, got-your-back Cole.

The very good friend she'd verbally trashed both earlier today and when she'd been a guest in his home. When, again, he'd been trying to help her.

Later. She'd make amends later. Right now—she gritted her teeth and headed toward her unconventional host—she had a date with an ancient signet ring.

"This you've seen before, but not since I found the accompanying bowl and lamp." Mr. Clermont had opened the golden box, and now that Claudia could make out the design and implements resting inside, she recognized what he was showing Mrs. Atmoor.

"An opium pipe," Claudia said, causing the strange man to stare at her like a startled owl. "Circa 1850, if I'm not mistaken. A real collector's item, even in those days."

He lowered the pipe and studied her, and for the first time since she'd entered the eccentric's lair, his eyes held true interest. "Yes. My, my. You are good."

Claudia smirked inside. *You have no idea, mister.*

Mr. Clermont looked at her shrewdly. "This has reportedly been in my family since before the civil war. An ancestor of mine was fond of the orient and all its," here he winked bawdily at Mrs. Atmoor, "guilty pleasures."

Holding the pipe with its delicately painted scenes of flowers and...nineteenth century porn, the man sighed and stared at the extremely ornate and costly drug paraphernalia. "I'd give anything to know what this sweetheart has seen. What my great, great, great grandfather might have done. Where he traveled. Whom he met."

Claudia's body went icily cool and alert all at the same time. Here was her opportunity. Revealing herself would be risky, but if she succeeded, the reward would be worth it.

She nailed Mr. Clermont with her eyes. "Would you really?"

Handlebar moustache twitching, the collector angled his head to the side as if confused. "What?"

Claudia edged forward and, breaking his first rule, tapped a finger to the pipe. "Would you really like to know all the stories this has to tell?"

She took a deep breath and steeled her backbone. Smiling like a cat, she practically purred, "Because I can tell you."

13

After over an hour of revealing the opium pipe's true stories, Mr. Clermont was adequately assured of Claudia's authenticity and had learned a great deal about the men of his family. Gathered around the tortoise-shaped table, he'd actually blushed a time or two after hearing what a colorful character his great, great, great grandfather had been.

So as part of the bargain for the ring, she and the others had also been sworn to secrecy.

With a deal struck and the signet ring packaged in a black box—which Cole held onto for the time being—the owner of the unique house insisted on a toast.

The dry wine caused Cole's throat to clench, but he participated in the ritual before they all went back upstairs. The day had been exhaustive for Claudia, and the strain showed on her face. He barely kept himself from slipping an arm around her waist to offer support.

The metal elevator ground down to open for them, then carried them back up to the main floor where Mr. Clermont requested that Mrs. Atmoor join him for a discussion of "board business." They were both members of a historical society operating in Southeastern Georgia.

"You're both welcome to have a walk around the house." Mr.

Clermont spoke affably to Cole and Claudia, a changed man and cordial host, now that he had been treated to such a vivid family narration. "I would suggest the library."

"Oh, yes," Mrs. Atmoor agreed. "If you need to leave before we're done with our meeting, feel free to do so. I'll be just fine on my own."

"Charles will drive you back to your cars whenever you're ready." Mr. Clermont took Claudia's hand and kissed her fingers. "An unexpected pleasure, Ms. Grant. Please come again."

After niceties had been exchanged, Cole studied Claudia to find that color was returning to her cheeks. She seemed to be amped up about seeing the library. "Your call," he said. "If you're too tired, we can go."

"I'm fine, but what about you?"

Strangely enough, his energy had also returned. Since he no longer felt the inexplicable fatigue, he inclined his head in agreement. He'd probably just not slept well the night before but, as the day wore on, he was beginning to feel better.

Being in Claudia's company didn't hurt either. She had a natural radiance about her, a spark. And he wasn't talking about the fire she could create with a finger snap. She delighted in the simplest discoveries, as excited to see the antique hardware installed on the interior doors as most women would have been over expensive jewelry.

He'd have to remember that. No shiny baubles for this lady. Unless they were from 1912.

He felt his mouth curve downward as he rebelled against his own thoughts. Why would he ever buy Claudia jewelry in the first place? They weren't involved, and if she had her way, they never would be.

So why does that make me so resentful? From afar, he watched her trail a hand over some kind of cabinet. He thought it might be called an armoire.

As they came to the end of the corridor Mr. Clermont had directed them down, they made a left turn and headed toward what Cole felt sure was the rear of the estate. The winding and strangely built mansion contained an elaborate network of intersections and oddly placed doorways. A map or diagram would have been helpful.

Claudia seemed to know her way, though, as if she could actually *smell* the books she was so eager to see. Finally they reached a set of doors that rose to the ceiling, painted white with flashy gold trim.

Claudia placed her hands on the dual handles and laughed. "This is the library, all right. Even the doors feel more erudite here."

"And you're already talking like a dictionary," Cole replied, hoping he didn't sound as fractious as he felt. Now that he was with Claudia again, alone, all he wanted was to back her against a wall and demand to know why she was so unwilling to consider him.

As anything more than a friend.

Each time they were flung together, he remembered how hard Trevor had fought his attraction to Hayden. And he also recalled how happy his partner had been when he finally gave in and let himself love her.

Cole tightened his jaw and let Claudia walk ahead of him, hoping she wouldn't notice his increasing agitation. He couldn't deny feeling drawn to the redheaded witch. He'd always felt it, even when surrounded by all the other beauties in the coven.

And he'd kept it to himself, even from Trevor. But the more time he spent with Claudia, the more he questioned his own motivations. His own desires.

Because lately, the woman who talked like an antiquarian but looked like a flame-haired goddess was all he'd been able to think about. Despite what he'd said earlier, he'd been glad to call in the favor from Mrs. Atmoor.

Because it brought him back to Claudia.

Once inside the doors, he could see they were on some sort of walkway. The railings mirrored the doorway of white and gold, as did the short flight of stairs that descended into the room.

Claudia squealed when she saw the rows of soaring bookcases situated throughout the chamber, enough for a public library. The bleached wood was silvery, light and airy, complementing the white and gray tiled floor.

They had, Cole realized, walked into a fairy tale.

In contrast to the gloomy cellar rooms, three large windows illuminated the space. The center frame arched while the ones flanking it were squared off. Those were Palladian windows, he knew, because his mother loved the look and had insisted on them for her parlor.

While Claudia ran from one area to another, he eased over to look outside. The lawn was open and natural, trimmed but without structural landscaping. Various trees were in bloom, their white and pink flowers creating a nice view from the library.

He sensed Claudia's approach and cursed himself for tensing when he smelled her sweet citrus and floral perfume. He kept his eyes riveted to the outdoor scenery. With the way he was feeling, it was way too dangerous to look at her legs right now.

Or her hair. Her eyes. The neck that curved to shoulders he knew were soft and warm.

"Dogwoods," she said, pulling him out of his forbidden fantasy. She slanted her eyes his way, and sunlight warmed the green.

Unable to hide his desire, Cole gave up and thought, screw it. Holding her stare, he let all the turbulent emotions knocking around inside him fuel his gaze.

Her face fell, shifting from elation to concern instantly. "What's wrong?"

Cole didn't want to ruin her fun just because he couldn't

contain his lust—or the very real frustration it was causing—so he turned back to stare at the trees again. "Nothing," he lied, focusing on the clear blue sky. He willed her to go back to the books, to find another distraction.

To take herself and her perfume far out of olfactory range.

"You're still mad at me." She sighed. "And you have every right to be."

Dropping the arms that had been crossed over his chest, Cole turned to her. "I'm not angry." That much was true, but he wouldn't elaborate on what he was feeling. He didn't think he could lie to her now. He could no longer cover it all up.

So better to just stay silent.

"I'm so sorry for what I said about you. *And* Mrs. Atmoor." She ran a hand over her ponytail, a nervous gesture that broadcast her regret more loudly than her words. "It seems like I never stop apologizing to you."

"I get it." There was a bite to his tone, but he couldn't help it. "You keep having to deal with me, so I could be part of your challenge. The true love answer to your trial. And that terrifies you, because you don't think I'm good enough."

"What? No!" Her face lost all color, and her hand clamped down on his arm. "Never say that. It's not that you aren't good enough. Never that."

Biting her lip as if she didn't really want to say what was coming next, she shook her head. "But even if it were easy for me to trust in relationships...Well, you know how you are with women."

"No, I don't know. Enlighten me." His arms went back up instinctively, crossing over his chest as he widened his stance and faced her fully.

But instead of letting her answer, he launched an attack instead. "Get this through your head once and for all. Admiring women and dating them is not the same thing as being a womanizer. You're free to ask anyone I've gone out with if they have a negative thing to say about how I treated them."

He took a step closer and leaned in, letting her finally see how her presumptions angered him. "And most of them would tell you we never went to bed together." He pointed at her and came close to touching her shoulder. "I don't sleep around carelessly."

Throwing up her hands, Claudia backed away. "Okay. It's really none of my business."

"The hell it isn't. You're making it your business by constantly telling me how untrustworthy I am. That you think I'm some philandering piece of shit."

Now her palms covered her face. Her shoulders sagged. "Oh, God. No. I don't think that." She hid behind her hands for a few more seconds before parting them just enough to peek out.

Her eyes begged for forgiveness. "I'm the piece of shit."

Hearing her say those words hit Cole in a way he never would have expected. Especially when she drooped her shoulders and stared up at him like a forlorn puppy. Laughter started deep in his gut. "Stop doing that."

"What?" Her expression transformed to slightly perplexed with a sheen of insult. "I feel really awful about how I've acted."

When his shoulders started to shake, she propped her fisted hands on her hips. "Stop laughing at me. I said I was sorry. I won't make any more snap judgments or further malign your character."

"Stop. Please stop." The more incensed she became, the more he wanted to pull her close and kiss her pouting mouth. She was so damned cute when she sulked. "You're forgiven."

With a toss of her hair, she pressed her lips together. "That's not the reaction I expected."

Cole knew he shouldn't push it, but getting Claudia rattled was pretty entertaining. "What?" He angled his head. "You thought we might go kick it in the stacks?" He moved closer. "It's not a *bad* idea. You know what they say about makeup—"

"Ugh!" Shock caused her mouth to fall open. She recovered quickly though, nailing him with a look that could only be described as professorial. He imagined what it would be like to be one of her students. The idea turned him on.

"Cole." Her voice dripped condescension. "The fact that you just said 'kick it in the stacks' virtually guarantees that we never, *ever* will."

Shrugging his shoulders, he said, "Hey. I'm just trying to live up to your image of me."

Claudia closed her eyes briefly as if praying for patience. But when she opened them, a smile tugged at her mouth. "You're hopeless. However, if I forgive you as you've forgiven me, then that will make us even. Besides, I don't like feeling guilty or angry. Especially with a friend."

Her long, slim fingers slipped into his hand, and Cole jolted from the contact. "Come on," she said. "There's a special section I spotted before. I'd like to show you."

He let her tug him toward one of the tall shelves, occasionally watching the way the hem of her gray dress hit the back of her thighs. Leveling his gaze was no better, because that just made him want to take her swinging ponytail in his hand. To slide the band off and let all that silky red fall freely down her back.

They stopped at a shelving unit in a corner of the large room. No direct sunlight fell on this aisle since the section was blocked on both sides by more towering shelves.

She pulled out a book with a black leather cover and handed it to him. He read the title. "Analytic Detection and Medicine." Laughter rumbled in his chest. "This is old, written way before we started using the term 'forensics.'"

"I thought you'd find it interesting." Claudia's voice and mannerisms were suddenly subdued. Wondering at the change, Cole studied her. He noticed how she bit her bottom lip.

A palpable force seemed to fill the atmosphere. Not sizzling with energy, but heavy and insistent. As if the two of them were encased in a capsule of their own, separated from the rest of the world.

"Thank you for showing me this." Heedless of returning the hardback to its proper spot, Cole turned it on its cover and set it atop a row of other books.

Claudia nodded almost imperceptibly, probing his gaze much as he was hers. There was nothing snobbish about her now. In fact, he didn't recognize the look she was giving him. Wonder and curiosity? Hesitation?

He could certainly identify with those sentiments. And more. The desire he felt for her was raging, and after months of being held in check, the need to show her was taking over. Breaking through the last chains of the principles that bound him.

And where was the honor in denying how he truly felt? Claudia Grant called to him, and the idea of turning away from her so she could go on with her life—either alone or with someone else—wasn't an option for him anymore.

"Maybe we should go." Her lips trembled as she spoke.

"Why?" Ready to press his advantage, Cole approached her.

Darting her eyes to the side, then over his shoulder, she retreated. Finally, she lifted her face, but uncertainty lived in her eyes.

Cole looked deep into the river green and let need take control. He lifted one hand to cup her cheek, then slowly smoothed his palm down her neck and to her shoulder.

"We shouldn't." Her voice shook. "It's too risky."

Widening his stance he confined her, so she had no choice but to flatten herself against the shelves. "Are you afraid to let me kiss you? Or afraid that we'll be caught?"

"Neither." The fierce independence that was pure Claudia came back to light a fire in her eyes. "You shouldn't be thinking about those things. But I'm not afraid of you."

"I'm not sure I believe you." When she gasped and started to respond, he shushed her denial with two fingers. Gently.

Seductively. "And if you don't want me to think of you that way, then you really should stop showing your legs all the time.

"I like dresses," she whispered, the pulse in her neck fluttering so prettily that he longed to cover it with his mouth. To feel her throb against his tongue.

But that would be too much too fast. First he had to know for sure.

Pressing his thumbs under her chin, he lifted her face and positioned her lips so they would catch his if he leaned any farther in. "You know what else I think?" He could feel her rapid breaths against his skin.

"I think you want me to kiss you again."

14

Claudia grabbed onto Cole's sides, afraid she'd topple over if she didn't. His hands feathering over her skin were making her dizzy, and his voice had grown thick, husky. The deep timbre was deliciously male as it brushed across her lips.

There was no going back now, she knew. No stopping the inevitable. But even more surprising was that she no longer cared. She didn't want to stop. Curling her fingers into his white shirt, she thought once again of the woman she'd seen him with at the café.

Despite a moment's guilt, she did a drive-by of his most recent memories, or what little she could pick up from his clothing. She didn't sense any other females and was thrilled by the confirmation. Actually, she was deliriously happy.

For about two seconds.

Until she analyzed her elation and asked herself *why* she didn't want Cole to be seeing anyone else. *Oh, no. No. No. No.* She couldn't be feeling territorial, could she? Possessive with just a dollop of jealousy on top?

Of course not. Lust. That's all she was feeling. She was only in lust.

Birds tittered somewhere outside, their spring song filtering through the windows. Sexual attraction could be a powerful thing, but with the right elements, it could also be spellbinding. This was an idyllic moment, so why not grab a small taste of happiness?

One afternoon cocooned in romanticism, enjoying the company of a gorgeous man she respected and admired. She was never going to allow herself to fall truly, madly in love, but that didn't mean she couldn't seize an opportunity when one presented itself.

True, Cole was the one man she'd also been trying to avoid. But since the fates apparently thought they could keep shoving him into her life and *make* her fall in love, she'd simply have to take advantage of their misstep. She'd beat them at their own game and outmaneuver destiny.

Starting now.

She drew in a deep breath of courage and whispered, "I want you, Cole."

Her fervent declaration made his eyes widen, but just barely. He couldn't hide his physical response, though. She felt his fingers tighten on her chin. Sensed the deep draw of air he pulled in so quietly.

Letting her hands fall to his hips, she gave one quick tug and slammed his lower body into hers. Thanks to her three-inch heels, his erection pressed against her in a way that made her new idea not only seem sensible, but like pure witching genius.

Inhibitions fled, and reticence no longer stood between them. She knew Cole. As a cop, a good man, and a reliable friend. If she was going to take a lover—that very rare and treacherous occurrence—then she might as well take one she trusted. At least with her body and her dignity, if not her heart.

Their familiarity over the months had been like carefully stacked tinder, though neither had even realized it. Now those sturdily arranged pieces erupted into something else, and the need to be with him roared through her like brushfire.

"Kiss me, Cole. In this beautiful library while dogwoods

bloom in the window." She licked her lips and slid them over his. "Do it."

For the first time, he looked a little nervous. "I don't want to push you, to rush you into something you don't want."

Hitching one leg up to run the toe of her shoe down the back of his calf, Claudia fought against any lingering indecision. She spoke against his lips. "When have you ever known me to be pushed into anything against my will?"

"That's true." She could see he was giving in, but the honorable part of him that always tried to do the right thing was still battling for domination.

Determined now to get what she wanted, Claudia narrowed her eyes like a cat on the hunt. Cole's continued presence in her life was becoming a problem, and she had to resume control.

So she'd take this chance, and they'd both get what they wanted. Then they could be done with lust and return to their comfortable friendship. A nice, safe place.

Using her tongue, she rimmed the inside of his bottom lip, moving slowly but thoroughly. And just like that, fuel was thrown onto the smoldering embers. Where his thumbs had rested gently under her chin before, now one hand glided up and around to tangle in her hair. The other encircled her waist.

He held her trapped against the bookshelf as he moved in and devoured her like a piece of the candy he was always carrying around.

The shivering pleasure that broke over her was stunning, and she had to remind herself this was only a means to an end. She could enjoy Cole and revel in their sexual chemistry, but nothing more. *Nothing* more. No attachment beyond what they already had. Simply an alliance against evil and shared acquaintances.

Yeah, she could keep telling herself that, but being wrapped up in him felt so damned good. His feel, his taste, his scent, everything that was Cole pulsed through her system like sweet intoxication. His hands were strong and talented, his tongue held the taste of sugar, and there was no way she could keep her fingers from his thick dark hair.

Bodies tight and hands searching, they couldn't seem to get close enough. She ripped open the button and zipper of his pants in one impatient pull, just as his hand slid possessively up her thigh to catch and hold her in place. When he paused and stared down at her legs, his eyes burned with a carnal hunger.

Claudia started to bask in the glory of feminine power, but Cole surprised her with a seductive move of his own. Lifting her in his muscular arms as though she weighed nothing, he braced her against the bookshelf.

Excitement pounded inside her, clutching and greedy, ready for all he had to give. Her breath caught as he reached beneath her dress and eased her panties to the side.

Their eyes clashed in a moment of mutual agreement. Of reckoning and acceptance. Then Cole slid into her in one smooth motion, and they both froze, still staring at each other as if unable to believe what they'd done.

Pleasure began to spread from where they were joined, sweeping through her body until her head fell back against the shelves. Her lips trembled open to emit a groan, but Cole's mouth was suddenly there to swallow the sound.

He kept his mouth on hers, his tongue teasing and exploring while his hips echoed the motion. He drove inside her until she was practically fused with the wood that supported her, but she loved every second.

Her breath was coming so rapidly now, and the need to take all of him had her stomach tied up in knots. Arousal was pummeling her sanity, but she needed to lay the ground work while she still could. When he started nibbling just beneath her ear, she said quickly, breathily, "It's sex, Cole. We're having sex."

He slowed, lifted his head, and shifted puzzled eyes to hers. "Yeah. I'm vaguely familiar with the process."

Sparing him a grin, she clarified, "No. What I mean is that it's *only* sex. Just a physical release."

She spoke hurriedly, wanting to make sure he understood but drowning in how *freaking wonderful* it felt to have the length of him moving inside her, stretching the most tender and sensitive part of her body. "We can get it out of our systems once and for all, then—oh, move a little to the right—then...we can be done with it."

His eyes narrowed, and she thought he might be upset. He didn't argue, but only gripped her tighter, leaning in so his voice growled near her ear. "Fine with me." Then he took her mouth again, brutally. Effectively shutting her up.

Claudia wouldn't complain. Quite the opposite. She lifted her leg higher to take him more fully. She'd known he was in prime physical shape, but...oh, the surprises he had hidden beneath his clothes.

Looping her arms around his neck, she held on and let his skillful undulations consume her, giving herself over to his overwhelming presence and strength.

Any woman would be thankful to have a man cherish her as Cole was doing now. And even if she was never with him this way again, she would always be grateful to have been in his arms, to have felt his stroking hands and sinful kisses. If only one time.

Claudia smiled as she gripped him tighter. She'd never forget their feverish afternoon spent in a fantasy-world library.

Their breathing was hushed but frantic as the tension built between them. Claudia's blood began to rush more swiftly. Pressure began to build in all the right places, and before she could even be sure what was happening, she tightened to an unbearable level of ecstasy. And shattered.

Again she cried out, and again Cole was there to meet her,

lips over hers, as he groaned his own release. Feeling his kiss as she lost control was somehow even more erotic, and tenderness ran between them, binding them, like a silvered thread of emotion.

He held himself still as they prolonged their final kiss, and when he pulled his mouth away, a strange emptiness washed through her. Smiling to cover the hint of sadness, Claudia lowered her legs to the ground.

She didn't realize the shelf had been slightly displaced in their fervor, but when Cole eased back, something toppled from above to land squarely on his head.

"What—" He jerked away from the offending object as it glanced off his shoulder and onto the tiled floor.

Spying the cover when it came to a rest, she tapped his chest with the back of her hand. "Oh, that's actually kind of sweet."

He looked at her like she'd lost her mind, so she laughed, letting humor wash away the last drop of desolation. "It's another history book about police procedures." Grinning like a hoyden, she ran a finger down the hard angle of his cheek and reeled him back to her, thrilled by his warmth. "Getting hit with that particular book is like...a blessing."

Cole rubbed his crown. "Yeah well, if another one falls again, maybe you'll be the one who gets blessed."

They both laughed lightly and shared a smile. Then an awkward silence fell between them, like an unwanted curtain neither one wanted to admit was there. One they didn't know how to deal with.

Cole's gaze went from her eyes to her legs before returning to her flushed face. Finally, he cocked up one side of his mouth, looking entirely too pleased with himself. "I guess I don't have to tell you what we just did."

Claudia bit back a groan, swallowing her pride. "Yes, Cole. Like you, I'm familiar with the process."

"Uh-huh." In a move that caught her off guard, he swept in

to nuzzle her neck. She was just beginning to enjoy his roving lips when he reared back again. "And you do know *where* we did it?"

Perplexed for a moment, Claudia glanced around to note the windows, high ceilings, and finally, the shelf still pressed against her back. She shook her head and grinned. "In the stacks."

With a smile that made her insides melt, Cole ran one of his talented hands up the inside of her thigh. "Want to kick it again?"

15

By the time Claudia got back home to the island, the idea that had been so "genius" in the throes of passion now seemed a lot closer to idiocy. She closed the front door a bit too soundly and stalked her way to the great room to find Kylie and Paige sitting in the dark.

The only source of light issued from the large flat screen on the wall, and the sounds blaring from the television were those of screaming heroines and torture-loving maniacs. Shaking her head at the two horror movie buffs, she attempted to slink behind the couch, as far on the opposite side of the room as possible.

"Slink" being the operative word.

But when Paige's head swung to the side, Claudia knew she'd been busted.

"Claudia? Is that you?" The tall, slim blonde whose bangs were in a perpetually shaggy cut was up and turning on the overhead lights before Claudia could protest.

Kylie repositioned herself and turned to sit on her knees, both hands clamped on the back of the green velvet sofa. "Hey. How'd it go? We expected to hear from you a while ago."

Cringing inside, Claudia gripped the plastic bag that held the jewelry box with the signet ring inside. "No problem.

I've got the ring. I promise not to touch it until we can all be together as planned."

The coven had unanimously decided she shouldn't handle any more of the items until she was within a well-cast and protective circle, with her sister witches around her, and inside the grand hall for good measure.

Not that they had any specific guidelines or anything.

Chiding herself, Claudia withdrew the catty thought. Her friends only wanted to make sure she wasn't hurt by one of her maverick visions. She loved them for their concern and wasn't opposed to the arrangement.

Truth be told, the only person she was angry with was herself, and she wanted nothing more than to get to her room where she could confide all of her troubles to Ashbi. The tomcat would listen without judging, yellow eyes half-closed as he snuggled against her side.

Her friends wouldn't judge either, but until she had a chance to sort through her volatile emotions, she wanted to keep the day's extra-curricular activities to herself.

She pushed onward, aiming for the stairs and increasing her pace, but Kylie the Ever Curious refused to be put off. "Well, what happened?"

"It was a great house." Claudia nodded emphatically with an enthusiasm that was…entirely fake. "I traded some information for the ring, along with a lot of cash, and there you go." She gave an exceptionally loud sigh. "Now I'd really love a hot bath. I'm heading up."

Her eyes shot to the side. The wide mahogany staircase was her escape route, if only she could make it that far.

Paige had returned to sit on the couch next to Kylie and faced backward like the younger witch. As both of them scrutinized Claudia, Paige tilted her head and squinted as if she saw straight through to their bones. "You've been gone since before noon. What have you been doing all this time?"

Clenching her fingers around the plastic bag, Claudia allowed her frustration to spew over like an unwatched pot. "If you really want to know, I'll tell you." She threw out her arms. "I've been out behaving like a complete Jezebel."

Kylie frowned and looked to Paige. "A what?"

Paige nudged her with an elbow. "Same thing as a ho."

Anna chose that moment to walk in. She stopped mid-step. "Who's a ho?"

Claudia clapped her hands to her head. "No one. Never mind. I'm going up to my room." With that said, she gave one hard nod for emphasis, pivoted, and marched up the steps.

Kylie and Paige turned to each other with mouths hanging open. Then they both scrambled off the couch in pursuit.

Anna frowned and gave it a moment's consideration, but she gave in and hurried after the others. The three women caught up to Claudia just as she reached the landing. They gathered a few steps below, looking up at her like three owls.

"What did you do?" Anna asked.

Kylie stood on her tiptoes. "Was it with Cole?"

And then from Paige. "Was it good?"

Letting loose an exasperated sigh, Claudia looked at each of her friends in turn as she answered their questions. "Too much. With Cole. And unfortunately, yes." She bit her lip. "Very."

Turning on her heel she headed toward her room just as Shauni appeared from hers a couple of doors down. Her dog, Skid, barked and jumped, wiggling from head to toe as he sensed the humans' excitement.

Claudia didn't stop but intentionally veered in the other direction.

"What's going on?" Shauni asked.

Kylie rushed past her, tossing a muffled response over her shoulder. "Claudia's been out being a ho with Cole!"

"What?" Shauni trailed after the parade of witches. "She fell in a hole?"

"No. Geez." Kylie glanced back, still hurrying after Claudia. "Haven't you ever heard of a Jezebel?"

Viv's room was on this floor as well and, before Claudia made it to her own door, she came face to face with the Asian beauty. Viv's glasses were askew. "What's all the clamor?"

"No clamor." Claudia wrestled with her door knob. "You can go back to reading."

Crossing her arms, Viv smiled sarcastically, "I beg to differ. *That*," she pointed at the convoy of witches, "is a clamor."

Lucia had joined the fray now, and by the time Claudia made it to her desk to dump her purse and the ring bag, every member of the coven had crowded inside her bedroom.

The Jezebel story got told and re-told. Soon the bunch of them were arguing semantics and women's lib like a group of avid scholars.

With no peace in sight, Claudia collapsed on her bed, grateful for the plush comforter with its coral and cream stripes. All she wanted was to hide. To cover her face and forget about Cole. So she reached for a pillow and tried to do just that.

"Oh, come out from there." Hayden tugged on the pillow until Claudia released it. "You've got nothing to be ashamed of." Then the soft-spoken woman gave her a sly smile. "We all know you're not a ho."

"Ohhh!" Claudia crossed her arms over her eyes. "I think I'm just in shock. You wouldn't believe where we were when we—"

"So tell us," Kylie jumped in, sidling up to Claudia's other side. "Every. Single. Detail."

"Nuh-uh. If you guys start that crap again, I'm gone," Paige said before switching to the military vernacular to drive her point home. "Seriously. I'm poppin' smoke." She leaned against the wall and eyed Claudia's cat. "You don't want to listen to that stuff either, do you?"

Rowan Von Ashbi yawned from where he was resting on a chair, having been woken by the loud mob of females so rudely invading his space. He blinked his yellow eyes at Paige as if to say, "Meh." Then he commenced cleaning his face.

In her gentle and considerate way, Willyn patted Claudia's knee from where she stood next to the bed. "You don't have to talk about anything until you're ready. Or not at all, if that's what you want."

"Thanks for that." Glancing around the room, Claudia noted the vase of orange daisies, but even the happy flowers didn't cheer her. Nor did the reproduction of van Gogh's *Sunflowers* in similarly bright tones. Anna had chosen the colorful picture long before the eight other women had made their journeys to Savannah, yet the warm gold and orange hues perfectly suited Claudia's style.

All of the witches had arrived to find their ideal bedrooms, each designed with them in mind. Which wouldn't have been nearly so amazing if not for the fact they'd never met Anna before the day they'd arrived on the island.

Anna's gift of premonition and foresight made her a wonderful hostess, one who could literally anticipate the needs of every guest. Now even the head witch, who was normally cool and composed, pressed her lips together as she studied Claudia with concern.

As the women began to quiet, Anna asked, "Are you all right, Claudia?"

Toying with a corner of her pillow, Claudia took her time before replying. "I'm not entirely sure." She sat up and plopped the cushion in her lap. "I thought I had everything under control and was making a smart, even tricky move to outwit fate."

"Oh, boy." Shauni stroked the top of Skid's shiny black head while the dog leaned lovingly against his human's leg. "How'd that work out?"

"Like a boomerang slinging right back at me, and loaded up with more of the very trouble I was trying to avoid."

Kylie leaned closer. "Does this trouble go by the name Detective Cole Lonergan?"

A strange *squeak-groan* type of noise lodged in Claudia's throat. "Yes." Panic fluttered in her chest as images flashed in front of her open eyes.

Cole's mouth as it descended on hers. Tree shadows dancing on the library ceiling. And the tenderness in his gray-green eyes when he'd looked at her and...

She smashed the pillow to her face again. "Oh, what have I done? What have I done?" She started hyperventilating into the peachy floral print.

Again the pillow was pulled away. "Deep breaths, Teach. There's no way it's as bad as you're making it out to be. I mean, have you *seen* Cole?" Kylie tossed a long lock of blonde curls over her shoulder. "If he is your true love, you should just be glad he's not the kind of guy you want to catch and release."

Claudia huffed. "That's part of the problem. He's *too* attractive. And caring. And the more I get to know him, the more I find he's got all these other great characteristics and interests." She flopped backward onto the bed again. "It's too risky to like him any more than I already do, and I don't even want to contemplate the possibility of falling in love with him. I don't want to love anyone. I can't."

Hayden rubbed her arm. "Of course you can. And you will. One day." The caramel-haired woman grimaced. "Or...sooner."

When her sternum began to feel like a vise, Claudia slapped a hand across the suddenly-oppressive bone. "I need a glass of wine."

"No. You're way past that." Kylie jumped up and headed for the door, nodding sagely. A physician diagnosing her patient. "It's time for the emergency rescue kit."

Paige clucked her tongue and winked. "Yep. I'll call it in on the way."

Kylie flung open the door. "We can take the boat to the

mainland and be back in thirty minutes." Then she and Paige looked at each other before declaring in unison, "She needs pizza."

~~~

Against her better judgment, Claudia let the girls talk her into going downstairs as soon as Kylie and Paige returned with four boxes of cheesy goodness. With a grumpy wrinkle still creasing her forehead, she helped herself to two pieces of supreme and assented with a small, "Please," when Lucia offered her some soda.

"I'm going to stop being such a crybaby and get myself together," she assured the worried faces still staring at her. "Any minute now. Promise."

Kylie doused her pepperoni with pepper flakes and wiggled her mouth back and forth as if trying to decide whether or not she should say anything. Then she did. "You'll probably feel better if you get it off your chest."

The younger woman was trying to be sincere, but Claudia could see the curiosity eating a hole in her patience. She chuckled and shook a finger at her. "You just want to know where we..." *Don't say kicked it...* "did it."

Kylie blinked once. "Yes. Yes, I do."

Chewing a mouthful of pizza, Claudia mulled it over, looking around the kitchen island where she and the others were gathered. Maybe she *would* feel better. Why had she been keeping her fears to herself anyway?

She'd come up with a supposedly brilliant solution all on her own. And look how well that had turned out.

She could still feel Cole's arms around her, holding her and making her feel so fragile. While she was anything but weak, she'd loved feeling so essentially female. Try as she might, she couldn't smell his clean, spicy scent anymore. The lingering memory of his cologne had finally evaporated.

And why was she so disappointed about that? Her plan to get over the physical attraction had obviously backfired. Instead of getting him out of her system, she'd ended up teasing a dragon. Now the fire-breather deep within her had been tempted. It wanted more.

More devouring kisses, more of those rough but steady hands on her skin, and more of the...aftershocks that, quite frankly, were still rocking her from the inside out.

Her vision went hazy as she stared at her glass of soda. Cole had been such an unexpected surprise. So masculine yet considerate. So...*thorough*.

"Aw, hell." Paige plopped her slice onto her plate. "I know that look." She wiped her hands on her napkin.

Claudia stiffened her spine at her friend's outburst. "What look? On whom?"

An expression of such distress covered Paige's face that it was almost comical. "Come on, Claudia." Her plaintive tone was the closest thing to a whine that any of them had ever heard from the rugged fighter. "You were the one person I thought I could count on to stand with me."

She blew her white-blonde hair out of her eyes and thumped her fist on the granite. "The last bastion of female independence."

"Hey, hey. I'm still in the game over here." Claudia twisted her mouth to show her own annoyance, as well as her restored willpower. "I'm not giving up that easily." Hoping she would shock the coven's warrior into silence, she said blandly, "It was just sex."

"Oh, please. You've got that dreamy expression all over you, so it doesn't matter whether you want to fall in love or not." Paige lifted her beer but paused before drinking. "You're halfway there already."

Claudia inhaled a chunk of sausage and started coughing.

"You're crazy."

"Am I?"

"Yeah." Hayden leaned over her plate. "Is she?"

Claudia drank her soda like a woman on the brink of dehydration. When her throat was clear and her wits about her, she made a passing sweep with her arm to encompass all of the witches. "Stop ganging up on me. It just happened, and yes, it was just sex."

Claudia closed her eyes. *It was just sex.* She couldn't help but remember the second she'd made her decision. The moment when she'd chosen to forge ahead and steal a piece of what she could never truly possess.

Happiness with a man. That she knew wouldn't last.

Picking up her pizza, she continued nonchalantly. "We were in this amazing library, and he—"

"Hold it." Viv started to adjust her glasses, then decided to take them off altogether. "A library?" Her face split into an amused grin. "That is so like you." She clapped her hands and hooted. "The professor. In the library."

Kylie giggled and added, "With the detective."

"Fine. Fine. Laugh it up." Claudia felt a tickle of amusement in her gut, but did her best to tamp it down. She was starting to feel a little better though, and even Anna and Willyn shot a glance to each other before adding in their own laughter.

Now if Paige would just stop being so dramatic.

When the chuckles faded and eating resumed, Anna was the one to return to the more serious aspect of the subject. "I have to agree with Kylie on this one, Claudia. You might feel better if you tell us what's really bothering you. You say you don't have feelings for Cole and, if that's true, you shouldn't have anything to fear in that department."

Opening her mouth to agree wholeheartedly, Claudia realized she couldn't make a sound. Just as she was about to state her complete and total lack of romantic inclination toward

Cole, she remembered his warm breath on her cheek, her ear.

Her shoulders slumped. "Oh, no."

Kylie and Paige both nodded, the younger witch smiling while the soldier only groused. Shauni, Hayden, Lucia, and Viv remained neutral, showing no overt reaction, but Anna and Willyn still evinced worry.

"So you do care about Cole." Anna's blue eyes were kind. "Why is that so terrible?"

Claudia lifted a shoulder. "The one thing our trials guarantee—falling in love—is the one thing I swore I'd stay away from forever. I've tried it before. I have." Now was the time to tell them all of it. "But the vulnerability that comes with it terrifies me."

Lucia reached across her plate to put her hand over Claudia's. "I understand. We all do to some degree. Each of us was forced to face something we were afraid of. Shauni had to fight to save Michael, even though she was against violence. And she had to use the animals to do it."

Shauni swirled her iced green tea. "Something I also swore I'd never do. As it turns out, I wasn't giving the animals their fair shake. They wanted to help us, but I just couldn't see the whole picture." She nailed Claudia with her emerald eyes. "Not until I was *meant* to see it."

Kylie jumped in to take over the recollection of trials gone by. "Then Willyn and Dare met. Two polar opposites if there ever were." That drew a round of nods and grins. "But they ended up combining their religions, getting past prejudices, and coming up with a mix that was all their own."

Willyn got a weepy look on her face. "I love my stubborn pagan."

"And you remember how mad I was at Shauni and Kylie for setting me up with Nick without telling me?" Viv bobbed her head, black silky hair brushing her shoulders. "But Nick was exactly what I needed. He taught me that it's all right to let someone else take control once in a while."

She sniffed and started to cut off another bite of her pizza. "But *only* once in a while." With a cunning smile she winked at Claudia.

"And I was so motivated by guilt, I was instantly at odds with Trevor." Hayden made a sour face. "Especially when he called me a con artist." She glanced aside to Lucia. "What was your challenge again? You had so much to do, it all gets confusing."

The Spanish witch rolled her eyes. "*Sí*. All I wanted was love. A true, abiding love." She wiggled in her seat. "And I eventually got him."

Claudia wagged her fork at her friend. "But that's exactly what I don't want. Love makes you susceptible to a whole new kind of pain."

She took another bite of her pizza and chewed thoughtfully. "I know you guys don't get it, but I have a long history—no pun intended—of relationships ending because of infidelity. And with my gift..." She shuddered. "Let's just say their liaisons were in high definition and tended to stick with me for a while."

Kylie sucked in through her teeth. "Yuck. Like a creepy sex horror movie."

One of Claudia's brows winged up. "Exactly like that."

"Yes, but this is Cole we're talking about." Hayden stared emphatically into Claudia's eyes. "*Cole*." The caramel-haired medium had been befriended by Cole right when she'd needed it most. She was squarely in his corner and was probably experiencing a split allegiance. "He wouldn't betray you like that."

Waving her hands near her head, Claudia wished for some Chardonnay to cool her palette. She would also like an end to the discussion. "This is all for nothing. There's no need for me to worry over Cole's quality rating as a lover or the likelihood of his monogamy. Because I'm not going to make the same mistake twice."

Intent on getting that wine, she slid her stool back and rose to go to the cabinet. Once she'd poured herself a glass and taken a substantial drink, she addressed her friends. "You were right. I do feel better. My head is clear."

She sipped again. "Whether or not I can trust Cole is a moot point."

"What do you mean?" Anna asked.

"It's simple. Cole and I aren't involved. Not really. And we aren't going to be." She gave her friends a buoyant smile. One she didn't actually feel. "If there's nothing between us," she lifted her chin, "then he can't deceive me."

16

On the mainland, Cole was dealing with his own aftermath. He'd tried working on the tile in the upstairs bathrooms, but in his current state of mind he'd been afraid he might do more damage than good.

So here he was, out on the street and headed for his favorite bar. He liked going to Nick's pub, especially since getting to know the guy. Nick had been through a rough childhood but had persevered, carving the life he desired out of brick and stone. And whiskey.

Cole had nothing but admiration for him. But Nick was also Viv's boyfriend, and Cole didn't want to be around anything or anyone that reminded him of the coven. Or more specifically, of Claudia.

Not tonight.

The Scottish tavern where he was headed had been his go-to hangout since he'd relocated to Savannah. The occasional outburst of traditional song made him feel right at home, and the Scottish malt flowed free and easy. Both would be much-needed comforts this evening.

Taking a high stool at one end of the well-worn bar, he caught the bartender's eye. "Hey, Stu."

"Cole." The tall man with deceptively wiry strength in his

long arms gave him a crooked smile. "Your usual?"

Cole considered the draft ale he often drank after work, but decided the light brew wasn't enough to cut through his foul mood. "Make it Longrow. Neat." He thought of how Claudia had looked when her climax had made her pliant in his arms. "Make that a double."

As if sensing his troubled mind, Stu set the whiskey down and left Cole alone with his thoughts. And dark musings they were, as thunderclouds of doubt and resentment circled in his head.

He had no regrets about what had happened with Claudia. Their sexual encounter had been pure and honest, and something he'd been craving for a long time.

But he could still hear her careless words. *Get it out of our systems. Be done with it.*

Cole sloshed back the whiskey and waved Stu to bring another. *Hell.* Cole fumed as he leaned against the bar. He wasn't used to this. He actually felt used.

The same woman who'd disparaged his dating life had just taken him to bed—or to the stacks—then cleanly wiped her hands of the whole affair before they were even done. He kept telling himself he was just surprised by her actions, and consummating their physical attraction shouldn't make a huge difference.

Like her, he'd just wanted to confront the attraction that fogged up his clarity where she was concerned. Get rid of the ball-gripping lust he suffered whenever she walked by. The feelings that made him yearn for her like some poor kid at a candy store window.

And so he had. Sex. Done. Over. He set his glass down with a clatter. Moving on.

But as the liquor started relaxing his mind, he had to admit the truth. He'd wanted to be with Claudia, that much was true.

Problem was, he *still* wanted to be with her. And the casual way she'd dismissed the act *did* matter. It mattered to him.

With a grunt Cole sat back in the stool, trying to give a damn about the game on the TV hanging at the far end of the bar. Attempting to convince himself he was cool with what Claudia had said.

Pretending it hadn't hurt his feelings.

Okay. This is my last drink. Else I might start crying like a girl into my Longrow. And eleven-year-old scotch deserved better.

He was still trying to mash his emotions into an acceptable man-sized box when someone took the seat next to him. The scent of musk and flowers surrounded him and he frowned.

"The place is pretty empty tonight." Her voice was low, subtly flirtatious.

Cole angled his head just enough to acknowledge her. During that brief glance he saw a heart-shaped face any movie star would envy. Not to mention the eyes, somewhere between blue and purple, and startling in their beauty.

"It is that," he answered with a half-smile, before returning his attention to the inch of liquor still in his glass. Deciding he'd had enough, he pulled a couple of bills from his wallet and pushed them to the inner rim of the bar. He caught Stu's eye, nodded, and stood up to leave.

"Have a good one," he told her, making his way out and hoping to avoid any drama. He was full up for the day, and she had a certain look about her.

He just wasn't in the mood, and his thoughts were still too caught up in a flame-haired temptress. One with long legs and a brain like a steel trap. A witch who'd burned him good, but not with her infamous fireballs.

Back out on the street, he inhaled the smell of barbecue chicken and wondered if he should pick dinner up on the way home. He wasn't hungry, but knew he should be.

Nah. He'd scrounge for leftovers at the house if he found the urge, but right now all he wanted was a shower and the cool, crisp sheets of his bed.

Soft clicks went unnoticed at first, then he realized they were getting louder. The smell of her perfume wafted closer, and he knew she had followed him. "Look, I don't mean to be rude—"

"I'm headed this way too," she said, cutting him off. A soft smile curved her lips. "Walk a lady home on a dark night?"

Put that way, he couldn't refuse. And he suspected she knew that. "Sure. Why not?"

They traveled a few blocks in silence, but when they made the turn onto Forsythe, she spoke again. Her tone was still mild, still velvety smooth. "You look lonely, is all. I hate to see you so down."

Cole stopped and looked at her in the shadows. Her violet eyes gleamed in the moonlight.

With her small hand, she reached out to touch his cheek. "I just want to keep you company." Then she withdrew her fingers and smiled. "We should spend some time together."

Shaking his head in amazement, Cole turned and carried on. He was almost to his block and would be home any minute. He felt as much as heard her fall into step beside him, keeping pace until he came to the walkway of his house.

He climbed the steps, opened his front door, and left it wide after he'd stepped through. The lights were out, he noted. He'd have to turn on a lamp.

Closing the door behind her, she brushed his shoulder as she slid past and walked down the hall. Her heels still clicked gently as she went. In her form-fitting black dress, and with a confident woman's rolling gait, she made her way to his study.

Cole watched her as she moved. As she disappeared into his room.

He watched.

But he didn't protest.

~~~

Sitting on her sunny yellow blanket, Kylie moved her head up and down in time with the music pouring from her speakers. Anna was still downstairs and had promised to let her know when she came up for bed. Until then, she was free and clear for some noise.

After Claudia had again declared the topic of her and Cole off-limits, Kylie had dragged herself away from the others to fill her head with Maroon 5. She wanted some time alone to think—okay, to brood—without bringing the rest of her friends down too.

Claudia's rejection of Cole bothered her, and she just couldn't understand her friend's reasoning. She didn't comprehend the logic. While she wanted to support Claudia—and she would, no matter what—deep in her heart, Kylie hoped her friend was proven wrong.

Hayden wasn't the only one cheering for Cole. None of them even knew what he wanted from Claudia, but Kylie really hoped he fell for her redheaded sister. And that Claudia fell along with him. Despite her fears.

Kylie was holing herself up in her room, because she didn't want anyone to guess what was really upsetting her. Part of her motivation was purely selfish, and she was afraid the others might figure her out.

She caught herself nibbling a thumbnail and tucked that hand under her butt. The nasty habit always resurfaced when she was distracted. Or really scared. Like now.

Yes, she was troubled over Claudia's determination to keep herself from Cole. Because if she completed her trial while managing to dodge the romance bullet, the pattern might be altered for the rest of them.

Love had been the only constant in the challenges. Each

of the women who'd gone before had found their mate, and it would be just Kylie's luck for everything to go all bugnuts before she had her turn.

Then she might never have a chance with Quinn.

Truthfully, Anna's younger brother had been a stuck-up pain in her ass ever since she'd come to Savannah. Over time, however, her opinion of him had changed. The two of them argued worse than anyone else in the house, and Kylie had finally been forced to ask herself why that was.

If she fell back on the old elementary school theory, any boy who teased a girl must secretly have a crush on her. Right? She rolled over on her stomach and flipped the pages of the fashion magazine she'd been trying to focus on.

But soon she gave up and stared out the window, propping her chin in her hand. If bad treatment actually equaled "I like you" in the male world, then Quinn St. Germaine must like her a whole hell of a lot. More than anyone in history.

Except maybe for Romeo and Juliet. She and Quinn hadn't reached the poison and dagger stage yet, thank the saints.

But his snide comments were really starting to get old, and she hated it when he called her a brat. As far as she could tell, he was doing his best to keep her at arm's length, so she was eager for her turn at trial.

One way or another, she had to know how he really felt.

When someone banged a fist on her door, she rolled her eyes. *That was a quick answer.* She didn't even have to ask who was there. "What?" she snapped, more than ready for a fight.

Sure enough, the blue-eyed devil swung her door open, and *Shocker!* he was pissed off.

Quinn marched to her iPod dock and pressed the button to turn the music down. "Other people live here, and it's almost eleven o'clock."

"I talked to Anna, and all you had to do was let me know you were back. I would have turned it down." Then she added snidely, "Grandpa."

She returned her attention to her magazine, a clear dismissal. "But I'm sure you knew that."

He didn't make a move to leave. "What's that supposed to mean?"

When she lifted her gaze to him again, she caught his eyes on her backside before they flicked to her face. So she rolled onto her side and propped her head on her arm, stretching in a way that was supposed to appear casual.

But was also meant to entice.

"I mean," she said sweetly, "that you never miss an opportunity to give me a hard time." She licked her lips. "Why is that, Quinn?"

She saw the flash of darkness in his eyes, but he quickly concealed the raw lust with a glare. He practically sneered at her. "What are you doing, Kylie?" Now he laughed cruelly. "Trying to play grown up?"

That does it! She sat up and swung her legs over the side of the bed. Wearing only small gray shorts and a fitted white T-shirt, she had plenty of bare skin to flaunt. Slowly, she slid one leg up and down the other in her best imitation of a seductress.

Forcing herself to smile instead of ripping him a new one like she wanted, she got up and went to where her iPod sat on a side table. With wicked intent, she bent over at the waist— more than was necessary—and turned the music back up a few notches. Not too loud, but enough to let him know that he wasn't her boss. Or her big brother.

Kylie faltered when she heard the song, though, and Adam Levine's sexy voice crooning about a girl who will be loved. Her heart clanged in response, a pitiful and empty bell that had been ignored for too long. *Let it be me next.*

Smoothing the pang of loneliness from her chest and whatever showed of it on her face, she turned to Quinn again and sauntered over to him with a hip-swing that would make Lucia proud. "If you hate me so much, why are you always trying to get so close to me?"

Quinn took a step back as if to deny her allegation. But he didn't say anything.

Could this be progress? Choosing to push her advantage, she tossed her hair back to reveal the curve of her neck, viciously delighted when he stared openly. His hungry eyes tracked down her body then back up.

"Do you want to be close to me?" Her finger hooked in the V of her shirt, tugging downward just enough as she looked up at him through lowered lashes.

When his handsome jaw clenched, she should have heeded the warning. When his eyes flamed like blue fire, she should have retreated. But she was committed now, and damned if he was going to call her a coward on top of everything else.

In a move too fast for her to avoid, Quinn reached out and hooked his arm around the back of her neck. With more force than she expected, he hauled her up against him.

Her head fell back like a damsel in a classic black and white movie, but she couldn't help it. He held her immobile, and when his other arm coiled around her waist, the first touch of unease flitted through her belly.

"Damn you," he ground from a mouth that was clenched in anger. He was enraged, both temples throbbing.

Unleashing every ounce of that fury, he trapped her between arms that were much stronger than she'd ever imagined. As she looked into his cobalt eyes, Kylie wondered what his kiss would feel like.

When his jaw tightened and his eyes locked on her lips, she knew she was about to find out. Joy leapt in her belly, but was swiftly replaced with an explosion of sparkling heat as his mouth crashed down on hers.

The tongue he pushed against hers was rough and insistent.

The sound that escaped him both fury and need combined.

His kiss wasn't sweet, nor was it gentle. He meant to teach her a lesson. To punish her. To threaten.

And his ferocity thrilled her.

Whimpering, she clung to his broad shoulders and lifted her chest to his while pressing her hips to the hardness she'd caused. She would take all of his anger, greedily. She would pull it inside of her and turn it into passion.

Kylie smiled against his assaulting lips, and let her hands roam. If Quinn had thought to scare her away, then he had seriously misjudged this witch.

Instead of releasing her, he took one long stride toward the bed, dragging her onto it before covering her from head to toe with his lean, muscular body.

His heated mouth traveled down her neck and continued its descent until his tongue delved into the V of her shirt. She'd only thought to tease him before, to make him look. But the pleasure of his mouth on her flushed skin was too good to refuse.

Her toes curled and liquid heat condensed in her belly. And down below. She glanced at his dark head and the strong shoulders and arms that held him above her. Was this really happening? With Quinn?

He took one breast in his mouth, scalding her through the thin cotton of her shirt. *Yes!* This was happening. *Thank you. Thank you.*

She felt him lift the hem of her shirt and plant his mouth on the soft flesh of her stomach. "Quinn." She ran both hands through his hair, holding his lips against her. "Oh, Quinn."

His body went rigid, and the incredible warmth of his mouth suddenly left her. In an instant, he was off the bed. In the next, he was standing by the door. As far away from her as he could get without leaving the room.

Facing the wall with his back to Kylie, he ran a hand through his hair. After several calming breaths he spoke. "Don't ever try that again." If he'd been harsh before, now his voice was disturbingly cold. Empty.

Distant.

A painful chill racked her insides. "Quinn? I don't understand." Part of her wanted to slip beneath her covers in mortification, but she didn't want to make an even bigger fool of herself. Or seem childish. "Please, tell me what—"

Without giving her the courtesy of eye contact, he opened the door and bit out the words. "Just don't. I mean it, Kylie." Then he left, the door shutting behind him with a soft *click*.

Humiliation and shame rolled through her, forcing out the pleasure and joy she'd felt only seconds before. Chills shook her all over, and an overpowering sense of dread clamped down.

She wanted to cry, or at least she thought she did. Her lungs weren't working, and she couldn't breathe. What was this feeling? It was horrible. Her head felt like it was about to burst.

Stupid. Stupid! She'd imagined herself falling in love with Quinn. Had been hoping for that very thing for months now.

Too late, she recognized the truth. Reality shoved up close, got in her face, and knocked her flat.

She was already in love with the jerk, and now she was pretty damned sure he didn't feel the same way. Her heart and pride had just been shredded, then tossed back at her like junk.

Quinn had made her feel like a fool. Like a stupid little girl not worthy of his attention.

Like a *brat*.

Suddenly her bodily functions returned with a vengeance, but tears and breathing took second place to another, more violent reaction.

Lurching to her feet, Kylie stumbled into her bathroom and prayed the tears held off for at least a few more minutes. Her body was finally succumbing to the shock, and to the awful, wrenching pain.

She was going to be sick.

17

As she entered the grand hall, Claudia fingered the ancient stone walls and recalled the first time she'd entered the huge dome-shaped chamber. She'd put her hand to the rocks that day—her first on the island—and had immediately felt the sanctity permeating the room.

This room was the only remaining part of the original structure built centuries before, and the coven still considered it the heart of the mansion. The three St. Germaine sisters had practiced their craft here, and their pure energy still lived within the walls, the foundation, and, of course, the massive pentagram on the ceiling.

Wooden beams intersected above them all, marking the grand hall sacred, a place of veneration to the gods and goddesses, all powers that created and ruled this world. As well as the realms beyond.

So it was here the coven came when they needed a boost to their strength. Or an extra layer of protection, as was the case today.

When Claudia let her eyes fall to the middle of the room, she laughed outright. "Whose idea was this?" She pointed to a lovely *chaise longue* upholstered in peacock blue. Judging by the color, the piece most likely belonged to Anna.

When the head witch gave an impish smile and shrugged, Claudia knew she'd found the culprit. "It seemed appropriate," Anna said, "given your penchant for passing out."

Laughter rolled in Claudia's chest again. She had such adverse reactions to all of Bastraal's possessions that she just couldn't seem to stay upright. So the *chaise longue*, known in the South as a "fainting couch," was definitely apropos.

And a pretty good joke.

She shot a wry smile to Anna. "I'm ready when you are." In her hand she clasped the plastic bag from Mr. Clermont's estate, but the ring was still safely ensconced inside the jewelry box. Insulated enough for her to hold.

She was still apprehensive about the burning pain she would feel when she touched the signet ring, as well as the disorienting voyage back to the eighteenth century. But gaining more knowledge about Bastraal's time on earth was a necessary evil.

She just wished she knew how many more times she would have to wade through these distorted visions. How many before her trial was complete? And what would be required of her when she'd finally collected the last item?

The rest of the coven filed inside, with Lucia and Hayden bringing up the rear. Above them the candle chandeliers were burning, as well as the torches around the perimeter. Lucia closed the door behind her and crossed the slate floor to take her place in the circle.

As ready as she'd ever be, Claudia approached the blue chaise. All preparations had been made, so there was no reason to stall.

No men were present today, and she found the purely female essence comforting. Maybe she just didn't want any more reminders of what her sisters had discovered during their own challenges. Commitment. Partnership. And...

Ugh. She was growing exceedingly sick of the L-word.

She pursed her lips, ready to forget about romance and all the helplessness that went along with it. She had no interest in relying on anyone else, even if that person happened to be Cole.

But is that still the truth? She nodded her head and continued the mental discussion with herself. *Yes. Of course it is.* This time when her inner voice called her a liar, Claudia blithely ignored the raving shrew and took a graceful seat on the fainting couch.

She did *not* want to fall for Cole. No matter how upstanding and trustworthy he might actually be. It was bad enough her heart picked up its pace whenever she pictured his charming half smile or pale, mysterious eyes.

And that was *only* because she found him attractive. Wasn't it? A natural female reaction to a man she found sexually appealing. Right?

Suddenly a transcendental trip to the past was sounding more like a much-needed getaway. Her recent ambivalence toward Cole was starting to chip away at her confidence. She should just focus on the demon and his flaming eyes of hate. Surely the monster was less terrifying than that other thing.

The. L. Word.

Shivering at the very idea, she raised her eyes to Anna. "Okay. Let's do this."

The ritual area had been spiritually cleansed that morning, and while many practitioners of magic cast protective circles with salt, the coven relied on an alternative barrier against evil.

Themselves.

Their union created its own power, and even now, Claudia could feel the low vibration that resulted when they were all together. A break in their connection would be sensed immediately, allowing them to fight off any invaders that dared cross their boundary.

Anna wasn't sure they would be able to draw Claudia out of

the vision, but at least they could help contain the mental path she traveled to get there. Essentially, her body and her mind would be defensible as long as she was inside their circle.

Claudia swiveled her head to watch as the second layer of protection moved into position. Only this one came in the form of fangs and fur. Cats had long been considered guardians against the underworld, and the deeper the coven was drawn into prophecy, the more their feline companions played a part.

The cats had also become more territorial, stalking the house at night like sentries and watching over the women as they slept. Their presence put Claudia at ease almost as much as the wards that shielded the island mansion.

Anna stood on the back side of the room, nearest the raised dais where she'd first addressed the women and revealed their fates. And clued them in to the fact they were all witches. What a day *that* had been.

Anna's pretty girl, Ivy, sat directly behind her human. The gray-haired cat was as secretive and serene as the woman with whom she'd been partnered. She observed the scene with guarded interest, her tailed wrapped tightly around her, tucked in close.

Next to Anna stood Paige, and at her back sat an equally tough and scrappy feline. Tiger-Lily, known familiarly as Tiger, looked almost eager for a fight. Still she held her position, as any disciplined warrior would.

Next came Lucia and her black-haired Persian. The feline was as high-maintenance as the Spanish witch but, when times called, Iris could also get down and dirty.

As Claudia's eyes shifted again, she found Kylie was next in line. But something was off about the young blonde. Her face broadcast misery. "Kylie, are you all right?"

She was right to be concerned, because a broken witch meant a broken coven. But more importantly, they all cared about each other, as true sisters did. Not only those of magic, but of the heart.

"I'm fine," Kylie said, but her face was still too pale. "My dinner didn't agree with me last night, that's all."

She's lying, Claudia told herself. "We can cast the circle with seven. Or we can wait."

Anna studied Kylie more closely. "Are you sure you're up to this?"

"Yes. I'm okay." Sassafras moved closer to lick Kylie's ankle, as if even the cat realized something was wrong. Kylie smiled down at her golden-haired partner and winked at her "Sassy" non-human twin.

"If you're sure." Claudia waited for a response, and Kylie worked up a bright smile. She nodded too vigorously, a clear pretense.

So they would continue, and the circle would be cast with eight. Not a magical number, but strong just the same. Willyn stood beside Kylie with a worried frown for the younger witch's strange demeanor. The healer's sweet and aptly named Snowball sat right behind her, composed and still.

Next was Hayden and her flighty tortoiseshell named Daisy, followed by Shauni and her sleek black Cuileann. The cat's Gaelic name referred to a type of holly, as all the felines had been named after plants.

Yet long before any of the women had ever met.

Now Claudia had come full circle, literally, and nodded to Viv who was on Anna's other side, opposite of Paige. Kiko had been named for the "bitter orange" tree in Japan, given his tendency to be a grouch.

Today, however, he was as solemn as the other cats, and his cute little face with tufts of orange at the cheeks helped Claudia manage a smile. She startled when her own Ashbi, like the ash tree, jumped up to sit beside her on the blue *chaise longue*.

Unwilling to be left out, he stared at her, as if daring her to send him outside the circle. Like the other cats, he would fight anything to protect his human. To defend his witch.

Claudia scratched the white spot under his chin and was rewarded with a mild rumble. "You can stay, Your Highness."

She was actually glad for the company, for something warm and living to hold onto as she ventured into the past. Into the dark swirling tunnel and the cold that awaited her.

When she was good and ready, she brought her legs up onto the fainting couch and leaned against the high back. After a nod to Anna, Claudia waited for Ashbi to readjust. He cast adoring yellow eyes her way and put one paw on her thigh.

With a grin tugging at her lips, she slipped her hand inside the bag and retrieved the jewelry box. She needed no pause to reconsider or review any second thoughts. She opened the box and extracted the ring.

She was barely able to clasp the silver in her palm before the whirling black swept over her.

Back through the familiar void she fell, only this time, the agonizing burn had been reduced to a mild tingle. It felt as if her skin was being tested by a thousand needle points, but very lightly, and with tiny needles. The circle her friends had cast was working in at least one capacity, and the absence of the crippling pain was a great relief.

She was still marveling at the difference when she found herself on the landing of a stairwell. Scanning her surroundings to determine her new location, she saw a wooden banister that led in two directions.

The split staircase had been a popular style at one time, but she felt far too exposed to both the room below and the hallways to her left and right. If Bastraal was on the premises, he could discover her at any second.

Still, she'd been sent here for a reason, so she had to perform a cursory search of the foyer below and whatever else she could see down there. Craning her neck and mindful of any movement, she combed the rooms below for anything that glimmered. For that special glow she'd come to recognize. But seeing nothing, she quickly pulled back and flattened herself against the green-papered wall.

Just like her hand had materialized during her last vision, she would swear she could feel her heart hammering and her breaths tugging in and out. A housemaid burst out of a hidden door to the left, and Claudia gasped aloud.

Luckily, the humans from this time couldn't see or hear her, just as before, so she remained undetected. For now. She would rather be hidden for a few seconds, though, so she could get her anxiety under control.

Going on instinct, she moved to the closing door and slid inside. The steps were plain wood, and the passageway cramped. No luxury in sight, because she'd stumbled into a servant's staircase.

This was perfect, she realized. There might be more foot traffic here, but it would consist only of harmless people. No demons.

She imagined Bastraal was far too arrogant to use the stairs designated for the help. Plus, if he was truly acting the part of American gentry, he'd certainly follow their guidelines to avoid attracting suspicion.

With her self-assurance flooding back, Claudia began to creep up the stairs. She'd only gone a few steps when a horrific scream carried from the other side of the wall. The sound was muffled, but the distress and pain wrenched at her gut.

She stopped all movement and listened, but the cry had her heart pounding in her veins, in her ears. So loudly she had to force herself to calm down again.

What was happening to the poor man? Should she try to help? Was that why'd been sent here?

No. Gritting her teeth, she closed her eyes and maintained focus. Whatever was taking place on the other side of the wall wasn't actually happening. Not anymore. His torture-filled screams were only an echo from centuries before.

She couldn't save him any more than she could truly travel through time. This was only a psychic visit, and trying to interfere would be fruitless. Still, his wretched screams and pleas for release made her stomach turn.

He's long dead. Long gone. In reality, he feels no pain. She had to keep her eye on the real goal, which was to prevent the same kind of torture and chaos from happening again.

Bastraal wanted to return to the human world, so he could revel in heinous acts like the one she was listening to. He existed only for pain and death, and her mission was to help stop him.

So she needed to keep looking for whatever object she'd come to find.

The man shrieked again, the sound biting into Claudia's spinal cord like jagged teeth, but she ignored the pitiful being and continued up. A door at the top gave her pause, since she didn't know who or what she might find on the other side.

Opening it a crack, she saw yet another hallway, and as she peered out, a neatly-dressed male servant exited a room. He was carrying some sort of jacket or coat. Could he be a valet? The man who saw to Bastraal's clothing and appearance?

If so, the room he'd just vacated was likely the master's chamber. Her intuition told her she should be inside that bedroom. The antiques she'd located thus far had been the demon's personal effects and were found in his private quarters.

So with a burst of bravery, she made a beeline for the room and slipped inside. Easing the door closed behind her, she turned to survey the room. She needed no more than a cursory glance before homing in on the large mirror that shimmered on the wall.

The rectangular shape was tall enough to reflect a large man. That, the opulence of the dressing area, and the dresser she recognized from her last visit confirmed her suspicion. The bedroom belonged to Bastraal. The vile master of this debauched household.

Studying the golden frame with its rope-like design, Claudia tried to find any distinguishing characteristics or craftsmanship that might serve as a signature. If she hoped to locate this piece back in her world, the real-time world, she would need more to go on than a superficial description.

Sighing as impatience started to get the better of her, she edged toward the antique for a closer look. Nothing stood out or drew her attention. Just a mirror in a frame.

Maybe she should look on the back side, but she had no idea how to heft the huge piece off of the wall. Her eyes swung to the surface, but from this angle, she could only see the masculine chamber reflected. Dark wood ran throughout, in both the moulding and wainscoting, adding refinery to the gold and maroon color scheme.

She saw only the room behind her. Two maple posts at the end of the bed, a corner of the dresser, and a clock affixed to the wall. Nothing more. Perfectly normal.

Until the center of the silvered glass began to shift, darkening to a brown cloud that didn't belong. She blinked her eyes to make sure she wasn't seeing things, but the image was still there. She whirled around to locate the strange haze behind her, but what she'd seen wasn't actually in the room.

It was only inside the mirror.

Beetling her brows, Claudia turned slowly back to the mirror. The brown shading had spread to encompass the glass surface, and inside the russet mists a picture began to take shape.

She staggered backward, knocking her thigh into a nightstand when she recognized the man reclining on a bed. The image was small, as if being viewed from a distance, but there was no mistaking the chiseled jaw and handsome profile.

She was watching a movie play out inside the mirror. A dreamlike reel of Cole lying on his back, his eyelids lowered as if he were drowsy. Or aroused.

She knew that room. It was Cole's study in his new house. And there—the brown fog was clearing—she could make out the clock he'd been working on just the other night. So what she was seeing was present time.

And that awareness ripped like a serrated blade through her chest. The sickening sorrow of betrayal exploded inside her as she stared. As she looked at Cole in his room. Shirtless. At ease.

And with another woman.

Claudia felt like she'd been punched in the stomach, and a keening moan squeezed from her tightened throat. The room began spinning around her as the alien sensation of being pulled back through time gripped her from all sides.

She was traveling again.

The hand that she'd clutched to her chest in the vision was still resting against her pounding heart. But when the spinning finally stopped, she was no longer standing in Bastraal's bedroom. Plush material cushioned her, and the fingers of her other hand were threaded through silky hair.

She opened her eyes, and relieved laughter rolled forth. She was touching fur. Rowan Von Ashbi's American Shorthair fur. Soft as satin.

"What happened?" Willyn rushed forward. "Are you hurt?"

Shaking her head, Claudia tried to catch her breath and calm down. "No. Why?"

"You were making one hellaciously weird noise," Paige said. Even the soldier's turquoise eyes were round.

"Oh. That." Claudia grumbled beneath her breath. She wasn't ready to think about what she'd seen in the mirror. And an even bigger question was why she'd seen Cole at all. With someone else. Was the force that controlled the prophecy trying to tell her something?

Or was her own paranoia sinking into her subconscious until the fear of deceit colored everything in her life? Refusing to dredge up that topic again, she reminded herself that Cole was no longer an issue.

They'd had their fling, and it had been nice. More like rockin' good, but who's keeping track? Either way, he was no longer involved in her trial. No longer a threat to her staunch singledom.

Boy, that was one desolate sounding word. Sing-le-dom.

Enough. You saw what you fear most, that's all. A psychological trick. Claudia winced as Cole's relaxed face swam in front of her eyes. If another entity had put the image in the mirror for her to see, then what or who? And why?

Patting Ashbi on his haunches, she swung her legs to the floor and stood. "I was caught by surprise in the vision. But Bastraal wasn't there. I was safe."

"Then what was with the moaning?" Kylie's fierce expression was the same as Paige's.

I saw a man I'd just shared myself with about to get it on with another woman. "Nothing." She frowned. "Just my past trying to mess up my present."

"Did you find the next item?" asked Anna.

"I did. Unfortunately, it wasn't very memorable," Claudia said. "There was a large mirror in Bastraal's bedroom. The design was unremarkable, so I have no idea how to begin searching for it."

"I'm sure we'll figure it out." Anna came closer and wrapped her arm around Claudia's shoulders. "But for now, why don't we all take a break?" The head witch lifted her head and added in an airy voice, "Then you can tell us everything."

Claudia huffed and quirked her mouth to one side. "It's hard to keep secrets from a psychic. You mean I can tell you all about the vision and be sure not to leave out the part that involved Cole?" She lifted her brows sardonically. "Is that the 'everything' you're referring to?"

Anna only smiled and patted her arm.

As the witches broke rank and the cats cleared their posts, Shauni opened the door of the great room to let them all out. The felines had done their job and were off to find well-deserved treats. The women weren't the only ones spoiled by Mrs. Attinger and her cooking.

"The circle was fantastic, by the way." Claudia met Anna's gaze. "I barely felt a thing. Going in or coming out."

"Good. That's one less thing for you to worry about." Her friend lifted a finger. "As long as you don't touch anything when we're not around."

"I'll do my best." Claudia fell into step with the others. The vision hadn't been as painful as the previous two, but she was preoccupied nevertheless. Seeing Cole in the mirror had been unsettling. She not only worried about his role in her challenge, in her life, but now she wondered if he was a target.

That didn't make sense but, lately, very little seemed to. Feeling another headache coming on, she rubbed her forehead, then her temples.

"Everything go all right?" Quinn was beside her now, walking with her through the great room to the kitchen. She'd been so entrenched in her thoughts she hadn't heard him approach.

"It did. Mostly." She shook her head. "I'm just disoriented." The strain she was feeling was apparent in her tone. "I'm confused, worried, and frankly, exasperated beyond repair. I never realized how many mixed signals the supernatural world could send. I can't tell reality from illusion, or suspicion from the ugly truth that's right in front of my face."

Quinn nodded. "You're in a bad place. You're far enough into your challenge to be overwhelmed, but not quite to the point where you can see the end in sight."

He took a breath, then paused, as if thinking over his next

words. "Plus, there's the love portion of the prophecy. That seems to be giving you a lot more grief than the Amara, or even Bastraal, for that matter."

Again she rubbed her brow. "You're right. It's all getting mixed together. No wonder I'm so keyed up all the time." She curled her fingers and lifted them. "I need something I can fight head on. A problem I can take care of with my magic."

She pictured the woman she'd seen with Cole. "Or even my fists. Whatever it is, I need a way to vent my frustration. Chasing antiques all over Savannah is great, but I'm ready to get my hands dirty."

Quinn laughed, the full-chested sound a welcome change from her irritability.

"Well, I'm glad you're happy," she said, but her lips were starting to curve.

He winked. "Don't worry. I think you're about to get happy too."

"Why?"

Leaning his head toward hers, Quinn spoke low, like a spy deep in collaboration. "Want to go blow something up?"

18

"Looks like the storm is moving out." Trevor indicated the roiling gray clouds visible through the windshield. "Blowing Northwest. Inland."

With his head laid back on the passenger seat, Cole shifted his eyes to the retreating haze then forward again. Trevor was at the wheel of the unmarked car they'd been using this tour, and Cole was more than happy to let him drive.

He was having a hard time keeping his eyes open, and the fatigue he'd been battling all day seemed to have roosted in the base of his skull. He never took naps unless he was seriously sleep-deprived or sick as a dog.

But he wasn't sure what was going on. He didn't have any flu-like symptoms, and whatever was affecting him seemed to come and go like the tide. Right now, unfortunately, he was swamped.

"You don't look good, man." One side of Trevor's mouth turned down as he studied his partner. "You don't have to go out there, you know." His eyes were understanding. "No one's expecting you, so if you don't show up…"

Cole shook his head in answer. No one would be disappointed if he couldn't rendezvous with the witches. That's what Trevor was saying. But what he meant, was that Claudia didn't know he was coming, so why bother?

"I'm not going to duck out of my obligations just because Claudia's going to be there." Cole picked up the bottled water in the cup holder and took a long swig. Hydration was supposed to make sick people feel better, but he'd been drinking round the clock and so far, he couldn't tell a difference.

"You're not obligated. To anyone." Trevor had been fully briefed about the *change* in Cole's and Claudia's friendship. If nothing else good came out of their library liaison, at least Trevor was firmly back on the side of male solidarity.

Even he'd been stunned by Claudia's casual dismissal of what had happened.

Cole crumpled the empty bottle and tossed it to the floorboard. "I have a responsibility to the people of Savannah, and I'm not going to sit by while they're being attacked." Then he tossed a mediocre grin to Trevor. "Besides, I can't let you hog all the glory."

Trevor snorted, and the two fell silent. They could do that, having been partners for a few years now. They had their own rhythm, habits, and system of communication. Sort of like a married couple.

Now Cole grumbled in his chest. Okay, not exactly like that.

As he stared out the window, he watched the landscape change. They'd been deep in rural neighborhoods for a while now, and the woods were growing thicker with each mile. The two of them were following up on a lead, but one that had nothing to do with typical detective work.

And everything to do with the coven.

Last night they'd overheard the drunken ramblings of a woman who'd been picked up for solicitation. Cuffed to a chair, she'd amused herself by telling stories, to nobody in particular.

But when she'd spoken of a door from Hell and the beasts that had poured from it, Trevor and Cole had made a point of questioning the woman in private. Eventually they'd gotten a location from her, so that's where they were headed now.

To a demon portal.

Most people couldn't see the monsters in their natural form, but somehow this woman had. That was a question best left to the coven. Maybe drugs had been involved?

Cole shook his head. He guessed they should be thankful the woman's john had been such a cheapskate, or else he'd never have taken her to a blanket in the forest. Cole couldn't imagine the setup had been very pleasant.

Not with the no-see-'ems in this part of the country. The almost-invisible gnats would bite into any naked flesh they could find.

Cole thought of the woman, then cringed at the mental picture that was disturbing on so many levels. He hooked a thumb to indicate the dive bar they were passing on the right. "That's the place she mentioned."

"Yeah. We're coming up on the culvert, and then we can pull off to park." Trevor knew his way around Chatham County and the surrounding, having grown up as a local. Sure enough, Cole thought he saw the flickering sheen of metal through the thick pines flying by at forty miles per hour.

They found a service road that curved back through the woods and turned off, following the bumpy, muddy lane to where the others were parked. Three cars sat hidden in the shadows, so he figured the entire coven had shown up to investigate.

Along with a few of the men now attached to them. Like amino acids creating a new strand of DNA, the witches just kept hooking up.

On the tail of this image, Cole searched for Claudia. It didn't take long, since her flame-red hair blazed brightly in the gloom of the woods. She was staring at him as well, and the creases in her forehead didn't translate to "I'm happy to see you."

Hell no. If anything, the woman looked cranky.

Irritated by how crappy and ill he was already feeling—and

by Claudia's ice-cold welcome—he averted his gaze and focused instead on Hayden. She was waving at Cole with a smile on her face, reserving some of her sweet charity for him in addition to her hulking boyfriend still sitting in the driver's seat.

"At least someone's glad to see me." Cole blew out a breath and unbuckled his seat belt.

As usual, his partner was supportive and sympathetic. "If you're going to cry or anything, just tell me now." Trevor gave him a shit-eating grin. "I'll shoot you first so you don't embarrass yourself."

Shaking his head but slightly mollified, Cole got out of the car and walked straight up to Claudia. Better to get the awkwardness out of the way. "Hey," he said with a nod of his head in greeting.

Claudia gave him a smile that looked more like she was clenching her teeth. "Hey." She rubbed one elbow distractedly, as if not quite sure what to do with herself. "Thanks for the tip. Having you and Trevor out in the city, and Nick at his bar keeping an ear out, it's been a big help in locating these portals."

Cole scratched his chest, also wondering how to act. "We all have a part in this. Nobody wants to see the city fall. Or see people die."

"No. I guess you don't." Kicking at some of the previous fall's pine straw on the ground, Claudia asked, "So is that why you're here? You feel like you have a part to play?"

"Relax," Cole said tersely. "Like I was just explaining to Trevor, I'm not going to any great lengths to avoid you or the coven." His edginess was riding on the persistent exhaustion he felt, as well as the nagging ache at the base of his spine. "That would be immature and, in a way, unprofessional."

"Besides," he turned hard eyes her way, "I thought you and I agreed to be adults about this."

A shadow of what might have been disgrace passed over

her pretty green eyes, now darker than the sunlit river they usually resembled. They were filled with emotion. Added to that, the day was overcast.

She regained her poise and inclined her head. "That's exactly right. Good to know we're clear on that subject."

Heat crawled up Cole's back, pride enflamed by anger. "Don't worry. We're clear."

As the bulk of the group moved deeper into the woods, Cole noticed Trevor at the helm. His partner was pointing with one hand while talking to Anna, probably relaying the prostitute's instructions.

Cole let his gaze travel to Claudia's back and the long, slender sword hanging across it. He'd always thought women with weapons were sexy, but the red-headed witch with a blade as long and lean as she was and sharp enough to cut a man in two?

He cleared his throat and forced himself to scowl. That comparison was uncomfortably accurate. She had, in fact, sliced Cole's ego into small pieces. A *Gensu* shredding a cola can, like in that old commercial.

He grimaced in annoyance. That was something for him to deal with privately. For now, he would just forget about it.

Claudia was walking with Lucia and Shauni, both of whom also carried their weapons of choice. The blades were made of titanium and instilled with mystical elements that Ethan had helped the witches formulate. The resulting alloy was able to store the coven's unique magic, the blue energy that destroyed demons on contact.

The women were prepared for anything it seemed, and Cole had to settle for sitting on the sidelines. He couldn't see demons like they did. In fact, only Ethan had that extra ability. But then, he'd had his own demon stalking him for most of his life and had picked up a few tricks along the way.

Lucia had been the one to help Ethan rid himself of the

beast. Something called a Seraphim? Whatever the thing had been, Lucia had risked her life to save the man she loved.

Cole bit down on his cheek, suddenly irritated that he wanted a woman who didn't want him back. If he wasn't meant to be with Claudia, he needed to embrace that reality and continue on with his bachelor lifestyle.

But instead of embracing any damn thing, he stared again at the history professor. Her long legs were clad in brown pants and nimbly stepped over the wet weeds they had to tromp through.

Disgusted with himself for being so entranced by her lithe form and alluring curves, he returned his interest to Trevor and Anna. They had stopped, and Anna was nodding. It looked like they'd found something.

When he drew closer, spanning out in a semi-circle with the others, Cole could see a disturbance in what appeared to be a cluster of pines. But they were much more than simple trees.

As if to prove his theory, Quinn picked up a pine cone and tossed it at the tall, thin trunks. The brown cone bounced off what looked like thin air, but ripples of disruption spread outward, confirming there was more there than met the eye.

"Ladies and gentlemen," Paige announced, "we have ourselves a portal."

With a few nods and silent agreement, Trevor, Quinn, and the other two men, Ethan and Dare, all trod to one side, giving the women room to surround the portal. The only two missing out on the excitement were Nick and Michael, but they both owned their own businesses and worked longer hours.

Cole had heard about the last portal destruction, and despite the tension between him and Claudia, he had to admit he was a little stoked to see this with his own eyes. None of them knew how many other underworld exit points there were, but each one they knocked out slowed the influx of demons into this realm.

Some of the beasts could masquerade as humans, which opened up a whole new set of possibilities whenever Cole and Trevor got called to a homicide scene. A lot of nasty options, and an explanation for some of the horrific mutilation they'd seen.

The memory of one young boy snapped into sharp clarity in his head, and he saw the portal in a whole new light. He not only looked forward to seeing the coven blow the thing up, he hoped a few of the sub-human bastards got pulverized along with it.

He wouldn't mind mounting a demon head on a plaque for his new study.

What the hell? Cole rubbed his eyes, wondering where the macabre thought had come from. He could think of only three possible explanations. His mysterious illness was really getting to him. Real-life monsters were becoming too much a part of his norm. Or—the most likely option—seeing Claudia again reminded him just how frustrated with her he really was.

Get over it. He spread his legs and crossed his arms, waiting for the light show to begin. *Plenty of other women out there.* He glanced at her bright red ponytail. *More receptive women.*

Just then, the witches all lifted their hands, palms toward the wavering oval that Cole could barely discern due to its enchanted camouflage. Azure beams surged from their hands, colliding in the center of the portal to create one great rush of power.

It wasn't until the portal was completely blanketed in the coven's special shade of blue that he could clearly define its shape. The massive gateway began to shudder and sway, as if the structure itself was trying to fend off the attack.

He glanced around at the women as they worked. They appeared calm, propelling their powerful magic without blinking an eye. And barely breaking a sweat.

Claudia, however, thrust her blue stream of energy with

more serious intent. Her delicate features tightened in concentration, like a woman on a mission. Or one bearing a grudge.

He wondered if she was mentally superimposing his face on the portal.

A rumbling noise began to build inside the gateway, like a huge sheet of metal being shaken to produce the sound of thunder. The oval-shaped mass was entirely blue now, sparking angrily in protest of the magic being shoved into it.

In a flash, the portal sucked in on itself to form a small blue ball that rotated in midair. Then it disappeared into a pinpoint and was gone, emitting a colossal *boom!* that vibrated throughout the forest. Birds were rousted from a nearby tree, springing into flight with aggrieved squawks.

With a beaming smile to replace her previous intensity, Claudia laughed. "*Now* I feel better." She elbow-bumped with Hayden as the other witches relaxed and broke into multiple conversations.

"So what did you think?" Trevor asked at Cole's side.

Trying to play it cool, Cole tilted his hand in a so-so gesture. "I expected more fireworks. The little ball was kind of anti-climactic."

Trevor punched his shoulder. "Bullshit."

"All right. All right." Cole started to grin himself. "It was pretty impressive."

Dare, Ethan, and Quinn were huddled together talking, three dark-haired men, each with supernatural qualities of his own. Ethan had studied and hunted demons for most of his life, and had coincidentally known Quinn in college.

He'd originally come to the island mansion to pay a visit to his old friend and to educate the witches on known species of demons. He'd stayed because of Lucia.

Quinn and Dare were both hereditary witches, but being called such didn't affect their masculinity. Another stereotype that had bitten the dust. In fact, magic reinforced their punches, adding an extra layer of hurt for anyone stupid enough to get in their way.

Then there was Michael, the veterinarian who could see the auras of any living creature. Cole wasn't sure exactly how that worked, but he could probably handle seeing rainbows on people if it would help him get a better read on Claudia.

That left him, Trevor, and Viv's boyfriend, Nick, as the only thoroughbred humans in the bunch. Though none of them were men to be trifled with. Nick had grown up fighting to survive, while Cole and Trevor had the drive and the well-honed instincts of cops.

Cole stilled and cocked his head, listening. Waiting.

Because those instincts were suddenly kicking in.

The woods surrounding them were too quiet, as if all the wildlife had purposely gone silent. As if they knew to become invisible. To hide.

Hackles raised on his arms, his neck. "Trevor?" He flicked the latch on his gun holster.

Just as his partner did the same. "Yeah. I feel it."

"What is it?" Dare skirted his gaze around the woods, picking up on the alert and vigilant body language of the two cops. "Is it the Amara? Surely the women would sense them if they were out here."

Quinn had backed up to them now and was watching the woods in the direction of the road. "I don't see anyone. Or anything." He looked to the black-haired man with eyes like burnished coal. "Ethan?"

"No. Nothing. But I'll get the girls, just in case."

"It's too late to run," Cole said, his Sig gripped firmly in his hand now. "I know this feeling well. I've been through it more than once."

"Like that time in Yamacraw." Trevor swiveled to Cole before he squared his shoulders and lifted his gun. "Shit."

"Yeah. Just like that." Glancing at Ethan, Cole nodded the okay to warn the women. "We didn't get lucky and stumble onto a good tip." He looked to Claudia and caught her worried stare, then spoke aside to the men. "We've been set up."

19

Claudia saw Cole and Trevor draw their guns, but before she could make a sound, an all-too familiar stench washed over her. "Demons." She turned to Anna and Shauni, who were standing closest. "We've got company."

By that time, Dare had reached Willyn, confirming that the men had already come to the same conclusion. Cole and Trevor stood with their backs to the witches and the spot where the portal used to exist. They were scanning the woods between themselves and the road.

Quinn had gone to tell the others, but Kylie shook her head, annoyed, and snapped something at him that Claudia couldn't hear.

"I feel the demons coming from deeper in the forest, but I can't pinpoint where," Anna said from behind Claudia.

"Me too." Scoping the tall swaying pines and darkened underbrush, Claudia opened herself up and felt tingling sensations emanating from multiple points. "They're all over the place."

"Guys," Cole called out, drawing everyone's attention to what he and Trevor were staring at. He'd lowered his mean-looking black gun as if unsure what to do with it.

And Claudia could see why. Mists were oozing their way

through the forest, meandering around trunks and coming closer and closer by the second. Cole's and Trevor's guns would be useless against the encroaching fog. Blood-red and sparkling, with a beauty that belied its evil.

"Willyn?" Claudia asked.

"That's the same stuff that chased Beth and me in the tunnels that day." She flattened her mouth into a grim line. "Scarlett's here."

Wordlessly, everyone backed into a circle, ready to face their enemies from whichever direction they charged. The women drew their weapons now, swords and daggers imbued with coven magic that would serve two purposes.

First, the blades would glow red or blue when in close proximity to a demon. Blue meant the person they were fighting was a human who'd been possessed. Those combatants required a little more work, but when exposed to a special herb mixture, the demon could be banished and the innocent human saved.

If the blades turned red, however, that would indicate option number two. A pure demon. Just waiting to be killed.

From within distant shadows, huge men started to emerge. Whether possessed humans or humanoid monsters, the Amara had chosen their fighters wisely. The attackers had arms the size of some of the nearby pine trees, and shoulders that looked capable of bearing the weight of five men.

Paige pulled something out of her satchel and yelled to Anna, "Ready to give these a try?"

Claudia furrowed her brow. "What are those?"

"Something Anna, Quinn, and I worked up. We wanted to get them right before we told anyone else, but it looks like we'll have to settle for a field test." Paige held small metal balls covered in short, curved spikes that looked suspiciously like barbs. Demonstrating the speed she was known for, she threw the spheres one at a time at the approaching brutes.

When the balls nailed their targets and clung like burrs, Claudia felt a sly smile creep over her face. "Nice." She understood the tiny barbs now, and almost laughed when each of the balls lit up a bright and undeniable red.

With a few more throws, the witches knew exactly what they were facing.

"All demons," Quinn said, glancing over his shoulder to the other men. His expression fell from excited to troubled. "Scarlett's getting closer."

Anna grabbed Shauni's arm. "Spread out. We need magic on all sides." Just as she started to step away, a black blur streaked from the woods to crash into Anna and send her flying through the air. She landed with a thud and lay there, stunned.

"I got her," Paige yelled, instantly registering what'd happened. Only one other person could match her speed and strength, and it was the black-leather-and-chain-wearing Amara member, Jack.

The small but deadly woman stopped yards outside of their circle and sneered at Paige. Her hair was the color of soot, and only slightly longer than the white-blonde shag of the coven's warrior. "You're getting slow," Jack taunted. "Is that what you call protecting your leader?" She tossed a smug look at Anna, who was still trying to catch her breath, and laughed.

A sound close to a growling scream ripped from Paige as she shot across the open area to meet Jack head-on. The two would keep each other busy, leaving the rest of the coven to take out the demons.

By now the monsters were charging, emitting fearsome bellows from fanged mouths. Death lived in their eyes, and each of them carried an instrument meant to deliver.

Distracted by the attack on Anna, Viv barely brought her two swords up in time to catch a swinging mace in the cross of her blades.

His weapon momentarily caught, she kicked the demon in

the chest, then whirled in a full circle while raising the sword in her right hand. Her attacker's head flew from his body, and the skin of his severed neck held a tint from the blue magic she'd sent singing through the metal.

"No time!" Kylie screamed, forgoing her own short sword to blast power straight from her hands. She managed to fell three demons, but her face was still marred by terror. "The red mist!"

Claudia couldn't spare a glance to see what the younger witch was talking about. She and Shauni were back to back, also shooting straight from their hands. These demons were moving faster than any they'd encountered before.

The beasts were enchanted somehow. Likely sent from Ronja and aided by a spell to help them destroy the coven.

"What is this?" Shauni yelled, panting from the effort required to fend off the monsters.

There was no time to respond. The demons were falling, but not quickly enough. Claudia turned to see how the men were doing, when she was blindsided.

An unbelievable force hit her in the ribs, and she thought she heard a *crack* before she went soaring. She hit the ground and skidded through wet pine straw. Pain tore through her as black mushroomed in front of her eyes.

She heard Paige yell her name, then her friend's feet were near her head, along with Jack's motorcycle boots. Heavy thuds exploded above her, followed by grunts and gasps.

This time it was Jack who hit the ground. And she was no longer laughing.

"You okay?" Paige had her hands on Claudia's shoulders, gently helping her sit up.

"I'll live, but I think she broke a few of my ribs." Claudia sucked in a breath and winced. "Oh, yeah. She did." She climbed unsteadily to her feet. "I'll get Willyn's help later."

"All right." Paige nodded and flashed away, meeting demons farther out in the woods to make sure there were no more surprises.

Kylie and Viv were knocking off stragglers when Anna—who'd gained her feet and was fighting again—yelled a warning to the men. "Get out of there!"

Lucia had gone to fight near Ethan, and the Spanish witch barely got out a muffled shout before she fell to the ground. Ethan went down next, both of them overrun by Scarlett's poisonous fog. The sparkling secretion covered them like a tide with a will of its own.

None of them had known what Scarlett's weapon would do. Now they did.

Hayden fell just as fast, though she attempted to blast the roiling fog with her magic. The radiant blue energy was simply absorbed by the red, morphing to a sickly purple, like a deep bruise.

"Go!" Viv yelled to Claudia and Willyn. "We've got this!" She and Kylie continued clearing out the final attackers while Paige circled the perimeter looking for any demons they may have missed.

"Where's Scarlett? I don't see her." Willyn raced to join Claudia, the two of them staring toward the road. The Amara witch was nowhere in sight. If they could confront Scarlett and attack her directly, they might be able to stop her lethal crimson flood.

Anna and Shauni began blasting the ooze with magic, but just like Hayden's, the electric blue was consumed by Scarlett's red haze. Diluted. Useless.

Hayden, Lucia, and Ethan were writhing on the ground, clawing at their throats. Lucia had been the first one to fall under Scarlett's magic, and her back was bowing now as she arched off the ground. She couldn't breathe.

"Move!" Cole's voiced roared as he shoved Trevor away from the shimmering, noxious vapors. Trevor stumbled but gained his balance, just as the blood-colored mist rose up to wrap around Cole's head and shoulders.

"Cole, no!" In that moment, every fiber of Claudia that had been rejecting Cole dissolved into horror. Crippling fear clutched inside her chest and hardened her body with shock. She stared as he collapsed and struggled to breathe alongside the others.

"We have to do something." Willyn spoke from somewhere nearby, but Claudia could only stare, immobile, and overcome with helplessness. Her feelings for Cole pulsed so strongly, forcing her to acknowledge them. To admit that she cared about him, and as much more than just a friend.

She couldn't lose him.

Jerking back to awareness, she looked to Lucia on the ground with the others, then back to Willyn. She couldn't lose *any* of them. "Our magic isn't working, but there's got to be a way."

The red mists seemed to be surging forward, leaping up in waves to surround anyone within range. Anna and Shauni were closest, and both went down together, unable to run away fast enough.

Each time the red mass covered a person, it seemed to grow stronger. Faster. Deadlier.

Paige, Viv, and Kylie now joined Claudia and Willyn. They all looked on in horror as Anna and Shauni dropped and started to struggle, ripping at their throats as they suffocated.

By now Lucia and Ethan had stopped moving. Their limp bodies were far more anguishing to see than the suffering they'd just gone through.

Lightning zigzagged across the sky, visible through the treetops. Thunder cracked and the smell of ozone wafted in the air. The skies seemed to resent the magic building inside the forest. As if angered by Scarlett's disruption of the natural order.

Claudia decided to lend her rage to the growing storm.

She latched onto Willyn's hand and let fear and fury

form the words she needed. As she gave life to the spell, her voice began to hum with power. "We call to the East, to the mountains beyond. To Sylphs and Zephyrs, and the yellow of the sun. Clear this poisoned air and set them free. As we will, so shall it be."

Her fingers tightened on Willyn's as she started repeating the spell. Then her sister joined in and reached for Viv, who in turn took Kylie's hand. The youngest witch then clasped palms with Paige.

It was up to the five of them now.

Claudia spoke with passion, her voice mingling with the others' and rising through the air. "We call to the East, to the mountains beyond. To Sylphs and Zephyrs, and the yellow of the sun."

Their words flew past branches, through whispering green needles. To the clouds above that churned and roiled. "Clear this poisoned air and set them free."

Claudia could feel her power binding with that of her sisters, magnifying the force of the spell. A huge gale rattled the tops of the pines, bending smaller trees over until they creaked and popped in protest. Sunbeams slid their way to the forest floor, and the pure light of white magic joined them. "As we will, so shall it be."

Scarlett's red fog quivered when the light struck. Its waves recoiled as torrential winds challenged the crimson death. Nature raged against the invading evil, light clashing violently with dark.

Air and light thrust repeatedly against the ruddy haze, battling it backward. Demanding a retreat.

The witches repeated the spell one more time, exercising the power of three. Soon Anna and Shauni were freed, gasping for the oxygen they needed. They rolled to their knees, drawing deep, sucking breaths, then with great effort, they stood.

Still swaying on her feet, Anna nodded to Claudia as she and

Shauni joined hands with the rest and added their voices to the chant. After another three repetitions of the spell, strengthened by two more witches, Scarlett's magic was finally driven back. The thick, vile fog had been beaten down to a few wispy mists on the forest floor.

As the red haze curled away and vanished for good, those who had been unharmed hurried to help the others. Willyn ran straight to Ethan and Lucia, but smiled at the worried onlookers when she reported, "They're alive. Just unconscious."

Still the gentle blonde put one hand on each of them and sent a quick zap of her healing magic to destroy any remaining toxins in their bodies. She continued on, doing the same for everyone who'd soaked in the venomous fog.

Cole had been affected near the end, so he was already kneeling when Claudia rushed to his side. She fell to her knees as well, so they were eye to eye. She clasped her hands to the sides of his face. "Are you all right?"

He nodded and coughed, expelling a tiny plume of pinkish breath. "Willyn," Claudia called, but her friend was already there, laying hands on Cole's shoulders.

"There you go." Willyn patted his arm. "Not much in you."

"*Merda!*" Lucia was still groggy but had awakened, and her outburst drew every gaze to where she sat patting the leaf-strewn ground around her. "My sword is gone. It's nowhere."

"My dagger too." Hayden looked everywhere in her vicinity, even standing to scour behind a nearby tree.

Lucia had her palms out, slowly rotating in a gesture that indicated she was using her gift to search for the lost weapons. "They're not here anymore." She looked to the witches and shrugged. "They're just gone."

"Not *just* gone," Trevor said, cursing and shaking his head. "Stolen. Because this whole damned thing was a setup."

He went to Hayden and wrapped her in his arms, stroking her caramel-colored hair. "I'm so sorry. We fucked up. Either that prostitute lied or she was influenced by someone. Either way, we led you all into a trap."

"It's not your fault." Hayden touched his chin. "We asked you to keep your ear to the ground. Even after this, if you got another tip, we'd still follow up on it. No matter what."

Paige had her hands on her hips and stood in a wide-legged stance. Her face was a mask of fury. "If they have our weapons, they have our magic."

"But it's not like they can use it," Kylie said.

Viv was still beside her when she answered, "No. But they can study it. Try to find a way to defend against it."

"Damn it," Cole said in a harsh whisper, so that Claudia turned back to him. "I can't help but feel responsible too." He stood, pulling her up with him. "We should have expected an ambush, or at least entertained the possibility."

"How could you?" Anna spread her hands. "What's done is done, and the important thing is we all came out alive."

"And detoxed, thanks to Willyn." Hayden smiled at the healer. "What would we do without our healer around to bring us back from the brink?" Then her face clouded with worry, and she let Trevor hug her again.

The same thing troubling Hayden was also eating at Claudia. And probably running through the minds of everyone there. They all knew death was just hanging around waiting for them to slip up or make a mistake.

It was a risk the coven had chosen to take. To accept.

But none of the men had to make that choice.

Claudia swung her eyes back to Cole. She hardened her stare along with her heart. "You shouldn't have come out here. You or Trevor."

She rushed ahead when Cole opened his mouth to respond. "It's bad enough that Dare and Quinn get involved. They have magic to fight with. But you, Trevor, Nick, and even Michael, none of you should be involved in this sort of thing."

Gesturing to where the portal had once been, she practically spit out her words. "Besides putting yourselves in danger, you're a distraction. We were fighting demons with one eye while the other was checking on all of you."

"Claudia, that's not fair." Hayden's expression was one of surprise. "I worry about them too, but we need their help. Yes," she added quickly, "even if they don't have powers. They all contribute in some way."

"That's right." Shauni nodded, rubbing her wrist as if she'd strained it. "I hate it when Michael's in danger, but I won't exclude him if he wants to fight. Either way, today is a victory as well as a loss. We lost our weapons, and that's a concern, but there's one less portal letting those monsters into our world."

Despite the encouragement and support of the other women, Cole stepped away from Claudia. His eyes did little to hide his anger. "If the coven needs my help, they'll get it."

With a jerk, he picked his Sig up from where he'd dropped it. He snapped the gun into his holster. "And, frankly, I don't give a damn whether you want me to or not."

Turning on his heel, he started back toward the service road where the cars were parked.

Trevor whispered to Hayden before kissing her mouth. He went after his partner, but not before shooting Claudia a look that spoke volumes about his opinion of her at the moment.

Facing the rest of her friends, she saw a mix of expressions. "What? Now everyone feels sorry for Cole, and I'm the bad guy?"

"I don't feel sorry for him," Dare said with a hint of a smile.

"We all have to pay our dues." Willyn elbowed her husband, but then she leaned into his side.

"I'm sorry if what I said upsets anybody, but I'm just being honest." When no one said anything, she added heatedly, "I have the right to protect him. And to protect myself."

Kylie marched over to Claudia, her hands balled into fists.

"That's not what you're doing. You aren't protecting anyone." The younger woman blew out an agitated breath. "You're being a coward."

"Kylie," Viv said in a warning tone.

"No." Kylie threw up a hand. "This needs to be said. You're afraid and that's fine, but your fear is making you cruel."

Claudia rubbed her chest, the spot that stung as if a dagger had just hit home.

But Kylie wasn't done yet. "Running from Cole and pretending you don't care about him is not going to fix anything. And it sure won't keep you from getting hurt." Her hazel eyes darted to Quinn then back to Claudia. "He may be the best thing to ever happen to you, but you're too stubborn to even try."

When she started to walk off, Claudia moved after her. "Kylie, you don't understand—"

"I understand more than you think."

When her friend's eyes started to tear, Claudia got the feeling Kylie's reaction was about more than Claudia and what she'd said to Cole. A quick glance to Quinn found him shifting his stance, apparently uneasy.

"I'm sorry, Claudia, but if no one else will tell you, then I will." Kylie blinked to clear her eyes. Then with a disgusted wave of her hand, she walked past Claudia in the direction of the cars.

She didn't make it far before turning to add one more thing. "Cole may be your soul mate and the one man in this world that you can trust. That you *should* trust. So do us all a favor." She firmed her jaw and stared hard into Claudia's eyes. "And deal with it."

20

Climbing the steps with a weighty conscience, Claudia entered the second floor of Nick's pub. Viv's boyfriend had finished renovations, opening up an additional area and more seating. The space was sectioned off by a wall, creating a room in the back for private parties.

That was the venue for tonight's after-portal-decimation party, although she expected the mood to be somewhat dampened by the loss of two of their weapons. Like advanced military technology falling into enemy hands, who knew what the Amara would now be able to create.

Several tables were set up at one end of the room, but close enough to allow easy conversation between their occupants. When her eyes lit on Trevor and Hayden, she made her way over to the couple.

Trevor was drinking a beer from a frosted mug, but he paused when Claudia gave them a weary smile. "I just wanted to say I'm sorry about earlier." Hayden looked sympathetic while Trevor listened calmly. "I do worry about you and the other men. That hasn't changed. But I don't get to make decisions for other people."

She shrugged a shoulder and met Hayden's golden eyes. "Or for the coven."

Hayden reached out and took Claudia's fingers briefly in acceptance of the apology. "We were all a bit out of sorts after what happened. And we understand the trial adds extra pressure."

Shaking her head, Claudia glanced around, searching for Cole. "Thanks, but that's no excuse. I've been difficult to be around since this whole thing started." When she didn't find the dark hair or broad shoulders she sought, she said to the two of them, "But I'm going to rectify that."

After studying her in shrewd speculation, Trevor took a long drink of his beer, set the mug down, and offered her a wide grin. "Then why don't you start that rectifying out on the balcony?"

A post-rainy day breeze filtered in through a set of French doors that stood open, allowing a clean scent to filter inside. The second floor veranda had also been restored, so customers could eat outside and watch the busy Savannah streets below.

While the air was crisp and fresh after the storm, the balcony was already dry. As was typical of local weather patterns, the rainstorm had blustered in with a fury, then fizzled out just as quickly. And all in under fifteen minutes.

Hope and nerves clanged around together, filling up the empty hole in her chest. She stepped to the doors and saw Cole. He was leaning against the green wrought iron railing, no drink in his hand but plenty of rigidity in his posture.

And she had caused the strain that was so apparent in the way he stood, tense and resentful, as he looked out into the night.

Only one step onto the veranda had Cole's head turning slightly to the side. Realizing who his company was, he frowned and twisted back to observe the dark skies. "Come to offer more apologies?"

Ouch. She had to admit, this routine *did* seem like a replay of previous events. "What else?" She tried for humor. "I'm getting to be so good at it."

When he didn't reply, she went to his side and leaned against the railing in imitation of his pose. She studied his profile, so well-proportioned and strong. Clean-cut lines and hard angles.

Cole was the epitome of masculine, yet she'd tasted for herself the softness of his lips. She'd stared into the depth and kindness that lived in his green eyes.

"How are you feeling? Honestly. Any after-effects from the poison?" She waited, but still he played mute. She reached for his arm and was stunned when he jerked away, finally looking at her face to face.

Derision turned his light colored eyes to a turbulent gray, like the skies before the storm had fully blown out. "I don't want false sympathy, or for you to pretend concern you don't feel." His hand clenched the rail. "Aftereffects? Yeah, I'm feeling some. But not from that witch's red poison."

He gave her his shoulder again. "No enemy can cut as deeply as a friend." His laugh mocked her. "Or someone who's supposed to be a friend."

Claudia fumed at the last remark but reminded herself he had the right to a couple of digs. "I am your friend. Why else would I care so much about you putting yourself in dangerous situations?"

"Yeah. Why else?"

Because you mean so much to me. Claudia swallowed and tried to collect herself. *You might mean too much.* But she didn't tell him that. "I'm allowed to be worried about someone who's important to me."

When he looked at her with a mix of regret and longing, she almost buckled. Almost grabbed onto him and begged him to make the feelings stop. To do something that would make her hate him.

"I don't have a problem caring about you." Now she was the one to gaze out onto the streets. "I have a problem with trust." The wind kicked up, cool and magical in all its spring sweetness.

Wispy clouds covered part of the moon, their silvered edges beautiful against the onyx sky.

She talked to the moon, to the clouds, because she was too afraid to face Cole. She wouldn't be able to stand seeing sympathy in his expression. She relied on him to tell it to her straight. No coddling. No evasion.

So far, he'd delivered on all counts.

"Something in me is broken," she continued. "I accepted it a long time ago and decided it was okay, that plenty of people lived alone. Happily solo. I decided I didn't have to let emotions control my life."

Cole was silent for a moment. "Seems to me that's exactly what you're doing."

"No." Claudia tilted her head up. She let the wind surround her.

"Yes." Cole's voice was made of granite. "You let fear dictate what you will and won't let into your life. How's that any different?"

Yeah. How is that? "Because...it's my choice. I'd rather go without a man because I say so than give myself to one completely just to have *him* decide to throw it all away. Slicing my heart wide open in the process."

He stepped closer suddenly, leaning in to speak. The warmth of his breath tingled over her cheek. "I wouldn't slice your heart open."

"But you *could*." Claudia whispered the truth that haunted her every night as she fell asleep, and again if she woke to the silent island mansion. "You're too close to being exactly what I need to stay away from. You're just too much."

He held her gaze and—damn him—his eyes were tender, making her blood pump almost painfully through her veins. "How am I too much?" he asked softly. "Tell me."

They'd taken a turn toward heartfelt honesty, like two lovers, whispering to each other beneath the ivory moon. Turning away with a shake of her head, Claudia tried to alleviate the seriousness of their conversation.

"Hmm." She gave him a brazen smile. "Wouldn't you like to know."

"Yeah." He nodded, never taking his eyes from hers. "I really would."

Flustered and out of sorts, she smacked her hand against the railing. "I don't know. I like you. You know, we're friends. But then there's that other stuff."

His brows arched up. "Your verbal skills are usually much better than this. What other stuff?"

"You know," she said in exasperation. "Like the *library*. That needs no explanation. Then there was the night at your house. That spark." She looked to the heavens. "When I passed out, then woke to find myself in your big, strong arms."

He stared at her for a moment, silent and considering. Then a wicked grin spread over his firm lips. "You think my arms are big and strong?"

"Ugh." His absurdity made her want to laugh, but all she allowed was an impatient sigh. "So now you know. I'm attracted to you."

"I think I figured that out in the library."

"Vulgarity," she said, cocking one of her own eyebrows, "will not gain you any points."

"Bullshit."

Now she did laugh. "What?"

"You call it like you see it, and you appreciate others who do the same."

"Well, you're right about that. I do appreciate honesty." Claudia felt the amusement drain from her as if a hole had opened up beneath her feet. Didn't she owe Cole complete honesty as well? Friends didn't keep secrets.

Especially friends who had a *spark*.

"I should tell you what happened during my last vision." She licked her lips but carried on. "I saw a mirror, the next item I'm supposed to find."

He listened without comment.

"I saw something in the mirror too." Claudia gathered her courage and spilled. "I saw you with another woman. In your house," she added when he looked at her with a blank expression. "Your *brand new* house."

"So you believe what you saw was real?" he asked. "And that I was with this woman recently, because you saw us in the house I've owned for only a short time. Is that what you're telling me?"

"Yes."

"Okay." He held her stare. "I haven't been with a woman, in any romantic sense, since that day I saw you, Kylie, and Lucia in the café."

"But you were with a woman then."

"And that was the last time."

Suspicion slithered through Claudia's mind, ugly, oily, and persistent. Why had the mirror shown her that image? Was Bastraal behind the whole thing? A trick to make her doubt Cole?

If that was the truth, then logic followed she *should* be with Cole. If the demon was trying to scare her away from him, then that was one hell of a good reason to do the opposite. To open herself up to him and see what happened.

Could she fall in love with him? Would the risk and her offer of trust be rewarded?

The thought was terrifying. Like jumping off of a cliff you knew had an eighty percent chance of having deadly spikes at the bottom. That's what love was to her. A skewering death trap.

Cole still hadn't shifted his gaze from hers. He hadn't looked away like a guilty man would. Like someone who was being dishonest.

Her legs trembled. Could she actually be considering this? Just fall into Cole's arms and let his words and actions be all she needed to accept his claims?

No. The answer slammed into her, and her own inability to trust suddenly felt more like a prison than a wall of protection. But she couldn't change who she was.

When Cole took her in his arms, she let him. Not because she was ready to consent, but because she was weak on her feet. The shirt he wore maintained a hint of the laundry detergent he used. Fresh and without perfumes, the outdoor smell blended with his natural scent.

So good. So tempting. When a picture of his morning routine—coffee at home while he showered—flashed into her head, she couldn't stop herself from reaching further in. Looking deeper into the past. She might not get anything of substance, but she had to—

"Stop it." Cole pushed her away, but held her at arm's length. His hands were locked around her wrists like manacles. "Don't steal a look at my memories like some damned voyeur."

He released her wrists with a small thrust. "You asked me for the truth, and I gave it to you."

Horrified by her own actions, Claudia put trembling fingers to her mouth. "You're right. I didn't mean to. You just smelled so good, so I leaned in and..." Her voice broke.

Cole shook his head and muttered something under his breath that sounded like cursing. Then he took her wrists again and pulled her to his chest, leaving her arms bent up between them while he glared at her. "Pull yourself together."

Then his mouth was on hers, burning through any remaining shame she felt. His tongue laved hers, rough and slick at the same time. His male taste traveled through her body and all the way down to her core.

But as soon as she started to melt into him, he released her and stepped away. Yet gently this time. "Just don't do it again."

Her voice sounded raspy when she asked, "Or you'll kiss me?"

When his face grew stern, Claudia's breath caught in her lungs. He was so handsome when he let his rakish side out. "I might," he said. Then a smile. "Or worse."

"I won't do it again. Invading the memories that cling to you…It was rude. Offensive. And I'll say it one more time, for the very last time." She winced. "I'm really sorry."

Cole angled his head as if to say they'd have to wait and see. "So, friend," he said with no small amount of sarcasm, "tell me about this mirror."

Blowing out a breath to release some of the pent up anxiety— and the added sexual frustration—she resumed her leaning position on the railing. Then he did the same.

"It's more of a challenge than the other pieces," she explained. "Harder to identify."

"To state the obvious," Cole slid his eyes to her, "I'm apparently meant to be part of your trial, regardless of how you or I feel about it."

Claudia couldn't pretend otherwise. Not anymore. "Yes."

"So I might as well do what I can to help you. In case you haven't noticed, I'm a pretty good detective, if I do say so myself." The smile was back in his voice, and Claudia marveled at his capacity for forgiveness.

Considering her fiery temper, maybe he was perfect for her after all.

"I also enjoy a good puzzle," he said. "So why don't you shoot me an email later with the details on the mirror? I'll see what I can find out." He heaved an aggrieved sigh. "I might as well do something, since we're apparently not going to be playing library tag anymore."

Laughing out loud and feeling like she meant it for the first time in days, Claudia pushed away from the railing. "Library tag. Good lord, Cole." She chortled as she eased toward the door to enter the bar. "I'm going to need a glass of wine."

~~~

The night went on for hours, and eventually all the men involved with the coven had joined them. Nick had his manager cover the downstairs for him after Michael arrived for a recap of the day's activities.

No one felt good about the loss of weapons, because the more they talked about the portal and how it had been used as a lure, the more they felt certain the stolen blades had been the true goal all along. Ronja had her despicable hands on the coven's magic now.

And who knew what she intended to do with it.

Theories were laid out and defense plans strategized, but despite the unwelcome turn of events, everyone managed to have a good time. Those lifting their glasses in the private room upstairs knew better than most how fleeting life could be.

Disaster could come at any moment, so friends and family were to be celebrated whenever possible.

But the witches laughed and socialized for another reason. Camaraderie and sisterhood didn't just make them feel better. It made them stronger.

The energy that filled the room and hummed around the tables was a positive vibe. A magic that recharged their souls and revived their spirits. Everyone was of one accord.

Except for Claudia and Kylie. The hard words from earlier were still wedged between them, so now, as the women entered the island mansion, Claudia resolved to set things right.

She didn't want to go to bed with hurt feelings clogging the air, or her mind. But more than that, she was worried about her friend. Kylie's accusations had been honest, and Claudia had no problem admitting that now.

But the young witch had been spurred on by more than her

annoyance with Claudia. Something was hurting her inside, and Claudia was going to find out what it was.

"Kylie." The blonde coed swung around when Claudia called her name. There was no more open animosity, but her hazel eyes were wary. "Come with me to the gardens?"

"I'm really tired. Maybe tomorrow." Wrapping her long blonde curls around one hand, she stifled a yawn and turned away.

"Please."

Claudia saw her friend's shoulders tighten momentarily, but then she relaxed and nodded. "Okay."

In silence, the two of them eased through the main level, down the stone-floored corridor, and into the back courtyard. Claudia felt the need for open air and an endless night sky. The sense of being small in such a vast universe was often soothing.

And she hoped Kylie would benefit from that calm.

As they strolled around a curving trail, Claudia bent to smell a white flower that glowed in the starlight. She didn't know its name, but the petals were soft as silk.

She plucked it and offered it to Kylie. A peace offering. "You were right in what you said, you know."

Kylie's eyes fell to the flower as she accepted the delicate stem. "Yeah, but I shouldn't have gotten angry with you. I shouldn't have done it in front of everyone either."

Claudia shrugged. "The time was right." She cast a look to her friend. "But something else was behind that anger. I may be completely off the mark, but my guess is that you were hurt."

She stopped so that Kylie halted as well. Their gazes locked. "And I think you still are."

Even in the dimly lit garden, Claudia could see the younger woman's eyes welling. "Oh, don't cry. I don't want to make you sad. I want to help."

"No one can help." Kylie's head shook back and forth in denial. "No one can do anything." The tears dried almost immediately and her jaw locked down tight. "He's an impossible ass, and I just have to accept that fact and move on."

Whoa. Violent mood swing alert. "Right." She needed to tread lightly here. Two of the people she cared most about in the world were at odds with one another. From a distance, it was easy to see that Kylie and Anna's younger brother would work it out in the end.

Or at least, that's what the rest of the coven wanted. What they expected.

Claudia frowned as she realized her optimism for Kylie contrasted starkly with her own dreary outlook on love. She fully trusted Quinn with Kylie's heart.

So why couldn't she feel the same about Cole?

She coughed away the sudden lump in her throat. Only one female crisis allowed at a time. Too many witches undergoing emotional calamities at once could be dangerous. And rather sparkly.

"I suppose the ass in question is Quinn?" She eased a strand of Kylie's hair back from her cheek, the motion so reminiscent of what a true older sister might do, that her throat clogged up again for an entirely different reason. "What happened?"

"The same thing as always. He treats me like a kid. Like I'm some coven mascot who's always in the way." Kylie started twirling the stem of the flower in her hand, the petals whirling like a pinwheel. "He thinks I'm too young. For him or just men in general? I don't know. It's not like he's a master of communication."

Claudia turned so the young witch wouldn't see the smile lifting the edges of her mouth. Quinn communicated clearly and concisely with everyone else. Couldn't Kylie see she made the poor boy nervous?

"And isn't that the most ridiculous thing you've ever heard?" Now the flower was in serious danger of taking off like a helicopter. Kylie's eyes were wide with exasperation. "I mean, he's only twenty-six!"

"Maybe that's part of it." Claudia tilted her head, letting Kylie puzzle it out for a few seconds. "Maybe it's not your age that bothers him, but his own."

"I don't understand what you mean."

Claudia sighed. Who was she to be giving romantic guidance? She imagined Cole would be laughing his butt off right now if he could hear her. So sage and wise. So logical. Ha!

But...she was going to give her opinion anyway. "You know how this pattern goes, Kylie. Each witch falls in love during her trial. It's part of what we have to do to succeed."

She balked at her own statement. The more she tried to convince Kylie, the more she felt her own advice bouncing back to slap her in the face.

Still, she explained, "If Quinn feels the same way you do, he may just be scared." She put her hand on Kylie's in an attempt to save the flower from decimation. "Especially," she said with meaning, "if he's only twenty-six."

Trying for humor, Claudia added, "He is a man after all, and you know how they can be."

As if completely baffled by the idea, Kylie pulled her head back and studied Claudia. Then she made a sound of dismay. "No. He just hates me. And I've never done anything to deserve it!"

The tears were back with a vengeance, racking Kylie's petite frame as she tried to hide the sobs that were bursting free.

"Oh, honey. No, he doesn't." Claudia wrapped her arms around Kylie, letting her cry on the much-needed shoulder. "He doesn't hate you."

Quite the opposite, she thought, though she couldn't tell Kylie that. Not now when whatever wound she'd been dealt was still so raw and tender. Just what had happened between her and Quinn?

While the tempest inside the young witch raged, Claudia let

her weep. She let her cleanse away the pain. She wouldn't offer false hope or encouragement, because in the end, Kylie's fate was all her own.

Whatever existed between the two young people, she had to believe their time would come. And when it did, Kylie and Quinn would likely suffer confusion and angst just as all the others had. Just as Claudia was enduring now.

They would eventually figure things out.

Together.

21

Cole studied the papers spread out on the desk he'd retrieved from storage. The scarred and nicked oak still begged to be restored, but stripping and refinishing the piece would have to wait until a later date. Right now, he just needed the work space.

After writing a name on one of the diagrams laid out in front of him, he looked back and forth between the documents. The connection was definitely there, and one side of his mouth slid up in triumph.

No doubt about it. He slapped the flat of his palm on the desktop. The mystery had been solved, so he could finally deliver on the promise he'd made to Claudia. For days he'd pooled resources from work and picked the brains of collectors and historians he knew from around town, including Mrs. Atmoor and Nathaniel Clermont. Then today he'd made a stop by the antique store where Claudia had found the first item, the pocket watch.

He'd gotten the last piece of information he needed from the saleswoman, allowing him to complete the charts he'd been compiling. Between the watch, painting, and signet ring, various people or estates had owned Bastraal's personal items during the last two centuries. The ring had been in the

Clermont family for years, but the pocket watch and portrait had changed hands multiple times.

Cole had essentially created three trees, dating from current owners all the way back to the demon himself. From these he'd been able to pinpoint a singular estate that had purchased the portrait of the woman with the owl, as well as the mirror Claudia was currently searching for.

Then, performing his process in reverse, he'd tracked the sale of the mirror forward in time—which had fortunately been owned by the same family for many years—to its most recent placement with a local buyer and seller. The mirror had been unloaded by that merchant one last time and, as far as Cole could tell, was still in the same place.

"Yes!" He highlighted the name on the receipt—one he'd pulled after searching the seller's financial records—and reached for the phone to call Claudia. As soon as he hit the screen, the time popped up in bright yellow. One twenty-eight a.m.

Damn. He'd done it again.

Researching on his personal time had meant late nights and full pots of coffee. He was invested in Claudia's trial, her success, as much as anyone else, but he wasn't going to wake her up in the middle of the night to give her the good news.

Leaning back in his chair, he thrummed his fingers on the desk. The hour was late, but he was too wired and excited to retire just yet.

Excited was an understatement. He couldn't wait to tell his favorite witch where the mirror was. If he had his way, he'd drive to the yellow house, rouse Joseph from sleep, and take a boat to the island this minute. Why? Because Claudia would want to be told right away?

No, he mused to himself. Nothing that altruistic. The selfish truth was that he wanted to see her eyes light up when he told her. To watch her lips spread into one of her beguiling smiles.

And maybe receive a peck on the cheek as reward?

That might be worth the effort he'd expended. Her lightest touch shook him in a way that was positively seismic. Hearing her voice over the phone just wasn't enough anymore.

He didn't just want to be with her physically, but in other ways as well. For support. To take some of the load off of her pretty white shoulders.

And hopefully regain some of the respect she seemed to have lost for him along the way. He needed to show her he could offer a lot more than just an afternoon quickie.

Looking back now, their romp in the library probably hadn't helped his cause. It was just the sort of thing a philanderer would do. Love 'em and leave 'em, exactly as she'd implied.

But he wasn't the one who'd left. If anything, Claudia was the lady Casanova in this scenario. Even though she claimed to care about him, and that he was—in her words—important to her, she still kept him in the friendship category.

But that classification just wasn't the right one for him, not if he had anything to say about it. He needed to see her, to help her, and to salvage their relationship.

He simply wanted to do it all within kissing distance.

Pushing slowly away from the desk, Cole rolled his chair until he was situated at the other table in his study. There he studied the dismantled lantern clock, the one he'd temporarily deserted. Tracking down Claudia's mirror had been another kind of puzzle, but solving it had been imperative.

He felt his mouth fall into a frown as he remembered what she'd said. That the mirror had lied, had tried to deceive her by showing her Cole with another woman. Why had that happened, and who or what had caused it?

As he picked up the brass dial and began polishing, Cole let his mind wander down a crooked path. If he was only meant to assist Claudia in her pursuit of Bastraal's lost items, then why hadn't another man entered the picture by now?

His fingers tightened around the circular part, and he eased off, reminding himself to hold his temper in check. But the thought of another man swooping in and whisking Claudia away made his head throb and the center of his chest tighten. A classic Neanderthal that-my-woman reaction kicking in.

He finally set the pivot down and decided to go to the kitchen for a drink. The last thing his blood pressure or his male hormones needed was a caffeine boost, so he'd sip some cool, clean water in the hope it would calm his ire.

The night was serene when he gazed out the back door. The towering live oaks stood undisturbed, and even the trailing Spanish moss hung straight and still. No wind out there tonight.

And he wished his mind could find the same even keel. The same peace.

Pulling his head to one side then the other to stretch his neck, he padded on bare feet down the hall and back to his study. He was the man in Claudia's trial; therefore, he was meant to be the man in her life. The *only* man.

And she was going to have to damn well get used to the idea. Even if he'd only just had the revelation himself.

He sat at the table to work a while longer and take his mind off his troubles. His father and grandfather had given him a gift when they'd taught him about clocks. Complexity churned beneath their elegant faces which required fastidious care. Long hours went into that care, but the results were well worth the time invested.

"Just like a lass," his Scottish grandfather had once told him with a wink and cackle. "Complicated and beautiful, but they need plenty of loving and stroking."

Cole grinned as he thought of the men he'd come from. He wondered if they'd also found solace in restoring the antiques. If they too had gotten lost in the attention to detail the old clocks required.

After his most trying and disappointing days on the job, he looked forward to coming home and escaping. Throwing himself into the painstaking work and getting caught up in the metal gears and ticking hands that had lived far longer than the humans who repaired them.

As he carefully took the clocks apart, piece by piece, arranging, cleaning, replacing as needed, whatever awful images he'd seen on the streets simply drifted away, falling deep below his consciousness.

The work was pure escapism, and he felt honored to refurbish what had been created by ancient artisans. The clocks held a fascination for Cole, offering small glimpses into the past, and a world that no longer existed.

What might Claudia see by gliding a finger over the brass curves? Much more than he could envision, but that was fine with him. He preferred leaving some things to the imagination, enjoying his own stories of what the clock had witnessed over the years.

He could be a patient man when need be, and the fine, intricate parts definitely required a slow hand. An appreciative touch and respect for the inner workings that had to be aligned perfectly to function.

He chuckled low. *Definitely* like a woman.

Again he thought of kissing Claudia. How she'd tasted under the moon, with both guilt and desire running through her lean body.

And there *had* been desire inside of her. He'd felt the voltage surge when they'd kissed. A special kind of energy only he could create.

Despite his desire to finish the clock, his neck was really aching after consecutive nights bent over paperwork. He turned off the desk lamps around the study and undressed by the light of the moon falling through the windows. He plugged his phone into the charger by his bed, but held onto the cell as he situated his pillows against the wall to lean on.

Claudia still didn't trust him fully, not the way he wanted. But he would make sure she found faith in him again, not only as a friend but as the man meant to love her. He would have to earn that confidence, though. Show her that he deserved her faith.

Now that he'd let himself admit he was falling for the stubborn redhead, he found the tumble to be a lot less painful— or terrifying—than he would have previously thought. Maybe her refusal to accept him had pushed the final button.

Or maybe he had been destined for her all along.

Whatever the reason, he'd made up his mind. He would stay in this fight, even if she didn't want him there, and over time, through actions—and possibly lack thereof—he would prove himself.

And he would start with the phone in his hand. Opening up his contact list, Cole surveyed the names in the electronic version of his little black book. As he scrolled through the A's, he grimaced.

He'd never been a womanizer, but he hadn't been a saint either. "This might take a while." He selected the female names that he considered strictly social, unrelated to work or business of any kind.

As he grew more and more definite about his decision, and solidified a plan to pursue his flame-haired witch, he smiled in the blue LED glow. One by one the names disappeared.

[Contact List> Options> Delete> Are you sure you want to delete this contact?]

Oh, yeah. He hit the button and went to the next listing. *I'm sure.*

~~~

In the pre-dawn hours when the city was quiet, Cole woke to

discover he was cold, shivering, with his sheet and blanket at the foot of his bed. The thought of reaching to pull the covers back up met resistance when he tried to move.

His arms were leaden, unable to lift an inch from the mattress. Exhausted, he peered from beneath lowered lids to search the room, but a veil of gray blurred the khaki walls and high ceiling.

What was happening? His vision was foggy. His limbs paralyzed. *Am I dreaming?*

He'd been stuck in this half-waking state before, but not since he was young. The only escape, he knew, was to let sleep overtake him. Relaxing his tense yet useless muscles, he closed his eyes and waited to fall like a stone into a deeper, more natural slumber.

As he dozed, a scent floated to him, cloying, heavy, and somehow…wrong. A woman's perfume.

He recognized the smell, but it wasn't the clean, tantalizing citrus and flowers that Claudia wore. Was someone here with him? Maybe. He couldn't be sure, and was too tired to get up and investigate. Too drowsy to care. *Must be dreaming.*

One thought stayed with him as he nodded off. He wanted Claudia to be there, sweetening the air with her presence.

But she wasn't, and that made the center of his chest feel achy. Bruised.

And for the first time in his adult life, he was lonely.

22

This is not your average antique store. As soon as Claudia entered the huge open floor plan with colorful and eclectic home furnishings, she knew she'd found a gem in the rough. Cutting-edge minimalism had been combined with vintage to create a clean space with both charm and pizazz.

Just inside the doorway, a variety of old ship lights hung from ropes. Their brass casings clearly authenticated their age, but bulbs of bright primary colors glowed within. She'd have to remember that idea. Maybe even purchase one or two before she left?

Rein in the shopping frenzy, she reminded herself. She'd come for the mirror Cole had assured her was here. Her patience was frayed, energy bouncing around inside of her, and shopping was an instinctual outlet for her.

She'd had to wait an extra twenty-four hours since he'd told her where the mirror was, because the store was closed on Tuesdays and Wednesdays. Even today, the place hadn't opened until ten-thirty. So she'd expended some of her excitement on a much-needed manicure.

She'd been neglecting her fingernails since the trial had begun, but now they shined a fierce yet subdued color somewhere between burgundy and brown. Raisin-in-the-Sun was the name of the polish, and the dark, shimmering color made her feel powerful. Feminine.

The easy confidence was in her walk too, as she made her way from a blown-glass vase of swirling yellow and lilac to a chair and ottoman of lipstick red. Golden upholstery tacks the size of dimes gave the set an extra-showy punch.

Most of the store walls had been painted a warm, pale gray, but the dividing sections were turquoise. A display of old apothecary jars and metal keys caught her eye, but still she had to keep moving. Keep looking.

Ignoring all the pretty-shinies was proving moderately difficult, so she promised herself a return trip once she'd completed her trial. Anything to get her past the gorgeous Chinese wine cabinet.

I'll come back with the girls, and we'll buy, buy, buy. After, she silently iterated. *After.*

A turn around the bottom floor revealed no mirrors large enough to be the one she sought, so with a friendly nod to the young salesman, she moved to the wide metal staircase. The building had been used for industrial purposes at one time, but the owners had preserved certain elements of the architecture.

Like the steps that clanged under her heels as she ascended, or the exposed brick walls that added that extra pop of old to blend with the new. At the top she found herself in a loft area that encompassed two large rooms. The layout was similar to the one below, but the design felt very different.

The first area was as chic and neat as the first floor with sunlight streaming through a balcony window. But past the dividing walls, the far corners were filled with furniture and décor that apparently didn't qualify for prominent display. At least, not in the minds of whoever managed the store.

Some of the items were dusty and stacked on top of one another. Claudia drew near and swiped a finger through the layer covering an old dresser. "*Tsk-tsk.* I'd save you all if I could," she murmured to the neglected antiques.

Her connection to ancient things was a true blessing, but at times, it was also a bit heart-breaking.

She should be grateful for the abandoned items though, or else the object she sought might have already been purchased and lost to her for good. Against the brick, near the back of the stockpile, she saw the upper portion of Bastraal's dressing mirror.

Cole had been right.

She was glad she'd committed the frame's rope design to memory, or she wouldn't have recognized it at all. Someone had painted the frame a glossy black, then added a barely-brushed on coat of silver.

While the mirror might have once belonged to a vicious and bloodthirsty demon, *no* antique deserved this. Classic craftsmanship Gothed over by cheap acrylics. She shook her head in dismay. *Tragic.*

Relieved to have found the next item, she turned to go back downstairs and make her purchase. The young salesman was thrilled to have sold something from the "junk pile," and Claudia had to bite her lip to keep from telling him about the small bronze sculpture she'd noticed. If the storeowner didn't know what he had, then she'd have to return another day and rescue the piece of art.

No. No way. She couldn't risk coming back to find it had been painted pink. "I'll also take the cute little fox I saw up there on the dresser."

"Oh, that? How about ten dollars?"

Claudia gulped and carefully kept her eyes from bulging. "Sold."

Giddiness danced in her historian's heart. She was now the owner of an Alfred Dubucand original. And from this day forward, the piece would receive the care it deserved.

Once the sale had been finalized, Claudia called Quinn to

let him know. She'd known there was no way she could carry the mirror out of there by herself, so Quinn and Joseph were hanging out at the mainland house. They were on standby, probably letting Claire feed them waffles and ham.

Joseph's mother cooked like an angel, and even Claudia had popped in this morning for one of her special coffees. Claire added wonderfully mysterious spices to her brew, but she refused to share the recipe. "Gotta' stay ahead of Mrs. Attinger in at least one area. And she hasn't been able to best my coffees yet."

That's what Claire had said when Claudia had begged. When she'd offered to make a blood oath of secrecy. But the dark-skinned woman of both African and Native-American heritage had only shaken her head. "Sorry, child. But some things are sacred." She'd winked then and made Claudia another cup.

Now, while she waited, Claudia continued to browse the store. The diverse inventory kept her happily occupied, and twenty minutes flew by. When a bell chimed, she glanced up to see Quinn and Joseph walk through the front doors.

A trio of college-aged girls poked each other and gawked at the two handsome men, both well-built and wearing blue jeans. The well-worn kind of jeans that Claudia swore had been specifically crafted to make women drool.

She laughed inside as the girls whispered amongst themselves. *Sorry, ladies, but those two are spoken for.* Sylvie had staked her claim on Joseph, and the hoodoo priestess was *not* a woman you wanted to mess with.

Quinn, she believed, had already met his end as well. He was just fighting it with everything he had. Given her own stalwart resistance, Claudia couldn't find much room in herself to lay blame.

Well, not too much. But she didn't want to see Kylie cry anymore either.

Quinn lifted a hand in greeting. "So, where's this magic

mirror?"

"It's still upstairs," Claudia said. "They said they'd bring it down when you got here."

Joseph angled his shoulder to indicate the front of the store. "I got a parking spot right outside but can pull around back if I need to."

The salesman waved to Joseph and Quinn then, so they went to talk to him. Quinn returned momentarily. "I'll pull around back to load up, but it will be a few minutes. The guys who work here are hauling the mirror down now." He gave her a roguish smile. "Joseph went to supervise."

"Good." Claudia glanced back to the stairs. "He knows how important this particular antique is."

With a nod, Quinn edged over to look at the same keys she'd appreciated earlier. Silently they waited, perusing and making the occasional comment on curious items.

"So," she said after they'd milled around the front area for a few minutes, "how's everything with you lately?" She cringed inwardly. *Smooth transition.* She'd been telling herself she shouldn't meddle, and that Kylie and Quinn didn't need, and probably didn't want, any outside interference.

But now she'd broached the topic, and she could tell by the wrinkles on Quinn's brow that he'd heard the hedge in her voice. "Everything's fine," he said, casually brushing the hair out of his eyes. "All under control."

"Hmm." *Might as well go for it. He knows what I'm getting at.* "I noticed some tension between you and Kylie."

"Nope." He picked up a blue bowl that she knew he had absolutely no real interest in. "No more tension than usual."

Claudia bit lightly on the inside of her cheek. She was going to have to be more direct. "I'm not sure Kylie would agree." She paused for a beat. "Did something happen, Quinn?"

Now he blew out an aggrieved breath. "We had a misunderstanding. That's all."

Evidently, the vault of Quinn was going to stay locked up tight. He didn't want to share with her, and he had every right to keep his private affairs private.

But Kylie's tear-ravaged face popped into Claudia's head again. "It's none of my business, so I won't press, but..." She met his bold blue eyes when he turned her way. "Just...go easy. Okay?"

"I appreciate the concern, and I'll keep it mind." He walked over to her and stood close. "But you know," his half-smile was reproachful. "I think I could say the same thing to you."

Her mouth opened as she tried to process his meaning, but before she could respond, Joseph called from the back. "Quinn. Bring the truck around?"

"Yeah." Pulling Joseph's keys from his pocket, Quinn started walking toward the doors. He turned halfway there. "Are you going to need a ride back?"

As she considered the implication of Quinn's previous words, Claudia felt a creeping sensation up her back. She abruptly changed her mind about going straight home with the mirror.

There was no reason she couldn't assemble her friends later tonight. And once they were around her, she could investigate the mirror further. See what story the reflective glass had to tell.

"No," she said, shaking her head. "I drove, so you guys go on ahead." She smiled at Anna's younger brother. The one who'd so deftly turned the tables on her. "I have something I need to take care of."

Quinn walked backward now, holding the keys to point at her. "I was hoping you'd say that." He pushed out the door, a wide grin on his face, and left to get the truck.

A quiver of both nervousness and excitement rippled over her skin. Yes, she had something she needed to see about. And it was long overdue.

~~~

The gate was open when Claudia pulled up to the back of Cole's house. She'd called after leaving the store and had been surprised to find out he'd stayed home from work. He'd sounded a little groggy over the phone, but she only wanted to stop in to thank him properly. Face to face.

Beside her in the front seat was a brown bag from the candy store on the Riverwalk. She knew the place was one of Cole's favorites, and she'd loaded up on sugar-filled tokens of appreciation. Pralines, of course, a caramel apple dipped in chocolate flakes and chopped nuts, and some pre-packaged sours she'd seen him with once before.

As her heels clicked on the back walk, a smile played around the edges of her mouth. She was happy to have a legitimate excuse to visit him. And she would stay cheerful as long as she didn't scrutinize the reason for her good mood.

Sure, she was pleased to have found the mirror, but even she—stoic rejecter of all things romantic—couldn't deny the flutter in her belly. Her anticipation had nothing to do with her trial or any of the objects she'd found. The curling pleasure she felt was all about Cole, and she was eager to tell him all about the mirror. To share her success. His success, as well.

She halted to re-examine that idea, perplexed and mildly alarmed that he was the first person she wanted to talk to. The one she couldn't wait to tell all the details to, and discuss her feelings with.

Nah. Her inner voice blew off the concern. Cole had helped her locate the mirror. That's all. It was perfectly logical that she would want to thank him for his contribution to the search. And for taking her to the gala. And for getting her into Mr. Clermont's house.

She knocked on the back door and waited for him to answer. Cole had been integral to acquiring three of the four items she'd needed, so there was no question he was part of her trial. The only thing open for debate was the role he was meant to play.

Lover? Those flutters in her stomach picked up again and warmth ran through her veins. Okay, so that part she didn't mind so much.

However, the leap from lover to love of her life was a wide, gaping abyss. She still couldn't see either of them having what it took to clear the distance.

The door swung open slowly, and as soon as she saw Cole's waxen face all thoughts of romance and its inherent pitfalls vanished from her mind. "Cole. You look awful."

He made a noise like a wheezy grunt before backing away to allow her entry. He immediately ambled back down the hall to the study and his makeshift bedroom. She trailed behind him with her purse over her shoulder and the bag of treats in her hand.

When he sat on the edge of his bed, she pulled a praline from the bag. "I brought you some candy to say thank you." She held the pecan-filled temptation out to him, then was shocked when he made a face and raised a deflective hand.

"Not right now, but thanks," he said. "I don't think I can handle anything sweet."

"Wow." Claudia was taken aback. "You really are sick."

With a pitiful laugh, he rolled back on the mattress. "I don't know what's wrong with me, but I feel drained. Nauseated. Headachy. I called out of work for maybe the second time in my career."

"Yeah. I was wondering about that." She returned the praline to the bag and set it all on a large desk she hadn't seen before. "I didn't think homicide cops took sick days."

His eyes were closed, but he gave a slight nod. "Rarely."

Glancing about, Claudia noted the empty glass on the floor beside his bed. "I'll get you some water." He didn't answer, so she made her way to the kitchen. The room was bare-boned with only the basics in place.

She assumed this area was on his project list, with an ancient Frigidaire, stove, and single white sink as the only components. The cabinetry had been removed, but some dishes were stacked on a small table beside a loaf of bread.

The faucet had a filter attached to the spout, so she filled the glass and got ice from the freezer. Opening the fridge, she found only cold cuts and sliced cheese, milk that was past its use-by date, and two eggs.

Back in his study, she set the water on the floor beside him and nudged his arm to rouse him. "I'm guessing you haven't eaten today, so I'm going to get you some soup."

He opened red-rimmed eyes. "You're going to cook me some soup?"

Already in the doorway, she turned back and put one hand on the frame. "Cook?" Her brows shot up, and then she laughed. "No, no. I said I would *get* you some soup."

He tried for a smile but seemed to be dozing off again. "Right."

Claudia let him sleep and left through the back. The trip to the Chinese restaurant she'd found by searching the web on her smart phone took about thirty minutes round trip. When she returned to Cole's, she crept in as quietly as possible, but he was looking at her through slitted eyes when she poked her head around the doorjamb.

"You're awake." She held up a finger. "Be right back."

With that she hurried to the kitchen where she'd set the soup container. She grabbed a bowl from what she guessed was the clean pile and poured the thick yellow goodness in. After locating a spoon and snatching a few more paper towels, she headed back to her patient-for-a-day.

Her weight settling onto the mattress jostled Cole to awareness. "I know you're tired, but just get some of this in you before you conk out."

"What is it? Chicken noodle?"

"Of a sort." She lifted a white waxed bag and poured wonton strips from inside. "It's egg drop, but the taste is similar, and... eggs come from chickens." She shook the bag. "You even get an accompanying version of crackers."

She cracked the strips with the spoon and swirled them around before lifting a spoonful to his lips. After taking a long sniff, Cole seemed to perk up and sipped the spoon clean. "Mmm. That *is* good."

She gave him a few more mouthfuls before he paused. He appeared to have just realized she was feeding him and, with a smirk, he took the bowl from her. "Thanks. I'll take it from here."

"All right." She sat with him until he ate his fill, and then took the dirty dishes back to the kitchen sink.

When she returned, she noticed his cheeks had a bit more color. And then, because it seemed the thing to do, because it seemed natural, she resumed her place beside him on the mattress and box springs.

"Better?"

"Yes, actually."

"I'm glad." She tucked the covers up around his neck when he nestled into the pillows again.

He laughed low and without much energy. "You don't need to play nurse for me, Claudia. I know you need to go." His eyes had cleared some but were still glazed. "I know you have to deal with the mirror."

She lifted her finger and ran it lightly down his forehead and between his eyes, then again and again. His lids drooped as she did, staying shut longer each time. "My mother used to do this to me when she wanted me to fall asleep."

"Feels good," he mumbled.

Content to see his body relax, Claudia angled her head. "And the only thing I *have* to do at the moment is take care of a good friend when he's in need."

When he looked at her and took her hand in his, she softened her voice. "Please let me do this for you." She touched his chin. "You've done so much for me."

He grinned then yawned. "I have, haven't I?"

"Yes." Claudia smiled back, but he didn't see it. His eyes were already closed again, and exhaustion was taking over.

She brushed the dark brown hair away from his forehead and studied his peaceful expression. "Yes," she whispered, to herself more than Cole. *More than you realize.*

23

Claudia reclined in a chair on the back porch reading while Cole slept. She hadn't brought her e-reader along, but had downloaded an app to allow access. Ah, technology. The mechanical savior for anyone who couldn't abide waiting.

The pleasant weather and sound of birds calling wasn't a hardship either, and she realized how little time she'd taken for herself in the last few weeks. Ever since her trial had begun.

She was watching a brown bird swoop and dive when the back door opened to reveal Cole in his plaid pajama pants. "I didn't know if you were still here or not." He scrubbed his jaw with one hand. "How long was I out?"

"About two hours." She closed the app on her phone and stood. Then she stretched, more soothed by the spring day than she'd been aware. "I came out here so I wouldn't wake you up."

His mouth kicked up on one side. "And because this is one of the few chairs in the whole house."

She laughed lightly. "There was that."

"I'm going to jump in the shower," he said, his hand pushing through his thick hair, deep brown and adorably disheveled. Before he stepped inside, he leveled his eyes at her. "Thanks for staying, and for the soup. I guess I was worse off than I realized, but the sleep and the food did wonders."

Nodding, Claudia gave him a soft smile, secretly thrilled to have played even the smallest role in helping him recuperate. She went inside, closing the door behind her, though there was no reason she should stay. It would be perfectly acceptable for her to say goodbye through the bathroom door and leave.

But she didn't do that. She still wanted to talk to Cole and spend some time with him. The impulse gave her chills, but in a good way.

She hadn't experienced this heightened sensitivity and light-headedness in a very long time. The euphoria was reminiscent of the shivering excitement one felt just before a first date. Anticipation, the nervous need to smile, and a weight in her belly from wondering what would happen and where things would go.

Cole was captivating. Every time she was with him, he revealed another aspect of himself, another facet of his life that made her curious to learn more. The candy-loving, laid-back guy she'd known for the past few months was only the icing on the cake. And the deeper she cut through the layers, the more she found to like about him.

But she could still appreciate the damn fine icing.

Moving to the table where he had the clock laid out, Claudia considered her changing perspective. Maybe Kylie's candid words had penetrated her thick protective shield. The outer casing was supposed to keep her from getting hurt, but had ended up doing the opposite.

She'd been the one to inflict pain. On Cole.

She'd never meant for that to happen. When the younger witch had pointed out her carelessness, her "cruelty," as Kylie had called it, the guilt beat at Claudia's conscience until it was all she could think about. Now she needed to make reparations.

The thought of hurting Cole was actually worse than the possibility of her own pain. But that was a daunting piece of self-discovery that could wait for another time. Today was about healing a rift.

She glanced to the bed where she'd sat with Cole, worried over his bouts of exhaustion and what might be causing them. She'd put his needs above her own, in a small sense, just as she was about to do again.

She would offer this truce, because that's what people did for those they truly cared about. They put them first.

Whether or not she would ever fall in love with Cole was no longer a cause for concern. Paige had been right when she'd said Claudia was already halfway there, and she was wise enough to know that sort of thing didn't simply unwind itself or disappear.

She'd developed a crush on her "friend" Cole weeks ago. She couldn't pinpoint the moment the attraction had started, but neither could she deny its existence.

Her heart beat faster and her breath caught when she pictured him, and he was the first person she thought of when it was time to share victories, develop tactics, or regroup from defeat.

Yes, tiny beads of hesitation still rolled through her mind, but she was ready to open herself up to Cole. She was prepared to assume the risk.

The shuffle of feet on wood had her turning to watch the doorway. Cole breezed into the study with a towel draped around his neck.

Unabashed, Claudia allowed her gaze to travel over him with slow deliberation, drinking in every delectable detail. Like the droplets that still clung to the firm cut of his shoulders, and the tips of his hair, so dark and slick from his shower. He wore only blue jeans leaving his feet and chest bare.

She held her breath. The trail of dark hair disappearing into his waistband was a punch to her gut, but one that was followed by a sweet, warm pull in regions farther south.

Cole's potent virility seemed to suck every particle of oxygen from the room. And when the air finally returned, it was with a vengeance, assaulting her with his clean scent.

She breathed in deep to get a better sense of him and couldn't keep the wicked smile from her lips, the promising glint from her eyes. She took three deliberate steps toward him.

Oh, yes. There was just something about a man fresh from the shower.

She saw his muscles strain and tense, his hands freeze in motion where they gripped the ends of the towel. "That's a dangerous way you're looking at me." His pupils dilated as he read her sexual signals and responded in kind.

"Not dangerous," she told him, stopping just out of arm's reach. "I don't believe that anymore." She pulled the band from her hair and let it fall around her shoulders, a sign of her intentions that he wouldn't mistake. "Just honest."

"Honest." His eyes were all over her now, hot and hungry. It was his turn to step closer. He lifted her hair from one shoulder and rubbed the length of it between his fingers. "You smell so good. Always do." His eyes darkened. "Too good."

Claudia let her head fall to the side when his hand drifted up the back curve of her neck to comb his fingers through her hair. Then she rolled back slightly, just enough to expose her throat. To invite him to take a taste.

He didn't disappoint. When his warm, skilled lips tasted her skin, worlds of passion opened up for her. The last time they'd been together, she'd still been chained by fear and the constricting need to control her emotions.

Now she'd shoved reluctance aside. Without it blocking the way, her raw, aching desire raged freely. Her heart was a piston, working itself into a frenzied pace, and when his hand palmed her breast, her head swam in a delightful way.

She felt his body inch closer, so she opened her eyes. Angling forward, she ran her tongue along the curve of his shoulder, cleaning those droplets from his skin. He was a dusky golden color, so rich and alluring against her lighter tone.

Just like that night on the pub's veranda, Claudia's knees went weak. "Cole," she began, but he had already wrapped his arms around her waist and was lifting her. Her legs encircled him naturally, as if they knew where they belonged.

He carried her in two long strides to his desk, swiping away papers until he'd cleared the top. Cole was wild and reckless in her arms, his energy surging and pulsing as his lips met hers in a fevered kiss.

He could feel it too, she told herself, the difference between them, the unhampered give and take. So much more sincere than the last time they'd made love.

No. They'd only had sex then, because Claudia had laid down the law about what it could and couldn't be.

But not today. She wouldn't prevent Cole from following his desires, and she wouldn't lie to herself anymore. Her needs were the same as his.

"Have I told you how much I love your short skirts?" he asked as he slipped his hands beneath said skirt and grasped her hips. She started to murmur some semi-intelligent response when he hooked two fingers in each side of her panties. He slid them all the way down her legs and over her high heels in one smooth motion.

Sitting on the edge of his desk, she reached for him, snaking one arm around his neck to pull him back to her. She had to feel his mouth on hers again. To run her hands over his muscled arms, down over rippling abs, and along that dark trail to happiness.

As she raked her nails over his chest—careful not to scratch too deep—Cole busied himself with her blouse. He started on the top button but quickly gave up the effort to simply pull it over her head. Her bra was gone just as quickly, but as soon as the cool air hit her skin, Cole was there, surrounding her with his heat.

Only her skirt and his jeans were between them now, so she fumbled with his button and ripped the zipper wide. They both sucked in a breath when she palmed his erection, then his eyes closed in response to her touch.

The contact affected her as well. Heat curled in her core, stirred by the smooth, hot length of him. For a moment she only stroked him, reveling in the memories from the last time they'd come together. Anticipating the pleasure he was about to give her, she found herself growing more aroused by the second.

Cole was way ahead of her, though, easing the denim over his hips just enough to free himself and give her better access. He reciprocated by sliding a hand up the inside of her thigh, his palm gripping her muscles lightly as he went.

When he neared her most sensitive flesh, Claudia stilled. His erection still pulsed in her hand, hard and ready. And the same glorious pressure was rushing through her bloodstream.

So when Cole eased two fingers inside and pressed the heel of his hand against her, the pressure spiked, then released. And she exploded. The climax was so strong she nearly wept. So unexpected she could do nothing but cling to his shoulders and ride the waves.

His breath was hot against her cheek, near her ear. She heard the groan in his throat as he continued pleasing her with his hand. And her whispered name was on his lips as the last ripple rolled through her.

Her breaths started to slow, now that she was languid. With her arm still hooked around his shoulders, she placed a light, teasing kiss on his chest. She trailed a hand down his body until she clasped his forearm and pushed it from between them.

Once again, she gave equal attention to him, with slow pulls on his manhood, soft and easy, and meant to tease. Laying her lips on his, she rubbed back and forth before taking his lower lip between her own. Gradually she deepened the kiss, pressing her breasts against his firm chest.

Her legs found their way back to his waist, locking around him as she nipped the side of his mouth. Now she was the one to whisper a name. *Cole*. In reverence. Acquiescence. And with tender emotion.

Their connection altered then, becoming deeper, more intense, but beyond just the physical sense. A certain sweetness flavored their kisses now and made her long to become one with him. To join with him and meet him there, halfway between friendship and love.

Ignoring the clothes still clinging to them, Cole eased himself between her thighs, but his hands held only her face. His gorgeous eyes locked on hers as he enfolded her, cherished her.

And as he claimed her.

Though the inevitable physical response rose up in her again, Claudia was entranced by another sensation. The joy of being with a man she cared for. The special bond they shared wrapped around her heart, filling her with bliss like she'd never known.

Burying her face in Cole's neck, in his hair, she held onto him as he brought them both back to the light. The man simply blinded her with ecstasy and, instead of looking to the past, Claudia opened herself up to something more.

She allowed for the smallest possibility, the tiniest and very optimistic chance...for a future.

24

Arms still draped around Cole and luxuriating in the feel of his broad shoulders, Claudia's heart rate was finally returning to normal. With her head still nestled into his neck, she opened her eyes and pulled back far enough to see his face.

"Cole?" She toyed with the hair curling at the nape of his neck.

"Mmm-hm." He sounded as worn-out as she felt, though she found the sensation of every muscle being reduced to the consistency of pudding to be a nice thing. Very nice.

She hazarded a glance back over his shoulder and chuckled. "Do you think we'll ever get around to using a bed?"

In answer, he lifted her and turned, taking only one stride to get close enough to the mattress and box springs. He laid her down in a smooth arc, making her stomach jump, and then he followed her to the bed. "Just give me a few minutes."

Rolling over to kiss his golden chest and breathe in the scent of his soap, she smiled against his skin. Then she raised her eyes to his. "I didn't mean right this minute." She tapped the pad of her index finger to his lips. "I was just wondering if you were planning to make this a habit."

"I promise," he told her, drawing an X over his chest with his hand. "Next time you'll have a bed beneath you instead of hard wood."

Content to lay her head on his shoulder and luxuriate in their well-earned glow, Claudia let her gaze track around the room. Other than the desk, he hadn't brought in any new furniture. "I noticed you've made a lot of progress on the clock." She stared at the lantern-shaped timepiece as she spoke.

"I fell into the project, using it to keep me distracted most evenings." He stroked her side, down along her ribs until the material of her skirt halted his exploration. "To keep my mind off of carnal fantasies and a certain red-haired witch."

She wouldn't tell him, but the admission thrilled her. Instead, she steered the discussion back to the clock. "You love working on old things, don't you? You appreciate their history. What they've seen and the fact they'll probably never be crafted the same way again."

She felt his nod. "I enjoy the mystery, the complexity. There's so much more to them than meets the eye." He sat up and propped himself on bent arms, his motion nudging Claudia upright as well.

He held his eyes on hers as he spoke. "If you take time with them, show respect for their frailties as well as their strengths," he paused, reaching out to stroke her cheek, "eventually they'll show you their secrets. What makes them—if you'll excuse the pun—tick."

Claudia bit the inside of her cheek, a nervous habit. "Why do I get the impression we're not talking about clocks anymore?" She willed herself to relax, then met Cole's probing gaze. His lips curved upward, but his eyes were inquisitive.

"I just wonder how much progress I've made with you. Will you pull away from me again, like you did after the library?" He tugged her down to lie across his chest. He kissed her firmly before gentling his lips on hers. "Or are you ready to take a real risk?" He swirled a finger in her hair. "And share your secrets?"

With a shivering hammer beating inside her chest, she

lowered her forehead to his and whispered, "Perhaps."

She laughed when his hands started working on the zipper of her skirt, and without any protest, she lifted her hips to help him ease the material away. Then his jeans went away too.

"Right now we're still in Phase One," she said with a grin.

Cole stroked her thigh. "Only Phase One?"

"All right, I'll give you Phase Two. But that still isn't the bones-in-my-closet phase. Not quite. But one day." She straddled him and ran her hands over the hard chest and stomach she couldn't seem to stop touching. "One day."

Cole made a sound that was part groan, part exhalation. When he opened his eyes, the sincerity in the green depths gave her pause. He clasped her hands in his, compelling her to look at him. "Does that mean you're starting to accept what's happening between us?"

Shaking her head, she softened the denial with a lurid lick of her lips. "I'm not accepting anything, and I'm still not letting fate make my decisions for me." She lifted herself up and lowered onto him, ridiculously pleased when he hissed through his teeth with pleasure.

This time, she was the one to join hands with him. To take his mouth in a fiery kiss. As she rode gently, unhurriedly, she spoke softly to her lover. Her friend. "I'm just not fighting it anymore."

~~~

When she woke, Claudia first perceived the pale light of stars falling over her sheet-covered body. The next thing she sensed was the heat of the man beside her.

Stretching languorously, she studied the length of Cole's arm, chiseled by muscle, then extended her examination to the long, powerful thigh protruding from beneath the blanket. Between the two of them, they'd managed to separate the bed covers completely, each stealing a portion for themselves.

Both used to sleeping alone, she mused. She and Cole shared more similarities than disparities, and she smiled to herself as she edged off her side of the bed, trying not to disturb him.

He'd showered on the first floor, so she decided to hunt down the bathroom he'd used. Maybe she'd be able to freshen up as well, though she knew her version of acceptable bathing space often differed greatly from that of the male species.

Searching silently, she finally located a wide door. Darkness lay beyond the frame, so she reached in to feel for the light switch. As it turned out, Cole was quite the rehabber, and his choice of ivory tiles with black detailing was both elegant and classic.

She had to admit, the clean grout went a long way toward encouraging that shower she'd considered, but first she needed to scope out the available products. She peered around the half-wall that enclosed the shower, dismayed to find only shower gel and shampoo, but no conditioner.

Regardless, she'd get a quick rinse, and her hair could wait until the morning. She made use of the brand new toilet, again approving of Cole's choice, then walked around the dividing wall to turn on the water.

She started to undress, relaxed and pleased to be in Cole's luxurious bathroom after a splendid night of lovemaking. She only wore her shirt and panties, slipped on as she'd crept from the room, but she took them off now with leisure. With decadence trilling through her satisfied body.

And they had made love, hadn't they? She smiled and stepped under the steaming spray, humming pleasantly when the wide showerhead rained warmth over her bare shoulders and back. Somehow, the term "lovemaking" suddenly didn't seem so horrid.

Not when used in reference to Cole. He *was* a good man, just as she'd known from the first night she'd met him. What a fairy tale beginning that story would make. They'd met in a morgue, waiting for Hayden to rescue a marked and bound soul.

Cole had been waiting there, dark and brooding, having just learned that real monsters existed. Yet he'd trusted the coven to do what they needed to save the young girl's spirit. He'd had faith in the witches and, by extension, in Claudia.

She turned off the shower and stepped out to towel off. Sniffing her shoulder, she found she quite liked having Cole's smell on her skin. Though she preferred it when he put it there himself. Via friction.

Quickly donning her clothes, she opened her purse to search for her brush. She'd do a quick repair job then slip back in beside Cole. Her palm was a bit wet, though, and she slung the brush to a far corner, the small plastic missile skidding across the tile to disappear beneath a linen cabinet.

"Nice," she said, kneeling down to stick her hand in the small space between the cream-colored wood and the floor. She fished around, telling herself there wouldn't be spiders in the brand new bathroom, when at last she latched onto the handle of her brush.

She slipped the small object out with ease, but was struck dumb by the small golden cylinder that rolled out with it. Staring mutely, she struggled for a plausible explanation for the lipstick's presence.

Cole had remodeled in here since she'd last visited his home. There was only one way the lipstick could have come to be here. In his new bathroom. And under a recently installed cabinet.

A woman had been here.

Pain and fury surged inside her like two tsunamis destined to wreak havoc. Knowing she would only be injured by what she saw, Claudia picked up the small tube and gripped it tightly. She opened herself up to the memories attached to the lipstick.

She had to see for herself. To know the truth once and for all.

Because she damn sure hadn't gotten it from Cole.

An image of Cole popped into her head, standing inside his front door, welcoming whomever was walking inside. Then she flashed forward to his study, where a woman whose face Claudia couldn't see, took off a jacket and threw it across the back of a chair.

Inside the woman's perspective, Claudia looked up when she did. She stood and held out her arms as Cole moved forward. Then she started unbuttoning his shirt. And as his eyes closed, she leaned in to—

Claudia dropped the golden tube as a cavern opened up inside her. Doubling over, she wrapped her arms around her midsection and clamped down on the keening moan that begged for release.

How could he have done this to her? He knew how she'd felt about falling for him, about the vulnerability she was so afraid of, but he hadn't backed off. Instead, he'd encouraged her, pursued her.

And I hate you for it. Gaining her feet, she splashed water on her face and in her mouth, trying to squelch the burn of acid rising in her throat. How could she feel so empty, yet ache so deeply at the same time?

Out. She had to get out. To get away. She couldn't face Cole right now, not after what he'd concealed. And especially after what they'd just shared.

Grateful for her bare feet, she clutched her purse in one hand and padded through the house, down the hall, and into the study where he still slept. Her skirt was on the floor, so she grabbed it and whirled, practically running for the back door.

Fumbling with the lock, she finally heard the click as it turned and opened. But then she stilled as another noise echoed through the empty house.

"Claudia?" Cole's sleep-roughened voice called out to her.

Screw him! She didn't answer. She didn't say a word.

But as anguish caused her heart to cave and a scorching sob

to rise in her chest, she ran out the door and into the backyard. The door was standing wide open, but she didn't give a shit. Let Cole find it that way and wonder what had happened. Let him feel confused because she'd left him in the middle of the night.

Claudia sniffed back the tears and got into her car, and as she roared out the gate in reverse, she saw Cole's silhouette in the door. *Good. Let him wonder.*

She was tired of being the only one in the dark.

25

Her phone had started blowing up as soon as Cole had time enough to step back inside and start calling her, so Claudia had turned off her cell. And had turned up the music.

Somehow she'd battled back the crying jag that had been her first reaction. Now she was in full-on rage mode and pissed at the world in general. Damn the fates for pushing her and Cole together in the first place.

Why did the powers-that-be want to break the coven's pattern? That was the only explanation for what was happening, because she couldn't love him now. Not after what he'd done.

And why did the break have to come in such a cruel fashion?

I never wanted this! She banged her fist on the steering wheel and drove onward through the night. Skidaway Island wasn't far, but the twenty-minute drive felt like forever. Her roaring stereo wasn't helping. Anger wasn't helping.

And she'd torch herself with her own fireballs before allowing herself to cry.

Damn it! She needed to do something, to feel anything besides this invading cold. What kind of sadistic, self-fulfilling prophecy would let her recognize her feelings for Cole on the same night she discovered it was all a lie?

Her headlights swept over the neat green lawn at the yellow

house, and she actually hoped no one was awake. If Joseph was asleep, she could drive the boat herself. She'd seen it done often enough to grasp the basics.

And if she capsized as a result of her own foolishness? Well then fate could just suck it.

Joseph, however, would not allow her to meet that end. He stepped into the garage just as she slammed her car door. One glimpse of her face and his deep brown eyes swam with sympathy.

She nodded without saying anything and made her way to the door, wincing with each resounding *clack!* of her heels on cement.

Wordlessly, Joseph waited for her to take a seat and started up the boat. As if understanding he carried bruised and fragile cargo, he throttled forward slowly and made the ride to the island as smooth as possible.

When she disembarked at the dock, she turned to Joseph and took his hand. "Thank you," was all she said.

Joseph squeezed her hand in return. "Always." Then he vanished into the dark.

For some unidentifiable reason, she watched until the boat was swallowed by the nighttime waters. Despite wearing high heels, she opted to take the trail through the woods, hoping the exertion would burn off some of the anger, the agony that still crashed around inside of her.

By the time she spied the lights of the mansion, she knew she would need more than a long walk to ease her frustration. The door was unlocked—considering there were magical wards to guard against any ill-intentioned visitors—so she entered into the foyer.

The immense house was quiet, with only the occasional lamp left burning. Claudia walked through the great room and stopped at the foot of the stairs. No one appeared to be awake, but then, time had rolled forward during her flight from Cole.

The grandfather clock now read one-forty-three a.m.

With a stubborn shake of her head, she turned away from the staircase and veered down a corridor. She followed the hallway, uncaring that her heels made noise, for no one would hear her from above.

She entered the grand hall, but here there was darkness. Total blackness, devoid of light. She reached out a hand in the shadows, using what little light filtered in from behind her to find the matches kept in a small recess in the wall.

Her fingers found the smoothness of the cardboard box, and within seconds, she'd struck for flame. Lighting only one of the wall sconces, she discovered the ancient light fixture cast enough light for her to see what she wanted. What she'd come for.

The mirror stood in the center of the room, directly beneath the overhead pentagram. The other, smaller items were on the white marble altar the coven used for various rituals and ceremonies. Considering the ancestry of the pieces, and that they'd once belonged to a man who'd actually been evil incarnate, the antiques were stored here for safety.

In the heart of the home, and the coven's most sacred place. Where they could do less harm, if for some reason, the pieces still carried malevolence in the shining silver or gold, carved wood, or even the colorful oil-based paints.

Cursing the mirror for its prophetic gift—and its accuracy—Claudia stalked closer. Shame, regret, and rage fueled her steps. "Why did I see him in you?"

She couldn't come to terms with the truth of her last vision. And what she'd seen reflected in its glassy depths.

The mirror had shown her what was happening with Cole, even as the man she'd decided to trust had deceived her. What backwards world was she living in when she couldn't believe a friend but had been aided by an enemy's possession? The mirror had told the truth when Cole hadn't.

"I knew I should've followed my own instincts. I've kept myself safe for years, and now this." She slapped the flat of her palm to her chest. "I'm doing my part!" She spoke to the mirror, and to any gods, creatures, or supposedly malevolent beings who might be listening.

"I shouldn't have to fall in love to fight the Amara. I shouldn't have to go through this just to prove myself." She stepped closer, emotions clamoring for release, and each as strong and demanding as the next. Sorrow, wrath, remorse.

But most of all, the fervent throb of treachery.

"I am stronger than this," she spat. "These games you play are trivial, but our lives are *not!*" Her breaths heaved now as she latched onto one particular feeling. As she rode anger until it came perilously close to madness. "If you want me to complete my trial, then stop fucking with my head!"

She reared back both hands, wanting nothing more than to punch straight through the silvered glass, but at the last moment, she restrained her strength. Instead, her palms smacked flat against the surface of the mirror.

As her spirit was ripped into nothingness to go hurtling into the past, she accepted the inevitable. She released all of her despair and fury in a violent scream.

Eyes shut tight, she swung her arms wildly, lost in the flowing dimensions she journeyed. Again and again she beat against the nothingness, until with a flutter of air near her face, she came to a stop.

This time her open palms met stone, hard enough to cut flesh. "Oh." Her eyes flew open, but all she saw was myriad shapes of gray, white, and beige. Blinking rapidly, she pulled her hand from the wall in front of her. A small slice in the shape of a crescent moon leaked a bright red line of blood.

Returning her scrutiny to the wall, she saw bits of shells embedded in a stone-like material. Tabby, the manmade mixture of sand, shell, and limestone found throughout

Savannah.

Stepping away from the structure, she looked up to the ceiling high above where wooden beams spanned the width of the building. While the upper portion of the area was open, the main level was cordoned off into sections.

More tabby walls reached a height of approximately ten feet on both sides and in front of her. Each contained a door, and for one chaotic moment, she flashed back to a Halloween house of horrors from her teenage years.

At the end, she'd had to find her way through a maze, and the torturous labyrinth had looked eerily similar to where she stood now. She put her back against the wall and drew even pulls of air into her lungs. She'd allowed her emotions to take complete control, and she'd behaved recklessly.

Her coven wasn't surrounding her back in the real world. None of them were even aware she'd come back to the island. If anything happened to her, in this slanted piece of history, she would have to face it alone.

Okay. Deep breath in. Slow breath out. She hadn't noticed her head was buzzing until the wasp-like hum began to fade. Had she felt pain during the transition? She couldn't remember. That's how embroiled in hysteria she'd been.

Normally, she despised the word "hysteria" for its root reference to female anatomy. Plus, the alleged "disease" had been used as an excuse to burn countless women during the Inquisition. They had, of course, been labeled as witches.

Nevertheless, her affair with Cole had ultimately caused her brief trip to lunacy, so in this case…well, the term sort of fit.

Logic was taking hold of her again, so she needed to put it to use. She'd thrown herself into this vision by accident, but she might as well get the job done while she was here. Flitting her gaze between the three doors, she resolved to take the one to her right.

From that point on, she would keep her right hand on the

wall and follow it around, the only sure way to avoid repeating her steps. She spared a glance for the wall behind her, disturbed to see even a small amount of her blood left behind.

The mark would serve to let her know if she returned to this room, but she didn't like the idea of being so physically grounded in this place. In this time.

All the more reason to get moving and locate whatever item she'd been brought here to find. The cut in her palm stung when she ran her thumb across it, a glaring confirmation that she could be hurt while inside the vision. She didn't know if her true physical body would be affected or not, but the prospect was staggering.

Once she walked through the door to her right, she saw two options. A short hallway with a dead end was to her right, and another doorway was to her left. She'd promised to abide by the right-hand-on-the-wall rule, so she traced along the wall down to the end, turned back around, and made her way to option number two.

The area on the other side of the door was darker, lit only by a few haphazardly spaced candles. She noted their wax was a deep color, possibly black, and the potential significance of that slithered in chills down the back of her neck. As her eyes adjusted to the shadows, another, even older line of dread snaked all the way down her spine.

Crude instruments were scattered on long wooden tables around the room, many of them stained, along with the wood they sat upon. Eyes darting to chains on the walls, she noticed a tall structure in one corner and a set of implements in a rack next to the door.

She swallowed terror-laced nausea. The place smelled of blood, urine, and beneath it, a harsher, more acrid odor. The pungent sting of death.

She was in Bastraal's workspace, where he could satisfy every brutal, heartless proclivity he possessed. She stiffened her body, arms locked close to her sides. She didn't want to touch anything in here, not even the walls.

This was a torture chamber. One that, by the looks of it, got plenty of use. "Oh, God." Her voice was a hoarse croak, anxiety tightening her vocal cords along with what felt like every muscle fiber in her body. Or her essence, whatever she had in this reality.

However this time interchange worked, she knew she could feel things, interact with objects, and be injured. So this was the last place on Bastraal's estate that she wanted to be caught.

Easing one foot backward, she started to retreat from the room of horrors. Her back bumped into something large. Something solid. With a gasp she jumped, whirling around.

But she hadn't backed into a wall.

Bastraal stood in front of her, smirking. And blocking the only exit.

Her mind shattered, so that no coherent thought could rise to the surface. She just reacted, her instincts making her skitter away from him. She hit a corner of one of the tables, and this time she did cry out.

But the striking pain made her reach for her natural weapon, the fire that lived inside of her. She opened her palm and sent the rage and fear through her arm. Nothing shot from her outstretched hand.

She tried the blue energy next, the coven magic specifically created to destroy demons. Even if Bastraal had taken a human's body, he was still a demon underneath his stolen skin.

Still nothing came from her. She had no weapons in this world. No defenses.

Instead of laughing at her, the tall, black-haired man crinkled his eyebrows, as if confused by her actions. "That won't work here." His tone was patronizing.

Like the gentleman he was imitating, Bastraal clasped his hands together over his stomach. He wore a white shirt with small ruffles at the collar, but it lay open at the throat and untucked over dark brown riding pants.

His eyes looked human now, not filled with flames like the first time they'd met. They were dark, such a deep brown the irises blended with his pupils. He inhaled through his nose and fixed those soulless eyes on her. "If you don't want my company, then why do you keep coming back here?"

He stepped forward.

Claudia took two steps back.

"You don't know?" Frantically she looked around the room while trying to keep him in her sights. She had no idea what to do. Should she try to make it past him and run? How strong was he in this realm?

When he answered, Bastraal's voice doubled. A deeper, more vacuous voice spoke along with his human tone, blending to create a sound that scraped at her brain. "I know everything."

Claudia couldn't understand the alien words beneath the English, but she knew the true monster was communicating with her now. In a language that was older and more wicked than anything she'd ever encountered. Demonspeak.

Talking to him was useless. He could only mean her harm, so she tried to calm herself. To gather her wits and think. But all she could focus on was the door behind him.

She edged around the back of the table, hoping he would follow. Her only chance was to make a break for the door and run. Even if the building was one huge maze, she had to get away from him.

"You came alone again," he said, the awful echoing voice underlying his human words. "Where are the other witches?" His smile turned evil. Knowing.

The bastard knew she was unprotected. She had to move. She had to go now!

Bastraal moved so swiftly that her eyes didn't register the motion. His hand was on her throat before she could draw her next breath. He lifted her up, dragging her body across the table between them, so the wooden edges bit into her pelvic bones.

"I've been waiting for this moment." He rolled her onto her back and pressed down on her neck. The pain was unbelievable. "You will pay in blood for what those three crones did to me."

With the flick of his hand, he tossed her from the table to the floor. He flashed again, appearing at her side before her body even stopped tumbling. His hand was in her hair now, pulling until she thought he would rip the scalp from her head. "And you will pay for what your coven has done as well."

Hauling her up by her hair, Bastraal shoved her against the wall so forcefully that her skull cracked against it. Chains rattled at her sides, hanging from iron loops embedded in the tabby.

"No!" She tried to shove him away, but her wrist was already clamped in his fingers. Then in one of the shackles at the end of the chain. "No!" Desperation flooded her mind. Isolation filled her chest. "Anna! Anna!"

In her panic she cried for her friend, the leader of her coven. She prayed Anna would hear her somehow. Through her gift, in a vision or dream. Anything.

Claudia was frantic and more afraid than she'd ever imagined possible. She was staring into the eyes of death. He'd finally come for one of them.

She was trapped in the world where he ruled. And she was alone.

Her lips were trembling so intensely that her breaths were making odd sounds, rhythmic emissions of the fear that filled her. Her entire face seemed to be shivering. Her arms and hands actually rattled the chains, but somehow she stayed on her feet.

After Bastraal had her securely affixed to the wall, he went to a roughly-constructed cabinet. He opened the front doors, swinging them outward to reveal more utensils hanging inside. But he didn't reach for the small chains with hooks, or the other long metal blades of varying shapes and lengths.

Instead he opened a drawer inside the cabinet. "Is this what you're looking for?" He'd taken something from the drawer, but with his back still to Claudia, she couldn't see it.

When he turned, the device in his hand glowed as waves of color emanated from its form, just like all the previous objects had. The thing was metal, she could make out that much, but could tell little else from this distance.

"This is what you want." Bastraal offered the item up. It was long and flat, though slightly rounded with one bulbous end. When he spoke, hundreds of fiendish voices rumbled beneath the man's. "Then by all means," he smiled again, "let me give it to you."

He peeled the metal instrument open, revealing hundreds of small spikes lining the inside. Claudia still didn't know what he was going to do with it, but she had an idea, and her head shook back and forth of its own accord. "Help me. Help me." She whispered the plea for anyone or any entity that might hear her.

Something inside her brain seemed to snap and even her pride couldn't stand against the sheer, quaking terror that engulfed her. "Help me." The words were unintelligible, and her eyes burned from being held wide open.

She couldn't blink. She had to watch him as he came closer, keeping her eyes on that *thing* for every single second.

Bastraal didn't move quickly this time, drawing out his torturous approach for his own sick pleasure. When he reached over to lift Claudia's hand, she wrenched her arm with all her strength, uncaring if her joints separated or her skin tore.

But her efforts were like those of a small animal against a much larger predator. He held her hand against one side of the contraption. Then he enclosed her hand and wrist before throwing a clasp to lock it down.

Claudia cried out in response to the tiny, sharp points pricking her skin, but the sensation was only uncomfortable. Not painful.

Not yet.

When his fingers pinched onto a small knob and started twisting, she finally understood how the mechanism worked. Like a thumbscrew, the two sides would tighten around her wrist and hand, driving the spikes into her flesh, her muscles, her joints.

But slowly. So slowly she would feel every centimeter of progress.

She didn't jerk away again, afraid she would hurt herself in the process. Instead, she drew ragged breaths and wished fervently to pass out. But despite the agony she could obviously feel in her visions, her body just wouldn't let her faint. She wasn't allowed to use her one and only means of escape.

Bastraal kept winding the screws, but all the while he watched her face. He spoke low, almost seductively. "Did you think you could avoid me forever?"

Claudia felt the first sharp points pierce her skin on the side of her hand. She perceived the smallest give of supple flesh.

Then he turned the knob again.

When the spikes bit into her knuckles, tapping against the bones so near the surface, she gritted her teeth and fought off the moan in her throat. She'd finally found her courage, when there was nothing left to do but endure.

She just hoped she managed to survive. The coven would fall without her, and so would the city of Savannah. The region, then the world.

Bravery or not, when the points drove deeper and she heard the sound of ripping skin, Claudia threw her head back against the wall and screamed. She screamed again when he increased the pressure. Her entire hand and wrist burned now. No area left unbroken.

With a growl, Bastraal emitted the black mist through his lips, the same that had spewed from his mouth in her first vision. He gave another hard twist as he glared at Claudia, his eyes finally lighting with fire from within.

But she clamped her teeth together until they ached. She wouldn't scream for this monster again. She wouldn't let him enjoy her suffering.

When her face started to tickle on one side, she instinctively pulled away, imagining a spider or bug. What else did the devil before her have planned? The torture he was inflicting wouldn't kill her. Only maim.

Tears threatened as she accepted her fate. She would endure horrors no human mind could conjure, torment and torture brought straight from the demonic underworld.

How long would she exist in this dimension? How much could she take?

Bastraal tightened the metal encasement again with a grunt. Claudia trembled and sweated, but still she didn't scream.

Her face started tingling again, more insistently than before. She rubbed her cheek with her shoulder and felt nothing. But the prickling strokes continued, soft and repetitive.

She saw Bastraal narrow his eyes, as if he understood what was happening, even when she didn't. "This is the final object." He twisted the knob violently, as if trying to cause as much pain as possible. "But you will *never* find it!"

His raised voice started to echo as she was dragged into the void that would take her home. Even the pain of traveling through the time channel was welcome in comparison. She closed her eyes and let the mystical cavity swallow her and carry her back to the present.

When she sensed hardness under her back and legs, she lifted her eyelids, worried she'd somehow been taken back to Bastraal's lair. It wasn't a tabby wall she felt, but the stone floor of the grand hall.

The strokes on her cheek continued, and the warm sandpaper kisses were ones she knew well.

Rolling completely onto her back, she wrapped her arm around Ashbi, burrowing her face into his side. "Oh, my sweet boy." Now the tears came freely, full of relief, lingering pain, and regret. For so many things.

"You found me." She ran her hand over the cat's back, still hiding her face against his dark, silky coat. As she sobbed in earnest, Rowan Von Ashbi sat steady and still.

Standing as sentry, he sat over his human, watching as she lay on the cold slate floor.

He licked her cheek again, offering what comfort he could. And in the vast empty room, he offered his tiny shoulder. And let her cry.

26

"Come on, Claudia." Kylie laid a towel across the spring-green grass of the side yard of the mansion. The freshly-cut blades emitted a scent which told them all that summer was on the cusp. "This will make you feel better."

"I doubt it. I don't have your golden skin. I'll burn." Claudia glowered at the other women participating in the outdoor meditation session. Shauni, Anna, and Viv were already seated, and Hayden, of course, was their Zen master for the day.

"You've never seemed to mind being in the sun before," Shauni said. "But we'll keep an eye on you." The animal whisperer had her raven-black hair braided and was wearing cotton pants with a tank top. She was breezily beautiful and seemed relaxed.

Which Claudia was not. "I don't want to ruin your good vibe. I'm going back in. Besides, I need to look for—"

Her words halted abruptly when a strong hand curved over her shoulder. "Sit," Paige instructed. "If I'm doing the butt-sniffing dog, then so are you."

Claudia's obstinate face cracked into an almost-smile just as Hayden rolled her eyes and said, "You mean the downward-facing dog."

"I know what I said." Paige flicked her towel out with an

impatient snap and sat. "And any dog who sticks their butt in the air like that is just asking for a sniff."

With a shake of her head, Hayden veered her serene gaze away from Paige and focused on Claudia. "A clearer head will help you in your search for the...item. So give me five minutes at least."

Claudia firmed her lips together and shrugged. Hayden was uncomfortable mentioning the device Bastraal had used to torture Claudia during her vision and, since no one had come up with a more appropriate word, they all just called it the "item."

Claudia had referred to it as the "pear" for a while, considering the rounded end where her hand had fit inside. But then during her research, she'd come across a different tool that had also been used to inflict pain. It was called the "anal pear."

After that, there was no more mention of any type of fruit.

With the disturbing image cemented in her memory center once again, Claudia struggled to breathe deeply, as Hayden directed, but she was having a hard time tuning out the surrounding noises.

The birds in the trees seemed far too loud and cantankerous. The breathing women around her sounded like multiple waves rushing to shore. Even Skid, Shauni's dog who rested under a nearby tree, sounded like a canine freight train.

She started to stand, to leave the circle without interrupting the others' peace, but again Paige clamped a hand on her, this time on her knee. "Stay."

"Sit. Stay." Claudia crossed her arms. "You've got dogs on the brain."

"No. I've got you on the brain." She tossed her head to the other women who'd all opened their eyes. "Just as everybody else does. We're doing our best to help you through this, but you're closing yourself off again."

With her unyielding strength reflected in the Caribbean blue of her eyes, Paige spoke softly but to the point. "We didn't betray you, Claudia."

Thorny vines of defensiveness grew their way into Claudia's rigid back. "I never said you did. I'm just trying to stay on task."

"You spend more time sitting at the computer with your head in your hands than you do actually using it." Viv stared straight at Claudia. "You're getting stress headaches all the time, because you won't let anything out. You barely even told us about this last vision."

"Because I don't want to think about it, and talking means remembering." With the warm sun beating down on her bare arms, Claudia still shivered. Icy dread was her constant companion after the torment she'd suffered at Bastraal's hands.

"Fine. We'll talk about something else." Kylie was in lotus position like the rest of them and lightly slapped her hands to her knees. "Have you spoken with Cole?"

"I'm leaving." Claudia tried to get up again, but this time it was Shauni who stopped her. With a single, soft-spoken word.

"No."

"Sorry?" Claudia stared at the coven's pacifist. Shauni was the one who said never to start a sentence with a negative, because it was off-putting. Now here she was using the big daddy of negatives.

"You heard me. You aren't leaving this circle until you hear us out." Shauni's emerald-green eyes shifted to Paige. "Even if one of us has to hold you down."

Claudia looked over their heads to the sky. In the distance, gray clouds were mingling with the blue, and she hoped they were carrying rain. And that they blew this way quickly, giving her an excuse to go back inside.

Anna had been silent up until now, but spoke as bluntly as Paige had before. "You don't have to relive the vision for us, but you do need to tell us why you won't talk to Cole. What happened?"

Another memory Claudia wished she could scrape from her data banks. One that hurt as much as the metal spikes clamping down on her hand. Only what Cole had done cut her inside. Sliced all the way to her hidden self.

"The last time I saw Cole, we were intimate." She waited for a smart remark, but her friends only listened patiently. "I found a lipstick tube in the bathroom, and because I wanted to be absolutely sure, I picked it up and let it show me what had happened. In Cole's house. With another woman." She plucked a blade of grass and threw it. "Recently."

A flash of orange made her jump, but it was only Kiko. He'd pounced on the blade of grass and was now digging into the ground with lethal intent. With a laugh, and silent thanks for the distraction, she picked a few more blades and tossed them to Viv's cat.

Soon she noticed Willyn's cat, Snowball, had come out to feel the sunshine, and trailing her like a male bodyguard was Ashbi. He cast loyal eyes at Claudia but still followed the white female cat.

"How can I trust him now?" She clutched more grass, her nails biting into the dirt. "He's been lying to me the entire time. It's like my worst nightmare has come true." Her fingers curled further. "I knew it. I just knew it."

Vexed by the fact she'd dug into the ground and gotten dirt under her nails, Claudia gave a disgusted grunt and clasped her hands together in her lap. "I never thought he'd do something so devious. Has he been laughing at me this whole time?"

Her chest cavity constricted as the ache of betrayal returned. "Could he be with them? The Amara?"

"No." Hayden's answer was sharp and flat. "I'm positive of that, and so is Trevor."

"Why ask me what happened if you've already heard it all from Trevor?" Claudia didn't like being the object of anyone's pity. Or speculation.

"Trevor and I both care about you." Hayden was serene and calm when she added, "And so does Cole."

"How can you say that?"

"Because something isn't right with this picture, Claudia." Hayden tamped her hands on her towel. "You know Cole better than that. And, if we're being honest, it's your trial and your obligation to find out what's going on with him."

Claudia was growing more agitated by the second. "I know what I saw, and my visions don't lie. I told Cole as much."

"So you have talked to him?" Kylie asked.

Those clouds were moving in faster, driven by a developing rainstorm. "No. I texted him when he wouldn't stop calling."

Paige laughed. "You are brutal, red." She shook her head. "Brutal."

Claudia tilted her head in a dismissive gesture. "He replied that he didn't lie either, and that's the last I heard from him."

The emptiness she'd been carrying with her since that night at Cole's reared up like an angry cobra to hiss through Claudia's mind. No, she couldn't concentrate on finding the next item. And yes, she was getting headaches all the time.

Because she couldn't stop thinking about Cole. She missed him and despised him all at once, and her head throbbed from all the crying she'd refused to do. Other than after the vision, but since that sob-scapade she'd been bone dry and determined to stay that way.

If she didn't cry over Cole, then that meant she didn't really care.

Yeah. Right.

Sensing the barely-restrained tears, Hayden said in an ardent whisper, "Call him. Or go see him. Claudia, I'm telling you." She reached for Claudia's hand, never-minding the dirt still present. "Something's not *right*."

"I don't know if I can." Hearing the crack in her voice, Claudia cleared her throat. "It hurts so much. I just don't understand."

She could feel the unshed tears glimmering in her eyes, but she didn't care anymore. She hadn't been fooling anyone, least of all herself. "How could he do that to me?"

Hayden angled her head to the side in sympathy. "Talk to him. Find out the truth."

"Maybe." Dashing away the wetness on her cheeks, Claudia tried to offer her friends a smile. "I'll have to think about it."

In response to the gloominess of Claudia's voice, Ashbi bounded over and sat next to her crossed legs. He brushed the side of his face against her thigh.

"Hey, sweet boy." She rubbed his white chest to generate a purr and smiled. But the smile was fleeting. She sighed. "At least there's one guy I know I can trust." Sadness overwhelmed her as she kissed the cat's silky head. "Besides my daddy."

"All girls trust their daddies," Kylie said quietly. "The trick is finding a man who measures up."

Paige stood and gathered her towel when the first clap of thunder vibrated the skies. She scowled down at Kylie. "Not all girls." With that she marched away, leaving the women to glance at each other in confusion.

When drops started pelting their skin, Skid and all of the cats bolted for the house. The dog was ever-joyful, even as he was getting rained on, but the cats in their stretching sprints were all business.

As everyone stood and started moving toward the house, Hayden came over to Claudia. "Feel a little better? Just a little?"

She looked so hopeful Claudia couldn't deny her friend this one small thing. "Yeah." She tossed her towel over her shoulder. "I do."

They both startled when another boom of thunder threatened from above, then they hurried for the house. She'd use the nasty weather as an excuse to go take a hot shower. The one place she could be by herself without question or concern.

Because, despite what she'd told Hayden, Claudia still felt ripped in two, flayed open, and emotionally exposed.

And she wouldn't classify that as feeling better. Not in the least.

~~~

Kylie had just stepped off the elevator on her way to her bedroom when Quinn intercepted her. He was coming from the direction of her room and stopped right in front of her, trying to block the hallway.

Keeping her eyes devoid of any emotion and straight ahead as if he weren't even there, she attempted to go around him.

He stepped with her, blocking her. "Kylie. How long are we going to keep doing this?"

"I don't know what you're talking about." She stared at his gray T-shirt and tried to ignore the tug of his masculine scent. He always reminded her of a library, but an expensive one, filled with leather and mysterious spices.

He started to reach for her arm, but her glare stopped him cold. "Don't."

Exhaling hard and throwing up his hands, he eased back. "Fine, if that's the way you want to play it. But we need to talk."

Her laugh was short-lived and caustic. "You see, there are two problems with that statement. First, I don't need anything from you. And second, I don't give a damn what you need. Not anymore."

"You're being childish."

Power crackled in her fingertips as insult soared. Her golden energy was far more deadly than the true lightning that flashed outside. "I'm done being patient with you. You've lost the right to talk to me that way." She poked a finger in his chest and let loose a tiny spark.

"Ow." He flinched but didn't release his stubborn stance. He did, however, grab her hand and hold it between them. "Don't slap your magic at me. You're only proving my point."

"I'm not being childish or emotional. I'm giving you a warning." Her teeth were clenched when she said, "Go play with somebody else's head for a while, because I...am..." She shoved him. "Done."

Finally he stepped aside to let her pass. "You tell yourself that if it makes you feel better, but I'm not the one who's been playing games. Shaking my ass all over the place and teasing like a—"

Too late. He stopped the words, but the intent hung over them both.

Kylie whirled around to face him. "Like a what? What were you going to call me?"

"You know how you've acted, and let's face it, when you girls talk, the room isn't always empty." He looked down at her. "What you do is your business." Now his face hardened. "Until it spills over onto me."

"What are you talking about?" She would swear she could feel fury curling the hairs at her temples.

"You don't remember?" His eyes grew so cold then. The sight made her skin bump with chills. "That all men are named 'Oh, yes.' I heard that one, along with so many of your other comments. I don't care to be dumped into your crowded pool of lovers."

"I don't have a pool of lovers. You don't know anything!" Anger and mortification had her searching for what to say to him. "You don't know anything about me!"

"I know what I saw the other night." He crowded her then, his face right above hers. "You put the moves on me like a woman who knew exactly what she was doing. Like a real *pro*."

She gasped and took a step back. "I hate you. Stay away

from me!"

She swung around to flee to her room, but his hand clamped on her upper arm and pulled her back around, right into his chest. "You don't hate me. Don't say that."

"Why?" Her eyes burned, but she focused on how she'd felt the night he'd kissed her. Then dumped her. She wouldn't bear that kind of humiliation again. And she wouldn't permit it. "You obviously hate me."

Quinn stilled, his eyes shadowing over with puzzlement and what looked like hurt. Kylie hardened her heart. She knew better than that. He'd have to care to be feeling any pain, and he'd proven that he lacked any bit of feeling where she was concerned.

"I don't hate you." His tone was deceptively soft. "Kylie..."

With a deep wrinkle on his forehead, he growled and lowered his head, all the while looking like a man who was drowning. When his lips met hers, they moved against her with a mix of exasperation and desire.

Kylie wanted to leap into his arms. She longed to finish what they'd started in her bedroom, but she knew the shame and heartbreak that only Quinn could deliver.

And he'd accused *her* of playing games?

When he gripped her chin to delve deeper with his tongue, she put her hands in his solar plexus and thrust.

His expression morphed into one of rage, but instead of leaving like last time, he grabbed her and tried to draw her closer. "Isn't this what you want? You're so determined we're supposed to be together, so let's go."

His full, handsome lips grew hard. Mean. "Both of our bedrooms are on this floor. Take your pick." He still hadn't let go of her, but Kylie could see the conflicting emotions bashing around inside him.

They were both boiling over, and if one of them didn't put a stop to the confrontation, things were going to get messy. And more destructive than either of them were ready for.

So she did the only thing she could. She drove the last stake between them by hauling back her hand and slapping him across the face.

Ignoring his shocked reaction, she jerked out of his grasp. She had to hurry, because the burning in her eyes was back and about to overflow. She stalked down the corridor toward her room, but turned back at the last second to yell at him.

"You know, Quinn, for someone who's supposed to be such a nice guy," she clenched her fists and banged open her door, "sometimes you're a real asshole!"

27

By the time Trevor walked into the great room the next evening, Claudia felt like she'd walked a thousand emotional miles. She'd argued the pros and cons of contacting Cole until late last night, and this morning, had finally decided to reach out to him.

As if the gods were laughing at her, she'd listened to the phone ring several times before finally being forwarded to voice mail after several rings. And again when she'd called at lunch, then one last time approximately an hour ago.

So when Cole's partner plopped down next to her on the green couch, she tensed, sure he was about to deliver a message from Cole. One of the stop-calling-me-you-crazy-witch variety.

"You look like crap," Trevor told her, perusing her loose hair and pajamas with a scowl.

She could have done without the honesty. "Thanks." She grimace-grinned. "You sweet-talker, you."

"Welcome." Settling himself into the corner of the sofa, he stretched his arms out. "Cole and I just got done with the case we've been chasing. Took us about twenty hours straight, but now we're free."

When Claudia only stared, he lifted his eyebrows the way one did when their hint hadn't been taken. "In other words, he'll have time to talk now."

She shrugged, sending the yellow daisies dancing on her PJs. "I left him a message."

"Not good enough." Shaking his head, Trevor rested one huge arm across the back of the couch. "You accused him of seeing another woman when he hasn't, so the way I see it, you need to make an overt gesture."

"Not you too," Claudia grumbled. "Hayden insists Cole wouldn't lie, and I know you have to back his story because you're his partner, but—"

"Hold it." Trevor spoke calmly but his eyebrows crunched downward with irritation. "You think I'd cover for him if he did something like that?" In a slow, deliberate motion, he sat forward and stared hard at Claudia. "First it's Cole you don't trust, now me?"

"I didn't mean—"

"You're all mixed up. I get that. But sometimes when things aren't adding up, you have to stop and figure out which column has more check marks." He nodded and smiled. "Happens to us a lot on a case."

"Right...I should..." Claudia tilted her head and dragged a hand through her unbrushed hair. "Okay. I don't know what that means."

"What I mean is that sometimes the evidence is clearly pointing in one direction, but when put in a different context and lined up with other facts, it doesn't seem logical."

He frowned when she gave him a befuddled look. "In other words, you're in the middle of your trial, and weird shit always happens to you witches when you're up. Based on what you know of previous challenges, and what you know of me, Hayden, *and* Cole, maybe it's time to reassess what you think is undeniable proof."

"Trevor," she said in awe, "I had no idea you could talk this much."

Silently she considered his analysis, and a trickle of hope began to drip, drip, drip. Her smile wasn't fake this time when she flashed it at Hayden's boyfriend. "You may be on to something. I trust Hayden's judgment, and I know what an honest man you are. If Cole was doing anything to hurt me or any of the women in this coven, any woman at all, really, you'd be the first one to call him on it."

"And?" Trevor prompted.

Claudia sighed, curling her hands into her lap. "And Cole just isn't that kind of man. No matter how hard I've tried to excuse my own fears by blaming him, the evidence just doesn't line up."

Feeling suddenly buoyant, she reached over and tapped her fist on his knee. "Not when I include the sterling character and past history of my prime suspect."

"Now you've got it." Standing and stretching again, Trevor yawned. "If you're good, then I'm going up to take a shower, spend some time with this hot witch I know, then lie down for eight to ten hours."

The plan forming in Claudia's mind started to collapse. "Oh. Cole probably needs to get some sleep too, I guess."

With his cocky smile in place, Trevor chucked her under the chin. "Nah. You should go wake him up." He headed for the staircase but called back to her, "I'm pretty sure he can handle it."

~~~

She hadn't phoned ahead, and part of her shriveled to admit the cowardice of that, but Claudia was going to see Cole face to face and get to the bottom of this once and for all. She still had Bastraal's hideous torture device to find and her trial to complete.

The last thing she needed was the distraction of the mystery woman from her visions.

Trevor and Hayden were both right. She knew Cole, both as a trusted friend and now as the man she couldn't stop fantasizing about. Despite what she'd seen when she'd held that lipstick tube, she found herself believing more in Cole than in her own gift.

And if that wasn't a big red check mark in his column, she didn't know what was.

The gate was closed and likely locked since he wasn't expecting her, so she parked on the side street and rounded the corner to the front walk. A light burned somewhere inside the house, so she took that as a sign he might be awake.

Her hand hovered over the doorknob as she waffled over whether to knock or go right in. He might have his gun handy, so it was probably smarter to announce her arrival.

She started to knock, but with the first rap of her knuckles on wood, the door swung open with a creak. "Cole?" She edged inside but was still apprehensive about invading his home this time of night without his knowledge.

The light she'd seen was coming from his study, but she didn't detect any movement. No squeaking chair or shuffling footsteps. No sound at all. For reasons that burst from deep within her, from the darkest place where instinct resided, Claudia stood very still and strained to listen.

Then the faintest sound filtered to her. A male grunt.

Followed by a very female moan.

The blood in her veins suddenly turned scalding hot.

Many women might have faltered. They might have scrambled out the door in shock and dismay. Or stood there in the foyer, listening and plotting how best to avenge themselves. But Claudia? No.

She just wasn't built that way.

Not only was her feminine pride stinging and raging, but so was her inner witch. And at this moment, she couldn't say which one was more lethal.

Uncaring that her heels clacked against the wood floors, Claudia took long, determined strides down the hallway. Again she heard the woman make a satisfied sound, and a tiny clutch in Claudia's gut made her hands ball into fists. She channeled courage.

Because she might be scarred for life by whatever she was about to see. If her psyche had been damaged before, Cole's perfidy would likely decimate her faith in men forever. Along with her ability to love.

But to hell with slinking out like a wounded mouse. She would see the proof for herself, and after she had her confirmation, no one would make her doubt her instincts again. No one.

She cleared the doorjamb but managed to keep her fury in check. She longed to unload her wrath on both Cole and whomever he was...*partaking* of, but miraculously she contained herself.

The gut-wrenching pain that assailed her when she saw them on his bed almost buckled her legs. Her fists tightened until joints ached and fingernails bit into her palms, but she ignored the tiny stabs into her hands.

She was too overwhelmed by the piercing jab to her heart.

Cole was on his back, wearing only pants as the lingerie-clad woman straddled him. His head was back against a pillow, and his eyes were in that half-closed position. The one she'd seen inside the mirror. In her vision.

She stared for a split-second, hoping to catch his gaze, and needing to see what flashed in his eyes when he saw her. Would he be ashamed? Would he be cold?

Would he even care that he was ripping her apart?

But Cole didn't open his eyes, and Claudia's attention was diverted by the woman's roving fingers. Her long, unpainted nails raked down Cole's muscled chest and abs, and Claudia ached to see another female with her hands on him that way.

Though she'd fought so hard to deny her feelings, she'd come to think of Cole as hers. Their connection was much deeper than she'd been brave enough to admit. Much stronger.

But now she embraced the blast of possessiveness. Damn it! He was hers!

What the hell was wrong with him that he'd intentionally hurt her this way? He'd been lying every day since this whole charade had begun. The cruel and deliberate behavior simply wasn't like Cole.

And hadn't Trevor tried to tell her precisely that? Hadn't Hayden?

Clarity and perception exploded to fill Claudia's entire body. The bright and blinding truth erupted from the spot that sat right beside her supposed intuition. The place within a person that often overruled gut instinct, or even visible and undeniable proof.

Some people called it faith, and right now her faith in Cole was battling for control. To make her see what she'd been ignoring all along.

Again she asked herself a question, but this time in a different context. *What the hell is wrong with Cole?*

He still lay recumbent, with his head on the pillow and lids at half-mast. He should have noticed her by now. She was standing in the doorway, well within his peripheral vision.

But his stare was fixed on the woman on top of him, his expression dazed. He looked like he'd been drugged.

The brunette had stopped rubbing his chest now and was leaning forward. Just as she'd done before in the lipstick-tube vision.

In one sparkling moment, everything made sense. The woman's connection to Bastraal's mirror. The way Cole had vehemently denied seeing anyone else. And the strange exhaustion that had been plaguing him.

She took a purposeful step forward, but stopped when pale

violet light flowed from the brunette's mouth. The pretty tendrils of magic curled their way through the air, beguiling and illusory. Just like the woman who spawned them.

Like tentacles the purple magic expanded, unfurling as it reached for its prey. As it moved toward Cole.

Rage still churned like a rusty machine, but now Claudia channeled it all at the mysterious female. Instead of keeping her fists clenched, she opened her fingers and aimed her palms at the woman.

She narrowed her eyes at the slender brunette and her lacy pink bustier. She fired up her magic, catching the woman's attention at last. "Bitch," Claudia growled, "get away from my man."

~~~

Cole was jolted by what felt like a knee to his ribs. His eyes were open, he thought, but all he could make out was a blur of pink. Then another hard knock to his thigh as the mattress beneath him jostled.

Abruptly, loud voices filled his ears. Women.

Where was he? Blinking fiercely in an attempt to clear his eyes and his mind, he tried to focus on what was a happening around him.

"You won't risk doing anything to me for fear of hurting him. Your anger will throw off your aim." The female voice was foreign to him. With tremendous effort, Cole lifted one hand and brought it to his face. He rubbed his eyes, struggling to wake up.

"You obviously don't know me very well." Now this voice he recognized. Claudia was here. But why? Wasn't she still angry with him?

At last the scene began to make sense, or rather, the place did. He was still in his own bed in the study. But he had no idea why a strange woman was standing over him in a pink lingerie top and white pants.

"Who are you?" he croaked. His voice sounded like he'd gargled nails. He hadn't been drinking, so why was his head so muddled?

"Lie still, Cole." Claudia again. "Everything's all right now. I promise."

While her words were cryptic, and he was beyond confused, Cole felt a swift kick of joy when he heard the warmth in Claudia's tone. *Everything's all right now.*

And somehow, he knew it was.

But that didn't mean he was going to just stay down and let her handle...whatever was going on. "Who are you?" he asked more forcefully. A surge of strength enabled him to push to a sitting position.

The woman spared him a sneering glance but kept her focus on Claudia. The very pissed off witch who had both of her magic guns trained on the stranger.

While the actors in this play were unfamiliar, the unfolding act was not. Cole was a cop, and he knew which way to throw his body. Away from the enemy, clearing the line of fire for his partner.

"The only thing keeping me from frying your ass is that I don't want to destroy Cole's house." Claudia circled closer to Cole, and the brown-haired woman copied the move but went in the opposite direction, toward the door. "But you can tell Ronja her plan failed. I will complete my trial."

She let her eyes land on Cole when she added, "And I do trust Cole. With my life." She glared at her opponent again. "And with my heart."

Bracing his hand on the wall, Cole struggled to remain upright. His legs felt like wood. "Claudia, who is she and what's going on?"

"Why don't you explain to him?" Claudia stepped nearer to

him, making them a unit. "Your name is...Valentina?"

The woman, this Valentina, bowed slightly. "At your service." Her lips lifted with carnality. "Actually, Cole has been at my service, but...all good things must come to an end." She edged closer to the door. "Alas, I have fulfilled my role. A small but crucial part in the overall scheme of things."

"Why don't you tell us about it?" Claudia lowered one hand, a sign of treaty. But Cole knew her better.

The woman lifted her hands and her shoulders simultaneously. "What does it matter? You said you trust him. How did you describe him? Oh, yeah. So sweet. You said that he's 'your man.' So you got me. No more sneaking around and taking a suck off of Cole."

"Now wait a minute." Cole thrust out his arm and sent irate eyes to Claudia. "I never—"

"I know," Claudia said. "I'll explain everything, as soon as this Amara trash gets her noxious-smelling self out of here. And don't forget." She flashed fire in one palm then lifted the other to reveal her blue magic swirling there. "Tell Ronja she failed."

The smile that played over Valentina's lips was anything but fearful. Or cowed. The woman was much too smug, considering her position. "Oh, I'll report to Ronja. You can bet on it."

Turning her vibrant violet eyes on Cole, Valentina mimed a pout. "I'll miss our times together, Cole." She ran her hand over her flat stomach. "I have to say, you were good. Real good."

"Enough. Get out before I burn this place to the ground with you in it." Claudia shot a flame toward the woman that made her scamper back a step. Then aside to Cole she asked, "You do have insurance, right?"

"Yes. But..." Cole wasn't sure what to say to the woman he loved as she held magic at the ready in both angry hands. After catching him in bed with another female. She seemed to know something he didn't, but why press his luck?

Valentina relieved his stress when she sauntered to the door. "I'm going. I'm going."

Her hands were still up as she faced Claudia. She didn't want to take her eyes of the fire-wielding witch either. She kneeled to retrieve a bag and jacket from the floor.

With her things clutched in her arms, Valentina stepped into the hallway and eased down to the front door, all the while keeping her steady gaze on Claudia.

The brunette reached behind her to open the door. When a breeze flowed in from outside, it carried a scent to Cole. Musk and flowers. He recognized the cloying perfume. "You," he said, as various bits of memory rushed to fill his head.

Valentina laughed like a vixen but grew solemn when fire burst toward her again.

"And one more thing." Claudia's eyes were alight with vengeance, glowing more brightly than the flames or the blue magic she brandished. "Your demon was wrong. I am going to find the final item. And I *will* complete my trial."

Again the lovely Valentina seemed far too superior when she stared at Claudia. Leaving the door wide open, she took a step back and onto the porch. Her violet eyes lifted at the corners. Her lips pursed in a mocking pout. "Sure you will."

28

Ronja had her legs stretched out in front of her on an outdoor lounge chair and was enjoying the midnight calm. The grounds behind her rehabbed plantation home were overgrown and wild, just as she preferred them. She loved listening to the struggles of life and death, imagining the furtive actions behind every rustle of shrubbery, hearing the hunt in each night creature's call.

The fight for survival was music to her immortal ears. And, as one who couldn't die, she took a particularly perverse pleasure in sensing the loss of life. If she paid close attention, she could feel when a vital source was permanently snuffed out. The earth gave an imperceptible wail, or maybe a sigh of relief, deep in those dark, Low Country woods.

Spring peepers serenaded each other, a thousand tiny frog voices that pleased her despite their hopeful notes. With her head lolling against the cushion, she sipped her glass of *glögg*. Though the Scandinavian beverage was classically a winter drink, the taste always reminded her of home.

Brandy and red wine, sweetened with sugar, raisins, cardamom and other spices, then simmered together and served piping hot. She licked her lips then grew still, alert, listening intently when she heard a crunch in the tall grass behind the house.

The potential entertainment of a death match was interrupted when Valentina opened the screen door and joined Ronja on the darkened porch. Tyr and Scarlett slid out behind her, neither one wanting to miss out on Valentina's report.

"The witch showed up unexpectedly tonight." Valentina sat in a cushioned wicker chair, one of the few Amara members who could take the liberty of sitting in Ronja's presence without express permission or direction. "I have officially been busted."

At ease due to the soothing night sounds and the steaming *glögg*, Ronja tipped her head to the violet-eyed woman. "It doesn't really matter at this point. You did what I asked, and you performed well. We needed to divert her attention."

She saw the gleaming whites of the brunette's perfect teeth as that one smiled in the shadows. Using her glass, Ronja gestured to Tyr and Scarlett. "It's so nice to have at least one person who can get the job done. Neatly. Efficiently. And within the specified time frame."

She didn't have to look at Scarlett and Tyr to know they were uncomfortably tense, and most likely seething inside because of her back-handed rebuke. Well, she mused, let them stew.

If she didn't crave them both so much, she would have stopped sharing her blood with the pair long ago. They would have withered and died after centuries of borrowed life, leaving behind nothing more than a gleaming black mane and a ruby-hued pile of curls.

Yet they were safe, because she did feel a certain *affection* for her lovers. Truly sadistic people with their hedonistic talents didn't come along every decade. And she so enjoyed the company of those she could relate to.

But Valentina. She was a different sort of treasure. A cool and composed woman whose true gift hid behind her angelic face and alluring eyes.

Though her skills were limited, she completed a task when

one was assigned. She was reliable. A delectable treat to look at. And completely devoid of a conscience.

Thanks to the woman's work with the sexy policeman, Ronja was closer to defeating the coven than ever before. Or, at the very least, making a huge leap forward in strategy.

The door burst open as Beth pushed her head outside. "Is everything still on track? What happened?"

Waving an impatient hand, Ronja shooed the younger woman back inside. Beth closed the door but looked out through the screen. "If everything goes well this time, does that mean I still get to—"

"Yes. Yes." Ronja cut the girl off, marveling at her own tolerance for the mare, a person who could affect people's dreams. And if she so chose, turn them into real night*mares*.

The sweet-faced Beth with her big eyes was like Valentina in one way. Hidden talents behind a beguiling face. Her burgeoning lust for violence also tugged on Ronja's heartstrings, and was probably the real reason for her lenience.

"We'll talk another time, Beth. Now leave us." Ronja listened to the sound of retreating footsteps, and once satisfied the girl was gone, she set aside her glass, swung her legs to the side, and sat up.

"You've created a monster with that one," Valentina said. "And I'm not speaking metaphorically."

"Yes." Ronja gloated and actually felt a sting of pride. "Yes, I did." Her laugh was rich and throaty. "I can hardly wait to see her in action."

"But only if we succeed this time." Tyr's voice rumbled from where he stood near the door.

"We will succeed," Ronja snapped. Her mood was spoiling, and she was ready to be left alone again. But before she sent the three away, she had one last question.

Leaning forward, she impaled Valentina with her stare, as surely as a spike driven through a pumping heart. "Tell me one thing." She perceived the brunette's silent nod. "Do you think the witch suspects?"

"No, Ronja. In fact, I'm positive." Valentina flashed her teeth again in the dark. "She hasn't got a clue."

~~~

"A succubus?" Cole topped off his coffee as if the extra caffeine would help him make sense of what Claudia was explaining. She'd tried talking to him last night, but as soon as Valentina had left, Cole had succumbed to whatever dark spell the woman—succubus?—had cast on him.

"That's what she meant by suck," Claudia told him, her face grave and sober. Her gaze was rigid and unmoving. Then she hiked a questioning brow.

"Yeah." He nodded. "I mean...no. She definitely wasn't talking about..." Cole stopped bumbling and slurped some coffee. He cleared his throat. "Anyway. Moving on."

"Mm-hmm." Claudia eyed him but with a teasing grin. "Well, all the pieces fit," she said. "You had no recollection of her visits, she left you drained of energy, life force, if you will, and there's no denying what I saw."

With a shiver, she exhaled a sharp breath. "I'll never forget the way her magic looked. Pale purple and enchanting, yet somehow I knew it was harmful."

"And now we know what the mysterious Valentina actually does. Why she's with the Amara." Cole set his mug aside and moved past her to the refrigerator. He pulled out eggs, a block of cheddar, cold cuts of ham, and then he took two tomatoes from a wooden bowl on top of the fridge. "I'm starved. Mind if I cook while we talk?"

"Not at all. Especially if you're making enough for two." Leaning against the wall, since there were no cabinets, Claudia drank from her own cup.

Cole glanced aside at her and made a mental note to pick up some of the sweetened creamers she preferred. Chocolate, caramel...and had she actually asked if he had tiramisu?

Cracking the eggs into a clear glass bowl, he quirked one side of his mouth up with satisfaction. He'd make sure to stock up on whatever she requested.

Because he'd liked waking up to her lying by his side this morning, especially with the worried wrinkle on her forehead that had been so cute. She'd bitten her bottom lip before asking him how he felt, her soft hands rubbing his shoulder.

Now here they were, having a chat over coffee and breakfast. So yeah, he thought, slicing the ham and cheese with a little more zest than usual, he could find it in himself to keep some girlie creamers on hand. Whatever it took to keep her coming back.

Still, he wanted to put the seductive woman out of his mind and put the issues of her visit to bed. Ugh. He grimaced. To bed? A bad and unintended pun.

"If Valentina is part of the Amara," he said, "then she didn't do this on her own. Ronja sent her here." He dumped the ham and cheese in with the eggs, then rinsed the tomatoes before placing them on the cutting board. "So what was the goal?"

Claudia heaved a breath. "There's no point in avoiding the obvious. You're a part of my trial, and we have apparently developed a somewhat romantic interest in each other."

Cole stopped slicing and gave her a look over his shoulder. "You really know how to stroke a guy's ego." Then a wink. "But seriously, what was Valentina's motive? To distract you? Or me?"

Claudia shook her head, her long red hair swishing across her shoulder blades. "To shake me up and make me distrust you. Anything to throw me off my game and prevent me from finding Bastraal's items. That's the ultimate purpose of my challenge." Her eyes narrowed. "I'm sure of it."

"Well, she made you doubt me. That's for sure." Cole whipped the eggs and other ingredients, adding a splash of milk for fluffiness. But instead of pouring the mixture into the pan he had heating, Cole set it aside and turned to speak directly to her. "We came through all right, though. Didn't we? Here we are, making eggs and not hating each other."

She managed a smile. "No. Not hating."

"So now we have to stay focused. Find the next antique."

She nodded as she swallowed a sip. "The final item."

Surprise lit up Cole's system. "How do you know that?"

Squirming, Claudia stared into her coffee cup. "Oh, um… Bastraal might have mentioned it."

"What?" Eggs forgotten, Cole moved to her, but Claudia met him halfway and did a slick one-two move around him to pick up the bowl.

"I'll take over," she said. "Don't want you to burn our breakfast."

"Claudia." Cole's voice held a wealth of warning.

"Well, obviously I had another vision." She filled him in on the mirror and her last trip to the eighteenth century. Cole tossed in the occasional curse word when appropriate, but when she told him about the torture she'd endured, he felt every drop of blood in his body drain down to pool in his feet.

He fell silent after that but kept his eyes on her as she cooked and plated the scrambled eggs. He'd meant to make some toast, but now he couldn't find the desire.

Her right hand, she'd said. Cole stared at the smooth milky skin, grateful there was no mark carried over from the other side. He didn't think he could handle seeing evidence of her pain.

As it was, he wanted to travel there this minute and take the demon bastard on himself. But that was his male pride talking without an ounce of rationale. The last time he checked, he couldn't do her time-traveling trick.

Not being able to find the one who'd hurt her and put him down was a hot wire scraping under Cole's skin. How was a man supposed to take care of a woman when she flowed with a magic he didn't possess and chased after monsters he couldn't see?

"Ready?" Claudia's question brought him back around. She was holding out the plates, and her hesitant smile told him she was upset by the retelling of her story. He shouldn't make her think of her torment.

Cole forced a smile he didn't feel. If he couldn't pound his fists into Bastraal's face, he could at least try to ease what was left of Claudia's misery. "This looks great." Then he narrowed suspicious eyes at her. "I thought you said you couldn't cook."

She sauntered past him. "Don't is not the same as can't."

They ate on the steps of the back porch, enjoying the breeze and discussing the azaleas that bloomed along the back wall of his yard. The colorful bushes were monstrous in size, proof they'd been planted many years ago.

When the sun grew too warm, they went back inside. Claudia insisted on washing the dishes, and Cole let her, sensing she needed a bit more time before they plunged into the hunt for the final object. The very device she'd been tortured with.

Cole stared at the brass clock in his study, finally completed and reassembled. As the soft sound of ticks whispered in the quiet, he pictured the delicate balance of mechanics that lived behind the white face.

If only Claudia's trial could be pieced together as easily. Nothing the coven faced was reliable or predictable, except for the continuous thread of love that seemed to connect the women.

Cole had no argument with that, but before he could gain Claudia's full attention, she had to find the final object. That is, if the demon could even be trusted.

How could she know Bastraal had told the truth? What if it

was a trick to keep her from continuing the search? In fact, how would Claudia even know when she was finished?

He thought of her necklace, the one she never took off. Her amulet would sing, that's how she'd know.

He heard her coming down the hall and was relieved to see her determined expression instead of the wariness from before. Damn Bastraal for hurting her that way. Far worse than any human male ever could.

"Here's what I know," she said, coming to stand beside him with her business face on. "The items I've located each correspond with a quality or trait possessed by the demon. Art equals beauty or humanity, the mirror his vanity or corporeal self, and the signet ring his position of power."

She raised a shoulder and dropped it. "It's just a theory, but for now it's all I've got. I'm not sure what to do with all the antiques once I've found them, but...one step at time."

With a frown that was more irritated than worried, she said, "I don't have to guess what the torture device represents. He was an evil, sadistic monster. Still is."

Cole refrained from trying to hold her. Tenderness wasn't what she needed right now, but support was. And he could offer that. As much as she wanted or required. "Let me show you the diagrams I made. That's how I found the mirror."

She nodded with enthusiasm. "Great. I'm ready to put an end to this." Her eyes tapered into slits. "I can't wait to strike back at Bastraal. To destroy him. I'm not sure I'll be the one to have the pleasure, but I'll be there cheering whenever one of us finally takes him down for good. No banishment this time." Her shoulders tensed. "But eradication."

The expression on her fine-boned face, the thousand-yard stare—these things transformed Claudia, and a jolt of awe raced through Cole. She was a little bit scary.

He guided her to the desk and spread the charts across the top, explaining his method of tracking items from their current locations back to the places they'd been before. Then he pointed out the original stash that had been sold from Bastraal's estate.

"There it is." She tapped a finger on the description of 'metal glove with spikes.' "How far did you track it forward, or have you done so yet?"

"The glove traveled in sync with the mirror, bought and sold until coming to rest with one man who had the items for years. His daughter inherited, then sold the mirror to the local dealer."

"Who later sold it to the antique store where I found it." She shook her head. "I bet she's the one who painted the mirror black and silver. Wonder what she did with the...the glove."

Cole silently instructed himself to continue on in a straightforward manner. Level-headed and distant, to keep her detached from the disturbing memories their discussion of the device might trigger. "I should be able to get a line on the item. I'll contact the woman and find out what happened to this piece."

"It's okay. You can call it the glove." She ran a hand through her fiery hair, a nervous gesture he'd never seen before. "It's as good a name as any."

Cole didn't respond but picked up the notepad lying on his desk. Better to keep moving and get past this part of the trial. He looked up the woman's contact information. "Could you make another pot of coffee while I make the call?"

"Sure." Claudia's shoulders sagged as they relaxed again, and she seemed glad to have a task set for her. Something to keep her mind occupied.

Which was exactly what he'd hoped for.

By the time she returned with two steaming cups, Cole had the answer they needed. "That was easier than I expected. She remembered exactly who'd purchased the glove." He took the coffee when she offered it. "Thanks." He sipped. "I'm afraid I know the woman who bought it too, and she might prove to be difficult."

"How so?" Her ginger brows beetled.

"She's a collector in the truest sense, like Mr. Clermont." When she only continued to stare at him, Cole added, "She prefers not to let go of her prizes once they've been acquired."

"But she'll have to, and I'll make sure she does."

"Correction. *We* will make sure." Cole sat on the edge of his desk and pinned her with a look that dared her to argue. "I've been involved every other time, and if you're truly coming to the end of all this, you can't leave me out now."

"True," she relented, her expression unreadable.

Cole knew of this collector, and there was no way Claudia was going in alone. Not because the woman was dangerous, but because Claudia wouldn't know how to make her give up the glove.

But Cole did.

"Besides, I already let her know we were coming." He tried to lighten the mood. "And despite all your talk and swagger, you're going to need me."

Claudia began to speak, paused as her mouth fell open, then, "I have swagger?"

He chuckled into his mug before drinking. "And then some."

"I was going to agree with you anyway. You should go with me. It's pretty clear that you and I are...that we're..."

Cole watched as her cheeks flamed pink, as her eyes clouded with angst. Crossing his arms over his chest, he grinned, musing over how beautiful she was when flustered. Just as she was when she got all fired up and righteous.

She was beautiful no matter what she did. To him, at least.

Because he loved her.

And he decided to interrupt her stammering to tell her so. "You're a complicated woman, Claudia."

"Not really, I—"

"And I'm a simple man, so I'm just going to put it out there."

He stood where he was—no touching, no kissing—simply the facts. That way her skeptical mind would know he wasn't being swayed by anything physical.

He studied her face as puzzlement and uncertainty took turns. He felt his eyes soften and his insides melt. "I'm falling in love with you," he said candidly. "No." He rescinded the statement. No stutter steps or half-attempts. "That's not right."

She stood frozen. "It isn't?"

"No, it's not. I'm no longer falling." He sipped his coffee again, casually, no pressure or anxiety that might send her skittering away. "I am *in love* with you."

"Whoa. Wait." Claudia held up her hands, trying to block the words. Cole had thought she'd been flustered before, but that was nothing compared to what he read in her body language now.

The pulse in her neck throbbed visibly, her pupils dilated, and her breathing hitched.

"I know that scares you," he said, "but you appreciate honesty, remember?" He wanted so badly to touch her face, to take her in his arms, to calm her racing heart. But he would stick to his rules. No more kissing or any other sexual behavior until she adjusted to the idea.

Until she was able to say the same thing to him. That she loved him.

"Yes, I do value honesty." She swallowed. "Especially after what's happened, even though you weren't at fault." She closed her eyes and blew out as if through a straw, then set her cup on his desk with a solid *clunk*.

Straightening her shoulders, she layered on some courage and met his eyes. "I can't seem to keep up with you. I mean, I just got comfortable with our mixing sex and camaraderie together. And now you're leaps and bounds ahead of me again."

She spread her hands, unable to contain her anxiety. "Cole, you're in an all-out sprint."

"And you're a marathoner. I know. But that's okay. I can wait for you." He grasped her hands and held on, forcing her closer to him.

He didn't let go until her pretty eyes settled on his. "Claudia," he whispered intently. "I can wait for you." She trembled in his grasp, and he sensed she was balancing on a very thin line.

He didn't want to influence her either way or add pressure to an already strained situation. "I don't need you to say anything. Not until you're ready."

He picked up her coffee and placed the cup in her hands, wrapping her fingers around the warm ceramic. "Now go on and stop worrying so much."

"Go where?"

"We need to get cleaned up and leave for our meeting. One step at a time, you said." He took her by the shoulders and turned her toward the door. "And our next step is to get that glove."

She just stood there, unmoving, and Cole could tell she was numb from his admission. So he slapped her on her backside to fire her back to life.

"What?" she asked, eyes still unfocused when he took her hand and tugged her into the hallway.

Cole gestured with his hand to get her moving. "You can have the first shower."

"Yes. Right." She shuffled away like a zombie, and Cole couldn't contain his roguish grin. He rather liked a surprised and unsettled Claudia.

When she turned the corner and looked back at him, he waggled his fingers. "Go ahead," he called, chuckling as she nodded slowly and trudged onward.

Once she'd gone, he finally let his love for her expand inside. He allowed it to fill him up and show in his eyes. Now that she couldn't see it and wouldn't freak out. "I'll be here," he said to the empty corridor, then he went back into the study for his coffee.

With his lips stretched in a grin that wouldn't die, he leaned against his desk and looked out the window. The day was going to be sunny and warm. "Take your time." Again he spoke to the empty space, but in his mind he pictured Claudia. "I can wait."

29

Claudia was still in a daze when Cole jerked his car into the first available parking spot. They'd traversed almost twenty blocks to reach Bay Street, but she was going to need a lot more time than that before she felt settled again. She couldn't seem to find her balance in this tilted and unfamiliar world.

Cole had told her he loved her. And the three simple words had changed everything.

Her logical brain and swooning emotions were shooting back and forth at each other like rifles in a Civil War skirmish. She no longer had any valid reason to mistrust him, and all the suspicions she'd been mired down in had been proven false.

He'd been reliable at every turn, dedicated to helping her get what she wanted, and ready to show her friendship and affection as needed. But she just couldn't let go of the doubt. Her fear of heartbreak had been ingrained for too long.

To compound matters, she still got that sinking in her belly whenever she remembered walking in on Cole and Valentina. He'd been without fault, and even while under the succubus' spell, they'd never been…they'd never done…

She clenched her eyes and channeled calm.

They'd never been together sexually. Valentina didn't crave that type of energy.

The only charge the succubus had been after was the one that came from draining Cole's vitality. His strength and stamina. But Valentina was naturally sensual, and she'd employed every one of her skills to get to the man Claudia wanted.

She cast her eyes to the side, drinking in his handsome profile. So rugged and fierce, yet sensitive and patient. A delicate balance that few men were able to manage. But love? *No. No. I'm not comfortable with that yet. Not yet.*

Her hand tightened on the edge of the car seat as she pictured Valentina's lingerie again. The jealousy—and she wasn't ashamed to call it what it was—jabbed into her and made her feel like molten lead had been poured into her stomach every time she envisioned that moment. When she'd seen Cole straddled and bewitched by another woman.

He'd played no part in it, she reminded herself again. He couldn't even remember the times Valentina had visited him. She fumed as she thought of that bitch's treachery. How she'd used Cole to get to her, driving a wedge between them.

But hadn't Claudia tried to keep herself apart from him as well? For her own reasons?

She focused on the anger instead of her own guilt. Cole hadn't deserved the poor treatment he'd received. He'd only been trying to help, and in return he'd just been used.

By Claudia as much as the succubus? Were they essentially the same in that regard?

No. Her nails curled into her palms. At least Claudia cared for Cole, she thought, sniffing with disdain. And she had much better fashion sense.

"That building there," Cole said, jerking her out of her vengeful fantasies. He pointed through his window and turned off the car. He exited on his side, prompting Claudia to disembark as well, then he went to the trunk and brought out a black duffel bag.

Good, Claudia mused. She was glad he'd thought of it. They

could transport the metal glove in the bag, and she wouldn't
have to look at it for long. That was Cole. Always thinking
ahead.

In silence, they crossed when the traffic light allowed and
followed the sidewalk toward the river. The ground was shaded
by thick and winding oak tree limbs. Dangling Spanish moss
moved with the wind, creating shadows that danced across the
grass and cement.

Drawing closer to the brick building—once a thriving cotton
exchange—she was struck by the beauty of an intricate black
fence and the fountain it encircled. The water feature was
brick-red, color-coordinated with the building it fronted, and
boasted a grim-faced lion with wings.

"She lives here?" She cast her eyes to the three-storied
structure. Who was this woman? Another old Savannahian?

"Top floor." As if hearing her questions by psychic link, Cole
explained, "Most local collectors have money, since these types
of acquisitions can make for an expensive hobby."

"So I've learned." Choosing to set aside her concerns about
Cole for now so she could concentrate on the deal they were
here to make, Claudia followed him to the front doors. Inside,
the air-conditioning created a wall of cold air that collapsed
onto her bare shoulders. They went to the elevator, and Cole
punched the call button.

On the third floor, they stepped off into a small lobby area.
Claudia estimated the space was only five by ten feet or so,
but the shiny gray tiles on the floor looked expensive. Directly
across from the elevator was a door, but one created for the
exterior of a home. For extra security.

Cole rang the doorbell, and within seconds, an attractive
blonde woman opened the door and offered them a nervous
smile in welcome. No butlers in residence, it seemed. "Detective
Lonergan. Ms. Grant."

Claudia inclined her head in response.

"Thanks for having us on such short notice, Ms. Lang." Cole held out his hand, so Claudia entered before him.

"I've already retrieved the artifact you requested from my safe room. If you'll come this way." Ms. Lang was dressed nicely, wearing cream-colored slacks and a pale yellow blouse of breezy chiffon. "I'll admit I'm a bit worried that you requested this meeting."

Cole remained stoic, offering no reply.

"Would you like a drink?" Ms. Lang stopped mid-stride, as if just remembering her manners.

"No, thank you," Cole said with a strained smile.

The living room where the woman led them was a mixture of exposed brick and ivory walls, with furniture and lamps in the same milk-white palette. Patches of color were found in rugs and large potted plants, but no additional adornment was required for this space.

The bank of windows down the main wall framed a gorgeous view of the Savannah River, as well as the green and brown marshland farther beyond. No photograph or wall art could begin to compete with the amazing vista.

But there was no time to appreciate the surroundings as Ms. Lang went straight to a plain wooden box and offered it to Cole. Her features creased when she asked, "Do you think this was used in a crime?"

Cole set his black duffel down to accept the box with a straight face. "Without a doubt, but nothing recent enough for the police to pursue."

"Then why is it so important? Crucial, you said."

He lifted his dark brows. "If you don't mind, I'll take a look first and make sure it's the right piece." He took a deep breath, and Claudia mimicked him as she waited for him to open the box.

She didn't relish the thought of seeing the spiked hand press again, and knowing she would have to touch it made her positively queasy. She rubbed her right hand absentmindedly when Cole lifted the lid.

After a meaningful moment of scrutiny, he stepped over to Claudia, angling his hold on the box and letting her see inside.

Faintness washed over her. "That's it." She backed away and sat in a chair without invitation, but Ms. Lang didn't notice. She was still too concerned with Cole and his interest in the metal glove.

"That's what? What do you know?" The woman wrung her hands.

"I'm sorry, but I can't share the details of this article's past. All I can say is that we have to have it." Cole's tone was unyielding, but Ms. Lang showed the barest hint of surprise.

Her lips crushed together, considering. "What will you offer in trade? This is a very unique relic. Old, from Savannah, and a custom-made piece."

Claudia sat in stunned silence. They were bartering? No discussion, just straight to the terms. Why hadn't Cole just tried to buy it? "We can pay," she interjected.

Ms. Lang held up a hand to wave the offer aside, her eyes never leaving Cole. He also ignored Claudia, so she sat back with a huff.

Cole knows what he's doing. And I owe him some trust. After her internal reprimand, she crossed her legs and chose to remain mute. She gave Cole his lead, observing the odd transaction with guarded interest.

Placing the box on an end table, Cole kneeled and opened the duffel. He extracted another box, although this one was newer. He opened the front to reveal a towel that swaddled and protected the contents. Then he pulled the material aside.

Claudia bolted upright when she saw the clock. "Cole. No." She stepped forward. You can't trade that. You've worked so hard on it."

He offered the box to Ms. Lang for inspection. "I can get

another."

"Not like this one, you can't." The blonde woman's eyes gleamed. "Don't you know what you've got here? This is an authentic—"

"I know what it is, and obviously, so do you. Then you also realize its value meets or exceeds that of your own artifact."

"Yes. More than."

Cole stood motionless. "We have a trade, then?"

"Wait," Claudia said, growing more alarmed with every word. This was moving too quickly. "Let's just take a moment." But the other two continued to act as if she wasn't even there.

"I would be a fool to refuse." Ms. Lang gave Cole a sideways smile. "But you knew that when you brought it here, didn't you?" In a flash, her expression turned doubtful. "You aren't going to want this back, are you?"

Cole paused, but the hesitation was long enough for Claudia to grasp its underlying sentiment. He didn't want to give up the clock.

"Cole," she said softly.

"No." His light green eyes hardened, telling her not to argue. He stuck out his hand.

Sparing no second for reconsideration on the side of either party, the woman grasped and shook.

The deal was done.

"I don't know what's so important about that thing." Ms. Lang's eyes flitted to the box that held the iron hand press as Cole set it carefully inside his duffel. "But I wish you good luck." She turned to Claudia then, a quizzical expression in place. "To both of you."

"Thank you." Claudia's answer was just above a whisper, her breath stolen by Cole's charity and sacrifice.

Again, the kind Ms. Lang offered them a drink, but they politely declined and were gone from the top floor condo before Claudia could gather her wits.

Once the elevator doors closed, she turned to Cole. "I don't know what to say. I wish you'd told me. We could have come up with another way."

"This was the only way. Neither of us owns anything she would have traded for, except maybe Bastraal's other items." He shrugged. "And we need those just as much."

She reached out and took his fingers in hers. Conflicting desires reared up and clashed in battle. But her romantic side had finally gained some ground. Her heart might possibly be winning.

But she still hadn't conquered her fear. She couldn't yet give him what he wanted, so she offered him a simple truth in its place. "I don't deserve you."

Cole closed his eyes, and after a moment, his strained face softened. He angled toward her to touch her cheek. "Claudia, you deserve everything. It's about time you realized that."

The elevator chimed and the doors slid open, cutting into their tender exchange. Neither of them had more words or admissions, so together they stepped out and walked across the lobby, then exited into the warm Savannah sunshine.

~~~

The first to greet Claudia and Cole as they entered the foyer of the island mansion was her cat, Ashbi. She held her hand down to scratch his head, but he was more interested in the duffel Cole still carried.

Ashbi sniffed at the bag, and then he pulled back sharply, his pink nose twitching. He walked backward on all fours before turning to dash through the great room.

"He certainly doesn't like what's in here." Cole jostled the bag as he stared after the cat.

"Felines are very intuitive. He's probably just picking up on the scents you and I have produced." Claudia tried to ignore the crawling sense of dread. "Cats read smells like we see pictures."

"So there's no way your cat could know what's in this duffel." Cole's statement half-sounded like a question.

She lifted a shoulder. "At this point, I'm not comfortable with any definitive statement."

Anna was lounging on the green velvet sofa in the great room, but she lowered the book she was reading when Claudia and Cole entered. Her eyes fell to the bag with dread. "You found it."

"We found it." Again chills raced through Claudia. Was everyone—including the animals—going to have this reaction to the torture device? If so, she'd prefer to tell them all at once.

Anna looked just as Ashbi had. Like a ghost had just trailed a cool hand down their backs.

"I'd like to take care of this tonight," Claudia said, confident her friend would understand. She was ready to see what the next—and hopefully final—vision would reveal.

"I want to stay." Cole's eyes were fixed on Claudia. "I can't go with you into the past, but..." His temple ticked with repressed anger.

Without thinking, she took his hand. "I'd like that." Then, in an attempt to downplay the roiling fear in her gut, she said, "I think you've earned a front row seat to the big finale."

Anna stood, closing her paperback and holding it to her abdomen. "You believe this is it? That whatever you...see tonight will complete your challenge?"

Something in the coven leader's hesitancy caused Claudia's heart to kick ferociously for several beats before settling back down to a normal rate. Did Anna sense something? If so, why wasn't she telling her?

Then Claudia recalled her friend's previous concern about sharing her prophetic insights before she was sure of them. Sometimes she needed the coven's help in figuring out one of her visions, as they often came in the form of riddles.

But other times, she feared her insight might alter the natural course of events. That pre-conceived knowledge would affect how her friends might behave, thereby disrupting what was actually meant to be.

Claudia could rest assured her strange visits to the past would soon return to the enjoyable, benign normalcy they used to have. Normal for her, anyway.

But Anna? Claudia studied her friend's serene expression. How had she maintained her sanity? Always getting glimpses of the future, but in convoluted images that may or may not even come true?

"Should I be worried?" Claudia asked suddenly.

Anna's face seemed made of stone, but her eyes were calm. "Shouldn't we always?"

"Wonderful. A cryptic question to answer my question." Claudia looked down at the black duffel Cole held, then his gaze followed hers.

"The danger is inherent. You've seen that for yourself." Anna sighed. "I also get the feeling tonight will be portentous. I just don't know why or how."

Cole's fingers tightened around Claudia's. He glanced to Anna. "So you're worried too?"

Anna folded her hands into a ball. "I'm not sure worry is the right word, but I feel..."

"Prickly," Claudia supplied. "So do I."

Anna nodded. "We have dinner planned, so let's rest for an hour or so, eat, and restore our energy. Then we'll be ready." She pointed to the duffel. "Why don't you take that to Quinn? He'll secure it."

"Fine." Cole turned to Claudia as Anna left them to walk toward the staircase. "I'll be here," he said, his voice conveying his will and determination to keep Claudia safe. To be there for her, no matter what happened.

Still holding his hand, Claudia offered a small smile of thanks. "Right where you're meant to be."

30

Sconces and candles illuminated the great room when Claudia entered, but tonight their flickering glow seemed ominous. She'd come to commune with history, with a past that had become far too real for her. And too menacing.

Bastraal had inflicted great pain on her during her last visit, and had been outraged by her escape. She stiffened when she thought of the black mists that had flowed from his mouth. And the horrid buzz she'd heard, like a million malevolent gnats.

Despite the bravado she was grappling to maintain, she paused in her steps. She shuddered.

What would the monster do to her this time? If she had truly found the final piece to her puzzle, perhaps the better question was…what *wouldn't* he do?

When Cole passed by she flinched, but he didn't notice and went straight to his black duffel. The bag sat on the dais in the back of the dome-like room, encircled by chunks of striped green malachite.

The green rocks were intended to block evil, and interspersed between them was a different mineral. Smooth brown stones with naturally-occurring black crosses in their centers. Chiastolite, Anna had called them. For psychic protection.

And for grounding.

The Chiastolite was an extra safeguard to keep her essence from being separated from her body. But the precaution terrified Claudia even more than the idea of being tortured again. Brutalization at the hands of the demon would undoubtedly be horrific.

But ending up trapped in the other world and tormented for eternity? That was enough to make her fortitude shrivel up and die.

Cole removed the box from the duffel and held it while the other women formed a circle, and he waited as the cats took up their posts behind each witch. He and Quinn were the only men in the room, though Trevor, Dare, and even Michael and Nick were waiting elsewhere in the grand house.

Claudia shook her hands and blew out through her lips, exhaling as many of her jangling nerves as she could. When she was settled as much as possible, she caught Cole's eye and nodded. "I'm ready."

Having already removed the spiked metal glove, he approached the white altar and set the device on top. With one last look of affection, he gave her a bolstering grin and stepped away from the circle to stand with Quinn.

None of her friends spoke, each one somber and weighted by the same trepidation she was experiencing. There was more to their dread than the sight of the hateful glove. The chance that she was about to finish her trial should have cheered them all. The potential triumph should have increased their morale.

But instead of eager smiles, there was an undercurrent of disharmony. The vibration that ran through the women when they all came together was off-kilter, unnaturally strained, and discordant.

When Claudia looked to each of her sisters, she could tell they all felt the same tension. But none of them could name the source.

Even the cats were more engaged than the last time,

watchful and on guard, aware of every movement in the room. She'd come to trust an animal's sixth sense, and tonight the feline guardians of the underworld were on tenterhooks.

Their vigilance shook Claudia to the core.

Taking a final breath, she stepped forward. Delaying the inevitable would only increase her anxiety, and she already had enough reasons to dread the looming vision.

Who wouldn't be intimidated, after what she'd been put through? But this was no time for cowardice or second-guessing. She knew what had to be done, and she was prepared.

Glaring at the metal glove, she let herself remember the awful pain it had caused. She embraced the horror and recalled the stench of her own fear. Then she channeled all of her rage and wrapped it around the memories, crushing them into oblivion.

This was her trial, and she would be the one in control. Not the demon and the putrid seeds of terror he'd planted.

She put both hands on the spiked glove and lifted it, ready for her final task.

But after several seconds, she found herself still looking at Anna and the back curve of the coven's circle. She was still in the great room. Nothing had happened.

"I don't understand." As if she could just reboot the process, Claudia laid the glove back on the marble altar, counted off three seconds, and tried again. Nothing. No vibe, no whirling void, no vertigo of any kind.

She saw Kylie and Paige glance at each other with furrowed brows, and like them, she was thoroughly confused. Talk about anti-climactic.

Viv spoke suddenly. "It's the final piece."

Pivoting her head to the Asian physicist, Claudia listened carefully to the woman who excelled at discoveries and breakthroughs.

"You told us your theory," Viv continued, "about each item

representing a part of Bastraal. Now you have them all."

The proverbial light dawned on Claudia. "Of course. Each antique led me to the next, because they were all meant to be together."

Claudia's chest expanded and air whooshed from her lungs. Yet the hype of adrenaline still pumped through her veins. "Quinn, could you set the others up here in the middle? I'll hold the glove and add it last." She retreated several steps from the altar.

The first item to be added was the huge mirror. Cole and Quinn propped it against the front of the altar and to the side. Then Quinn carried over the pocket watch and signet ring to place atop the cool white marble. Cole came behind him with the painting he'd helped Claudia win at the benefit gala.

Once the antiques were in place, Claudia shot a glance to Cole and Anna. She eased forward to place the glove in the middle, between the watch and portrait.

As soon as she set the glove down, the earth seemed to crumble, dropping from beneath her.

The vacuous tunnel she normally traveled through began to open up all around her, but she could still see her sisters and the curving stone walls of the great room behind them. She hadn't gone anywhere, but she was linked to the other plane of existence.

Disoriented by the colliding realities, she called Anna's name. Her friend only stared into the center of the circle, focused and meditative, like all of the other witches.

No one seemed disturbed at all. No one could see or hear her.

Shaking her head, Claudia put her hands out to wave them around in the darkness of the tunnel. Instead of holding firm, the walls spread like a dense fog, shifting and swirling. And enlarging. The walls thickened until she was only able to catch an occasional glimpse of her friends.

Soon the rest of the room was blocked out by the haze,

leaving her cut off from her circle, bewildered. And increasingly alarmed.

But it was the figure stepping through the mists that caused a ripple over her skin, a cold so intense it struck all the way to her bones. Caused her hands to shake.

Bastraal was with her. But how? Why here?

Where the hell was here?

The demon tilted his head to the side, then a malevolent smile formed on his full lips. The outer shell was dignified, handsome even. But she knew firsthand what depravity lurked beneath. "There you are." He lifted a finger. Twirled it in her direction. "My Claudia."

The possessive endearment had her spine snapping back into place and fire raging in her belly. "No, Bastraal. Never yours."

"No?" The demon began to circle her and with each step he took, Claudia turned in time with him, always keeping him in her sight. The filmy wall of darkness still dipped and spun around them. "You and I are eternally connected." His coal-dark eyes burned, as if hiding a dirty secret.

"I feel no connection to you." She practically jerked to one side when he tried to touch her. Her voice was a snarl of derision. "And you will have no eternity. My coven will make sure of that."

"Oh, but I will." He moved so swiftly then, swiping his fingers through her hair. She whirled but he had already shifted back to her other side. His speed was incomprehensible. "I will." He leered at her. "Thanks to you."

"I don't know what you're trying to do, Bastraal, but I won't fall for your lies. Not again." She glanced aside as the black cleared long enough for her to see Cole and Quinn. They stood back from the circle of witches. Still watching. Tense, but not affected.

They didn't know she was trapped inside a vortex. With the

demon.

"My lies?" Bastraal echoed her as he waved a hand to the tall mirror. Its center reflected the rushing walls around them, and her face when she turned to stare into it. But then the surface blurred, revealing an image she'd seen once before.

Like an eerie movie screen, the mirror played the movie reel of Cole and Valentina.

Jealousy flared briefly but was extinguished by stronger sentiments. Wrath. Protectiveness. The desire for revenge.

Valentina wasn't here, so Claudia directed her hate at the only available target. The deceptive demon. "I know the truth now, Bastraal. Cole never lied to me." Anger renewed itself as she thought of how suspicious she'd been. How hurt.

In response to the blast of emotion, her power sparked to life. A trickle of the cool blue magic flowed through her arms. "You and your succubus tried to stop me, using my own deep-rooted fears about men. About love."

Her palms began to burn like ice. "But you failed." She threw back her head and pierced the demon with her glare. "I love Cole, and he loves me."

The words sent wonder and revelation shooting through her, even more potent than the mystical power she wielded. The glory of truth shone inside, lighting up her previous denial like a spotlight.

She did love Cole, so much. And she was no longer afraid.

"Even if you kill me, you'll never change that. *I love Cole.*" She said it again. Because it felt so damn good.

The blue glow in her hands caught her attention then. Raising them to her line of sight, she felt the first creeping sense of dread. She shouldn't be able to call her magic. Not if she was in the past.

"Kill you?" Bastraal drawled. "No. Not now." His voice began to deepen, rattling with a strange vibration. "After you've served me so well."

What was he talking about? Claudia's mind was torn between what he was saying and her worry over what was happening. She could still see snatches of reality through gaps in the rotating haze, faces of the people she loved.

"What is this?" Her throat felt like it was the size of a straw. The attempt to speak wheezed from her mouth. "Where are we?" she demanded in a stronger tone.

Bastraal's voice had doubled a hundred times over. She heard legions of unclean souls when he answered her. "We are together." His face began to morph, as if the bones beneath his flesh were enlarging. His brow grew heavier, more pronounced, deepening the shadows of his eye sockets.

His flesh darkened to a roughened brown, like cooked meat, and his eyes were fully black. She saw a tiny speck of herself cast back from the soulless depths. *Why is he changing? Where are we?*

His clothes began to shred as his body grew. "I have come to you, Claudia." His mouth spread wide in a smile that bared sharp teeth. "Because you called me." He laughed and the voices laughed with him. "You summoned me."

"No! You're lying!" Claudia shook her head back and forth, so violently her vertebrae spiked with pain. "This wasn't supposed to happen!"

As she watched, his skin began to crack. The vortex around her spun faster and faster and, as it did, the force of the winds scraped pieces of Bastraal's flaking flesh from his bones.

Suddenly, raised voices carried to her through the twisting walls. Alarm. Fear. Could her coven see the funnel?

What was left of Bastraal began to fragment into tiny dark specks, just like the spew she'd seen coming from his mouth. His body was dissipating, the filthy skin dissolving into particles that were lost in the rushing storm.

"Claudia!" Cole was calling for her now, but she couldn't tell where he was. She didn't know what to do.

The demon was almost gone, and as he vanished, the winds accelerated and began to wail and scream. She could see larger strips of her world through the streaking black. She caught Cole's anguished face on one pass.

Bastraal had almost disintegrated completely, so she threw herself into the churning mass. She tried to escape, but the force of the spin tossed her back.

Bastraal's voice called out to her, but no humanity remained. All she heard was the forgotten tongue of ancient devils. The dissonance reverberated around her, through her, penetrating her ear canals.

She screamed her fury and shame as she attempted to push through the wall again. She'd been used. Manipulated. Deceived. And she'd set that monster free.

What have I done? Oh, God. What have I done?

Standing with her hands clapped over her ears, she fought back tears of despair. She had to get out. She had to warn the others.

Leaning into the winds, she made her way to the spinning wall. She struggled to hold her ground, then shoved an arm through.

A strong hand clamped down on her wrist. She could feel the heat of his fingers just before he yanked her to the other side. Tumbling through the vapors, she let Cole guide her and fell with him to the floor.

Hands brushed her hair from her face. "Are you hurt?" His frantic eyes raked her from head to toe.

"No. I'm okay." *But I'm not.* "Cole." A sob burst from deep inside. "I've made a horrible mistake."

"What is it? What's wrong?" He held her close, cradling her. The women all rushed to them, each with their own questions, but Claudia could only clutch the front of Cole's shirt. How could she tell her sisters what she'd done?

A subtle sound began to hum then, so faint she barely picked up on it. Soon it expanded into a clean, strong note, like a finger rimming the edge of the purest crystal.

She grasped her amulet and closed her eyes, absorbing the sweet, sweet sound. But the song that should have filled her with joy left her feeling hollow instead. Gutted and thrown aside, because she'd served an awful purpose.

"What is that?" Kylie screamed as the soot-like mass continued to roar and spin.

Claudia grabbed onto Cole's forearms and climbed to her feet. She stared into the dark whirlwinds, wondering where Bastraal had gone. What he would do next.

"Cuileann!" Shauni cried out, staring at her cat with frantic eyes. They all turned to the animal-whisperer as she screamed again. What had she heard in the feline's mind?

Claudia looked to find Ashbi aligned with the other cats, his back arched and fangs bared. Their circle still held, and their eyes were focused like lasers.

Anna jerked her head to lock her gaze with Claudia's. Her face crumpled into grief when she yelled, "I'm so sorry!"

Just as all of the cats leapt into the swirling black.

31

Anna gripped Claudia's arm. "I didn't know this would happen. I'm so sorry."

"Sorry for what?" Lucia leaned closer to speak to them over the howling winds still churning at a frenzied pace. The spine-scraping sound of angry, fighting cats made the Spanish witch jump and clutch a hand to her chest. "*Dios!*" She yelled now to be heard. "Are they okay? What are they doing?"

"Their jobs," Quinn said loudly. But his brow was wrinkled with concern as he too looked into the whirlwinds where a deafening moan intermingled with snarls.

"I didn't know," Anna said again, and the pain in her wretched expression broke through Claudia's own self-loathing. "Anna. It's not your fault."

"It's not yours either." The coven's leader drew herself up and tightened her hands on Claudia's arm. "You did what you were supposed to do. Don't forget that."

Unable to form any words of agreement, Claudia nodded and bit her lip. She would try, but there was no changing the fact that she'd released their most feared enemy into this world. She had set him loose on innocent people. On her friends and loved ones.

Her stomach twisted when she heard a raging scream that

sounded like Ashbi. And what about her cat? He was fighting for her now. For all of them. *Please let him be okay.*

She didn't know if her plea had been answered, but abruptly the churning dark mass began to lighten, changing to gray. The spinning slowed gradually as the noise quieted, and soon she was able to see inside the strange tunnel-turned-tornado.

A flash of orange sprung from the center and over to where the women stood. Kiko went to Viv and stood next to her ankles. The staid scientist dropped to stroke his side, crooning her concern and love.

The foggy vapors were almost completely transparent now, and then in a wink they were gone, leaving the felines exposed. A few of them looked worse for wear.

Ashbi stood proudly in the center, his dark stripes gleaming along his sides and white chest bowed from the battle surge. Claudia allowed relief to rush in, but the absence of the tunnel didn't mean the threat was gone.

"Now that we can hear each other, tell us what happened." Paige had Tiger-Lily in her arms. The small brindled female had a bloody scratch on her ear, but she seemed oblivious to the wound. Another battle scar for the soldier's little soldier.

"It's Bastraal." Claudia spit the words out. "He's here. He's out." She was grateful Anna still held onto her. Her sister's support helped force what she had to say next. "I set him free by bringing all of his things together. They did represent parts of him, and I..."

She took a breath, steadied herself. "I summoned him."

Hayden gasped. "Have we lost? Is it over?"

"No," Anna said firmly. "I didn't see this coming, but it makes sense."

"How?" Cole asked just as Kylie screamed. "Willyn!" Her hazel eyes were wide with fear. "Help her. Sassy's hurt."

The healer rushed to where Kylie kneeled by her cat. Long blonde hair was matted with blood. Three crimson slashes oozed.

The coals started burning in Claudia's gut again. *Bastraal.*

The demon's handiwork was all around them. Commotion. Injuries. Turmoil. She looked again to Sassy as she lay still. Too still.

She could add grief to that mix as well. Sadness so deep that it rolled straight into righteous fury.

One of the golden legs kicked then, and Kylie collapsed into tears as Willyn hugged her. Their gentle nurse had worked her magic, and it looked like Sassy would recover.

"He's still here," Claudia said gravely, warning the others to stay calm and aware.

Just then the door leading to the main house flung open, its aged wood slamming against the stone wall. Everyone jolted.

"Was that—" Lucia began, but she was startled when her own Iris hissed and darted toward the open door. One by one the other cats followed. Tiger jumped from Paige's arm, making her call out after the feline.

The only one who didn't bolt was Sassy. Willyn had her hands on the cat, but her sky blue eyes were aimed at Claudia and the rest of the coven. "What's going on?"

Beneath her palms, Sassy rose unsteadily and started walking, despite Kylie's hand on her back trying to hold her. With her strength back in full force and apparently healed, Sassy bolted, heading for the fray.

"Let's go," Claudia said, wise enough to follow the creatures who'd just jumped into Hell and tangled with the devil. She might not be able to see the bastard, but his ability to do harm was absolute.

Willyn and Kylie stood as the witches passed through the grand hall. "It's Bastraal," Paige told them in a short, no-details clip of words. But enough comprehension filled Willyn to send her flying out the door ahead of the others.

Claudia didn't have to wonder where she was going. Her

husband and child were out there, somewhere in the mansion.

And so was the demon.

The rest of them all ran down the hall to the great room, and Claudia noted Cole was right at her side. He gave her a rigid stare. "I'm with you. No arguments."

She thought of the defiant declaration she'd thrown at Bastraal's feet. She'd been trapped in a maelstrom with a powerful and supernatural entity, and the one thing she'd wanted this world to know before she left it...was that she loved Cole Lonergan.

If fear for her friends and the blameless population of Savannah wasn't forefront in her mind, she'd pull him aside and tell him this minute. She'd show him.

But the beast was in their home, the coven's most protected place, and she'd been the one to put him there. Prophesied or not, she still felt responsible for the outcome.

The vast open area of the great room was dark when they all rushed in. High above them pale beams of moonlight streamed through windows, but not enough to light the area.

Michael and Ethan were both standing in front of the couch. Their eyes darted, and each wore an expression of puzzlement. "The lights just went out," Michael said, moving to Shauni.

The raven-haired witch put a hand on her boyfriend's shoulder, as if to confirm he was unharmed. "Where's Willyn?" she asked.

"She ran upstairs, but Dare had already gone up to check on Tadd. As soon as the lights went out." Michael's face turned grim. "Why are all of you that color?" He was an empath and was reading the witches' moods.

Claudia was sure she was a nasty mix of deep blue fear and uncertainty combined with scarlet rage.

Quinn's deep voice rumbled in the dark. "*Illuminaria.*" Throughout the area, candles flickered to life.

"Quinn," Viv muttered. "You've been holding out on us."

Kylie twisted her mouth to one side. "I'll do you one better." She went across the room and through a door that led to the lower level. Sassy darted to the door as it was closing, but she was too late to squeeze through.

She wailed to the other humans to let her in, wanting to go after Kylie.

"He's a demon." Paige was standing with her fists hanging by her sides. "Maybe our magic will work on him."

"We can't fire if we can't see him," Viv replied.

"You better fill us in," Ethan said. He took up post next to Lucia, just as the Spanish woman's cat returned to circle around her feet.

Lucia spoke softly. "Bastraal is here."

"Ethan, could you see him?" Claudia hoped the demonologist's ability to see underworld creatures might still be in play.

"No." His jaw was tight. "I was up as soon as the door slammed open. If he was coming down that corridor, then I didn't see him. I didn't see anything."

The electricity popped back on then, blinding them all with the sudden brightness. Kylie had used her special talent to juice the system.

Now that they could take a better look, they spread out and watched for any signs of movement. Claudia noticed the cats were each aligning with their witches. Ashbi patrolled with her and Cole now, and Cuileann scouted near Shauni and Michael.

All eyes—human and feline—scoured the mansion for signs of activity.

Willyn and Dare leaned over the railing to look down from the upper level walkway. They didn't speak but moved stealthily down the balcony toward the stairs. Dare held a sleeping Tadd in his arms, the small boy's light blonde head resting on his stepfather's shoulder.

Kylie returned from downstairs and Sassy leapt to put her front paws on the young woman's thigh. She meowed in reprimand for having been left behind.

A loud "*Oof!*" and a thud of body against wood made them all look upward. Dare was leaning his shoulder against the wall but was barely keeping his balance. As they watched, the dark-haired man was shoved again by an unseen assailant. Still he managed to shield Tadd as he crashed against the wall, catching his body weight with the one shoulder.

Willyn lifted her hands, both a bright blue. "Bastraal!" she yelled, challenging the fiend she knew was there but couldn't see. "Come for me, you son of a bitch!"

More than a few eyebrows hiked up in response to the language. Considering it came from Willyn.

She didn't shoot her magic, but let it seep from her hands like a net, slowly expanding in search of her quarry.

"Smart little witch," Paige mumbled as she watched. None of them had done anything like this with their magic before.

But a mother's protective instinct should never be underestimated.

A roar of indescribable depth and resonance blasted through the air, then Willyn was shoved into the wall, just as Dare had been. She screamed in pain when several gashes opened up on her shoulder and slashed around to her back.

Her eyes remained fixed on Dare and Tadd. "I'm okay," she cried, answering the worried expression on her husband's face. She reached around and clamped her hand to her back, healing herself.

Snowball was suddenly screaming like a banshee behind Willyn. The cat leapt forward once, twice, swiping her extended claws and hissing so deeply in her throat the sound sent chills down Claudia's back.

A table turned over in front of the cat, then a large picture flew from the wall. Farther down and around the corner, a huge potted plant upended, spilling dirt across the gleaming mahogany of the landing.

Nick and Trevor suddenly appeared on the stairs, running down from the third floor. They stared at the mess, and Trevor started to call out. But he was thrown forward and down the steps, his body hitting hard and wrapping around the banister.

"No!" Hayden dashed for the staircase, her eyes on the man she loved. But she was too far away. Her cat, Daisy, was running in front of her, but she wasn't going to make it in time either.

Nick lunged forward to help his friend, but an invisible force threw him back onto the stairs. His head hit with a *thunk!* and he collapsed like a rag doll.

Bastraal returned to Trevor, hefting the muscular man into the air as if he weighed nothing. Still dazed, Trevor lifted his head and shook it. "Wha—" He was tossed over the railing before anyone could react.

Hayden's shrill scream filled the cavernous room as Trevor went flying higher, arcing twenty feet or more in the air before his weight slowed his upward momentum to bring him crashing down.

Claudia's mind was scrambled, but she tried to focus and conjure powers of levitation. Others did as well, but Trevor was still falling.

They weren't fast enough. They weren't good enough.

But Viv was. The black-haired beauty propelled her waves of magic forward, catching Trevor and lowering him gently to the solid slate floor.

Hayden reversed her course and ran back down the stairs, throwing herself at her boyfriend.

"What do we do?" Michael was rigid, staring at the last spot they'd seen evidence of Bastraal's damaging strikes. They could track the demon by the destruction he caused, but he didn't stay in one place long enough for them to attack. "He's invisible."

"And he's fast," Claudia added. "Extremely fast."

Paige was unsettled. Even her speed and strength were no match for this particular enemy. "We aren't prepared for this."

Anna looked around. "No. We aren't."

"But they are." Shauni pointed to a couple of the cats, each standing vigil around their people, protecting them. "I can hear them, and they have no trouble seeing the demon. But their thoughts are scattered. Lots of hate and determination." She shuddered. "Bastraal and his kind are not only our worst adversaries, but theirs too."

Doors slammed in the vicinity of the library. Then they slammed again. Paige tore through the great room in a blurry streak, then Claudia saw the far hallway and foyer light up with a blush of blue. Paige was trying to blast Bastraal with the coven's magic.

But it didn't work. "He's coming!" she yelled down the hall, her voice bouncing off the stone floors and mahogany wainscoting. She sped back to the great room, but the beast was ahead of her, knocking aside large paintings on the wall, overturning lamps and scattering anything in his path.

Paige skidded to a stop near the group as glass began to shatter in the kitchen. "He's just screwing with us." She swiped her white-blonde bangs to the side with a jerk of her hand. "We should see what we can do with a direct hit. We can use both entrances and flank him. He'll have no choice but to meet us head-on."

"What about the greenhouse?" Kylie asked.

Anna shrugged. "If he breaks out through the glass, then so be it. He's destroying our home anyway." She gave a fierce nod. "Let's do it. We have to learn what we're dealing with."

Paige and Anna went to the kitchen door that exited off the great room while Claudia hurried with Shauni and Viv to the side corridor. There, another door entered into the breakfast room connected to the kitchen.

They'd only just flanked the doorframe when a freezing

numbness burst from inside and embraced Claudia. The overpowering cold picked her up and carried her down the vestibule. Then it shoved her to the ground and restrained her.

What felt like multiple hands began to grope and stroke her body, but they were so cold. Unnaturally devoid of heat.

She'd always imagined the netherworld as a hot, burning place, like Hell. But now she knew the opposite was true. A stinging, stabbing pain racked her body as evil covered her, as it molested her.

One of the hands clamped onto her breast, and she screamed from the brutality as fingers dug into the soft tissue like frozen daggers. She released the magic inside of her, letting it flow without direction.

Bastraal was all over her, pinning her down, so she struck out blindly. Desperately.

This was no normal form attacking her, but a polymorphic entity. She'd seen the demon change shape before he evaporated, but he'd transformed again.

He was unbelievably strong. Unpredictable. The beast he'd become was foreign to her, and she had no idea how to fight him.

The agony was intense, as if a hundred monsters attacked her, mobbing her with their vile thoughts and deeds. Her heart stuttered from disgust and paralyzing terror. Her valves seemed to clutch and pinch, as if they might stall out completely.

What felt like a giant oily tongue slicked up the inside of one thigh and she almost vomited.

With another shove of energy, she channeled the blue light into the area surrounding her. She heard Viv and Shauni call to each other, preparing to join their magic with hers.

The entire corridor lit up like center of a blue star, and at last the awful cold released her.

She rolled onto her side in a fetal position, clenching her teeth against the nausea and lingering pain. *I will not scream for you. I will not allow you to feed off my fear.*

She was on her knees then, lunging into a run toward the main portion of the house. Viv and Shauni were close behind.

The entire house shook and the sound of an explosion resonated throughout. The lights flickered and died again.

"Damn," Kylie swore.

Horrendous pounding came from the foyer. Banging, banging.

"This is insane." Hayden's golden eyes practically glowed. She was as livid as the rest of them, frustration bubbling just beneath the surface.

Claudia continued through the main room in search of her foe. The beast had finally let go of her, and perhaps it had been the united strike of three witches that had forced his retreat.

Regardless, she was ready for a blowout, and with this intention, she ran for the foyer. She could see a corner of the front doors, twin massive slabs of oak that had been in Anna's home for decades, maybe over a century.

The deep-hued wood was straining, as two giant hands were pressing the doors out before pulling in the reverse direction. The outward bulge and release happened again, creating the tremendous noise that filled the mansion and throbbed in her ears.

"Claudia," Cole called loudly from behind her. She could hear his footsteps and many more as the rest of the coven and the men chased along with her. She paused just long enough to look back at him. To mesh her gaze with his gorgeous light green.

And the doors exploded.

Shards and arrows of wood bulleted in every direction. A chunk shot across her arm, leaving a gash. Other fragments hit the back of her head, her torso, her legs.

Cole threw up an arm reflexively and caught a sliver the size of a pencil in the underside of his wrist. A few screams rang out as everyone ducked, and Dare threw Tadd on the velvet sofa, covering the small boy with his body.

Claudia took the brunt of the detonation, but the damage was minimal. So much less than it would have been if she hadn't looked back to Cole. If she hadn't answered his call.

She would have run head on into the blast, and her face would not have fared well.

Slowly, she turned to survey the wreckage. Night winds tore through the ragged edges of a hole where the doors had been.

The howling shriek felt like a final mocking insult from Bastraal. And as the gale receded, she thought she heard the legion of strange, ancient voices fading into the island forest.

But promising their return.

Only candles burned in the house now, but by the dim yellow light she saw Cole's anxiety. His handsome face was rutted with lines of concern. He yanked the wood from his wrist and clamped his hand on the bleeding wound, walking toward her the entire time.

"Let me see." He barked out the order, easing around her to take inventory of her punctures and cuts. His fingers moved lightly on her back then picked a shaft of wood from her hair. "You're okay," he told her, comforting himself as much as Claudia. "You're okay."

"We'll have Willyn take a look," he said, turning her around. "I want to hold you, but that might hurt."

She laughed, half relief and half lament. The beast she'd called forth had destroyed much of the mansion. She tried to smile. "I'll make sure you can hold me before the night is over."

Paige passed them and went to the foyer. Her yell into the night was one of furious loss. When she made as if to go outside, Anna's voice stopped her. "Paige, don't." She went to the blonde warrior and clasped her shoulder. "There's nothing we can do. Not now."

"He's out there." Paige was still but her body hummed with

the tension of a jungle cat ready to pounce.

"You won't find him, Paige." Claudia tried to walk, but the injuries to her back screamed with the movement. She took smaller, easier steps and made her way to Anna and Paige.

"Bastraal is here now. In the human world." The quaking fear they all felt was etched on the blonde soldier's face.

"But it's not over, and we aren't defeated," Claudia said.

"No, we're not." Anna shook her head, but her jaw trembled. "As terrible as this is, his release had to happen. I understand that now."

With a weary sigh, Claudia edged closer, staring into the peaceful spring night. The woods were silent. Nothing moved. "Bastraal will bring mayhem. He will cause agony and death before we're done."

"Yes." Anna's shoulders were strong and regal as she stood there, sable hair flowing down her back. "And he will take full advantage of his freedom. He came here for a reason."

Claudia's muscles ached as the memory of the monster's freezing, clenching hands came back to her. "He'll begin his search. For the body he wants."

Anna stared into the darkened woods as she whispered, "And the man he's going to take it from."

32

After an hour of working together, the bulk of the debris had been cleared away, and Cole and Quinn had boarded up the front entry to the mansion. Most of the cleaning had occurred in the kitchen, where the demon had cleared shelf after shelf of glassware, sending it all crashing to the floor.

After repairing the cuts in her shoulder, Willyn had seen to Claudia, Cole, and anyone else who'd taken some of the door shrapnel. The mood of the house remained grave, each of the men and women lost in thought and coming to grips with the unforeseen disaster.

Now as they returned to the great room, Anna waited for everyone to settle before she addressed the gathering. "I've already spoken with Claudia, but I want to make sure everyone understands." As ever, she was cool and collected. "It was inevitable that Bastraal would come back to the human realm. That he would have to be brought back."

Claudia listened quietly, having already accepted Anna's explanation. The coven was in a battle with an enemy of interminable power, and it was naïve to think there would be no loss for their side. No defeats.

No one questioned Anna, so she continued. "If we are going to defeat him once and for all. If we are going to destroy him, we have no choice but to face Bastraal. And that can only happen if he's here in this world."

Paige had one hand in a fist, resting on her knee. She stared at the floor when she said, "We saw what he's capable of. Even without the possession of a human body." The fist elevated then hit her knee again softly, with restrained ire. "We have three more trials to complete, so that means he'll have at least that much time to hurt people. To destroy as much of our world as he can."

Anna drew a breath, paused, then said in a soft voice, "Anything is possible."

"This sucks." Kylie, succinct as always, crossed her arms over her chest. "What do we do? Should we attack the Amara? Bastraal must have gone to their plantation, or...I don't know. Does he even have to be in one place at a time? Whatever he is? Demon just doesn't seem a sufficient enough description anymore."

"It's not," Claudia said, shivers coursing and hairs prickling. "I don't think we have a word for what he is."

"Calling him evil incarnate doesn't do him justice either." Shauni was sitting with Michael on the sofa, their hands clasped between them. "And the wards here are still down? Can we fix them?"

Quinn stepped up to answer. "Not tonight. I've never encountered anything like the energy Bastraal used. Then again, I've never dealt with a being like him either. The best way I can explain it is he left a sort of magical virus. The network around the mansion is...scrambled. It will take some time to redo everything. We can start from scratch, but first we have to cleanse what's left behind."

"And our magic isn't responding." Anna glanced worriedly to her brother. "But we'll find a way."

"We will," he said.

"Ugh." Claudia rested her head in her hands. "I understand

your logic, Anna, but that doesn't change the facts. I did this. I brought him here."

"And if you hadn't," Cole interjected fiercely, "the prophecy would never come to completion. I helped you find those antiques, don't forget. I bear some of the responsibility too. And some of the guilt."

Claudia tensed. She'd never considered he might feel this way. "But you couldn't have known."

"Neither could you." Viv gestured with her glass of white wine as she spoke, her gray eyes earnest, supportive. She was sitting in Nick's lap, both of them crowded into a fancy velvet chair.

Now that Claudia took in the scene, all of the witches were sidled up close to their men. Tonight had brought too many close calls. Their sanctuary had been invaded, and no one felt safe anymore.

Even little Tadd remained with the group of adults. He was sleeping in Willyn's arms, and Claudia doubted he would be far from his mother or Dare until the wards were back in place.

She was still getting used to the fact that she had someone to lean on now. Someone she could count on and trust to take care of her. A partner who would help her and, on occasion, tell her when she was wrong.

Warmth suffused her when she studied Cole's stern expression. He had stood by her side in the face of incomprehensible danger. When she had chased after a monster, he had gone right along with her.

"Good thing we had the cats around," Ethan said. His dark eyes were on Iris, Lucia's black Persian, as he stroked the animal's back. "I've heard tales in several different cultures about the feline ability to see into the other world. To defend against devils and creatures beyond human comprehension."

He smiled as he rubbed the purring cat under the chin "But let me just say...they were some real badasses tonight."

Shauni's dog, Skid, whined from his perch on the floor. Shauni looked down at him then laughed. "He's sorry he missed the action, but he was sleeping." Her eyes widened. "You were where?" Her chuckle was low when she added, "Better not let Mrs. Attinger catch you."

"Don't feel bad, Skid." Trevor spoke to the dog. "My pride's taken a beating too." He knelt to pet Daisy, the tortoiseshell who had yet to leave Hayden's side. "I've gotten used to a bunch of women being on the frontline, but now I have to stand behind cats?"

Hayden lifted one brow. "A bunch of women?"

"You know what I mean." Trevor stood and had the grace to look sheepish. Then a smile lifted one side of his mouth. "A bunch of beautiful, gifted, and very, very powerful women."

"Good save, so you're forgiven." Hayden tipped up on her toes and kissed him. "That and the fact you almost fell to your death."

He grunted. "Thanks for the reminder."

The last tiny knot of regret loosened inside Claudia then slipped away. No matter how bad things got, her friends were always able to find their balance. To grasp the happiness they'd been blessed with and continue living life to the fullest.

There was a kind of magic in their connection, and not one of the mystical world, but of human nature. Love and friendship would always bear the weight of malice, and even when life was lost, the bond would persist.

From this world into the next, only one thing could ever truly be counted on. Only one thing could be trusted.

Claudia stood and took in the faces of her sisters, the men she'd come to depend on, and the animals who hid such bravery beneath their sweet, furry faces. She could always rely on them.

Finally, she rested her gaze on Cole. She could rely on *all* of them.

"All this time, I was just being used." She didn't know where this speech was going, but for once she set her busy mind aside and followed wherever her full heart might lead. "I didn't know I was helping Bastraal get what he wanted, and I absolutely hate that."

The others were all listening, so she pressed on. "But Anna's right. When I set him free, my amulet sang. I did my part and completed my trial. Even if I despise how it all came together, I know it had to happen."

With a shame-faced grin, she said, "It's really hard for me to admit when I'm wrong."

"No kidding." Paige chuckled.

"But," Claudia nodded acknowledgement to the comment, "I should have had faith in whatever great powers control our prophecy, and our destinies."

She turned to face Cole. "I should have had faith in my friends. And you." She softened her eyes as they lit on his. "You have always been that to me." Moving to him, she took his hand. "A very dear friend."

The corners of his eyes crinkled, letting her know he was smiling on the inside.

She shook her head. "The irony is that the one thing I thought was true, the goal I had to pursue, well…it turned out to be the biggest lie of all."

Her tone changed, grew thick with regret, but the remorse was tempered by the love that filled her chest. "And the person I doubted," she stepped even closer to Cole, "was the only one who could help me. The man I was always supposed to be with."

Pressing his lips together, Cole's eyes shifted to encompass the very large gathering of people around them. "This isn't exactly how I imagined this moment."

Claudia's joy burst free in a laugh. "I want to do it here. Right here, in front of everyone. A sort of tribal recognition."

Paige threw up her hands. "Now we're a tribe."

"Shush." Kylie poked the blonde warrior and sniffled. "I've

been waiting for this."

Behind them Trevor muttered, "You and me both."

"Cole," Claudia said, "I love you. So much I'm still trying to wrap my brain around it. And I promise you, from here on out, I will always trust you." She took his hands and shifted toward him.

He froze. "Are you about to propose?" His face tilted down to her with skepticism. "Because if you are, I'm going to have to put my foot down. That part is *definitely* my job."

"In fact," he turned his head and gave the others an excuse-us-folks wink, then dragged her toward the kitchen. "I'm going to transfer the rest of this conversation to somewhere more private."

"Ohhh," Kylie whined when they relocated the unfolding drama.

"Whatever you say, Detective." Claudia was giddy with the relief of her admission. That and the energy coursing through her that she still needed to burn off.

And Cole was looking mighty manly in those jeans.

When they got to the kitchen, he surprised her by hauling her up against his chest and burying a hand in her hair. "Now that I'm not feeling side-swiped anymore." He pressed a kiss to her lips briefly.

"I want to tell you something," he said. "After you came back to my house and found...*her* there, I was so glad to have you back. Even angry, hesitant, or a little scared, I was just so happy you'd come back to me."

He traced the curve of her cheek with his thumb. "But I made a promise to myself. That I wouldn't kiss you again until you felt the same way about me as I do you."

He leaned closer. "Or until you admitted it, anyway." He smiled, the warmth of his curving lips so close to hers that she felt the motion. "You did just tell me you loved me, right?"

Her breaths were shallow when she whispered, "I did."

"About damn time." His lips on hers were still tender, but she could sense the desire flowing beneath. Hot and insistent. Together she and Cole were so much more than friends. More than buddies. Or comrades.

Together they were *explosive*. They had been since their first touch, but now love flowed between them in addition to the amazing chemistry. And that made their connection even better. Stronger.

Magical.

When they parted at last, and she had a chance to catch her breath, Claudia told him about what had happened in the grand hall. When she'd held the final item and had faced the fiend.

Afterward, she wrapped her arms around him and reveled in his heat. His strength. And knew the precious gift she'd found in him. "I should have been able to tell you before, and I'm sorry it took being more afraid of Bastraal than of love for me to admit my feelings."

She lowered her head to his shoulder. "I've been a terrible coward."

"A coward?" Cole nudged her back up to look at him. "Claudia, you were sent alone into an unknown world where you were forced to stand up to a powerful demon. Fate wouldn't have chosen you for this level of trial if you weren't up to it."

"I suppose. Yet the thought of you breaking my heart seemed worse than any of that. Why was it so hard for me?"

"Maybe you had to make it hard." He shrugged. "Every one of us is different."

"What do you mean?"

"If you'll recall, I wasn't exactly thrilled about being forced into a relationship either." His handsome visage grew arrogant. "I was pretty happy with my single life."

She pursed her lips. "Oh, really?"

"But I always had a thing for you." His grin turned carnal.

"You and your legs. I guess I just needed a few slaps to my ego to make me sit up and take notice of what else was behind those short skirts."

She twirled her fingers in his hair, loving the way it was just long enough to curl over his collar. "I had to run to get you to chase?"

"It worked, didn't it? And honestly, I wouldn't change a thing. Our love has been hard won. It's already withstood more hardship than most relationships ever have to."

"So we've been thoroughly vetted." She stepped closer to him, stepped into him. How had she ever refused this wonderful, reliable, and virtuous man? Not *that* kind of virtuous. Thank the stars.

The clean scent of him was arousing and reminded her of another time. When he'd just come from the shower, wet and warm.

Hmm. But there would be time for that.

Her thoughts turned serious as she touched his face. "You know, I keep going back to that day we saw you in the café. The day my trial began."

He grimaced. "Uh-huh."

"You were with that perky blonde." She teased him with a sideways glance. "I can tell you now." She bit the inside of her cheek. "I was a little bit jealous."

"Yeah?" His hands fell to her hips and held on. "Tell me more."

"Actually, envious would be a better word. I pictured you and how happy you'd make someone someday." Her lip and her heart trembled. "I remember thinking what a good man you are, and that some woman was going to be very lucky to have you."

He lowered his forehead to hers. "I'm just glad that woman finally came around to my way of thinking."

Claudia gave him a shy grin. "So am I." The smile slipped a

little as love clutched her in a painfully sweet hug.

Just when she was about to bare her deepest wish, her secret need, Cole looked past her shoulder to the pantry. "You think Mrs. Attinger has some cake stashed around here? Some cookies?"

With a shake of her head and a tear in her eye, Claudia chuckled. Her man needed sugar.

"She usually does. But before you get a cookie," she lifted her eyes to his and stared into that beautiful and unique shade of green that was pure Cole, "I want you to make me a promise."

"Name it." His arms tightened around her, sturdy as an oak.

"I want you to smile at me, in that way you do." Her voice changed to an impassioned whisper. "Smile at me for a lifetime."

When Cole's hand slid up to brush her cheek, the smile she'd requested touched the corners of his eyes. "From this life into the next."

Her stomach's romantic butterflies went wild.

Then, with a burst of energy, he spun her out and back, just as they'd done on the dance floor at the gala. All the while he grinned at her, and Claudia swooned. Like a woman who'd truly been swept off her feet.

"And, Claudia," he said when she came to a stop, as she pressed against him so tightly their hearts beat together, "I keep my promises."

She maneuvered him toward the cabinets and the sweets she knew were inside. "Oh, I know you do." She kissed his full lips and reached for a bag of chocolates. She sighed dreamily. "I know."

If you enjoyed this book, we would love to read your review on your favorite retail or review site.

Thank you!

Suza Kates writes both paranormal romance and suspense. She lives in Savannah, Georgia with her family and three ridiculously spoiled cats.

For more on Suza and her books visit

www.suzakates.com

www.ingramcontent.com/pod-product-compliance
Lightning Source LLC
Chambersburg PA
CBHW020225180626
46810CB00006B/2048